MAFIA VOWS

L. STEELE

1

Elsa

"Did you know the enemies-to-lovers trope is superior to the rivals-to-lovers trope?" The woman in front of me turns to her friend.

"It is?" The friend leans forward.

"In enemies-to-lovers, two people on opposite sides of a feud fall in love and work together to put an end to the conflict, while in rivals-to-lovers, there's no battle or feud. And even if there is, they're on the same side; they just hate each other. Know what I mean?" The first girl angles her body so their shoulders touch.

"Nope, but thank you for the information I can do without." Her friend scrunches up her face.

The door of the nightclub opens and the music pours over us, drowning out the rest of their conversation.

When was the last time I went to a nightclub? I stopped going out at night in order to avoid temptation. But when my best friend Theresa called me up and asked me to accompany her, I couldn't refuse.

When I lived in London, I supported myself by working in a supermarket while I studied to become a pianist; I had been so hopeful for the future. And then, everything changed. I only have myself to blame. The pressure builds behind my eyes. *Do not cry. Do. Not. Cry. How many tears are you going to shed about the past, eh?*

You can't alter what happened. All you can do is stay in the moment. Stay in control. *You can do this. You can get through the evening without giving in to the need which wants to split you in half and rip its way out.*

A black Maserati with tinted windows rolls up. The door on the driver's side opens and a man steps out. Polished black shoes, black pants which encompass powerful thighs, and a black jacket which is tailor-made and clings to his broad shoulders. He's wearing a tie in—you guessed it—black, against a black shirt. He tugs on his cuffs, and glances up and down the street. Tattoos peek out from under his collar, a vibrant splash of color against his skin. In contrast to the perfection of his suit, his hair is unruly. A thick curl flops onto his forehead and he pushes it away. Alertness clings to every muscle in his body, and he has that whole 'don't mess with me vibe' going for him. Either he's a cop or—nah—can't be. No cop would be dressed in such an impeccable fashion. In fact, he wouldn't seem out of place in a boardroom. Except, this man does not work in an office. Confidence oozes from his pores. The light from the overhead street lamp highlights his body, but casts his face in shadow. I crane my neck to see his features, but he turns and walks around to the passenger door. He pulls it open and a girl steps out. Dark hair, slim figure, about the same height as me. I know her. *What's he doing with her?*

"Theresa." I walk toward her, only to come to a stop when the black-jacket guy from earlier plants himself in front of me.

I tilt my head back, and further back, to meet his gaze—golden-brown eyes, flares of fire, the sunlight shining straight at me. I blink, and when I open my eyes again, I find him staring down that patrician nose at me. I catalog his features—full lower lip, thin upper lip, thick eyelashes, and a scar that runs up from the edge of his eyebrow in an inverted comma toward his temple. Aren't scars supposed to be a badge of honor in some cultures? And don't they indicate high levels of testosterone and good genetic qualities that can be passed onto offspring or something? Hold on, why am I thinking along these lines?

The behemoth crosses his arms across that massive chest, and his biceps stretch the sleeves. His gaze narrows, and he glares down at me like I am a piece of chewing gum stuck to the bottom of his over-priced, black leather shoe. Jeez, what climbed up his butt?

Except for the fact he resembles Keanu Reeves—a much more muscular and angrier Keanu, with eyes the color of sunlight—I wouldn't have given him a second look. Ha, who am I kidding? The man has the kind of presence which absorbs all of the oxygen in his vicinity, leaving us mere mortals gasping for air.

The muscles of his shoulders bunch, stretching the suit jacket he wears. He must work out every day. Either that, or he has the kind of job that demands he is at peak fitness. Come to think of it, if Keanu Reeves and Henry Cavill had a lovechild, he would look like this guy. Only, while I love their intensity and smoldering good looks, not to mention the don't-give-a-damn attitude of the characters they portray, I prefer my alphaholes on screen or between the pages of a book. This man, though, has all of the tell-tale makings of one in real life. Which means I need to give him a wide berth. Besides, he's too good-looking. Too mouthwateringly gorgeous. Definitely not a guy to be trusted.

"Who're you?" I scowl up at Mr. Grumpy Grumphole.

"This is my uh, my bodyguard for the evening," Theresa explains as she draws abreast with him.

"Bodyguard?" I shoot her a sideways glance. "You have a *bodyguard*?"

"Yeah, um..." She moves closer to me and lowers her voice, "The Sovranos insisted I get ferried about for my own safety." She's referring to the family at the head of the *Cosa Nostra*, the clan which rule this part of the country. The clan she's marrying into in less than a week.

"Hmm..." I look Mr. Bodyguard up and down. "We don't need you this evening." I wave my hand in the air, dismissing him. "Why don't you go off and do whatever it is bodyguards do on their time off?"

Seb glares back. Next to me, Theresa chokes.

"Jeez, you are crotchety, aren't you?" I flutter my eyelashes. "Maybe you should come along with us and have a few drinks to loosen up?"

Mr. Bodyguard's features harden. He turns to Theresa. "I assume you know her?"

"Oh, yeah. Sorry. I forgot to introduce her. Seb, meet my friend Elsa." Theresa glances between us. "Elsa, this is Seb."

"Pleased to meet you." I hold out my hand.

He ignores it, then spins around and prowls toward the entrance of the nightclub. The crowd parts in front of him and we follow in his wake.

"He's rude." I glower at his broad back.

"He's a Sovrano." She shrugs.

"There seem to be more of them than the Baldwins," I grouse.

"What?" Theresa blinks. "What does that mean?"

"Nothing; just a film reference joke. It's from one of my classmates in England —Summer West, was her name. She was so into movies, all of her conversations were peppered with movie trivia. Some of it rubbed off on me."

"You moved to Italy to be close to your daughter, didn't you?" she asks.

"It was the only way I could see her." My lips firm.

"Sorry, didn't mean to upset you."

"No, it's fine." I shoot her a smile so patently fake, Theresa winces. She opens her mouth, no doubt, to ask me what's wrong, but I shake my head. "Let's have some fun, shall we?"

I hook my arm through hers, and we follow Seb into the nightclub.

A wave of noise hits us as we walk down the short flight of steps and into the large room. The beats echo throughout the space, sink into my blood, and sync with my heartbeat. The scent of perfume, sweat, and sex hang in the air like a heavy cloud that's going to burst at any moment. The space is crammed with men and women, from the bar to the dance floor and across it. It resembles a mass of humanity all welded together by their common desire to dance and fuck.

"Umm, I'm not sure I want to be here." Theresa begins to turn away.

I grab her arm and pull her along with me.

"Elsa, please," she begins to protest.

I turn on her. "Do you want to stay home moping for your Sovrano?"

"N-no..." She hunches her shoulders.

"This was your idea. Clearly, you want to prove a point to yourself. Let's loosen up a little and have some fun, okay?"

She sighs and I drag her into the sweltering hot cavern.

That's when I realize I haven't seen Mr. Alphahole Bodyguard for a while. For a big man, he sure seems to disappear with ease. Well, that's good. At least, I don't have to worry about his glowering looks. Or hiding the attraction I feel toward him, which is surely a mistake. Why should I feel so drawn to a man who clearly hated me on sight?

The strobe lights dance over us as I elbow my way through the crowd. I keep a firm grip on her, until I reach the very center of the dance floor. Bodies push in on us from all sides. Sweat beads my brow and trickles down my temple. My dress clings to my back. I grip Theresa's arms and we sway in tandem to the music. The beat ricochets around my head and I close my eyes, letting the rhythm overpower me. Releasing her, I turn around, then lean forward and jut out my hips as I squat down. With a snap of my lower body, I push out my butt and straighten. For a few seconds, I am one with the cadence of the beats. I shimmy my upper body, long-forgotten dance steps that I picked up through my university years flowing back to me.

When was the last time I allowed myself to flow with the music with such abandon? I cut it all out of my life. Abstained from anything that could fire up my urges. Yet here I am, back in the eye of the storm, and... The feeling is so heady. A ripple of awareness flutters under my skin, I pop open my eyelids. The crowd in front of me shifts and I spot Seb at the bar.

His gaze clashes with mine, intensifies, and for a second, it's just me and him. All other sounds fade away. I try to breathe, but all of the oxygen seems to have been sucked out of the room. My lungs burn, my scalp tingles, a throb of heat swells my core. My lips part and those golden eyes of his seem to flare... With rage? I'm a sucker for punishment, for a shiver zings down my spine. My thighs clench and my core dampens.

Then the crowd moves again, and I lose sight of him.

"Elsa," I hear Theresa call my name above the music, "Elsa."

I turn to find her watching me with a disagreeable expression on her face.

"Come on, babe." I throw my arms about her. "You need to loosen up a little." I grind my hips into hers with an exaggerated flourish.

"What are you doing?" She laughs as I pull back, then twirl her around and back in. Then I turn my back on her and do another bump and a grind.

"Elsa, I need to get off the dance floor." She grips my shoulder.

"Aww, and I was just beginning to have fun," I gripe. And really, I am. For the first time in a very long time, I finally feel so close to the edge.

"Well, I'm not." She scowls.

I take in her flushed features, the sweat on her brow. "Hmm, I know what you need." I grab her hand, and we push through the crowd, until we burst out of the throng.

"Phew, it's hot in here." She pushes the hair off of her neck.

"I know how to cool off." I head for the bar, and she follows me. I get the attention of the bartender. "Two tequilas, please." Within minutes, he places two shots in front of us then slides over a plate with salt and lime.

I pick up the glass, and she eyes hers with distrust. "Um, I'm not sure I should—"

"You absolutely should," I lick the skin between my thumb and forefinger, sprinkle it with salt, and pick up a slice of lime. "You know the drill, lick, shoot, suck."

"Is that an euphemism?" she snickers.

"You bet." I pick up the other shot glass and thrust it at her. "Bottoms up!"

She copies my action with the salt and lime, then holds up her own glass.

"That's the spirit. On the count of one-two-three." I clink glasses with her, then lick the salt, throw back the liquor in the shot glass, and bite the lime. The alcohol slides down my throat, hits my stomach and tendrils of heat radiate out to my extremities.

"Whoa..." She shakes her head. "That was—"

"Excellent," I gesture to the bartender. "Two more, please."

"Oh, no." She backs away. "I am *not* drinking more."

"Oh, yes, you are." I shove one of the freshly-filled shot glasses into her hand. "Come on, keep me company."

She begins to protest, and I scowl. "Come on, Theresa, we need to celebrate." I refer to her upcoming nuptials to Axel, one of the—you guessed it—Sovrano brothers.

"Right..." She tosses her hair over her shoulder. "But you don't need to get drunk to celebrate."

"Maybe not, but it helps," *especially when you want to forget what a mess you have made of your life.* I raise my glass, "Come on!"

After downing the glass, she plants it upside down on the bar and backs away. "No more for me. I'm going to the bathroom."

"I'll come with you." I begin to follow her, but she waves me off.

"You go ahead and get another drink; I'll just head to the bathroom and back."

"Let me come with—"

She cuts me off, "I'll be fine. I just need a minute to cool off." She brushes past me and heads for the hallway that lead to the restroom.

O-k-a-y... I didn't piss her off, did I? Theresa is, literally, my only friend in Palermo. She hired me to work at her flower shop, *The Tilting Tulip*, which helped me find my feet quickly in this place. I often wish I could confide more in her, but if I revealed the fractured side of me it'd likely only put her off. No, I need to figure out how to hide the side of me that got me into trouble in the first place. I shouldn't have come here today, really. It's taking me too close to the edge, where it would be so easy to fall over and lose myself.

For that matter, I shouldn't have had the alcohol or indulged myself with the dancing. Especially the dancing. But gosh, did it feel good to be there in the crush of the bodies, with the music pounding down on me and drawing out all of the worries in my head. Just one more drink couldn't hurt, right? I turn to the bartender and gesture for another shot of tequila.

A shiver spirals through me, up the hair on the nape of my neck, and pours down the valley between my breasts. My nipples swell. The heat of his body envelops me, and a second later the bartender glances over my shoulder.

"*Grappa Quater.*" His low growl thrums in my ear, "She'll have the same."

2

Elsa

The vibrations from his voice seem to ricochet down my body and settle in my core. He's so close, I can feel the tension radiating off of him. Even without looking at him, the force of his dominance seems to pin me in place. *Thud-thud-thud.* I can feel the blood pounding in my ears. I cannot let him overpower me like this. I cannot allow him to see how attracted I am to him.

My stomach lurches, and my throat tightens. My pulse rate booms in my ears with such force that the world seems muted, like someone turned down the volume. I turn around to tell him off, and promptly lose my voice because he's standing so very close to me. I tip up my chin and he scowls down the length of that patrician nose at me.

I clear my throat. "*You* are in my space." I scowl.

"No, *you* are in mine." He takes a step closer, and I flatten myself against the bar. Not that it helps, for the tips of his shoes brush my stilettos.

"I'm not scared of you."

"Good." He rakes his gaze across my face. "That will make our interactions so much more interesting."

"Interactions?" I laugh. "I don't plan on seeing you ever again."

"The feeling's mutual." He reaches past me and scoops up both glasses of grappa. The spicy masculine scent of him is in my nostrils; I drag it into my lungs and my entire body seems to light up. My thighs clench and my toes curl. No, no, no. This kind of a visceral reaction to a man is exactly what I've been trying to avoid.

He holds out one of the tulip shaped glasses, and I snatch it from him. Before he's raised his own glass, I've tossed mine back. The alcohol leaves a trail of heat in its wake. It hits my stomach, and a ball of heat radiates out from the point of contact. I cough as my eyes water. "Jesus, what is that? Paint remover?" I glance up through my spiky eyelashes to find him watching me with something like disdain.

"What?" I sputter. "Never seen a grown woman act like a wuss?"

He merely tosses his own drink back—the action is so elegant I want to lean in and follow his every move, with my tongue—then places it on the table with a controlled snap. The kind that manages to be authoritative and demanding. Bloody hell, how can one man convey all of that with such a small gesture?

Out of the corner of my eye, I spot the bartender hurrying to refill his drink.

Seb takes the glass from me, and his fingertips brush mine. A current of electricity shoots out from the point of contact. *Oh, shit.* Not good, not good. Don't want to have this kind of a reaction to this man.

"I'm not going to sleep with you. Even if you were the last man on earth," I blurt out.

A touch of humor sparks in his eyes. "We'll see." He tilts his head. "You're a little thing, aren't you?" He frowns, as if only now noticing my lack of height. Well, I'm five-feet-four-inches, which is pretty decent, or so I'd thought until I stood before this monster of a man.

"You're a big, mean alphahole, aren't you?" I scoff.

His jaw drops, but he recovers quickly; I'll give him that much credit. "That's not a word in the English language," he says in a tone that could have chilled my grappa if I were still holding it in my hand, which I'm not. More's the pity. I would have dumped it on him, just for the satisfaction of taking him by surprise again.

"It is now," I inform him, "and by the way, I may be small, but I pack a punch."

"Somehow I don't doubt that." He lowers his head until we share breath, then murmurs, "But whatever it is you're offering, I'm not interested."

It's my turn to gape. "What the—?" I sputter. "I'm not offering you anything. I'm not sure what makes you think—"

He chuckles, the sound so deep, it seems to reach all the way to my toes.

"Jerk," I snarl. "Stop laughing at me. I don't know who you think you are, but—"

"I have to admit, your response was most satisfying." He smirks. And damn it, that shouldn't be so hot. And I shouldn't still be staring at that beautiful face of his. But honestly, while I've only heard of men being referred to as fallen angels before, now I get where the phrase comes from. If that description fits anyone, it's this larger-than-life guy who's looking at me like he's the most superior thing ever to have walked this planet.

"Only because you caught me by surprise." I poke my finger in his chest. "I'll have you know, normally, I am far cooler and more collected."

"No doubt, it's my presence that unnerves you," he drawls.

"It's your presence that makes me want to leave this bar," I retort.

"No one's stopping you." He raises his hand in a dismissive gesture, much like the one I used on him earlier. "In fact, I'll give you a drink to go." He jerks his chin at the bartender.

For the second time in a few minutes, I gape at him.

"And I thought Italian men were such charmers."

"Only with the right kind of women," he shoots back.

"Which I am not—when it comes to you— thank god." I pretend to wipe my forehead. "I wouldn't be interested in you if you were the last man on this planet."

He yawns. "I believe you already mentioned that. Are you done with your childish tantrum?"

I resist the urge to stamp my foot; that would only confirm his misogynistic remark, and I am *not* going to validate his misplaced perception.

"I'll have a beer," I say in a casual voice.

"Eh?" A line appears between his eyebrows, marring the expanse of that gorgeous forehead.

"A beer." I stab my thumb over my shoulder. "Tell him I want a beer to go."

"Instead of grappa?" He wrinkles his nose like I've suddenly developed a bad smell.

Not that I didn't like the taste of it, but there's a reason I'm asking for beer. "In fact, make it a pint. You know us Brits; we never settle for anything less."

He shoots me a look filled with disgust.

"There, there, it can't be all that bad." I pat his chest. The heat of his body instantly soaks through his shirt to bleed into my skin. I shiver. To say the man is ripped is an understatement. I mean, I have touched walls which were less firm. Okay, maybe a tad exaggerated on my part, or not. I swear, the man must spend all of his spare time working out.

He glances down at where my hand seems to have developed a relationship with the front of his shirt.

"Oops, sorry." *Not.* I lower my hand to my side.

"Your hair..." He points to where I have piled my hair on my head. Half of it has come undone, and strands now hang about my face. The curse of having thick hair. Not to mention, the humidity in this establishment pretty much means my hair is frizzy and escaping from its messy bun.

"What of my hair?" I scowl.

"I've seen bird's nests that are tidier."

"Such sweet compliments. Keep that up, and I'll be sure you have a crush on me."

He smirks.

I glower up at him.

The skin around his eyes creases. Then he reaches over and tucks a strand of hair behind my ear. Tendrils of loathing—it has to be loathing—shiver out from where his fingertips brushed my earlobe.

Someone clears their throat. That's when I realize Theresa is standing beside us.

"Erm... hello, everything okay?" she finally asks.

Her voice breaks the fugue state I seem to have descended into. I blink. Seb lowers his hand to his side at the same time.

"Elsa? Seb? What's going on?" she questions.

"What's going on is that your grumpster bodyguard seems to think he owns the place," I snap.

"I do, actually." Seb looks me up and down. He seems to notice my dress for the first time and his features harden. "What the fuck are you wearing?" he growls.

"Excuse me?" I open and shut my mouth. "What did you just say?"

"You may as well be parading naked, for all that you have on."

"What the hell?" I plant my hands on my hips. "Who the hell do you think you are, you asshole?"

"That's alphahole to you," he says through gritted teeth. "Also, we're leaving!"

"You can take her; I am not going anywhere." I turn away.

"Don't turn your back on me," Seb orders.

"I'll do what I want, when I want," I shoot back.

I can't see his features, but I'd wager he's grinding his teeth so hard, he probably split a molar.

I sense him lean forward, but out of the corner of my eye, I notice Theresa tug at his sleeve. Something hot stabs at my chest. Damn it, why am I jealous? She's in love with another man. She's only trying to calm Seb down. Besides, what do I care who touches him? *I don't. I don't...*

"Don't," she says in a soothing voice. "Let me handle this."

There's silence for a second, then he must nod, for she touches my shoulder. "Elsa, I think it's time for us to leave," she says softly.

"Aww, I'm just starting to have fun." I glance at her sideways. "Besides, who does he think he is to order me around?"

"The Sovranos can be a bit overwhelming. Why don't we get out of here, and I'll explain on the way home?"

"Fine." I toss my hair, most of which has now escaped from the messy bun on top of my head. "There's one thing I have to do before we leave." I bare my teeth.

"Oh?" Her gaze grows worried.

I reach past her to seize the tall plastic cup the bartender filled with beer, and dump it on Seb.

3

A week later

Elsa

"Open up." I bang on the front door to the mansion. "Open the hell up."

I hear footsteps approaching, but it's not quickly enough. My heart hammers in my chest and adrenaline laces my blood.

"Help," I scream, "help me, please."

I raise my fist to bang on the door again, when it's flung open. I stumble forward and smash my face into what feels like a brick wall. A wall that emanates heat, which slams into my chest, pours over my shoulders, and pins me in place. My breasts swell, my thighs clench, and all of the pores on my skin pop. I know who it is, even before I raise my head and those golden-brown eyes meet mine. What the hell is he doing here?

"Help," I pant. "Help me, Seb."

His hands grip my upper arms. Then he glances past me, and his gaze widens. "*Cazzo*," he swears. The next second, he hauls me inside the house, then throws me down on the floor. The open door is too far away to reach.

"Get down," he yells into the room, then lowers his head so his cheek is plastered to mine.

He covers my body with his, and the breath whooshes out of my lungs. Shots ring out above us.

"What the—" my heart leapfrogs into my chest, and adrenaline spikes my blood.

My throat closes, my pulse rate ratchets up, and a trembling grips me. I lay there as the shots seem to go on and on. When they finally stop, silence descends. Something crashes to the floor inside the house and I flinch. He wraps his fingers around the nape of my neck and holds me in place. It should feel threatening, but instead, some of the panic abates. The heat from his body pours over me and sinks into my blood. Sweat beads my brow, and it's as if I have stepped into a sauna. His chest rises and falls, and I can feel every ridge, every cut of his sculpted muscles that dig into my back. His big body surrounds me; he's all around me. I should feel claustrophobic, but instead, I feel protected, and safe, and secure. Then his weight is gone.

Cool air flows over me. The sound of people moving, of footsteps approaching us, of voices raised in concern, pours over me. I try to move, but my body doesn't obey. Try to open my mouth to speak, but nothing comes out.

"You okay, Frozen?"

Huh? Did he just call me what I think he did? He grips my shoulder, turns me over, and once more, I am staring up into those golden eyes. It's the first thing I noticed about him, because they are startling. Bottomless orbs of power that can see right through to my insecurities. He's so goddam gorgeous with those thick eyelashes, sculpted cheekbones, and a nose hooked enough to lend him an air of arrogance. That pouty lower lip that hints at the sensualness that clothes him, that thin upper lip that warns me he could be mean. Cruel. He could cut me off at the knees with the charm that radiates from him, and surely, fills any room he enters. He'd chew me up, spit me out, and damn, if I wouldn't enjoy every bit of sensation he'd wring from me.

"John," I croak.

His gaze intensifies. "Who's John?"

"Who's Frozen?" I counter.

"Touché." His lips twitch. "Princess suits you better."

"Keanu Reeves played John Wick in the movie by the same name, and PS, you must have been sleeping under a rock if you haven't heard of it. Also, I hate Princess even more," I grumble.

"I'll call you whatever name I want," he announces.

"Definitely John Wick," I mutter under my breath. "No, actually, you're grumpier, and that's some feat, I can tell you."

"Eh?" He searches my features. "Are you hurt?" He runs his hands down my torso, my waist, over my hips, and something inside of me sparks to life.

"Stop touching me, you oaf." I slap his hands away. "I'm fine."

"Don't look fine." His forehead furrows. "And what the hell were you doing outside the door?"

"Getting shot at, what do you think?" I glower back at him.

"You could have been fucking killed," he growls.

"Not if I can help it. I like my life just fine, thank you very much."

I try to sit up, but he flattens his palm on my chest and pushes me back down.

"Hey, stop manhandling me," I protest.

"Not letting you move until you've been checked out by a medic."

"I said I'm fine," I huff.

"I'll believe it when a doctor tells me so."

"Elsa!" I glance up as my friend Theresa's face comes into view.

"Thank god." I raise my gaze skywards. "Please, can you tell this jerk that I'm fine and he can let me up?"

"Umm..." She takes one look at his features and her eyebrows shoot up. "I think he's right."

"What?" I scowl at her, but she's too busy waving at another woman, who walks over to us. She's wearing a simple, dark-colored dress that hugs her curves, before dropping to below her knees. Her eyes are intelligent, and her auburn hair is pulled back from her face.

"I'm Dr. Aurora Sovrano. Is it okay if I check you out?"

I glance from her to Theresa, who nods vigorously. "You're safe with her," she assures me. "She's Christian's wife."

Christian is one of the Sovranos; I know that from what Theresa's told me about the brothers. In fact, she's spoken about the Sovranos in enough detail, I'm confident I could pick out each of them in a crowd.

I turn back to the doctor and nod at her.

She smiles, then glances over to the man who's behind her. "Can you get my medical bag, honey?"

"Sure, baby." The tall, broad-shouldered man, who looks very similar to Seb, and even more like Axel, spins around and disappears through a doorway. I know they're married, but somehow, the very cozy endearments of 'baby' and 'honey' still feel out of place in relation to one of the Sovranos.

Another man—the tallest and broadest in the room—walks over to us. "Everything okay here?" he asks.

"No," I say at the same time that asshat here growls, "I have it under control."

The man—who has to be Massimo, going off Theresa's description—smirks.

"I'm going to go check on the guards outside." He walks past us and out of the house.

Aurora sinks down next to me and reaches over to take my pulse.

By the time she lowers my arm, Christian has returned; he hands over her medical bag before stepping back. The doctor pulls out a small flashlight and shines it in my eyes. She checks my heart beat with a stethoscope, performs a few other tests, and pronounces that I am fine.

"You'll need to take care of that cut," she says as she points to my forehead.

For the first time, I become aware of the throbbing sensation above my eyebrow. I touch it and wince. When I glance at my fingers, they're bloodied.

Seb rises to his feet and holds out his hand. "Come on, let's get that cleaned up."

"Umm," I fold my arms across my chest, "no, thank you."

He merely stares down at his proffered palm, then back at my face.

"What?" I scowl. "I am not going anywhere with you."

"You do have to get that cleaned up," Aurora says in a reasonable tone.

I turn to her. "I'd rather you do it."

Aurora hesitates.

"I can do as good a job as you, Doc," Seb interjects.

Aurora begins to speak, but he holds up a hand. "I have training in first aid."

"You do?" I whip my head around to look at him. The scrape on my forehead protests, but I ignore it.

He tilts his head.

"Are you lying?" I scowl up at him.

"Would I lie to you?"

"Wouldn't you?" I retort.

He surveys my features. "One of us was always getting hurt growing up. It made sense to get some basic training so I could take care of wounds. Thanks to the good doctor here, that occasion has not arisen until now, but you'll be pleased to know, I'm going to make an exception in your case."

I scoff. "And if I decline?"

"Not giving you a choice. I'm not letting you go anywhere until I ensure your wound is bandaged by me personally," he explains reasonably. *Damn him.*

I glower. He holds my gaze. Those gorgeous, golden orbs of his bore into me. Damn it, he's not going to back off, is he? Well, too bad. I'm not going to simply fall in line with whatever he asks me to do.

I gasp as he bends down, wraps an arm around my back, the other under my knees, and straightens with me in his arms.

"What are you doing?" I hiss.

"You could have done this the easy way, but you left me no choice."

"Let go of me." I shove at his chest.

"Once I've seen to that cut on your forehead."

I notice Aurora glancing between us. "Don't make me regret this," she warns. She narrows her gaze on him. "You take good care of her, you hear me?"

"Oh, I intend to." He smirks.

Is there a hidden meaning to his words? I peer into his features, but the expression on his face seems sincere.

"Here," Aurora holds out her medical bag.

"We're better equipped than whatever you're carrying in there, I assure you," Seb throws the words over his shoulder as he marches toward the inner part of the house. He passes the rest of his brothers, who are deep in conversation—presumably plotting the end of whoever was crazy enough to shoot at the house of the grandmother of the Don of the *Cosa Nostra*. OMG, someone was shooting at me. Someone was trying to kill me, and if Seb hadn't pushed me out of the way, they might have succeeded.

A trembling grips me and my teeth begin to chatter. I try to squeeze my lips together, try to curl into myself, to bury myself in his shirt, but nothing makes it better.

"Shh..." He holds me closer to his chest. "It's okay, you're safe now."

For some reason, I believe him. And it's nothing to do with the fact that his chest is broad, and the heat from his body is furnace-level hot, or that he smells soooo good. I draw in a huge lungful of Seb and my head spins. Nothing can hurt me as long as he has his arms around me. Why do I feel so safe in the embrace of one of the Mafioso who rule this city? Or is it precisely because I know what he does for a living that I'm confident he wouldn't hesitate to hurt anyone who'd dare come after me? OMG, he really is John Wick come to life, isn't he?

"Who...who was that, who shot at me?" I ask, mainly because I want to stop the line of thought buzzing through my mind.

"Whoever it was, he doesn't have much longer left to live," he answers in a grim voice.

I swallow. A shiver runs down my spine. The menace in his voice is a reminder of how his way of life is so different from mine. The confidence with which he speaks is also a turn on. I shouldn't find the violence inherent in him so appealing, but my elevated breathing, the way my pulse flutters as he tucks my head under his chin, the moisture that laces the flesh between my legs—all of it, insists otherwise.

He shoulders his way inside a bathroom and comes to a stop in front of the sink. I try to pull away from him but he only tightens his grasp around me.

"Hush," he says in a voice that brooks no argument, "calm down first."

We stay that way for a few seconds, during which time I allow myself to relax in his embrace. Allow myself to rub my cheek against his shirt, to draw his musky, edgy scent into my lungs, and close my eyes and pretend it's okay that a well-known Mafioso is comforting me after someone shot at me. Jesus, I was shot at.

"Feeling better?" his voice rumbles against my cheek.

I nod, and he lowers me onto the counter.

He peers into my face, then swears. "You're still bleeding."

He grabs a fresh cloth, wets it under the tap, and presses it to my wound.

I wince and his jaw hardens further. He takes my hand and presses it against the washcloth. "Hold it there," he orders as he moves away. Every time he speaks, authority drips from him. It must be nice to know that whatever he says, us mere mortals will obey.

He reaches up and grabs a first-aid kit from the shelf above the sink, then shakes out cotton balls and a bottle of antiseptic. He moves to stand between my legs, and when I lower the washcloth, he presses the antiseptic-soaked cotton ball to the wound.

I hiss out a breath.

A pulse tics to life in his jaw and his features seem to grow stormier. His actions, however, grow gentler. He dabs at the blood, tosses away the bloodied cotton ball, repeats his action with the next, and with the next. When he's finally satisfied, he places a bandage on the cut.

"There." He surveys his handiwork. "Does it hurt?"

"No," I say truthfully, "it's just a surface cut."

"On your face." He scowls. "They hurt your face."

"Technically, I think I hurt it when you pushed me down and threw yourself on top of me and—"

He glares at me, and I forget my train of thought. My stomach twists. *Bam-Bam-Bam*, my heart collides with my ribcage. Wariness trickles down my spine. I lean back from him, trying to put distance between us. To my surprise, he steps back and I slide down to place my feet on the floor and straighten. Unfortunately, that also means my breasts brush his chest. Heat sluices through my veins and my breath catches.

Every muscle in his body seems to tense. The tendons of his throat move as he swallows. Is he as affected by my proximity as I am by his?

"How do you feel?" he growls.

"I am fine, really." I peer into his features. "You, however, seem agitated."

His lips firm and he wraps his fingers around my wrist. Goosebumps pop on my skin. Little frissons of sensations arrow out from the point of contact. "Wh-what are you doing?" I croak.

"Accompanying you back to the others."

Before I can protest, he's turned and pushed open the doorway of the bathroom. He drags me along, and I could protest, but weariness grips me and I allow him to tug me along. We reach the living room, where the group of men I'd seen earlier are talking in low voices.

The doctor sees us and rushes forward. She surveys my forehead and nods, "Good job."

Seb grunts.

"Do you need a painkiller?" she asks.

"No," I say at the very same time that Seb snaps, "Yes."

She glances between us, then pulls out a pad from her handbag, writes out a prescription and hands it over to me. Before I can reach for it, jerkface here has snatched it from her and pocketed it.

"Hey," I scowl, "that's my prescription."

He ignores me and nods in the doctor's direction, "Thanks, I'll take care of it."

"I'm sure you will." The doctor turns to me. "You take care, and if you need anything, make sure you call me. Seb has my number." She smiles again, then pats me on the shoulder. She turns to leave, and Theresa runs over and hugs me.

"Oh, my god, you gave me a scare. Are you okay?"

"I am." I squeeze her shoulders. "Sorry I barged in on your dinner like this. I didn't know where else to go when I realized that I was being followed."

"You were followed?" Seb snaps from behind me.

I draw in a breath. I will not lose my temper. I will stay calm.

"What's it to you?" I shoot him a sideways glance. "And in case you haven't noticed, I'm speaking to my friend."

"Axel's calling you." He nods over Theresa's shoulder. I follow his gaze to find that, sure enough, her new husband is trying to get her attention. They were married a few days ago.

"You sure you're okay?" She peers into my face. "If you want me to stay with you—"

I shake my head, "No, go. I don't want to keep you."

"I can stay, really," she insists.

"I'll be fine." I kiss her cheek. "Go, be with your new husband."

"You sure?" she whispers.

"I'm sure." I step back.

Her features break into a smile, and she turns and almost skips across the floor to where Axel waits for her. The two of them lock lips in a kiss that seems to go on and on.

"Pussy-whipped motherfucker," Seb snorts.

"What do you mean?" I turn on him. "They're in love."

"Like I said, pussy-whipped," he says with a smirk.

"Why do men have to be so macho when it comes to admitting that two people can be in love?"

"Because love is an illusion?" His lips thin. "It's one way that women and men con each other into believing that they have feelings, when really, all they want to do is jump each other."

"You don't believe that, do you? If that were true, how do you explain Theresa and Axel, who are not only in love, but married?"

"They got lucky, I guess?" He raises a shoulder. "Doesn't mean most people do."

"What do you have against falling in love?"

"It's not for me," he says in a tone that brooks no argument.

"With that grumpy attitude of yours, I'd be surprised if anyone were rushing to fall in love with you, anyway" I mutter under my breath.

"I heard you." His grin widens. "You're feisty, aren't you?"

"Hate that word." I toss my hair over my shoulder. "Also, I think I should be getting along."

Massimo returns, followed by Luca. "Seems whoever shot at us also knocked out the guards."

"Hmm..." Seb glances from him to me. "They didn't try to stop you when you ran toward the house, did they?"

"Truthfully, I was too busy trying to save my life to have noticed anyone, but no, no one stopped me."

"Strange," Luca murmurs, "so they were already knocked out when she came to the house."

Seb stiffens. "What are you implying Luca?" he asks.

"Just stating a fact, is all." Luca tilts his head. "Better not let your emotions get the better of you."

"You done?" Seb says in a hard voice. The tension between the two stretches. Anger leaps off of Seb's big body, but his face doesn't change expression.

The two men glare at each other, then Luca jerks his chin. "I'd watch your back if I were you." He walks past us, and Seb's shoulders relax a little.

"What was that? What was he talking about?" I ask.

"Nothing you need to concern your pretty little head about."

I firm my lips. "You're a sadistic asshat, you know that?"

He raises a shoulder. "I'll drop you at home."

"I can see myself home, thank you very much."

"You're not going anywhere without me." He closes the distance between us.

Suddenly, someone screams behind us.

4

Seb

I glance over her shoulder just in time to see Nonna swaying on her feet. Cassandra, our housekeeper, has her arm around Nonna. She staggers under the weight of the other woman. In two quick steps, Adrian reaches her and steadies the both of them. Nonna presses a hand to the side of her chest and her fingers come away bloody.

"Fuck," I race toward Nonna, Elsa right behind me.

Adrian and Cass lower her gently to the settee and she leans her head back against it.

Aurora reaches her at the same time as me. She places her medical bag on the floor and sits down next to Nonna. She takes Nonna's pulse and her features shutter. "Call an ambulance," she tells Christian, who grabs his phone and walks a few feet away as he dials.

"Here," Elsa shrugs off the scarf she's wearing and gives it to Aurora, who uses it to staunch the flow of blood.

Nonna's eyelids flutter. She glances over the faces of all those assembled.

"It's good that everyone is here." She coughs.

"Don't try to talk, Nonna." I sink down to my knees next to her and take her hand in mine. "Save your strength."

"Don't stop me, Seb." Her lips kick up at the edges. "You've always been the most stubborn of all my boys. Once you get an idea into your head, you won't stop until you've found a way to make it happen. I wish I could have been around long enough to see you get married."

"The air-ambulance is on its way; it should be here within four minutes. I'm going to alert the guards so they can come right in when they arrive." Christian walks off.

Nonna coughs again. My heart hammers in my chest.

"You're going to be okay," I say the words aloud, not only to convince her but also myself. "You will be around long enough to see me get married."

"You promise?" She squeezes my hand. "Promise you'll get married. Promise you won't let what your father did to you get in the way of finding true happiness."

"Why are you talking like this?" I bring up my other hand and envelop her thinner, more fragile one between both of mine. "You'll be around to see the rest of us boys get married."

She smiles sadly. "I had hoped so, but I don't think I'll be alive that long."

"Nonna," I protest as the sound of an approaching chopper reaches us.

She tilts up her chin in my direction. "Promise me you'll get married within the next month."

"I promise," I whisper.

A smile curves her lips.

The sound of the helicopter grows even louder, and I suspect it must have landed on the back lawn. Within seconds, we hear footsteps, followed by voices, as two paramedics race toward us. One of them squats down next to us.

"I'm a doctor," Aurora says crisply. "Patient has been shot in the chest. She's lost a lot of blood, she—" Her voice fades away as I survey Nonna's pale features.

She's going to be fine. She has to be fine. She's been more than a mother and a father combined to us, and I never let her know that. Never let her know how much I appreciate everything she's done for us. If something happens to her... No, nothing can happen to her. She's going to be okay. She has to be ok—

"Could you please step back, sir?" The paramedic's voice cuts through my thoughts.

I release Nonna's hand and take a few steps back.

The paramedic slides a needle into her forearm, tapes it in place, and begins to run an IV drip.

I rise to my feet and watch as they move her to a stretcher, then wheel her toward the doorway, followed by Aurora.

Karma, my oldest brother Michael's wife, presses her hand to her stomach and sways. Michael catches her around her waist. "You okay, babe?"

"Yes," she nods. "It's just the shock of everything that happened. I'm sure I'll be fine."

"You need to be in bed." He glances from her to the doorway through which the medics are wheeling Nonna outside with Aurora in tow.

"I'll go with Nonna, too," I state.

"I'll come with you." Elsa steps up next to me.

I turn to her and she raises a shoulder. "Least I can do after you bandaged my wound." I glance up at the bandage on her temple. Was it only a few minutes ago that I took care of her wound? It seems so long ago already.

"You may as well." Michael looks from me to her. "We need to find out what you noticed about the man who shot at you earlier."

She pales, but nods. "Of course, Don Sovrano." She sounds uncharacteristically meek. "I'm happy to help in any way I can."

"Massimo, you, Luca, and Adrian head over to the hospital." He turns to Christian. "You, Axel and I need to talk."

"Me?" Axel scowls. "You need me for this conversation?"

"You're one of us now, aren't you?" Michael says in a hard tone. "You pull your weight, then. Your family is in crisis; we need your help."

He seems like he's about to protest, but Theresa grips his arm. "Please," she murmurs, "you promised, Axe."

Something passes between her and Axel, then Axel nods, "Fine, then." He turns to Michael. "How can I help?"

An hour later, I pace the floor of the waiting room outside the operation theater. I accompanied Nonna and held her hand throughout the ride in the air-ambulance. The paramedics worked to stabilize her the entire time, then rushed her into the hospital. Aurora accompanied them, and Elsa and I were told to go to the waiting room.

Massimo, Adrian, and Luca arrived about thirty minutes later by car, at which point Elsa retreated to one side of the room, and took a seat. I asked if she wanted anything to drink, but she refused. She did, however, pull out her phone to check... What? The time? Messages? Does she have somewhere to be? A boyfriend, perhaps?

As I walk away, Massimo corners me.

"Did they say anything?" he demands.

"How is she?" Luca adds.

"Give the man a chance to breathe," Adrian murmurs. "He's as stressed as the rest of us."

"They said she's in surgery." I shake my head. "We won't know anything more until they finish." I glance past them to where Elsa's eyeing her phone with a frown on her face.

"What's between the two of you?" Massimo growls. "The way you're watching her, it's like you can't stay away."

"She was hurt—"

"A scratch on her forehead," Adrian says in a mild voice.

"They shot at her," I insist.

"Which begs the question, why did she come to Nonna's house in the first place," Luca drawls.

I turn on him. "What are you trying to say?"

"Me?" He raises his hands. "Nothing."

"Say what's on your fucking mind, Luc-*ass*," I call him by the name he hates and am rewarded when his features harden.

"You want me to say it aloud, fine. If your girlfriend hadn't come knocking on Nonna's door, the gunman wouldn't have fired at us, and Nonna wouldn't be in there fighting for her life."

In my peripheral vision, I notice her glance our way. Her color fades, and she slides the phone into the pocket of her jeans and walks over to us.

Luca glances at her, then falls silent.

The four of us glance at each other, but no one says anything.

"You're right," she says in a low voice, "it's my fault the bullet hit Nonna."

"Don't blame yourself," I murmur, "it's not your fault. It's no one's fault this happened."

"Why didn't you go to Theresa's house? Or Seb's? Or Michael's? How did you know that we were all at Nonna's place?" Luca growls.

"Luca," I growl, "shut the fuck up."

"Why?" He folds his arms across his chest. "It's a simple enough question. Why can't she answer it?"

I glance between Massimo and Adrian's faces, and their expressions indicate they agree with him.

"The fuck you guys?" I widen my stance. "This is not an inquisition."

"Luca's only voicing what all of us are thinking," Massimo points out. "Although, I'll admit, our brother lacks the finesse with which to word his questions."

"It's true," Adrian tilts his head, "and you know it. The faster she tells us why she came to us, the sooner we can clear all of this up."

"*Cazzo*." I ball my fingers into fists. "They shot at her. She was in as much danger as the rest of us. You saw that, so why are you—"

"It's fine." Her touch on my arm stops me. A current sizzles from the point of contact and up my arm, aiming straight for my dick, apparently, for the blood drains to my groin. *Gesù Cristo,* why is it that just her touch is enough to make me want to haul her to me and kiss her lips, then throw her down and bury myself inside her, when my grandmother is fighting for her life across the hallway? I pull my arm from her grip.

Her face pales further, hurt flashes in her eyes, and she glances toward my brothers.

"Theresa had mentioned to me where she was going to be, and that all of you were gathering at your Nonna's home today. I was on my way to the shop—"

"The shop?" Massimo frowns.

"The florist's shop that I run with Theresa—when I noticed a car following me. He sped up when I increased my pace, slowed down when I did. I, uh, knew that Theresa had married into the *Cosa Nostra*—"

"So, you concluded that one of our enemies was after you?" I frown.

"Theresa and I do not just work together; we are also good friends. We hang out a lot, go out together. I figured people have seen us together, and something like this has never happened before. I didn't think it was a coincidence I was followed so soon after her being involved with Axel. I... I panicked." She squeezes her hands together. "I didn't know where to go. And then when they tried to run me off the road—"

"He tried to run you off the road?" I explode. "*Stocazzo!*" I drag my fingers through my hair.

"N... nothing happened." She turns her gaze on me, and this time, there is no hint of emotion in her blue eyes. Interesting. She's more in control of her feelings than she lets on.

She swallows. "I was on a strip of road where there's not much traffic when it happened. Then, another car crowded me, so I had no choice but to take the next turn.

"I realized I was near your nonna's house, so when I reached it, I slammed on the brakes, jumped out, and raced toward the front door, hoping to get help. I'm sorry I wasn't thinking. I just knew I was in danger, and that someone here would be able to help me, but then the gunshots rang out and—" She bites down on her lower lip and a shudder grips her shoulders.

So, there was more than one car following her? *Cristo Santo!* My stomach knots. A ball of emotion hooks its claws into my throat. Why am I unable to see her in distress? My fingers tingle. I want to reach for her, hold her close and calm her down, and promise her nothing like this will ever happen to her again. Except, we are the *Cosa Nostra,* and I'm an integral part of it. Our lives are always at risk from our enemies, and so are our family's and friends'. It's the price we pay for the path we follow. It's a lesson I learned early.

It's why I swore to never get married... Until Nonna made me promise otherwise earlier. *Cazzo!* I tuck my elbows into my sides and try to wipe all expression off my face.

"Looks like she was coerced into coming to the house." Massimo leans forward on the balls of his feet. "Whoever was in those cars knew where we were and wanted her to come to us."

"What about the guards?" Luca asks in a hard voice. "How do you explain them being knocked out so you could get past them and to the door?"

She bites down on her lower lip, and hell, if I don't want to go over and pull out her lip from under her teeth and bite down on it myself. I take a step toward her, then stop myself. Luca has a point. Why were the guards knocked out before she came on the scene? Something doesn't fit.

She glances at me, and I want to nod in encouragement, but I stop myself. If she had anything to do with Nonna being shot... But no, that makes no sense at all. It's a coincidence, is all. But I want to hear it from her.

"I..." she tips up her chin, "I don't know why they were knocked out, to be honest. I didn't see anyone as I ran through the gates."

"—which had been left open." Luca widens his stance.

"Whoever steered her in our direction made sure to remove all obstacles from her course," Adrian muses.

I whip my head in his direction. "You think she was set up?"

"By someone who knew where we all were, and who counted on Seb recognizing her and letting her in," Massimo completes my train of thought.

Luca, Massimo, Adrian, and I exchange glances.

"Cazzo!" I drag my fingers through my hair. "This means there's someone inside our clan who is sharing information. Someone who knew we'd all be here under one roof. Or someone overheard Theresa's conversation with her."

Elsa hunches her shoulders. "I... I'm really sorry I burst in on you guys, sorry that I brought the gunmen to your doorstep, sorry that Nonna was hurt. If I could do it all over again, I wouldn't stop at Nonna's house, but continue on to the shop—"

"And he'd have shot at you as you entered the shop, if he hadn't pushed you off the road, forced you out of your car, and put a gun to your head." I dig my fingernails into the palm of my hand. My stomach churns. *Porca miseria*, she could have been killed. She almost *was* killed.

"You should have never left home today," I say through gritted teeth. "You should have stayed in bed. That way, all of this could have been avoided."

"Excuse me," she snaps. Color rises on her cheeks, she juts out her chin, and scowls at me. "You don't tell me how to live my life, mister. No one does. I am my own person, and I've worked hard to build my life exactly the way I like it, and—"

Someone clears their throat and we all turn.

5

Elsa

My phone vibrates in my pocket; I slide it out and glance at it. At the same time, the surgeon in his blood splattered scrubs looks between us. Seb moves toward him, followed by his brothers. The doctor speaks with them in a low tone as I move to the side to check the message.

I need to leave soon Elsa. When will you be back?

I'll be there within the hour. Can you hold on until then? I text back, then pocket the phone and glance up to find Seb's gaze on me. His features are pale; his eyes are dead. It looks like he's lost his best friend in the world... Or his nonna.

Oh no, no, no. I press my knuckles to my mouth and move toward him. I brush past the other men who are standing around with shellshocked expressions on their faces. I reach him, close the distance between us, and wrap my arms around him. His entire body feels as if it's frozen, his muscles locked in place. A palpable sense of disbelief emanates from him. I glance up to find his gaze fixed on a point in the distance.

"Seb?" I whisper. "Sebastian?

When he doesn't reply, I stand up on tiptoes and press my lips onto the strip of skin exposed between the lapels of his shirt.

A shudder runs through him and his shoulders bunch. He glances down at me, and my breath catches. That light in his amber eyes is gone, replaced by a darkness that both frightens me, and beckons me. His skin is pale and the hollows under his cheekbones seem to have become even more pronounced. I guess this is what a forsaken angel looks like. He's looking at me like he doesn't actually see me, yet he'd reacted to my touch, so I know that he feels me.

"Seb," I swallow, "are you okay?" My phone vibrates in my pocket, and I wince.

A frown creases his forehead. "Are you going to answer that?" he asks.

"No," I shake my head, "but I have to go."

"Go?" He repeats the word as if he hasn't quite comprehended what I'm saying.

"I have to leave Seb, I'm so sorry. It's just I..." I bite my lower lip, and his nostrils flare. His gaze drops to my mouth, and a nerve flicks to life at his temple.

My phone vibrates again. Damn, I can't ignore it. "I'm so sorry, Seb. I really have to go." I step back from him, but he swoops his arm out and around my waist, pulling me close and holding me in place.

"You're leaving me?" he asks in a voice devoid of emotion.

"I'm sorry, but I have to. I know how much pain you are in, and believe me, if I could, I would stay—"

"So stay," he says in that same remote voice.

"I can't." I glance past him at the door. "I'm truly sorry, but I can't." I try to pull away, and to my relief, he releases me. I brush past him, rush out the door, and run straight into Michael and Karma, whom I've already met through Theresa.

"Elsa." Karma grips my arm. "How is she?"

"She..." I swallow, then turn to Michael. "I'm sorry for your loss," I say in a soft voice.

Michael's gaze widens before he wipes all emotion from his face.

"Oh, no!" Karma's features crumple. She releases me, only to turn to Michael and throw her arms around him. "I'm so sorry, baby."

He leans into her, and for just a few seconds, I see the vulnerability of the Don of the *Cosa Nostra*. Feeling like an intruder, I walk past them and down the corridor to exit. I scramble out of the way of incoming paramedics with a woman on a stretcher, and I'm reminded—that could have been me. Simultaneously, I remember I left my car at Nonna's place. I hesitate. *What do I do?*

I reach for my phone to call a car when a town car with tinted windows pulls to a stop in front of me. The driver rolls down his window and addresses me, "Sebastian told me to bring you home."

"Eh?" I blink rapidly. "But he didn't tell me anything. He—" My phone buzzes. I pull it out of my jeans pocket to find there's a message from an unknown number:

. . .

Michael's bodyguard Antonio will take you to your car and follow you home.

I blow out a breath. Only one person would message me in that imperious tone, and somehow, I'm not surprised he's gotten hold of my number. He is a part of the Mafia, after all. I assume he has minions in his pocket almost everywhere—people who are only too glad to drop everything and do his bidding.

Antonio—I assume he's the one driving—gets out of the car, then opens the back door for me. "Please, Miss Elsa, let me make sure you get home safely."

I hesitate.

"He has a lot on his plate at the moment; it'll help if he knows you're safe," Antonio adds.

That's true. And damn, if I don't feel manipulated. On the other hand, this means I'll save time and reach home faster.

I slide into the backseat and he shuts the door behind me. He gets into the driver's seat, shuts his own door and eases onto the road.

In half an hour, we are back at Nonna's place. I find my car parked in the driveway, behind the now-closed gates, with the windows rolled up. I left the car on the street, with the engine running and the keys in the ignition. The gates to the house had been open and I'd darted through and up the pathway to the front door.

"I got the car off the main road. Seb told me to," Antonio explains as the gate opens and he parks behind my car.

"Thank you." I nod at him, before getting out of the car and heading toward my own.

Inside, I find the keys still in the ignition and my hardback where I left it on the passenger seat. I adjust the rearview mirror and spot the cut on my forehead. It's crazy how just a few hours can change everything. Now, his nonna is gone. And I know that the simmering connection between us is more than I had imagined. The entire situation is so messy. On the other hand, I caught his attention. Mission accomplished. But at what cost?

I draw in a breath, start the car, and follow the circular driveway out and onto the main road.

Twenty minutes later, I am home. Antonio had followed me at a safe distance, and waited until I had walked up the steps and into the door of my apartment block. Only after I shut the door behind me, do I hear him drive off. No doubt, he's following Seb's instructions to a T.

The flat is quiet as I place my handbag and keys on the table near the door. I walk into the living room to find my babysitter, Sara, fast asleep on the couch. I head toward the smaller of the two bedrooms and peek inside. The night light is on, illuminating the stars stuck to the ceiling. I walk over to the crib and find Avery fast asleep. She's on her back, chubby arms flung out to the sides. Her chest rises and falls as she breathes. Her eyelashes lay against her cheekbones and her mouth is slightly parted. Warmth coils in my chest. I lean forward and slide my finger inside the tiny half-curled fingers of her hand. She stirs, then clasps her fingers firmly around mine. I wait a few seconds, to ensure she is completely still, before I kiss my fingertips and touch them to Avery's forehead. Her baby smell fills my lungs and it's all I can do not to scoop her up and cuddle her close. I'd do anything for this little girl. Anything to ensure that she has every happiness in her life. She deserves everything I couldn't have. I never knew my father, and I'm going to ensure she has one, bastard though he might be. I'd sacrifice myself so she'd go to sleep every night with a smile on her face.

I slowly slide my finger out from between hers, then straighten and leave the room. I walk over to the sofa where Sara is sprawled out, her hair about her shoulders.

"Sara..." I touch her shoulder, and her eyelids snap open.

"Oh, hey." She yawns. "When did you get back?"

"A few minutes ago."

She stretches, then bolts upright. "Shoot, what time is it? I promised Mom I'd be home by ten."

"It's nine-forty-five."

She rubs her eyes. "I guess I should get going. Good thing I live just upstairs." She rises to her feet, then peers into my face. "What happened?" She gestures to my forehead.

"Nothing, it's just a scratch."

"You sure?" She takes in my features. "I can stay, if you want."

"No, that's all right. You've helped me a lot by babysitting her already."

"Any time. She's a sweetheart. She ate most of her dinner. Then we played, I read her a bedtime story, and she was out like a light."

"That's good." A wave of exhaustion overwhelms me and I clutch the back of the sofa.

"You sure you're okay?"

"Sure." I smile. "Hell, I forgot to pay you." I walk around her and head to where I dropped my purse on the table. I pull out a few notes and hold them out to her.

"It was a pleasure. You don't have to pay me; I love babysitting Avery."

"I insist. You earned it." I push the notes into her hand, then walk to the door and hold it open. "Thanks again for being available on short notice."

After she leaves, I head toward my own bedroom. Too tired to even shower, I simply step out of my clothes, pull on a soft camisole, and slide into bed. I close my eyes, and what seems like only a few minutes later, I'm awakened by a cry from the other room.

Avery! I jump out of bed and race to her room to find her sitting up in her crib. "Hey, baby, did you have sweet dreams?"

She holds up her chubby arms, and I scoop her up and cuddle her.

She settles down instantly, then begins to fuss again. "Time for a diaper change, Bubu?"

I set her down and quickly change her diaper. As I toss the soiled diaper in the receptacle, the doorbell rings.

I glance down at myself, then carry her back to my bedroom. Placing her on the bed, I pull on my robe, then cuddling her in my arms, I head for the front door. The doorbell rings again.

"I'm coming," I yell. I look through the peephole and my breath catches. I take a step back then fling the door open. "What are you doing here?"

6

Seb

She has a baby. She has a baby who looks exactly like her. Blonde hair, big blue eyes, pink lips, and glowing skin. I glance from the little girl in her arms to her, then back to the child, who begins to fuss. My reports had indicated she had a child. Still, knowing about it's one thing; seeing her with the child is another. And feeling this weird sensation in my chest that tightens my rib cage is something else altogether.

"How did you know it was safe to open the door?" I thrust my chin forward.

"I *did* look through the peephole," she retorts.

"What if it had been someone else? Someone like the guy who chased you yesterday?"

She pales, then tips up her chin. "But it wasn't, and I recognized you. Although, I'm beginning to think maybe I shouldn't have opened the door."

The child in her arms wriggles, then holds her arms out to me.

I blink, almost take a step back, then stop myself.

"Oh, she wants to go to you..." Elsa seems as dumbfounded as me.

I stare at the little girl, who all but throws herself at me. I grab her and tuck an arm under her to support her weight. She stares at me, unblinking, then begins to babble. The words make no sense; they are in some kind of completely made-up language.

"Uh, what did she say?" I study the baby who holds my gaze. Huh? No one, and I mean no one, dares stare back at me. Except, apparently, this child here.

"I think she wants you to feed her breakfast," Elsa ventures.

"Breakfast?" I blink at the girl again.

"Children get hangry if they're not fed on time." Elsa leans past me to shut the door, and the scent of cherries fills my senses. I don't realize I've leaned in toward her until she turns and slams into me.

"Oops, sorry." Her breasts push into my chest, her nipples so pointed that I can feel them through the robe she's wearing. She tries to brush past me, but I wind an arm around her waist and keep her in place. She glances up at me as her daughter babbles again, then reaches over and socks her head.

"Ow." Elsa laughs. "What was that for?" She cups her daughter's face, then rises up on tiptoe to kiss her chubby cheek. She makes a loud mwah sound.

With my arm around each of them, a weird sensation fills my chest. Clearly, Nonna's death and the promise I made her is affecting me more than I expected. It's the only reason I can't shift my gaze from her as she ruffles her daughter's hair then tries to pull away from me.

"I need to get her breakfast," she explains, and I release her.

She brushes past me and heads to the kitchen, where she bustles around getting a small bowl out of the drawer. She proceeds to cut up some fruit, which she places in the bowl. When she returns, she places it on the tray of a high chair.

She holds out her hands for her daughter, who turns away and clings to my shoulder.

"What's her name?" I ask softly.

"Avery," she murmurs.

"Avery." I hold the baby's blue gaze as she stares up at me. She suddenly laughs, then smacks my cheek.

I burst out laughing, and something releases inside of my chest.

"Avery," Elsa exclaims in a horrified tone. "Sorry," she turns to me, "this is something new that she's picked up. It seems to be her chosen way of communicating right now."

I've been put in my place, all right, and by a kid.

"How old is she?" I ask as I lower her into the high chair.

"Almost two." Elsa snaps the tray in place and pushes the bowl in Avery's direction.

The child bashes her hand into the bowl of fruit. Half of a grape goes flying, then a bit of apple. She manages to grab a piece of banana and brings it to her mouth. She chomps on it, then exclaims, "Umm." She makes smacking noises with her lips.

"I know, baby." Elsa turns to me. "That should keep her occupied for a little while."

"So," I glance between them, "you have a child?"

She raises one eyebrow and looks at me like I'm stupid. "It would appear so," she replies.

"You're fighting for custody of her," I state.

"Excuse me?"

"You're currently only allowed to have her on weekends, and if your ex-husband, who just happens to be one of the most powerful cops in the police force, has his way, he'll take that away from you. In fact, you are one step away from losing all rights to your daughter, aren't you?"

The color fades from her cheeks. Her muscles seem to coil until she is a mass of vibrating tension.

"Get out," she says through gritted teeth. "Get out of my apartment."

"Oh, but I haven't even told you the real reason for my visit."

"I don't want to know."

"Oh, but you should." I fold my arms across my chest. "In fact, I think it's in your best interest to listen to what I have to say. It might go a long way toward alleviating many of your problems."

"I don't want anything to do with you," she snarls.

I allow my lips to curl in a smirk. "Afraid you may not have much of a choice in this, Princess."

"Don't call me that."

"You prefer Frozen?"

She squeezes the bridge of her nose. "Why are you even here? Shouldn't you be—" She waves a hand in the air. "Taking care of whatever needs to be done after what happened yesterday?"

"If you mean, shouldn't I be mourning my grandmother, I am. In fact, that's why I'm here."

She looks at me suspiciously. "I don't follow."

"Before Nonna died, she asked me to get married."

She frowns.

"Within the next month."

"What does that have to do with me?"

"It has everything to do with you." I grin.

"It's a little too early for riddles." She rubs her temple.

"How's the head?" I jerk my chin in the direction of her still-bandaged wound.

"It's sore," she admits, turning toward her baby to make sure she's okay, I guess, before she glances back at me. "You were saying?"

"That I have a proposition for you."

"Oh?" She folds her arms around her waist. "I'm really not interested in anything, especially if it has to do with you."

"Don't be too hasty." I glance around the room. "Have you eaten breakfast? Babies are not the only ones who get *hangry,* you know?"

I circle the table, then begin pulling open the doors to cabinets.

Something hits me in the back. I turn to find Avery waving her hand in the air. She laughs at me, then goes back to playing with her food.

"See? Even my daughter knows you're not welcome here."

"On the contrary, I would argue she's quite enjoying my company."

Avery grabs a grape and flings it on the floor, then smiles at me again.

"See? She definitely wants me here."

"Well, I don't," Elsa huffs.

"Definitely *hangry,*" I conclude, then turn and pull out a skillet. I place it on the stovetop, then walk over to the refrigerator and pull the door open. There're jars of baby food, two eggs, some butter, one head of lettuce, and one tomato. Does she not like to stock her refrigerator? Or does she simply prefer not to eat, or—

"Hey!" She charges toward me and pushes against the door of the refrigerator, trying to shut it. I hold onto the door so it won't budge. "It's impolite to peer into other people's refrigerators," she points out.

I pull out the eggs and butter, then step back. She slams the door shut and the entire refrigerator wobbles.

I brush past her, grab a fork and a mixing bowl from one of the shelves. I tap the egg on the side of the bowl.

"What are you doing?"

"Making you breakfast."

"I don't want you here."

"Too bad." I whisk the eggs together, and light the flame under the skillet. "Why don't you make yourself useful and slice some of that bread?"

She hesitates, then does as she's told.

"Lay the table." I point with my spoon in the direction of the table.

She opens her mouth to protest, and I click my tongue. "Don't argue with me."

She huffs, then grabs cutlery and thumps it down on the table before she drops into the seat next to her daughter.

I whip up the scrambled eggs, divide them into two plates, butter the bread and add some to each plate, then walk over and slide a plate over to her. Taking off my coat, I place it over the chair opposite her, then take my seat.

Avery beams at me, then picks up a piece of apple and throws it at me.

I snatch it out of the air. "Thanks, sweetheart." I pop it into my mouth.

The kid smiles at me, then points at Elsa's food. "Egg, mama."

"You want some eggs, baby?" She scoops up some of the food and offers it to Avery who chows it down like she is starving.

"She has an appetite, eh?" I watch the little girl closely.

"She likes to eat everything... At least, I think she does, based on the little time that I have her."

Her lower lip trembles and she looks away. She reaches for her plate, shovels some of the eggs into her mouth, and chews.

I scoop some of the eggs onto the bread, take a bite, then place it back on the plate. I watch as she makes her way through her food, as if it's a chore.

"How is it?" I point to the food.

"Good," she admits. "Sorry, I'm just not used to eating breakfast."

"From the way you look, you're not used to eating at all," I observe.

"What's wrong with the way I look?" She scowls.

I look her up and down. "Nothing." I raise my gaze to her face. "Absolutely nothing, and that's the problem."

"What do you mean?" She carefully places her fork on the plate. "What is this all about? Why are you here, trying to be all cozy and domestic with me, when you should be with your family."

"I am with my family."

She opens and shuts her mouth. "Okay, I'm not sure what game you're playing, but I really don't like it." She pushes her chair back and starts to rise, when I reach over and grab her hand.

"Sit down, Princess."

She glances down at where my fingers are curled around her wrist. She's so thin that my fingers look obscenely large against the delicacy of her frame.

I release her, then hold up my hands. "I think you'll find it worth your time to listen to my proposition."

She folds her arms across her chest and leans back in her seat. "Not that I'm even remotely interested... But in the interest of getting you out of my home, what is it?"

I lean forward, lock my fingers together, then fix her with my gaze. "Marry me."

7

Elsa

"What?" I gape at him. "I think I heard you incorrectly."

"You heard me right." He looks back at me placidly. "Marry me."

I burst out laughing, and Avery turns to stare at me. I reach over, pick up half a grape, and hold it to her mouth. She flicks her tongue around it, then closes her lips around my fingers, and begins to chew on it. I pull my hand back, and she proceeds to smash her fist into the tray next to her food bowl.

"And I thought I was the one to take a blow to the head," I mutter under my breath.

Anger radiates off of him, and I can't stop myself from glancing at him. His features are set in uncompromising lines, his lips firm. He glares at me and my insides flip-flop. "Whoever chased you yesterday is not going to stop until he gets to you." He jerks his chin in Avery's direction. " What happens to her then? Have you thought of that?"

"I'm a mother. What do you think?" I snap at him.

"So, then you know what I'm offering you will help you take care of all of your problems in one stroke."

"You're joking, right?" I half laugh.

His face grows even more stormy and a nerve throbs at his temple. He seems to be barely controlling himself, if that set jaw of his is any indication.

"Anger leads to high blood pressure, which leads to all sorts of other problems," I murmur.

"Excuse me?" He frowns.

"You're perpetually frowning. It's also bad for your skin. Not that the lines don't look good on you... They do add a certain distinguished air... But still, when you smile, the whole world smiles, you know?"

His scowl deepens. "Don't change the topic of discussion."

"I wasn't aware we were having a discussion."

He pulls something out of his pocket, and places it on the table between us.

"What the hell—?" I gape at the blue diamond surrounded by golden-yellow sapphires in an intricate setting. The ring is not store-bought. Everything about the piece points to it being a family heirloom. This was not a spur of the moment decision.

"What... what is that?" I finally mange to force the words out through a throat gone dry.

"It belonged to Nonna." He glances at the ring, then at me. "I want you to have it. I want you to be my wife."

"W-wife?" I shake my head. "I barely know you."

"You don't need to know me to marry me."

"Oh yeah?" I reach for a glass of water, take a sip, then choke on it and place it back on the table. I cough so much that tears run down my cheek.

He jumps up, grabs a napkin, and hands it to me.

"Thanks." I nod to him as I dry my eyes.

At which point, Avery begins to cry.

"Sorry, honey, I didn't mean to scare you." I scoop her up from the highchair and cuddle her. She instantly subsides and begins to play with my hair.

"So, what do you say?" he persists.

"About what?"

"You, me, getting married." He jerks his chin in Avery's direction. "You do realize it's the best way to get full custody of her, right?"

"What, by getting married to you?" I frown at him. "I'm really confused by this conversation."

"The *Cosa Nostra* is more powerful than the police, more pervasive than the government." He drums his fingers on the table.

"You mean, you would kill him?"

"Only if you want me to."

"No," I burst out, "he's her father, I... I wouldn't want that."

"As you wish." He tilts his head.

"My ex has enough money to afford the best legal help."

"I have more money than him," he drawls.

My head begins to spin. "Are you saying that if I marry you, you'll help me get full custody of my daughter?"

"If you want, I'll make sure your ex never looks at either of you again. Also," he flattens his hand on the table, "you don't have to worry about anyone coming after you. As the wife of the Capo of the *Cosa Nostra*, you and your daughter would receive round-the-clock protection."

I rock Avery, who wriggles against me. I place her down, and she waddles over to Seb and throws her arms around his leg.

"Up." She looks up at him expectantly.

"Oh, you don't have to..." Before I can complete the sentence, he lifts her up in his arms.

"Hi, beautiful," he murmurs.

"Play." She grabs at his hair and tugs. "Play," she says more insistently.

Even though Fabio speaks to her in Italian, I speak to Avery in English, and when she's with me she tends to use more English words.

"You want to play?" he asks her in a serious voice.

She nods. "Play, Scooty, play," Avery chants.

"Scooty; that's the name of her toy bunny. Guess she wants you to play with him," I murmur.

"Where's this Scooty then?" He turns that brilliantly golden gaze in my direction.

I hesitate.

"She wants me to play with Scooty. I think you should take me to him." He arches an eyebrow at me.

"Fine, fine." I blow out a breath, then turn in the direction of her room. He's on my heels as I reach the cordoned-off play area in her room.

"There," I point to the raggedy toy.

He carefully lowers her to the floor, and Avery pounces on the bunny and begins to chew on its ears. She drags it out of her mouth and offers it to Seb, who accepts the toy.

"Thank you," he says.

She purses her lips together and makes a kissing noise.

"You want me to kiss Scooty?" Seb asks.

When she nods, he does just that, then offers the toy back to her. Avery takes it from him, then grabs another, a toy airplane, and begins to make a humming sound as she weaves it through the air.

"That should keep her busy for a while. I hope."

"Good." He turns to me. "I'm still waiting for an answer."

"And I'm not ready to give you one."

"I'm not leaving you alone until you do." Those golden-brown eyes of his hold mine. Heat from his body surrounds me and sinks into my blood. My heart rate ratchets up and my pulse skitters. I lick my lips and his gaze falls to my mouth. His nostrils flare and I wonder if he's thinking of kissing me.

He weaves his fingers through mine and guides me out of the room.

"Wait." I grab the baby monitor on the way out.

He leaves the door to her bedroom open, then leads me into the living room. Once there, he takes the baby monitor from me and places it on the coffee table. I tug on my hand, and he releases it. Thank god.

It had felt so right to have my hand in his, to follow him, to not have to think, or make decisions, or do anything but allow him to direct my actions. I shake my head. *What the hell is wrong with me?* I've come so far. I have a steady job, friends who have my back, and I'm doing everything possible to get more time with my daughter. *And how is that going for you?*

Fabio will never allow me more time with Avery. He's convinced that I'm a bad mother. He has the money and the influence in this city, and access to the best legal help. Also, he's Italian and I'm English, which means the courts in this country will always favor him. I'm fighting a losing battle and I know it.

"What do you get out of it?" I tip up my chin. "You could marry anyone you want. Why me?"

"Nonna was very clear that I should get married within the coming month. As you know, it was her... dying wish." He pushes out the last couple of words, and I swear, I hear his voice crack. He glances away, then drags his thumb under his eye.

Was that a tear he wiped away? Or is he doing it just to get my sympathy? But there was that change in his voice, and he was genuinely shattered when he heard the news from the doctor at the hospital, wasn't he?

He turns back to me. "As to why you?" He raises a shoulder. "You're as good as anyone else. Only, you need this marriage more than I do."

"And you want to marry someone who is beholden to you? Someone who would be dependent on you so you could control her?"

"Someone who would benefit greatly from this arrangement, too," he points out.

But it's only an arrangement; this is not a real marriage, is it? "And what about..." I shuffle my feet. "You know what I mean."

He frowns. "Afraid I have no idea what you're referring to."

"We'll have different rooms, won't we?"

He still seems puzzled.

"You know, bedrooms, sleeping at night—"

"We'll be sharing the same bed."

"Excuse me?" My cheeks heat. "The same bed?"

"Once we're married, yes."

"B-but…"

He arches an eyebrow.

"I don't know you at all," I burst out.

"I don't need to know you to fuck you."

I firm my lips. "If you think this is going to convince me to marry you—"

The doorbell rings. I scowl at him, then at the door. "I wasn't expecting anyone."

The doorbell rings again and again.

"Coming," I call out as I head toward the door with him right behind me.

I wrench it open, to find a guy standing there, holding out a packet. I sign for it, and he leaves. I close the door, lock it, turn, and once more, crash head-first into that wide chest. The dark male scent of him fills my lungs, and I'm ashamed to say that I take in big gulps of it.

"Did you just smell me?" He sounds amused.

"What?" I pull back. "Of course not." I march around him, head for the living room, where I grab the letter opener from the side table. I slide it under the flap of the envelope and open it, then take in the official looking sheets of paper. My heart begins to race and my throat closes. I sit down on the settee and pull out the documents. I scan through them and anger squeezes my lungs.

"Goddamn it!" I throw them down on the table and jump to my feet. "You knew that this was going to happen. You knew my ex was going to file for full rights to her. You knew it, and you manipulated things so I would have no option but to marry you, you—"

"Hold on," he snaps, "don't go shooting your mouth off without any evidence, woman."

"The evidence is that I was served with papers immediately after you told me you'd make sure I get custody." I grab the papers off of the table, then walk around it until I reach him, and slap them against his chest. The papers slide down to the floor around him, and he makes no move to pick them up. He also doesn't seem too upset by my outburst. That entire attempt at not allowing my temper to get away from me? I failed in spectacular fashion.

He folds his arms across his chest and taps his foot against the floor. "Are you done?"

I pivot and walk around the sofa, so I can put some distance between us.

"My inquiries showed it was just a matter of time before your ex filed to strip you of your parental rights. It's why I came here today. We both stand to gain if we go through with this marriage as quickly as possible."

"You mean, you get what you want, without any delays."

"And you." He steps over the papers, then closes the distance to stand on the other side of the sofa. "The sooner we marry, the sooner I can put pressure on my contacts to have him retract his actions."

I grip the back of the sofa. I don't want to marry him, especially not when I'm so attracted to him. The last time I thought I liked a man, see what happened? He not only slept around, but also turned out to be the kind of bastard who won't rest until he's taken everything from me. And now, I'm considering walking straight into another marriage... In order to redress the consequences from the previous one. If that isn't a recipe for disaster, I don't know what is.

"I cannot... *Will* not let anyone take my daughter from me. She is my top priority. She is my heart. I cannot separate me from her." I tip up my chin. "I'd fight anyone and anything for her. If I lose her, I won't survive."

"And I'll make sure that never happens. We'll make sure no one dares take her away from you. That no one dares harm either of you."

We. He said 'we.' When did I last feel like I was part of a unit? Maybe with Theresa and her friends, who had taken me under their wing when I'd moved here from England. But this is different. This would mean being part of a team... A family... My family. My unit. I'd never thought I could have that again. Never thought I'd marry again. Definitely not to a Mafioso.

"Well?" He tilts his head. "What do you say?"

"I'll marry you," I tilt my head up, "on one condition."

"Oh?"

"No sex."

8

Seb

I throw back my head and laugh. "You're crazy, if you think I'm going to agree to that."

"You need me as much as I need your help." She firms her lips.

I need you... and that's what bothers me so much about you.

"Okay, fine. I accept the condition, but I have one of my own," I retort.

Her forehead wrinkles. I guess she wasn't expecting that. But if she thinks I'm not going to take advantage of this situation, she's sorely mistaken.

"What is it?" she finally asks.

"An open marriage."

"Eh?" She blinks rapidly. "What does that mean?"

"Exactly what it says. I'm free to see other women during the time we're married."

She gapes at me. "So, you'd ah, you'd—"

"Fuck other women," I helpfully supply. "Clearly, if I'm not getting it at home, I'm going to have to go elsewhere."

"No," she snaps.

"Yes," I insist. "You don't expect me to deprive myself when you've determined our marriage will not meet my needs."

She juts out her lower lip, then shuffles her feet. "Fine, but I get to be with other men, as well."

"No fucking way." I scowl. *If anyone else dares to lay a hand on her I'll... I'll kill the bastard.*

"If you can see other women, surely, I should be allowed to see other men."

Anger thuds at my temples. I curl my fingers at my sides. "During the time that we are married, you will not see anyone else," I growl.

She gapes. "So you can see other women, but I'm not allowed to see other men?"

"Exactly."

"I don't understand why we wouldn't have the same rules for each of us."

"You're the one who doesn't want sex to be a part of our marriage. Hence, sex is not important to you."

She hesitates, then says, "That's not what I— But that's not fair."

"It's not; deal with it," I drawl.

"Then you can't see other women, either." She folds her arms across her chest.

"Are you jealous?" I smirk.

"Of course not. I'm trying to level the odds here."

"How about a compromise?"

She glances at me with suspicion.

My lips quirk, and I manage to wipe the smile off of my face. "During the time we are married, I won't bring any of my women back home."

"What the—?" She opens and shuts her mouth. "You were thinking of bringing them home?"

"On occasion." I raise a shoulder. "I wouldn't fuck them in our bed, of course. I'd keep a room in our house just for that, and you wouldn't even know I was there. Well, unless one of them was particularly loud." I bite back a laugh. I can tell she's about to explode, but I continue, "In fact—"

"You will *not* bring anyone home with you. I have a child, or have you forgotten?" she says in a dangerously low voice.

"It's the main reason I proposed to you; lends an air of authenticity to the proceedings, you know?"

"You're a... You're a horrible, horrible man. I don't think I want to marry you, after all."

I widen my stance. "I've pretended you have a choice, but we both know that you don't."

Color fills her cheeks; her chest rises and falls. Those blue eyes of hers grow stormy, and honestly, it's the most beautiful thing I have ever seen. Her skin is so creamy that her every emotion is reflected on her face.

"Why are you doing this?" she whispers. "Why are you making everything so difficult?"

"I'm doing you a favor, and you know it." I tilt my head. "Without my help, you're going to lose all rights to your child. You need this arrangement, Princess."

"Aargh!" She closes her eyes. "You are a piece of work, you know that?"

"So I've been told. What's it gonna be then, Frozen?"

"Stop calling me that."

"You prefer Princess, I take it?"

"Call me by my name, will you?" She snaps her eyelids open and frowns at me.

"And you can call our arrangement by any name you want, but it's the only way forward for you."

"And for you." She props her hands on her hips. "At least, admit that you need me to marry you, and that you have no one else who fits the bill on such short notice."

"You're a persistent little thing, aren't you?"

She scowls at me.

"You do realize that I could have any woman in this city agree to this arrangement."

"So, go ask them, then," she scoffs.

"However, the chemistry between us makes this a much more believable proposition to the rest of my family. Besides," I close the distance between us, "you're not too hard on the eyes, either."

Her features contort. She raises her hand to slap me, but I grab her wrist. I twist her hand behind her back and haul her close to me. She brings her other arm up, but I grab it and bend it behind her back, shackling both wrists together. She struggles, but she's trapped. I bring my other hand up to grip the nape of her neck.

"Let go of me," she hisses.

I pushed her earlier, wanting to see what it took to push her over the edge, wanting to feel her anger, see the crackle of those silver sparks in her eyes. She wriggles against me and I fit my hips to hers. She must feel my hardness against her thigh, for she stills. Color suffuses her cheeks; her gaze grows wary. She swallows, and her chest rises and falls.

"You sense it, too, don't you, this connection between us?"

"All I sense is a man who thinks he can use his dominance to get his way in anything."

"If I were using my dominance, you'd be bent over the back of your sofa, ass out, and me, balls deep in your pussy as I fuck your impudence out of you."

Her breathing hitches; her gaze drops to my mouth then back up to my eyes.

"No church wedding."

"Excuse me?" I frown.

"I am not marrying you in church. It will be a quick wedding at City Hall, without any of your family in attendance."

"It will take a few days to make the arrangements," I say slowly.

"That's fine. I need time to organize things at the shop so I can take a half-day for the wedding."

"You'll take the entire day off."

"No, my job is important to me."

"The day off, and you'll attend a wedding lunch with the rest of my family."

She seems like she is about to hesitate, and I slide my fingers around her neck. My fingers almost meet in the front. "What do you say?" I squeeze gently, and her pupils dilate. Well, damn, she likes that, hmm? I press my thumb into the skin right where her pulse skitters. "Do we have a deal?"

She swallows. "You promise to make sure I get full custody of my daughter?"

"It's my top priority," I murmur.

She peers up into my eyes, and whatever she sees there must satisfy her.

"Fine," she says in a low voice.

"I didn't hear you," I drawl.

Her gaze narrows. "Fine. I said fine. Okay? You jerkass, you asshole, you—"

I lower my lips to hers.

Mistake, mistake. All of my senses go on alert, but goddamn it, her nearness is driving me insane, and while technically, I've agreed to no sex in the marriage, we're not yet married, so I'm allowed to kiss her, right?

Her muscles lock and tension pours off of her. She freezes in my arms as I brush my lips against hers once, twice. I want to taste her, to consume her. Instead, I nibble on her lower lip, then lick her mouth until, with a sigh, she parts her lips. I thrust my tongue inside her mouth, suck on her tongue, drag my tongue across her mouth, and drink from her. A moan bleeds from her mouth. I release her hands, then wrap her thick blonde hair around my hand and tug. Her head falls back, and I trail kisses down her chin, down the length of her creamy neck. I suck on the skin at the base of her throat and feel her body shudder. She brings her hands up to grip my shoulders and digs her fingers in. I trail tiny kisses as I retrace my path back to her mouth. I bite down on her lower lip and her entire body jolts. I close my lips over hers, thrust my tongue inside her mouth, and deepen the kiss as I grind my thickening arousal into the soft flesh between her legs. A groan trembles up her throat, and I swallow it down, tilt my head, slide my hand between the gaping folds of her robe to cup her breast and squeeze as I shove my thigh between both of hers. She grinds herself against me, and begins to ride my leg.

"That's it," I growl into her mouth, "get yourself off, Princess." I release her breast, only to untie her bathrobe and shove it off of her. Then, I grip her ass and haul her even closer, until every part of her torso is plastered to mine. She throws her arms around me, pushes her body into mine as she rubs her soft center against the thickness of my cock that tents the crotch of my pants.

A trembling seizes her and her back arches. I know she's close, that she is going to come, when a cry emerges from the baby monitor.

9

Elsa

He tears his mouth from mine at the same time that I push away from him. I stumble back, and the cool air rushes between us. My pulse pounds at my temples; my chest rises and falls. He rakes his gaze down my camisole-covered chest, and my breasts hurt. He raises his gaze to mine, and I notice those golden eyes have gone even lighter. Flecks of green spark within them. His nostrils flare and he takes a step toward me, when another wail from Avery fills the tense silence.

He freezes. His features wear an expression of panic. I almost giggle at that. Guess the reality of living with a baby is setting in, eh?

I bend, grab my bathrobe and slip it on, then spin around and head for the bedroom. I slip inside and walk over to where Avery is standing up in the play area. I scoop her up and rock her. "It's okay, honey. What's the matter? Do you need your diaper changed again, baby?"

I carry her over to the changing table and lay her down before opening the sides of her diaper. I carefully change her. When I'm done, I glance around to find him lurking in the doorway.

"Do you mind dropping this into the waste basket?" I hold out the poopy package containing her soiled diaper.

He seems taken aback, then prowls over to me. He pinches the parcel between his forefinger and thumb, his features slightly frozen, like he's horrified but also fascinated by what I've asked him to do.

"It's in the bathroom," I gesture.

He stalks away, walks inside the bathroom, and emerges a few seconds later. By which time, I am bent over a warbling Avery.

She grabs my fingers, and I pull her to standing. She glances past me and her gaze fixes on him. Her features instantly crack into a wide smile. She releases my finger and raises one hand toward him. Damn it, of course, she likes him. A bit difficult to resist that larger-than-life asshole, isn't it? And she's only female, after all.

She wiggles her fingers at him. I sense him move, and he comes over to stand next to me.

"Up." She laughs up at him. I turn to find his features have softened. He reaches for her, and she latches onto his hand. In fact, she releases my other hand and holds that arm up to him. He scoops her up and holds her close to his chest.

"Scooty, play Scooty." She warbles a few other unintelligible words, then smashes her fist into his face.

His gaze widens, and I hold my breath as he laughs. "You're a strong girl, aren't you? Just like your mama, huh? As beautiful and as stubborn, eh?"

He thinks I'm beautiful? Heat flushes my cheeks.

He bends his head and pretends to bite her finger. Avery bursts out laughing. He tickles her and she wriggles in his grasp. She grabs his hair and tugs. He raises his head and the two stare at each other.

Something hot tugs at my chest. Jesus, my daughter is going to fall for him. *I'm* going to fall for him. And then when we leave him—which we'll have to do when he finds out the real reason I agreed to marry him, we're both going to be heartbroken. I haven't even married him, and his charisma is overpowering us. I jump up to my feet, walk over, and take her from him.

"Hey," he holds his hands up as if still holding her, "what was that for?"

"I think you should leave," I mutter.

Avery's lower lip trembles just before she begins to cry.

"Hush, baby." I turn away and begin to pace, rocking her in my arms. "Don't cry, sweetie pie. See? Mama's still here, isn't she? Do you want to play with Scooty?" I walk over to the play area, grab the ragged toy and hold it to her. She shoves it aside and continues to cry. I snatch up her rattle, hold it to her; she takes it, puts it in her mouth, and her cry stops just as suddenly as it started. My breath rushes out of me. I rock her a while longer, then turn to find him still staring at us.

"I really think you need to go."

"Nonna's funeral is tomorrow," he says in a low voice. "I need you to accompany me."

"Oh," I blink rapidly, "I have to work tomorrow."

"The flower shop is closed tomorrow for the funeral," he points out.

Of course, it is. Theresa sent me a text last night, but it slipped my mind.

"Do I have to?" Not that I don't want to. I mean, the few times I met Nonna, she was amazing to me. And considering I'm probably indirectly responsible for her death, it's the least I can do. But to go with him?

"It's best the family start seeing us together, so I can tell them about our upcoming nuptials."

"Is it wise we marry so soon after Nonna's funeral?"

"She wanted me married within the month." He folds his arms across his chest. "Also, you need to move in with me."

"What? No."

"You're not safe here. The man who chased you the other day... We still haven't tracked him down. If he's still out there, chances are, he's going to come after you again."

"I... I'll be safe here, surely?"

He leans forward on the balls of his feet. "If you stay here, I'll have to post guards outside your door."

"That would draw too much attention," I protest.

"It's your choice. Either I post guards outside your door, or you move in with me."

I begin to pace again. "This is crazy. You can't just walk in and turn my life upside down."

"You're the one who banged on our door, barged in, and turned our lives upside down," he points out.

I turn to him. "That's not fair." I swallow. "You know it's not my fault that the bullet hit Nonna."

"That's not what my family thinks."

"So do they... Do they blame me for what happened?"

He tilts his head.

"So, they *do* blame me." I chew on my lower lip. "And you? What do you think?"

"I think you should move in with me so we can start getting used to each other's company."

"So that's it. I just move?" I glance around the nursery. "I'll have to pack Avery's things. And my things. And I need to swing by my ex's place and drop her off in an hour."

"I'll get people to help you, and I'll have a nursery set up for her by next weekend."

I hold Avery closer. "What if this entire situation only upsets my ex further? What if he uses the situation to prove that I'm an unfit mother—living with a man before we're married? Not to mention, marrying into the mob. What if he wins the case against me? What if I lose her?" I squeeze her so tightly to me that she protests.

Seb closes the distance to us, then bends his knees and peers into my eyes. "Do I look like someone who's going to lose?"

I shake my head.

"You're not in England; you're in Italy. Here, the judges tend to favor the mother over the father. Also, the *Cosa Nostra*'s power is second only to God. Believe me when I say that in Italy, the law isn't upheld, it's interpreted."

I blow out a breath. "I don't know if that's good or bad."

"All you need to know is that no one dares go up against us. If we want something, we get it and I... I want... you."

My heart begins to race.

"Once you're my wife, whatever makes you happy becomes my priority."

Holy shit, hearing him speak with such conviction makes me almost believe him. "But it's only a pretend wedding, isn't it? I mean, you don't plan on staying married to me for long, do you?"

"There are no divorces in the *Cosa Nostra*." He pulls himself up to his full height. "Take what you need for the day. I'll have my men come in and pack everything else for you."

He turns to leave, and I stare after him. "Wait," I call out.

He pauses at the door and levels that golden gaze of his at me.

"You want me to move out so quickly?"

He simply stares at me.

"B-but... Can't we wait until we're married? How will it look to the judge if... when I have to go up before him?"

"Leave that to me. There is no judge here who cannot be bought by the *Cosa Nostra*."

"But Avery... This is her home, too. I-I need more time to allow her to adjust to a new place."

"Avery's only here on the weekends, so it's probably always like a new place for her anyway," he points out.

I shuffle my feet. "Still, she's more used to this place than your home."

He hesitates then nods. "I suspect it's more a "you" issue than an "Avery" issue, but how about this? We can alternate between the two places, as needed. After all, you'll still be keeping this place."

"I... I will?"

"I'll make sure the rent is paid up for the next six months, so you'll have it in case you need to use it for Avery."

"Okay," I say in a small voice. Gosh, he has an answer to every question. Apparently, once he's made up his mind, nothing can stop him.

"Anything else?"

I shake my head.

"Good." He jerks his chin. "Now, what can I help you carry to the car?"

10

Elsa

"You have a baby seat in your car?" I stare through the open door of the stunningly beautiful SUV, and at the most stylish baby seat I have ever seen.

"You have a baby, don't you?" he retorts.

"I thought all you Mafioso only drove sports cars?"

"This *is* a sports car." He pats the hood of the silver-colored beauty. "It's a Fornasari RR99."

"Is it a cousin to R2D2?"

He glances at me strangely. "It's made in Italy, but the horsepower is completely American."

I place Avery in the baby seat and strap her in. I hold up her bunny, and she grabs hold of it and immediately begins to chew on it. I place the bag with all of her essentials on the floor in front of her, then walk around to the passenger seat. Before I can reach for the door, he opens it for me. "Thank you," I murmur, then slide into the seat.

He shuts the door, rounds the hood to the driver's seat, and straps himself in.

"Seatbelt," he reminds me as he turns the ignition key. The muted purr of the car's engine fills the space. I buckle in and he eases the car onto the road. There's something about an expensive vehicle: you can feel the power under the soles of your feet, sense it as it glides down the road. But when you glance out of the windows, the world is still the same. The scene is exactly how it would be if you were looking out through the windows of any another vehicle. But somehow, everything is different.

He joins the stream of traffic, keeping well below the speed limit. The throb of the vehicle's engine, though, hints at the latent power possessed by this machine. A bit like the man next to me. His broad shoulders are encased in a tailor-made jacket, his tie is dark against the stark white of his shirt. His wide palms and thick fingers caress the steering wheel as he guides the SUV along. His thigh muscles flex as he depresses the accelerator. His entire being is a mass of tightly restrained control. Authority pours off of him. The little I've seen of the Sovrano brothers has made it clear to me that Seb lucked out with the best features of all his brothers. Almost as tall as Massimo, as gorgeous as Axel and Christian, as mean looking as Luca, as authoritative as Michael, and as deceptively easygoing as Adrian.

Yeah, he's gorgeous, larger-than-life, someone who's a real catch. Not that I'm bad looking. I mean, I've never put myself down in comparison to a man, but still... When I take in his beautiful profile, his larger-than-life presence, the way he carries himself as if he owns the world and expects all of us mere mortals to fall in line with his commands, which is exactly what I did... Well then, I can't help but wonder why he wants to marry me. He's given me all of the reasons, but somehow, it still doesn't make sense.

"What are you thinking?" His deep voice cuts through my thoughts.

"That you need to make a right up ahead."

"I know." He nods at the GPS. "I have the address keyed in."

"So, you know where my ex lives?" I shake my head. "Of course, you know where my ex lives." I turn to face him fully. "Is there anything about me you don't know?"

"I don't know the color of your panties," he shoots back.

"Shh." I turn to glance over my shoulder and find Avery nodding in her car seat.

"That was a very effective change of topic." I place my hands in my lap. "I'm really not comfortable with this whole thing. My ex... He's not a nice man. It's one of the reasons I left him. He took Avery and moved to Italy, and I had no choice but to follow. He's the Police Commissioner, so he has the system behind him. It was ridiculously easy for him to prove I was an incompetent mother without the means to take care of my child. Avery was barely a year old when he got custody of her. I was sure I wasn't going to get to see her at all, but at the last minute, the judge took pity on me and ruled that I would get to see her on weekends. It's not much, but it's better than nothing."

I lean over and glance at Avery's sleeping face again. I'd managed to give her a quick bath and dress her in her favorite pink dress while Seb had made his phone calls from the living room. I'd also managed to pack some essentials for myself in the little time I had.

The car eases to a stop, and I notice the long line of cars in front of us. We remain stationary for a few seconds before the vehicle behind us honks. It's taken up by the car next to us, then the one in front of us, until all of them seem to be honking in a rhythm that shouldn't be synchronous, but somehow, is.

The honks fade away, then the driver in the car next to us pushes open his door, steps on the running board, and yells at the cars ahead.

"What's happening?"

"Traffic jam." Seb thrusts his chin forward in a very Italian gesture that means 'it's out of my hands.'

I pull out my phone and glance at the time on it. "We're going to be late." I shuffle my feet. "I can't afford to be late."

I turn to glance at Avery, who's still snoozing. I pull out a tissue and lean over and wipe the drool off her chin.

"If I am late, he'll report it to the judge, and they'll use it against me again."

I move around in the seat. "Please, Seb, we can't be late." I unsnap my seat belt, and he reaches over and grabs my hand.

"What are you doing?"

"We're only ten minutes away; it'll be faster if I walk."

"I'm not letting you out on your own."

"I'm not staying in the car." My heart begins to race and a bead of sweat slides down the valley between my breasts. "You don't understand. Fabio is not a patient man. If I'm even a minute late, he takes it out of the next visit. If I'm more than five minutes late, he takes away half a day from the next visit. And he... he has a temper."

His hold on my hand tightens. "Did he hurt you, Elsa?"

I swallow.

"Did he beat you when you were together? Is that why you left?"

"I left because we were incompatible, because I married him in haste. I didn't find out I was pregnant while I was with him, or he might not have let me go at all..."

His gaze grows thunderous. "What does that mean? Did he use force with you? Did he, Princess?"

I shake my head. "Please, let me go. I need to make sure I get Avery to him before it's too late."

The traffic in front begins to move slowly. Horns sound all around us. He curses, then releases me to focus on his driving. A few minutes later, we come to a stop again. I grab the handle, twist it, and shove the door open on my side.

Seb curses, "*Cazzo*, I should have locked the doors."

I open the door to the backseat, and reach over to Avery to unbuckle the straps so I can scoop her out of the baby seat. Then, I reach down to grab the bag with her essentials.

I straighten to find Seb has crossed over to stand next to me. He grabs the bag from me.

"What are you doing?"

"I'm coming with you."

"But the car—"

"I've messaged Adrian to come get it."

He slams the door shut behind me, then locks the car. The man in the car behind us rolls down his window and gestures rudely. "*Stacazzo! Dove pensi di andare?*" He yells.

I know enough Italian to understand that he's asking Seb where the hell he thinks he's going?

Seb shoots him a glare and the man pales. He must recognize Seb as Mafioso, for he instantly retreats back into his car. I cross over to the sidewalk, with Seb leading the way. His long legs eat up the distance, and I struggle to keep up with him. Sweat pours down my temples as I move Avery to my other arm. A few more steps, and my arms begin to ache. Damnit, am I not strong enough to carry my own child? I try to increase my pace and trip on a crack in the sidewalk.

Seb grasps my arm. "Easy," he murmurs, "easy."

Avery begins to cry as I continue to walk with Seb guiding me forward with an arm around my shoulder. "Shh, baby, it's okay," I assure her, but I'm not even sure I believe that myself. She cries louder, fat tears rolling down her cheeks.

"Here, let me." Seb takes her from me. He holds her against his chest with one arm, the same arm over which he flung the bag over his shoulder. He grabs my wrist with his other hand, and begins to walk faster. I almost have to run to keep up with him, but at least I'm not carrying the bag or encumbered by Avery's weight. We reach the corner, turn right, then keep going until we hit the turnoff to the road for Fabio's house. We turn in and the noise of High Street fades away. He picks up his pace, and so do I.

"It's this house," I pant as we reach a pair of white gates.

I reach for Avery, but he steps to the side. "I'm coming inside," he murmurs as he depresses the button below the security camera.

"This is a bad idea." I shift my weight from foot to foot. "He won't be happy."

"Too fu— Too bad," Seb growls.

The gates swing inward and we walk through.

11

Seb

How did I find myself in this situation? Carrying another man's child, leading another man's ex-wife, walking to his door with the purpose of telling him to back the fuck off from them? Not that I mind. Everything I've seen on Fabio reveals that he's an asshole of the first order—a corrupt cop who works both sides of the system. I'm looking forward to taking him down, but why the hell is she so afraid of him? What did he do to her to put that terrified look on her face? She brushes past me and stops in front of me. "Please, Seb. Please give her to me."

I glance from her to the door up ahead.

"Please, it's bad enough you're with me. I don't want him to see her with you; it will drive him crazy."

It's driving me crazy, hearing you talk about another man in my presence. It's making me insane thinking of you with anyone else.

"Please." A tear rolls down her cheek. "Please, Seb, please don't do this."

A hot sensation stabs at my chest. My insides knot. *Porca miseria*, I am going to regret this. I hand Avery over to her. The kid begins to cry again and reaches for me, but Elsa grabs her bag from me, then walks toward the front door of the house. She walks up the steps and the door opens as she reaches the top. A man stands framed in the doorway. He's wearing the uniform that identifies him as the *Polizia*. He's also wearing his hat. *What a prick.* Clearly, he's trying to fluster her with his authority.

And didn't you try to do the same?

I push the thought aside, and watch as he smiles at Elsa. Charm drips from his features, fucking *pezzo di merda*. What a phony *bastardo*.

He holds the door open and beckons her to come inside. Elsa refuses. He glances past her and spots me; his shoulders stiffen. His smile disappears and his features harden. He folds his arms across his chest and lowers his chin. Another woman appears next to him. She takes the bag from Elsa, then reaches for Avery. Elsa kisses Avery, whose cries seem to turn up a notch. My guts twist. I can only imagine how upset Elsa must feel right now. If I, a Mafioso, with a string of murders under my belt, am disturbed by the kid's tears, then she must be close to her breaking point.

Fabio and Elsa speak. Elsa waves her hand in the air. Fabio glances at me again, then the two exchange more words. Elsa grows more agitated by the second. I narrow my gaze as their voices rise. They are still too far away for me to hear the words, but it's clear things are getting heated.

Elsa finally throws up her hands and steps back. That's when Fabio swoops down and grabs her wrist.

Motherfucker. My vision tunnels. Adrenaline laces my blood. My feet connect with the ground, and that's when I realize I'm moving. I reach them, grab Fabio by his collar, and haul him up to his toes. "Let her go, motherfucker."

"Seb," Elsa yells, "please stop."

"He laid a hand on you." The blood thuds at my temples.

"She's my wife." He leans forward on the balls of his feet, a nasty smirk on his face. "I can do anything I want with her."

"You're not married to her anymore, you *testa di cazzo*." I pull my fist back, but Elsa grabs my arm.

"Please, Seb, please don't do this."

"Let. Go. Of. Her," I say in a low voice.

"Or what?"

"Or I swear—" My voice trails off. Goddamn it, he's the head of the police force, and while the *Cosa Nostra*'s reach is deep within the force, there's a tacit agreement we won't mess with the guy who's the face of the force. Not only because it'd draw a lot of attention to us, the kind we can do without, but also because it would completely disturb the balance of power between both sides of the law in this part of the world.

The asshole knows I can't kill him and his smirk expands into a grin. "That's what I thought." He lowers his gaze to where my fingers are locked onto the front of his shirt, then back to my face. "Get your hands off of me, you Mafia *figlio di puttana*."

"First release her," I growl.

"No." He laughs in my face. "Now turn around and leave, motherfucker."

Anger slices through me. My vision tunnels. Adrenaline laces my blood and I throw up my fist.

"Seb, no." Elsa grabs my sleeve. "My daughter's inside; she's on the other side of this door. Please. Don't, Seb."

Her voice cuts through the noise in my head. I draw in a breath, and force my shoulder muscles to relax. My vision clears, and I lower my arm to my side.

"Let her go," I say in a calm voice, "or you're going to regret it." The threat is clear.

Fabio scoffs. Color flushes his cheeks. He seems like he is going to refuse me, then releases her so suddenly that she stumbles back.

I let go of his collar and grab her shoulder before she can fall. Once she finds her balance, I wrap my arm around her and draw her to me.

Fabio's gaze narrows. His face pales as he glances between us with a strange look in his eyes.

"Sleeping with the mob now, Elsa?"

"Don't talk to my fiancée in that tone of voice," I snap.

His gaze widens, then he bursts out laughing. "Good one. You don't want to marry that piece of ass, trust me."

"Shut the fuck up." My fingers tingle. Fuck, if I don't want to bury my fist in his face, but she'd never forgive me if I did. And her daughter's inside, goddamnit. Even though I want to teach this guy a lesson, I'd never do anything that might emotionally scar a child. I dig my fingernails into the palm of my free hand and glare at him.

"Get the hell out of here," he snaps.

"Or what? Are you going to arrest me?"

His features harden and his gaze narrows, but he doesn't say anything.

"That's what I thought."

Remember, I said I can't kill him or the balance of power will go to shit? Well, it goes the other way, as well. The pigs can't touch us, unless they want to invite the wrath of the *Cosa Nostra* on themselves.

"Elsa, let's go." I turn to find her face ashen. She's standing motionless, her gaze on the door beyond him.

"Elsa?" I lower my voice, "Let's leave, right now."

She draws in a breath, then turns and walks toward the gate.

I close the distance to Fabio so we're standing chest to chest. "If you dare touch her again, I will kill you, regardless of the consequences, this I promise. She is under my protection from now on, you *faccia di merda*."

His features contort. "I am going to come after you, you *fetente*, and I'm going to make your life miserable."

I laugh. "I'd like to see you try." Turning, I follow her to the street.

Thanks to Adrian, my car is parked in front of the house. When I help her inside, she glances to the backseat, spies the car seat, and almost dissolves in tears.

"Shh-shh-shh, baby. It's okay."

I hold her while sobs wrack her body. Within a few moments, she takes a deep breath, pushes away from me, and sits down in the car.

"Okay, let's go," she says.

We drive for ten minutes without saying another word to each other. I glance at her, and find her staring straight ahead. Her shoulders are stiff and her hands are folded in her lap.

"Elsa, are you okay?"

She doesn't reply.

"Princess?"

She turns away and glances out the window. "Can we go by my apartment first, please... I... I forgot something."

I am almost positive she's lying, but that's okay. I'm not going to push things, given our recent interaction with her ex-husband. I'm also not going to tell her I've already arranged for everything she could possibly need to be at my place. For now, I'm going to take her to her apartment, so she feels a little more at ease.

For the rest of the drive, she stays quiet. I reach her home, turn into the small parking lot, and pull into a space adjacent to the steps that lead to her building.

She makes no move to leave the car.

"Elsa..." I turn to her. "Talk to me; tell me what you're thinking."

"Don't you want to know why he said that?"

"Said what?"

"That you shouldn't want a piece of ass like me."

I shake my head.

"Aren't you the least bit curious about why he doesn't want me to see my own daughter?" she asks.

"Firstly, I don't believe a word of what he said, and secondly—"

"Let me stop you right there. What if there is truth to what he said? What if I am such a horrible mother that I agree I shouldn't be allowed to have custody of my daughter? Maybe I shouldn't be trusted with her."

"I wouldn't agree with that."

"You hardly know me." She firms her lips. "We've met just a handful of times, and hardly spent any time with each other. You have no idea what I'm capable of."

"I've seen you with your daughter. It's clear how much you love her. That you'd do anything for her."

"That's just the thing. There are some things I don't have any control over."

She shoves the door of the vehicle open and springs out. She runs up the steps to her building, opens the door, and is inside before I round the car. I sprint up the steps to the entrance and grab the door before it closes. Entering the lobby, I allow my eyes to adjust to the light. Then, I catch sight of her down the hallway, rounding the corner. When I make the turn, her door is closing, and I hear the click of the lock engaging.

I bang on the door. "Open the door." I jiggle the handle. "Open it, Elsa, or I swear, I'll kick it in." I put my shoulder to the door and push. It shudders. I step back, and am about to plow into it, when it's wrenched open.

12

Elsa

I spin around and walk toward the small room with pink walls, aware he is on my heels. My foot brushes against something soft. I pick up a teddy bear and toss it into the play area, then bend again to retrieve the doll she was playing with earlier. Tears squeeze out from the corners of my eyes, and I wipe them away. What's the use of crying now, when the fact that Avery is not with me is no one else's fault but my own?

I rub the back of my hand against my nose, then tuck the soft toy under my chin. I hear his footsteps behind me. The heat of his body envelops me and a shiver spirals down my spine. This... right here... It's a complication I can do without. What the hell was I thinking, allowing him to get anywhere close to me? Why the hell am I not able to control myself when it comes to him?

I was doing so well. Stayed away from anything that could complicate my life. But one look at him that one time at the nightclub, and something came over me. I haven't been able to get him out of my mind. I lay awake nights, thinking of him. Allowed myself to get myself off as I imagined him peering into my face —those big, blunt fingers of his sliding across my skin as he buried his face between my legs and bit down on my clit while he gripped my hips and held me in place when I tried to wriggle away.

He touches my shoulder, and I shudder.

"Don't, please." I pull away, drop the toy in the play area, then walk to the window.

Footsteps approach, then the heat of his body sears my back, and I know he's standing behind me.

"Princess," his low voice rumbles. The vibrations sink into my skin and arrow all the way down to my feet. I flinch.

"What do you want? Why are you here?"

"I'm worried about you."

"Don't be. Why don't you leave, and do whatever it is you Sovranos spend your time doing?"

"You mean shooting down my enemies, and spending nights with different women."

"Exactly." I wipe the tears from my cheek.

"Thought you'd have better sense than believing the cliche that Hollywood has painted of us Mafiosos."

"Are you trying to tell me you're different?"

He hesitates.

"That's what I thought." I try to brush past him, but he grabs my wrist. Goosebumps pepper my skin and my entire body shudders. *No, no, no; this is so wrong.* I can't allow my body to react with such intensity every time he touches me. I raise my gaze to his, and in his golden-brown ones, I see concern and something else I don't dare define. I can't allow him to care for me. That would simply make this entire arrangement untenable. It'd soften me toward him even more, it'd dissolve all the defenses I've built up against the world. It would put me in a situation I'd never be able to get out of. And I can't afford that. I have to save the best parts of me for my daughter and I won't be able to do that if I begin to lose myself again.

"I'm a masochist"

He blinks. "What?"

The words spill out of me like grains of sand from an hourglass. "I like to be spanked; I like to be beaten. I like to be blindfolded, then tied up with my legs spread wide apart, and brought to the edge over and over again. I like to be owned. I like to be told what to do. I like to have my choices taken away from me, and be directed every second of my waking life. I want to be in a twenty-four-seven Dominant-submissive relationship. I crave it so much that I went into therapy to find a way to control my urges. I met Fabio when he was stationed in London on a project for the Italian police. I knew the only way he would marry me was if I didn't reveal my submissive tendencies. By then, I had managed to control my urges enough that I could stay loyal to him, and have an ordinary relationship. I stayed that way until Avery was born."

"What happened after her birth?"

"I had post-partum depression. I found myself, once more, craving the lifestyle." I shuffle my feet. "I managed to curb it until she was a year old. Then, when Fabio was away on a trip, I had my babysitter stay the night, and I visited an S&M club. There, for the first time since even before her birth, I felt like myself. I finally felt grounded and alive. After that, I began to visit the clubs frequently. All of my hard-won control was gone."

His jaw tics and a nerve throbs at his temple. "Did you sleep with other men?"

"No." I lock my fingers together in front of me. "You have to understand that I was always faithful to him, even if he wasn't to me, but I couldn't stop myself from being there, and watching what was happening. Even if it wasn't me being bound, seeing someone else getting off that way helped." I draw in a breath. "One day, I returned from a club to find that Fabio had arrived home early from his trip. It was clear, from the way I was dressed and how I smelled, what I had been up to. That was the first time he hit me."

He fists his fingers at his sides. "He hit you? The bastard hit you?"

"I deserved it." I glance away. "I knew it was wrong. I was a mother. I should have known better than to hang around the clubs and spy on other masochists with their Doms, but I couldn't stop myself. I'd wait, and as soon as I managed to find an opportunity, I'd slip away to one of the clubs."

"What happened then?"

I open my mouth, but can't bring myself to say it.

"Tell me, Princess. What did that bastard do to you?"

"The beatings became more frequent. You'd have thought that as a masochist I would enjoy them. At least, that was Fabio's justification for hitting me. Turns out, even a masochist can tell the difference between being beaten for pleasure and being beaten to be abused." I wrap my arms around my waist.

The skin around Seb's lips tightens; he curls his fingers into fists. "What else did that *pezzo di merda* do?" he growls.

"He began keeping my daughter from me as a way of trying to control me. It was horrible." A teardrop slides down my cheek. "I tried to stay away from the lifestyle. Honestly. But I found... I found I missed it so much. I wouldn't let him sleep with me. I lost interest in having sex with him."

"Good," he says in a hard voice.

"That made him really angry. He... he..." I swallow.

"What did he do, Elsa?" he growls. "Tell me."

"The abuse grew worse, and it didn't matter what I wanted. He threatened me, told me that if I didn't stop, didn't start acting like a good mother and a good wife, he'd take Avery away from me. For a while, the threat worked. I stayed away from the clubs. Things seemed to go back to normal—well, as normal as they could be, considering..." I draw a breath. "Then one day, when he was away on a trip, I couldn't fight the urge anymore. I tried to stop myself. I really did, but one night when Avery was asleep, I called the babysitter over and went back to the club. That day... For the first time, I allowed myself to be tied up and whipped." I squeeze my eyes shut. "I'll never forgive myself for it. I returned home and Avery was gone."

His shoulders stiffened. "What do you mean, 'gone'?"

"He had taken her and left for Italy."

"And he didn't tell you?"

I shake my head.

His eyes flash, a nerve twitches at his temple. He seems angry, not at me, but on my behalf. Huh?

"So, you moved to Italy to be closer to her?" he finally asks.

I nod. "I was lucky to find a job with Theresa. It's what's saved me, giving me a place to go to every day, and money to survive. I begged Fabio for a divorce, and he refused me initially. When he finally signed the papers, I couldn't believe it, especially since he seemed to resent me even more afterward. My instincts told me he was up to something, but I couldn't figure out what it was."

"He had an ulterior motive?"

I nod. "Now I know the reason he signed the papers was so he could file for sole custody on the grounds that I'm an unfit mother. And he's right. No mother who has the best interests of her daughter at heart would have done what I've done. I don't deserve her, but I can't live without seeing her. I need to be in her life, Seb. I do."

"Just because you're submissive, doesn't mean you're an unfit mother, Elsa." His voice sounds deeper.

I chuckle, "That's a very nice thing to say, but—"

"I am not saying this to humor you." He grips my shoulders. "Look at me, Princess."

I raise my chin.

"I've seen you with Avery; you love her."

"More than my life."

"You're an amazing mother who cares for her child deeply and will do anything for her happiness."

Something hot stabs at my chest. Why does it have to be an almost-stranger like this guy, a man who can also be a big-time jerkass, to tell me something I've longed to hear? Why does it take this alphahole to build my self-esteem? I shake my head. "So why can't I stop myself from being a masochist?"

"Just because you are a mother, doesn't mean you have to stop being a woman, or being sexually active. And if it means you need to indulge your masochistic side, then you're entitled to that."

I peer into his eyes. "But how am I supposed to reconcile the two? How can I be a mother, yet also explore my sexual identity? Especially when I need to be treated a certain way in order to feel anything. It's wrong Seb. I don't want to go to those nightclubs. I don't want to look at others getting it on."

"You don't have to."

"You're not listening to me. It's a part of me I cannot cut out completely."

"You don't have to."

He holds my gaze and there's decisiveness in his features.

"I don't understand."

"I'm saying, there's a way for you to be a mother, and my wife, and not have to give up the part that makes you feel fulfilled as a woman."

My heart begins to race and my pulse pounds at my temples.

"What… what are you saying?" I whisper.

"I'll be your Dom."

13

Seb

After that pronouncement, I told Elsa to take her time thinking about my proposition. Clearly, she wasn't expecting that—she paled and froze on the spot. After allowing her to grab a few things, I led her out of the apartment, and she didn't protest. I walked her into my house and showed her the guest bedroom I'd readied for her. I even showed her the closet full of clothes I'd purchased for her, and pointed out the bedroom opposite hers, for Avery. Her eyes brightened as she realized what I was showing her. I explained my room was up the corridor, and I needed her to be dressed in the morning to accompany me to Nonna's funeral. She nodded, and I left her with instructions to head down for dinner when she was ready.

Then, because the thought of her so close by was playing havoc with my mind, I headed down to the gym in the basement and worked out for an hour.

When I returned from my work-out, I found the house silent. My housekeeper informed me that Elsa never came down for dinner.

I headed to her room with the intention of making her eat, but found her under the covers. I'll admit, I stood over her and watched her sleep. Her pale skin, the shadows under her eyes, and her hair strewn over the pillow called to me. I sank down to my knees and pushed a strand of hair away from her cheek. She didn't stir. I inhaled a lungful of her scent—cherries laced with a feminine scent that is uniquely her. If I stayed any longer, I would push her legs apart, kneel between her thighs, and bury myself inside of her. Which would be okay; she agreed to be my wife, after all. But I also want to be her Dom, which means putting her pleasures before mine. Which is why I walked away from her, then proceeded to jerk off to images of her in my mind, before skipping dinner and falling asleep.

When I headed down this morning, she was already in the kitchen, whipping up breakfast. We ate in silence, then headed over to the cemetery.

Now, I watch as the coffin with Nonna is prepared to slide into the family crypt. The sun shines down, reflecting off the polished surface of the wood. Elsa stands beside me. On the other side, Massimo stands at attention, Luca on his other side. Then Adrian, Christian and Aurora, Michael and Karma, and finally, Axel and Theresa. We form a semi-circle around the casket.

Axel and Christian seemed to be getting along better, especially after Christian made that trip to London to convince Axel to return to Palermo and woo back Theresa.

The priest begins to speak and his words wash over me. I glance around at the people from the community who have gathered. An old woman about the same age as Nonna sheds tears. She's supported by another woman, younger than her, probably her daughter. There are other old-timers, friends of Nonna who grew up with her in this city where she lived all her life.

I spot a tall, broad-shouldered man standing to the side: Nikolai Solonik. And next to him is an older man with greying temples: JJ Kane. Our one-time rivals, now partners, all of whom have turned up to pay their respects to the matriarch of the *Cosa Nostra*.

She should have survived that bullet; the old bat had seemed invincible. Spry enough to be independent and on her feet until the end. She had been such a staunch defender of the Mafia. In the end, it seems fitting that a bullet took her life. In a strange way, I think she would have liked that.

She led a full life. A largely happy life. Her presence was a towering force in all of our lives. And now she's gone. A pressure pushes behind my eyes as I watch the priest shut the Bible. There's silence for a few seconds. The wind rustles the branches overhead.

Then Michael moves forward. He picks up a rose and stands with his head bent for a few seconds, then he places it on the casket.

He steps away, and I know it's my turn next. As the *Capo*, I follow after the Don on these occasions. I try to put one foot in front of the other, but my arms and legs feel too numb. Until this moment, I didn't realize just how much her death has affected me. She was a mother to us after our own mother died when we were young. She was our protector, our defender... Some might point out that she didn't protect us completely from our father's wrath, but she tried her best.

And even as she was dying, all she worried about was us. She wanted to see all of her grandsons married. It was her last wish. It's something I'll ensure I fulfill as soon as I can. My eyes smart. I try to draw in a breath, but my lungs burn. I can't take my gaze off of the dark doorway where my grandmother will be entombed. My arms and legs tremble, when a soft hand grips mine. Elsa twines her slim fingers with mine. She grips my palm, and warmth floods my veins. I draw in a breath, and oxygen fills my starved lungs.

"You okay?" she whispers.

I tear my gaze away from the casket and to her face. Those baby blues of hers hold mine. Her blond hair has been pulled away from her face and into a chignon. Her cheekbones stand out in her pale face. Her pink lips glisten, and I can't stop staring at them. She's real. She's alive. She's here. And she's mine. *Mine. Mine. Mine.*

Even though she hasn't said 'yes' or 'no' to my proposition of being her Dom. No matter. It's not like I'm going to give her a choice in the matter. I only backed off because it didn't seem prudent to push it. That, and the fact that she already agreed to move in with me. Baby steps. After driving her home and showing her to the guest room, I decided to give her some space and time to adjust to the changes. I was patient and stayed away from her last night. But now, I feel that resolve crumbling.

I move toward her, and her gaze widens. She shakes her head, tilts her head toward my grandmother's open grave, then back at me.

Cazzo! What's wrong with me? I shake my head to clear it, then pull away from her. I pick up a rose and walk toward the casket. *Rest in peace, Nonna. I'll see you on the other side.*

Two hours later, we're gathered in the drawing room of Nonna's home. Even though the rest of us called it the living room, she preferred drawing room, so... I guess I feel like it's one small thing I can do for her. The rest of the mourners, including Nikolai Solonik and JJ Kane, left after sharing their condolences with us.

Cass, Michael and Karma's housekeeper, who's really more like family, walks into the room, her usually neat hair loose and disheveled. She rubs her palms down the dress of her skirt, then heads straight for the bar.

Adrian follows her. He walks around the bar, reaches for the bottle of wine, but she shakes her head.

"Whiskey." She points to the half-full bottle on the counter.

He raises his eyebrows, but doesn't say anything. Instead, he pours her a healthy measure. She snatches up the glass, tosses it back, coughs a little, then points to the bottle. "More, please."

He frowns. "I won't have you getting drunk."

"Oh, please," she scoffs, "stop trying to control me."

When he doesn't move, she reaches for the bottle but he holds it out of her reach. "You've had enough."

Her entire body stiffens. She opens her mouth, no doubt to chew him out, when Michael walks over to stand next to her.

"How's Gino?" he asks, referring to Nonna's butler who'd been with her since she married into the Sovranos.

She draws in a breath, seems to gather herself, then turns to him. "He's fine. Maybe too fine. He's been silent since she passed. No tears. No outbursts. He refused to come to the funeral, and said he'd prefer staying in to cook the snacks for the wake." She runs her fingers through her hair. "He also says that he wants to return to his home in the village in the countryside. He feels his work here is done."

"Understandable. He can stay here as long as he wants. If and when he chooses to return, I'll make sure all of the arrangements are taken care of. Either way, he will be taken care of."

She nods. "Thank you, Don. I'll let him know." She turns to leave, and Adrian walks around the bar and toward her.

"I'll come with you."

She scowls at him. "I don't need you with me."

In answer, he brushes past her and heads for the door. Her scowl deepens. She looks like she is about to protest, then thinks better of it and follows him out.

"What's up with those two?" Massimo murmurs next to me.

"Clearly, there's some serious chemistry there, though neither of them seems to have acted on it," I muse.

"You'd think he'd just fuck her and be done with it," Luca scoffs.

"Cass is part of the family. He can't just fuck her and be done with it." Massimo scowls at him.

"Well, then he needs to stay away." Luca raises a shoulder. "Although, the way things are going... What, with first Michael, then Christian and Axel, and now Seb is next in line to get married... If I were him, I'd stay the hell away from her."

"You do realize it was Nonna's wish that we get married as soon as possible, don't you?"

"I loved Nonna, and would love to fulfill her wishes, but marriage?" He shakes his head, "No thanks. Not for me. Not for a long time, if ever."

Massimo gives him the side-eye. "You do realize, it's those who claim they'll never get married who end up tying the knot first."

"Not me." Luca takes a step back, as if the very thought is repulsive to him. "I'm getting another whiskey. What about you, Seb?"

I shake my head, and he heads for the bar.

I turn to watch Elsa speaking with Karma. She grips Karma's shoulder, and the two of them embrace. Theresa, Axel's wife joins them, and the three speak in hushed voices. On the other side of the room, Christian and Aurora are talking intently, their heads bent, their arms around each other.

I turn to glance back at Elsa, and this time, she glances in my direction. Our gazes hold, and she seems to falter in the middle of her conversation with Karma. Karma glances between us, then bends and says something to Elsa whose cheeks heat. Karma walks past her and toward us. She slips into Michael's side, and he wraps his arm around her and pulls her even closer.

Christian glances in our direction, then walks toward us, leading Aurora.

Elsa swallows. Then, as if hearing my unspoken command, she walks in my direction. She reaches my side, and I take her hand in mine.

I look around the group and realize all of my brothers, and their spouses, are here.

"As you all know, Nonna didn't want to have a wake; she wanted to be directly buried. Much as she sought the limelight in life, in death, she wanted to be allowed to leave with little fanfare. Still, it feels wrong not to say a few words to celebrate her life." Michael glances down at his drink, then back at us. "Some people leave a void so big, it will never be filled. Nonna was one of those people." He takes a deep breath, then leans forward on the balls of his feet. "When I was a child, she was the biggest influence on me, more than our father—thank god—or our mother, who was too gentle. When I hesitated to take my place as Don after killing our father, she's the one who told me not to question my birthright. She was reluctant to step in when our father physically beat us and our mother, and she always regretted that she didn't act earlier. She told me not to think twice, but to follow my instincts. That future generations would thank me."

He draws in a breath and Karma touches his shoulder in empathy. He smiles down at her, his expression brightening.

"She's the one who told me I'd be a fool not to recognize what a rare find my wife was. That, although I may have started our relationship on the wrong footing—which is putting it mildly—" a titter runs through the assembled crowd, "it was never too late to fix things. She warned me I'd be a fool if I didn't find a way to keep her happy."

His lips kick up.

"Believe me, I followed her advice and I've never regretted it. I credit my return to the human race to my wife, and in no small measure, to my grandmother, as well."

He glances down into his glass, then raises his head. "In losing her, I've lost a piece of myself." His voice wavers, ever so slightly. "As Don of the *Cosa Nostra*, there aren't many people I can go to for advice. She was one of them."

"You do know you can discuss things with us, don't you? As your second in command, I'm here to be your sounding board." I lean forward on the balls of my feet.

"I appreciate that." A ghost of a smile curves his lips.

"She will be missed." I shift my weight from foot to foot. "She was not only our grandmother, but also our protector. There was a certain strength to her that I've never seen in anyone else, and probably never will see again. We owe our lives to her."

"She never put up with my mule-headedness. She never took shit from me." Luca rubs the back of his neck. "That woman knew how to put me in my place."

We all laugh.

"Amen to that." Massimo widens his stance. "Not that she didn't have her faults. She never could understand Xander's need to explore his sexuality—something he mentioned to me in passing—even as she encouraged his need to pursue his muse. I think she was the only one who understood how important it was for our brother to follow his creative calling. Something he was eternally grateful to her for. As for me?" He rolls his shoulders. "She always told me to use my strength wisely. There are two types of men: those who abuse, and those who protect. Our father was among the first; she insisted I strive to be the second."

"I only knew her briefly." Axel brings his whiskey glass to his lips and takes a sip. "I admit, I was very angry with her for not pushing our father to do the right thing by me and my mother. But I'm glad I forgave her and made my peace with her."

"She appreciated it." Michael tilts his head. "She also wanted us to make amends with the *Camorra*. They are, after all, your family."

"They are no family of mine. They may have taken my mother in when she needed help, but they didn't treat her right. It's why she decided to leave and make her own way." Axel frowns.

"No doubt, it's something we need to discuss moving forward," Michael acknowledges. He raises his glass, and says loudly, "To Nonna, see you on the other side."

"To Nonna."

All of us raise our glasses.

Michael takes a sip of his whiskey. "Since we're all gathered here in Nonna's home today, and we all heard a certain promise someone made to her..." He turns to me. "Something you want to tell us Seb?"

"I'm not sure what you mean," I say slowly.

"Don't pull that on me," he replies in a mild voice.

O-k-a-y.

He glances at Elsa, then at me. Of course, nothing gets past my oldest brother. He didn't become the Don without reason.

"I had hoped to get a little more time before sharing with the *famiglia*, but now that you mention it," I widen my stance, "perhaps it's time to share my announcement."

Next to me, Elsa stiffens. "What are you doing?" she whisper-screams.

"Nonna's last words to me were that she wanted to see me married within the next month. Even in death, it seems, she can't stop herself from manipulating my life." I chuckle.

Smiles break out on everyone's faces.

Elsa begins to pull away from me, but I wrap my arm around her waist, and pull her into my side. Karma's gaze widens as she glances between us.

"I have asked Elsa to be my wife," I declare.

Karma gasps.

Theresa breaks into a smile.

Luca stares at me aghast, while Michael's lips twist into a smile.

Aurora's forehead creases and she narrows her gaze on Elsa. "And what was your answer, Elsa?"

She shuffles her feet. The silence in the room grows.

"Yes, I'd like to know that, too." Karma turns to her.

Theresa's brow furrows; she watches Elsa with an anxious look on her face.

Everyone's attention is directed toward Elsa, who doesn't reply. The tension radiates off of her.

I release her and turn to face her. I raise an eyebrow. "So, are you planning to tell them what your answer was?"

14

Elsa

Why is he doing this? I thought we had an understanding. That we'd go off and get married quietly, and only then, announce it to the family. Maybe I should have been clearer in my communication with him. But I had been so overwhelmed by the events of the past few days—first, Nonna's passing; then, him asking me to marry him; then, the altercation with Fabio, which still has me shaken.

If not for the fact that I believed him when he said he'd ensure I don't lose access to my daughter, I wouldn't be here today. And of course, I had promised to attend the funeral with him this morning. And seeing him silently grieving for his grandmother had melted my heart. I'm glad I'm here by his side to support him and comfort him. I really don't understand why I feel so moved by his emotions, or why I feel compelled, even now, to stay with him. I mean, I could simply walk out, and given his entire family is here, I don't think he'd try to stop me. I could go back to my job at Theresa's florist shop, and figure out how to tackle Fabio.

And the bastard would continue to ride roughshod over me. He plans to make sure I lose all rights to my daughter. There's no way I can take on Fabio on my own, especially not in Italy, where he has the police force behind him, and no doubt, far-reaching influence within the legal system. No, I need Seb's help in this. I need access to the power and influence he has. If there's anyone who can take on Fabio, and ensure that my daughter is restored to me, it's Seb. And if Seb fails—and let's face it, there's a chance he might—I need to ensure that I don't burn my bridges with Fabio completely, so I'll have a chance at changing his mind.

"Elsa," Theresa interjects, "are you okay? You don't have to agree to marry him, if you don't want to. You know I'm here to help you. Axel and I will make sure that you and your daughter are taken care of. You don't have to feel compelled to marry him."

I glance at her, then at Seb, who's watching me closely. He slides his hand inside his pocket, his entire demeanor casual. Only the ticking of his jaw indicates that he's tense. That, and his shoulder muscles that are bunched under his shirt. His biceps strain the sleeves of his jacket as he trains his gaze on me.

"Elsa," Karma says softly, "you don't have to do this."

"You're right. I don't have to..." I pause long enough for Seb's entire body to stiffen. Tension vibrates off of him. "But I want to." I turn to him. "I want to marry you."

The tension in his body seems to dissipate, though his facial expression remains unchanged. Then, he closes the distance between us, dips his head, and presses his lips to mine. It's a hard kiss, a punishing kiss, a kiss that hints at the power inherent in his body. A kiss that reminds me that I need him. A kiss that he softens before coaxing me to part my lips. A moan shivers up my throat. He swallows it, then wraps his arm around my shoulders and pulls me to him. He slides his tongue in between my lips, and a shudder grips me. He deepens the kiss, and heat flushes my skin. Then, just like that, he pulls back, brushes his lips over mine, and steps back. The sound of clapping cuts through my lust-addled brain.

"You move fast, don't you?" Massimo slaps his back with an audible thump.

Theresa walks over to me and holds her arms wide.

I glance at Seb, who presses another kiss to my lips before murmuring, "We'll talk about this later."

He steps back, and Theresa envelops me in a hug. "Are you sure?" she whispers. "He isn't putting pressure on you or anything, is he?"

I shake my head, "No." I press my cheek to hers. "I'm sure. I want to be with him."

"Do you love him?" she whispers back. "I didn't even know you two knew each other that well."

"You don't need to know someone well to be sure they're the right person for you, and Seb is the right person for me. He's the only person for me."

She leans back and peers into my features. She must see something there, for she nods. A relieved smile spreads across her face. "Oh, my god, I'm so happy for you, I can't even tell you. The Sovrano men are tough, but they're all gooey inside, once you get to know them better. Getting them to open up can be a challenge, but if anyone can do it, it's you. And we're going to be sisters! Can you believe that?" She throws her arms around me and hugs me again. Karma moves in to join us and hugs the both of us. Out of the corner of my eye, I spot Michael walking over to congratulate Seb, followed by Christian and Axel. Aurora comes over to join us.

Something rough touches my foot. I step back from Theresa to find a cat licking my feet.

"What the—"

Karma laughs. "Oh, sorry, that's Andy. He's convinced he's a dog." She bends and picks up the cat. She snuggles him against her chest, and the animal stares at me with unblinking eyes.

"He's gorgeous." I scratch him behind his ear and he purrs at me. "Where have you been hiding him?"

"Lately, he seems to prefer hanging out in our bedroom, even though he has his own cat-cave in my studio."

"He has a cat-cave? Does he have a cat-mobile, too?" I smirk.

The girls all laugh at that before Karma answers, "No, but what a great idea." She starts to stroke her chin like a comic book villain might do. "I wonder if I could design a kitty mask for him so he can be the masked-cat?"

I chuckle. "That's funny."

"Thanks." She giggles. "If you think that's funny, you should meet my sister, Summer. She has this amazing comedic timing, and she weaves film trivia into her conversations, which is—"

"Wait," I interrupt, "you're Summer's sister? Summer West's sister?"

"Now Summer Sterling, but yes. Why, do you know her?"

"Oh, my god, it's such a small world. I went to school with her."

"You did?" Karma tilts her head. "I mean, of course you did. Of course, I could tell by your accent that you're English, but what're the chances that two Brits meeting up outside of the UK, will end up knowing someone in common?"

"That is weird," I laugh, "but maybe not that unusual, considering we are both here in Italy, and in Palermo. How many other Brits do you know living here?"

She shakes her head.

"Exactly. We met, thanks to the Sovranos. It stands to reason we have more than them in common. Not that I knew Summer that well, but we were in the same class and had a shared passion for reading books, which is why we ended up hanging out together a lot. How is she, anyway?"

"Oh, I haven't seen her in a few months." Karma's laugh is forced this time.

"It's just, meeting Michael and getting married... All of it took place so quickly. And then I was in an accident, and lost the child I was carrying."

"Oh, my god, I'm so sorry for your loss."

"Thank you." Her eyes glimmer with unshed tears. "It wasn't easy, but I survived, and it helps that I'm pregnant again."

Aurora jumps in, "And the pregnancy is going well so far, although you definitely need to take the weight off of your feet more often."

"Not now, Aurora." Karma cuddles Andy closer. "This is Elsa's day—"

"It's actually Nonna's day," I remind her gently.

"True, and it was Nonna's wish that Seb get married soon, so she must be very happy, wherever she is. And if she were here, she'd encourage me in what I'm about to do now."

"Which is?"

"Give you all of the support you need, because marrying into this family can be a bit of a rough ride in the beginning." Karma rubs her cheek against Andy's head.

"The Sovranos don't make it easy on their women," Aurora warns.

Theresa nods. "They tend to put you through the wringer, and when you think they must be the biggest assholes—"

"Alphaholes," I cut in.

The three women look at me, then burst out laughing.

"What? What's so funny?"

"You calling them alphaholes," Karma sputters.

"Well, I don't know about the others, but Seb can sometimes be a completely full-of-himself asshole. Somehow, I've made it this far without slapping his face."

"Do it," Theresa pipes up.

"It helps to knock some sense into their big, dumb heads," Aurora agrees.

"Just be sure you are ready for the repercussions." Karma's lips twitch. "Not that I'm complaining."

Aurora clears her throat. "It can be very rewarding... As long as you're sure you can stand on your own and not give in completely, if you know what I mean."

My cheeks heat. "How do you do it?" I turn to Theresa. "You're the sweetest, nicest person I know. I'd have thought Axel would have chewed you up by now, but you seem to be able to hold your own—no offense." I raise a hand.

"None taken." She shakes her hair back from her face. "To be honest, in the early days, I found I simply couldn't say 'no' to Axel. It was like he'd narrow his gaze on me and use this voice, which would completely entrance me, and I'd find myself doing anything he asked. But as I've gotten to know him better, I've realized I want him not only to love me, but also respect me. I know the only way to do that is to hold my own against him."

"And you've done it." I touch her shoulder. "I'll bet it wasn't easy for you to go against your natural personality."

"It's not so much that I changed myself. I've always had it in me to stand up for myself. I just had to find the incentive to activate that part of me." She glances between us. "Does that make sense?"

"It does," I say slowly, "and I wonder if there isn't a lesson somewhere in there for me." I reach over and scratch under Andy's chin. He meows then wriggles out of Karma's grasp, and lands on my shoulder.

"Oh," I gasp, then laugh. The cat turns around, draping himself about my shoulders like an expensive scarf, then he licks my cheek.

I giggle. "Ooh, that's rough."

"Told you, he thinks he's a dog. He's been so spoiled by Michael, it's not even funny."

"He's practicing for when he's a daddy." Theresa reaches over and rubs Andy's forehead. "Is Michael as protective of you as Axel is with me since you became pregnant?"

Karma starts to speak and Theresa holds up her hand. "No, don't tell me. That was a stupid question. Of course, he's protective and possessive and everything in between." She turns to me. "Well, this is what you have in store," she flings out a hand, "so take notes."

"I already know."

"I assume you're getting married in the same church as we did?" Karma asks.

"Umm," I shuffle my feet, "no church."

"Eh?" Theresa blinks.

"Yeah, I already told Seb I'm not getting married in church."

"You're not?" Theresa frowns, then her forehead clears. "Oh, is it because of your daughter?"

"Wait, you have a daughter?" Aurora turns to me.

"Yeah," I blow out a breath, "and my ex lives in Palermo, which is why I moved here, to be closer to her."

"Is she with her father?" Karma's voice is soft.

"I have her on weekends, but—" I glance to the side then back at her. "I'm afraid he's petitioning the court for sole custody."

"What?" Theresa gasps. "Why didn't you tell me?"

"It's been an eventful month for you," I remind her softly. "I didn't want to bother you with my problems."

"Oh, Elsa." Theresa grips my hand. "You should have told me. Nothing is more important than this. We're talking about your future with your daughter."

"I know." I withdraw my hand from her grasp. "But seriously, don't worry; it's all in hand, now that…" I jerk my chin in Seb's direction.

"Ah," Aurora makes a noise at the back of her throat, "is that what he held over you to make you agree to marry him?"

"Ah…" I shift my weight from foot to foot. "I'm marrying him because I want to."

"So, did he bargain with you, he'd help you get custody of your daughter if you agreed to marry him?"

"Does it matter? The important thing is, he's going to ensure I don't lose my daughter."

Aurora grimaces. "Damn these Sovranos. Couldn't, at least, one of them go about trying to woo their woman in a more conventional fashion?"

"And where would the fun be in that? You have to admit, half the appeal is they're unconventional in the way they go about showing their love," Theresa murmurs.

"Love?" I shake my head, "No, no, no, this has nothing to do with love; it's merely a marriage of convenience."

"Do you actually believe that?" Karma laughs.

I stare at her.

"You really *do* believe that." Her face grows serious.

"No one knows the true nature of any relationship." Theresa tilts her head. "But if Karma's experience, then Aurora's, and now mine are any indication, the Sovranos marry for keeps and when they do, it's because there is an affair of the heart involved. Except, they're too damn pig-headed to admit otherwise."

I snort. "Next, you'll be telling me it was a *Colpo di Fulmine* for him." I refer to the Italian translation of love-at-first-sight which means, literally, being struck by a bolt of lightning.

That's when Seb's voice rings out from behind me, "It was."

"What?" I turn to find him walking toward me.

Theresa releases my arm as he draws abreast.

"You dumped a pint of beer on me the first time we met, and while it may not have literally been a bolt of lightning, it was definitely a shock that roused me out of my stupor and made me notice you."

"Wait, what? You dumped beer on him when you first met?" Karma chortles.

"Well, he made me so mad." My cheeks heat as he pulls me close to him. I direct my attention toward him. "Anyway, you deserved it." I try to pull away, but he doesn't release me.

"I don't know if I deserve you, but if you marry me, I promise to put your interests before my own. I promise to cherish you, and protect you, and ensure you're always happy."

I stare up into those golden eyes of his which haunt my dreams. Damn, but he is a fine actor. I almost believe him, and this is despite knowing the reality of our situation.

"What are you doing? You don't have to lie, you know," I whisper under my breath.

"I'm not lying. I wouldn't have proposed to you if I didn't mean it."

I open my mouth to protest, but he pulls a velvet box from his pocket.

What the—? My jaw drops as he goes down on one knee.

"Marry me, Elsa."

Why the hell is he making such a big deal about it? I already agreed to this arrangement, didn't I? So why is he rubbing it in, in front of his family? And to think, I wanted to keep the entire affair discreet, maybe even pretend it wasn't happening. But he's dashed all of those hopes into the ground with this gesture.

"Marry me, else I'll call you Frozen, and you know how much you hate that."

A chuckle spills from my lips. "Very funny," I say in a voice that indicates the exact opposite sentiment.

He stays there on bended knee, with his chin tipped up and a very intent expression on his features. Goddamn, he deserves an Oscar for his performance. The silence in the room stretches. Every person there is watching me, waiting for my reaction. My skin prickles and my scalp feels too tight. Heat flushes my skin, and bloody hell, what choice do I have? Besides, I already 'agreed' to this earlier, so what's stopping me from replying in the affirmative right now? Maybe because this feels too real? Because after Fabio, I swore I'd never get married again, only to agree to Seb's plan because it ensures the future of my daughter.

But this... romantic proposal, in front of his family and on the day of his Nonna's funeral? Goddamnit, it doesn't get more serious than this. A pressure grows behind my eyes. *Wh-a-t?* Why do I want to cry? It's all an act, probably to convince his family we're for real. Don't want them thinking we're sullying Nonna's memory, do we? Especially considering he's only marrying me because of the promise he made to his nonna, after all.

I draw in a breath, then hold out my hand. "Yes, I'll marry you."

He slips the ring, the one I left sitting on my dining table, onto my finger and kisses my hand. A shiver runs up my arm. My entire body seems like it's on alert. He rises to his feet, pinches my chin and tips my face up. Then he lowers his lips to mine.

15

Elsa

Twenty minutes later, we are in his car-slash-SUV, the one with the baby-seat, and on our way back home. And my lips are tingling from that hard yet tender kiss that seemed to go on and on. My heart still feels raw from the emotion he seemed to pour into it. My gut is in knots.

What is the meaning of all this? Why is he complicating an already messed up situation? Like it isn't enough I need to focus on my daughter, or the fact that soon I'll be married to this almost-stranger, or that if he finds out what I'm doing to him and his family, he'll definitely hate me—there's also the other thing. The one that's the cause of this mess I've landed in. And I've been trying so hard to be good. I've been trying not to slip up, and I've succeeded over the last year, by staying away from all temptation and ignoring the yearning inside of me. Then, he has to come along, and open up the vault to all of my secrets. Argh!

I must make a noise because he side-eyes me. "Stop thinking so much," he says in a mild voice.

"Ha, easy for you to say. You weren't put on the spot by an alphahole who thinks he can manipulate you and get away with it."

"Do you think I manipulated you?"

"Why else would you propose to me in front of your entire family?"

"You already agreed to marry me," he reminds me.

"I know." I wring my fingers in my lap, and spot the ring on my left hand. "It's just... It seems so much more real."

"That's exactly why," he murmurs.

"Oh." Something deflates inside of me. Of course, it was all a charade. He wanted his family to believe we're in love. He didn't mean any of that—not what he said, not the beautiful ring he gave me. I hold up my fingers, and the late afternoon light catches on the yellow sapphires in the ring. It's beautiful, exactly the kind of ring I'd have chosen for myself. How did he know the sapphire is my birthstone?

"I guess I should return the ring, now there's no one here to watch us?"

I move to take off the ring, and he makes a sound deep in his throat. "It's your ring," he says in a hard voice, "and as long as you are my wife, you'll wear it. And as I've already told you, there are no divorces in the *Cosa Nostra*."

I firm my lips. "Is that an order?"

"Do you want my help in ensuring Fabio doesn't get sole custody of your daughter?"

I turn on him. "Is everything a transaction with you?"

"If it's needed to get my way."

I turn and face forward, watching the houses go by. How could I have thought he meant anything he said earlier? And I almost believed him when he said those words. We ride the rest of the way in silence.

When we reach the house—his house—I push the door open and get out without waiting for him. He follows me, pausing only to speak with the security detail outside. I don't think I'll ever get used to living in a place with so much security, but it does make me feel safe. Surely, there's an oxymoron somewhere in that statement, considering I'm in the heart of the Mafia clan. Then again, maybe it's just ironic. Dontcha think?

One of the guards pushes the door open for me. I thank him and walk through. The door shuts after us, and the noise echoes around the space. I walk past the hallway, and toward the stairs that lead up to my room. His house is big, one of those common Italian homes built in the early 1900s. It's built from sandstone in a style that is Arab-Norman, so typical of the homes here.

It's a beach-front house, offering a panoramic view of the ocean from my room, while the sliding doors on the far side of the living room lead to a deck with stairs leading down to the sand.

I reach the hallway on the second floor and stop at the first door. I peek inside of the room with a crib on the far end. The rest of the furniture is expected by Friday. He told me he engaged an interior designer to make sure the space is completely set up by the time I bring Avery home for the weekend. Her room is across the hall from mine, while Seb's room is next to mine, the two connected with an adjoining door I made sure to lock last night.

Footsteps sound, then come to a stop behind me. "She'll be home this weekend."

"I know." I brush past him and head toward my room.

"You're a good mother, Elsa," his voice follows me.

I walk inside my room and head to the window.

"You're worried about her?" he murmurs.

"I only get to see my daughter on weekends. What do you expect?"

"You also put your own happiness on hold by entering into this arrangement; and you did it so you could ensure the future of your child."

"Don't make me out to be something I'm not." I stare at the sea that stretches into the horizon. "If I were a good mother, I wouldn't have landed in this situation at all."

"Don't allow someone else to define what a good mother is. You can't change the past, but I can help you ensure the future is more to your liking."

I turn to find him leaning against the doorframe.

"You're in my future, so I'm not sure that's going to happen," I mutter.

His jaw tics. He straightens, then takes a step forward, only to pause. He shakes his head. "It's been a long day. I'll let you get some rest." Turning, he leaves.

I shouldn't have said that, after all he gave me a ring. Not just any ring his nonna's ring. Worse, I like the ring. Why is he trying to be nice to me? He manipulated me into marrying him, after all. And then, he was understanding when I told him about my proclivities. I had expected him to throw a fit, maybe tell me the wedding was off... A part of me had hoped he'd say he couldn't go through with the marriage any longer, considering I'd confessed to liking kink. And don't these Mafia guys like their brides to be virgins? Which I, clearly, am not. I'm a mother, and I'm divorced, *and* I confess to skulking around in S&M clubs. Maybe I hadn't slept with anyone there, but still, I'd been a voyeur, and then a participant. Not very Mafia-bride-like behavior, if you ask me. But he wasn't fazed by it. Instead, he offered to be my Dom. And I don't think he said that just to make me feel better. I have a feeling he knows exactly what that means.

A shiver runs down my back. We haven't had a chance to discuss that further.

Why can't he continue to be an asshole—which would make it easy for me to continue hating him? Instead, he's trying to be understanding, and the problem is I like that part of him too much.

I grip the window frame, then blow out a breath. He's just up the corridor; I should go and apologize. Much as I want to stay angry with him, I'm already regretting my outburst. I blow out a breath, then walk up the corridor and to his bedroom. I peer inside, but he's not there. Eh?

Did he leave the house? Where could he have gone? I walk down to the living room, then peek into his study but there's no one there.

I return to my room and begin to pace.

It was Nonna's funeral today, and instead of being empathetic, I was nasty toward him. Sure, he gave me a ring, but he only did it to make sure our engagement seemed genuine to his family. I can hardly fault him for that. All I did was piss him off... And he left. Damn it, he could have argued with me. He could have confronted me about my remark. Instead, he turned on his heel and left, not only my room, but apparently, this house.

In all likelihood, he went to Venom, the place where we met the first time. And I imagine, as I wear a hole in the carpet, he's with another woman. Someone who would be all sweetness to him and lend him a shoulder to cry on. No doubt, while I dither and try to figure out what to do, he's stripping her... and kissing her... and pushing her down to her knees, and— I shake my head. Why am I torturing myself with these images? There's only one way to find out.

I pull out my phone and call a cab.

16

Seb

I aim the gun at the target and fire again and again. I don't stop until I have emptied all of the bullets. Then I lower it, pull out my earplugs, and pull the paper target toward me. All of my bullets, except one, found their mark. Huh? That's never happened before. Not that I'm a bad shot. It's just… I've never managed to hit all of them on the bullseye before.

The sound of clapping reaches me. I glance up to find Luca walking in my direction. "And I thought I was the crack shot here."

"I missed one," I point out.

"That's as good as me on a bad day," he humblebrags.

"Fuck you very much, too," I growl.

"Everything okay, ol' chap?" he murmurs.

"We just buried Nonna, who was shot by a rival gang's bullet. Do you think I'm okay?" I lean forward on the balls of my feet. "Also, what's this 'ol' chap' bullshit? You've been spending so much time with our resident Brit, you're beginning to sound like him."

Massimo walks over to join us. "Were you envisioning the head of someone in particular?" He gestures to the figure on the paper target, now riddled with bullet holes.

I tear off the paper, then crumple it and toss it aside.

I head for the exit... A-a-and, here comes Adrian.

"Just the person I was missing—the man who never seems to lose his temper, no matter how messy things get." I glower at him.

"Hey." He holds up his hands. "What did I do?"

"Nothing, and that might be the problem." I make sure my shoulder bumps his as I walk past him and into the adjoining bar. Rarely do I contemplate the fact I belong to the most famous family in Italy and have enough money to rival the economy of a third world country. Today, I can assure you, is not one of those days. Today, I am fucking grateful we're rich enough to have our own bar and adjoining shooting range. Both are situated on the top floor of the building that houses Venom, the nightclub owned by our family. We spent so much time in Michael's office above Venom, he eventually refurbished the entire floor. In addition to the shooting range and the private bar, there's also a gym, a pool room and a sauna. All of the comforts under one roof, without having to go anywhere outside the building.

This way, we don't have to compromise on our lifestyle. And we don't have to come in contact with the rest of the populace. Especially important on a day when I'm liable to point my gun at whoever gets in my way. Not that I have anything against killing people... But I do prefer to take a life when there's a real reason. Like someone who is out to get me or one of my own. Someone who has hurt her. Someone like that *coglione*, Fabio Costa.

I walk around the bar counter, grab a bottle of Macallan forty-year-old, and pour a healthy dose into a glass.

Adrian walks over to join me, followed by Massimo and Luca.

Adrian takes the bottle and pours whiskey into their glasses. He slides one over to Massimo as Luca picks up his own glass.

"To Nonna," I murmur.

"To Nonna." My brothers raise their glasses and we clink.

"Remember how all seven of us would spend most of our time here at Venom?" Luca comments.

"Michael and Christian are married. It's natural for them to spend more time at home," Adrian remarks. "And Xander..." He stares into his glass. "I miss Xander. And now Nonna. Damn, everything's changing."

"Change is good." I drain my glass. "Change is what keeps us from losing our edge."

"So that's why you proposed to her, because you want change in your life?" Massimo asks.

"I proposed to her because I promised Nonna I'd get married within the month."

"And it has nothing to do with how you've developed feelings for her?" Luca smirks.

"What are you talking about?"

"You pushed Elsa out of the way of a bullet and threw yourself over her to protect her, then insisted on dressing her wound and driving her home, by way of the hospital, only to appear preoccupied for the next few days... Well... Clearly, you're developing feelings for her."

"Anything else, Montalbano?" I ask, referring to the well-known fictional Italian detective who has achieved cult status in this country.

"You mean Sherlock, don't you?" Luca grins.

"*Cazzo*, and I thought you and Axel didn't get along," I reply.

"We don't." His gaze narrows.

"And yet, that's the second British reference you've made in passing today." I place my elbow on the counter. "Is the Brit your new best friend?"

"As you well know, Axel and I are not friends." He points his finger at me. "Don't change the topic, *fratello*. We're brothers. We have our differences, but when one of us is threatened, we stand up for each other."

I rub the back of my neck. I hadn't expected to hear that from Luca, but I have to admit, it's reassuring. And much as I hate to accept it, Fabio's a formidable enemy. If there's anyone who could stand up to the Mafia in Italy, it's him. The man's corrupt, of course, but he's been taking bribes from our rivals, the *Camorra*, who hold sway from the *Campania* region in Italy. He owes his allegiance to them, which means he's out to get us. And this gives him a perfect excuse. What's worse, now he knows my weakness. If he does anything to her, I'll kill him, and that would only spark a full-fledged war, which could bring the kind of destruction that wouldn't be good for anyone. And he's the father of her child.

"*Cazzo!*" I drain my glass and slap it down on the counter and reach for the bottle.

Massimo snatches it away from me. "Talk first," he growls. "It's not going to help if you get so drunk you're not thinking straight."

"It's a start." I pivot and begin to pace.

"If nothing else, it will help to get it off your chest," Adrian says in a reasonable tone.

"Do you have to be so fucking reasonable and calm about everything?" I round on him. "You've never been in my position, so don't attempt to give me advice."

His jaw tightens. "Haven't I?" He holds out his hand and Massimo passes the bottle to him. Adrian drinks straight from the bottle and I blink. The gentlemanly Adrian, who believes in following the rules in every aspect of his life, acting out of character? Have I touched on a nerve?

"It's Cass, isn't it?" I prop my hands on my hips. "If you feel so much for her, why don't you do something about it?"

"Why don't you get your own house in order first? Why are you so twisted up about marrying Elsa anyway? What's the deal there?" Adrian points at me with the bottle. "Is she in love with someone else?"

I stiffen.

"*Gesù Christo.*" Adrian straightens. "She *is* in love with someone else."

"*Cazzo*," Luca exclaims, "and you proposed to her? There's so much other pussy out there, why do you have to go after someone who belongs to another man, you—"

I whirl around, close the distance between us, and grab his collar. "She doesn't belong to him, you *coglione.*" I haul him up to his feet. "She's divorced."

"Watch it, I was only trying to be helpful." Luca scowls.

"Well, don't." I release him and begin to pace.

"And the *Cosa Nostra* doesn't believe in divorce," Massimo points out.

"Fuck that."

"What's the problem, then? She's not with her husband, so you can move in, can't you?" Luca asks.

I shuffle my feet and glance to the side, then back at my brothers. "She has a daughter."

"Ah," Massimo nods, "that does complicate things."

"*Cazzo*, that's messy." Luca takes a step back as if trying to distance himself from the situation.

"You're telling me?"

"And you still want to marry her? Being divorced is one thing, but having a kid?" He shakes his head. "I mean, you're probably better off without her."

"Luca!" Massimo and Adrian say at the same time.

"What?" He raises his hands. "I'm trying to save him from making a mistake."

"You really have no idea, do you?" I rub the back of my neck. To think, I was just like him only a few days ago, when all I'd been focused on was my role within the *Cosa Nostra* as Capo, and of course, getting as much pussy as I could. Until I had run into her at Venom.

"The first time we met, she dumped a pint of beer on me," I murmur.

"What?" Massimo laughs.

"Now that's something." Adrian chuckles.

"Wish I'd been there, if only to see the look on your face," Luca adds.

"So, what did you do?" Massimo leans his bulk against the bar counter.

"I drove her home."

"Hold on. Let me get this straight. She dumped beer on you, and instead of retaliating, you dropped her back home?" Luca stares at me like I've grown a second head.

My neck heats. "We were at Venom; she was with Theresa. Besides, I probably deserved it." I raise a shoulder.

"*Che cazzo*," Luca chortles, "look at you being all honest and shit."

"Hey, I'm an honest person... Mostly."

"So, she has a child." Adrian drums his fingers on his chest. "But that's not what's stopping you, is it?

Goddamn, I forgot; Adrian's also the most insightful of all of us.

"So, what's the real issue?" Massimo strokes his chin. "It'd have to be something serious for you to be shooting at a paper target, instead of going after a live one."

I blow out a breath.

"What is it?" Luca shuffles his feet. "You're making me nervous, *fratello*; why don't you just spit out what's on your mind?"

"Is it the husband?" Massimo drawls.

"Ex-husband, and can you guys back off or what?"

"It is the husband. The ex, I mean," Massimo adds when I bare my teeth at him. "Want me to off him?"

"If it were that easy, wouldn't he have done it already?" Adrian retorts.

"Don't all of you try to put words in my mouth all at once," I say dryly.

"Well, come on then *fratello*." Luca rolls his shoulders. "Just tell us, will you?"

Fuck this. "He's Fabio Costa," I say through gritted teeth.

Silence.

Luca's gaze widens. "The Police Commissioner?"

"Bingo."

Massimo rocks back on his heels. "You don't pick your adversaries lightly, do you?"

I fold my arms across my chest. "What do you guys think?"

"I think we should use this opportunity to clean house, once and for all," Luca retorts.

"*Porca miseria*, are you even thinking straight?" I narrow my gaze on him. "Do you have any idea what the repercussions could be for killing him?"

"So, the cops get pissed off. Too bad." He raises a shoulder. "We can handle them."

"And the *Camorra*," Massimo says slowly. "You're aware he's affiliated with our biggest rivals—"

Luca doubles down, as usual. "It's time we taught them a lesson. Those *stronzi* have been infringing on our territory for a while now. It's time we show them who's stronger."

"Do you have any idea what you're talking about? Perhaps we could take on the *Camorra* on their own, or the cops on their own. But together?" I shake my head. "And while we do control a part of the police force, it would put us in a difficult situation even to contemplate going against both of them at the same time."

"Not if we had help," Adrian points out.

"What are you talking about?"

"The Bratva and the Kane Company; they're our allies."

"Joint ownership of a single company does not make them allies," I snap.

"Whoever represents us on the board of the company could sway them to work with us on something as strategic as this. Perhaps just the fact that we have them in our corner might be deterrent enough to stop the *Camorra* or the pigs from trying anything."

Michael recently stepped down from the board of Trinity Enterprises, the company in which we have joint ownership with the Bratva and the Kane Company. He left it up to the four of us to decide who will represent the *Cosa Nostra* in his place.

"Hold on." Luca props his hands on his hips. "Is this conversation headed the way I think it is? If so, the answer is no."

Massimo scowls. "Luca, come on. Surely you can see it would benefit all of us for Seb to join the board. He could use the position to strike a deal with the Bratva and the Kane Company, which would help him with his predicament, and with ours."

"So that's it? We've decided he gets the seat on the board?" Luca's jaw hardens.

"I have no interest in being on the board. You know my ultimate aim is to set up my own media company. It's what I've been working toward for a while now."

"So, leave the seat on the board to me," Luca retorts.

"You're an enforcer. Are you really interested in boardroom maneuvers related to a company which deals with cryptocurrency trading?"

"Whether fighting on the streets or in the boardroom, how different can it be, eh?" He widens his stance. "Besides, this is my chance to increase the scope of what I do and learn something new. I can't be stuck as an enforcer forever."

"That's true," I move toward him, "and I think you're right thinking of growing your skillset. I think you'd be a natural in the boardroom, actually. It's just right now, I really need this position. If it means I can get in with the Bratva and the Kane Company, and work out a plan with them, perhaps I stand a chance at putting this *stronzo* Costa in his place, without disturbing the balance of power too much."

Luca's jaw tics. "Fuck." He drags his fingers through his hair. *"Porca puttana!"* He drains his glass then throws it at the opposite wall, where it shatters. The shards crash to the floor. He shakes his head as if to clear it, then jerks his chin. "Fine, but you owe me."

"*Grazie, fratello*, you have no idea what this means to me." I grip his shoulder but he shakes it off.

"Just because I agreed to this, doesn't mean I'm happy," he warns.

"I'm aware, and I'll make it up to you."

"We'll see," he says in a grudging tone.

Before I can respond, there's a knock on the door.

17

Elsa

I peek inside the doorway, and the tension in the room hits me like a kick to the face in *47 Ronin*. Jesus, it feels like a war-room in here. There are four men, but my gaze hones in on him.

He tilts his head, no change in expression on his face. He's wearing another of those black suits he seems to favor. Expensively cut, they cling to the breadth of his shoulders. His silk tie—also black— is a contrast to his snowy white shirt. His hair is swept back from his face, and the length is a tad too long to be considered stylish. A lock of hair falls over his forehead. He slides his hand inside his pocket and surveys my features. Damn, he's going to force me to make the first move, apparently. Not that I blame him, after what I said to him the last time we spoke.

I mean, what was I going to say? Sorry I was nasty to you the last time we spoke. Sorry I didn't respond to your offer. Sorry I'm not sure if I could have you for my Dom. Sorry… if you were my Dom, I wouldn't be able to stop myself from getting too deeply involved with you. The thought of him commanding me, ordering me, dominating me, telling me what to do, what to wear, what to eat, and taking care of my needs in bed, sends a shiver of anticipation down my back.

No, no, no. I can't do this. One taste of his power and I'd be addicted. I'd grow dependent on him. I wouldn't be able to live without him, and then what would I do when he decided he'd had enough of me? How would I be able to function? How would I be able to take care of my child if I couldn't even take care of myself?

On the other hand, if anyone can stand up to my ex, it's him. Seeing them together had shown me how much more overpowering Seb is. Oh, Fabio isn't a weakling, by any means. But face-to-face, Seb easily wins in the personality department. Fabio's more classically good-looking. He seems like the respectable kind of man you'd take home to meet your mother. But looks can be deceiving. Seb, on the other hand, looks darker, meaner, and even wearing one of his suits, there's something so untamed about him.

Next to him, Luca widens his stance.

Adrian pushes away from the bar and walks toward me. "Elsa, how are you?" He takes my hand and kisses it.

There's a low growl from behind him. I glance around him to find Seb glowering at the two of us. Is he jealous? Surely not.

Adrian chuckles. "We were just leaving." He turns to glance at his brothers over his shoulders. "Weren't we, *stronzos*?"

"Yes, we were," Massimo agrees. He prowls over to us. He's the tallest and the broadest of the brothers. "I'd kiss your hand like Adrian here, but I fear my brother would have a cardiac episode if I did." His lips twitch. He follows Adrian through the door.

Luca is the last to follow. He and Seb exchange a look before Luca stalks over to me. He jerks his chin in my direction before he walks around me and leaves.

I shuffle my weight from foot to foot. Should I go in? Should I leave, maybe? Why did I come here, anyway? "Umm, maybe this was a mistake."

I spin around, and am about to step out of the room when Seb calls out, "Stop."

I hesitate.

"Shut the door, then turn around and face me."

The command in his voice is unmistakable; a shiver runs down my spine. My nipples tighten. Jesus, what is this crazy reaction to him? I've known for a long time I'm submissive. I've hung around clubs, wanting to find the right kind of Dom, but I've never found anyone I felt comfortable approaching. It's always been experience-by-proxy, where I'd see Dom's get subs off and imagine myself in that role. Even then, the sensations had been intense. But I have to admit, nothing I've visualized has come close to being here, knowing he's a few feet away, ordering me to return to him.

"Princess." He lowers his voice to a hush and a shudder grips me. "Do it, now."

His voice fills the corners in my mind. I reach out, pull the door closed, then turn to face him.

"Good girl," he murmurs, and heat sears my cheeks.

"Now take off your coat and place it along with your handbag on the table near the settee."

I do as he says, noticing a velvet box on the table, then straighten.

"Come 'ere." He quirks his finger, and I put one foot in front of the other until I'm standing in front of him.

"On your knees," he orders.

"What?" I swallow. "What are you doing?"

"Isn't this why you came here?"

"No, of course not."

"Don't lie to me," he says in a hard voice. "Since I told you I'd be your Dom, you haven't been able to stop thinking about it. You haven't been able to reign in your imagination. You've thought of how it would feel to be dominated by me, to be controlled by me, to obey me, to be..." he leans in close enough for his body heat to envelop me, "owned by me."

"No." My voice trembles and I clear my throat. "That's not true."

He laughs. Asshole actually laughs. He grips my shoulder and presses down. "Do as I tell you, Princess."

"And if I don't?"

He holds my gaze. Silver sparks flare to life in the depths of his gaze. A plume of heat spools off of his body and slams into my chest. I gasp and a bead of sweat slides down the valley between my breasts. His gaze darts there and stops. His nostrils flare. He raises his gaze back to my face. "Either do as I say or—"

"Or?"

"Turn around and leave." He pulls his hand back, and I instantly miss the weight on my shoulder. "It's your choice."

Bloody hell. I shift my weight from foot to foot. *Should I leave? Should I stay? I don't want to have to make a decision.*

"If you leave, I'll still fight Fabio to ensure you get custody of your daughter."

"You... you would do that?"

"And you wouldn't have to marry me, either."

"I... I wouldn't?" I gape at him. "Are you sure? This doesn't sound like you."

"You mean, because I'm giving you a choice?" One side of his lips kicks up. "You forget that if you come into this relationship willingly, I'll have much more control over you."

"So, all of this is just manipulation?"

He merely tilts his head. "You can give it any name you want. You and I, we want the same thing."

"Which is?"

"Your happiness."

I scoff. "So everything you've been doing so far is to make me happy?"

"Sometimes we don't know what we want."

"You're saying you know better than I do about what I want?" I resist the urge to wrap my arms about myself. I'd only be revealing just how confused I am by this entire conversation. "First, you almost blackmail me until I agree to marry you, and now... You're telling me I can leave and you'll still help me?"

He holds my gaze, unblinking. He slides a hand inside his pocket, and the rustle of the fabric is loud in the empty space.

"Maybe I should have a drink." I gaze past him at the bar.

"You may, once you make a decision."

I draw in a breath. "I don't know what I want. I thought... I wanted to be free of you, to get on with my life, but..."

"But?"

"But now, when you give me the choice to leave, I find I can't."

Something hot flickers in his eyes, then recedes.

"You must think I'm pathetic." I shake my hair back from my face. "I can't even make up my mind what I want from you."

He stares at me steadily.

I've never been able to stand silence, so my mouth starts moving, and before I know it, I'm spilling secrets. "I was ten when I stripped my Barbie doll, tied her up, put a patch on her mouth, and had her lay down waiting for Ken to do god-knows-what to her. I didn't even realize it had anything to do with sex, you know? It was just this yearning, from somewhere deep inside of me. And before you ask, no, I wasn't abused as a child. It's just... I always sensed this need inside of me, but it took a long time for me to give it a name." I fold my fingers in front of me. "Of course, once I learned to google about my cravings, I realized they had a name. Even then, I couldn't allow myself to completely accept what I truly craved. I began to haunt BDSM clubs. I lurked around and spied on Dom-sub pairs. I used to be so envious of the subs, of how the Dom was so focused on them, of how they were high from the ministrations of their master."

"Princess," he interjects, "I—"

"No, let me finish." I glance to the side, then back at him. "I did have boyfriends, and while the sex wasn't bad, it didn't blow my mind, either. I knew what I was looking for, but I never could acknowledge to myself just how much I needed it. Then I met Fabio and—"

"Don't talk about other men in front of me," he says through gritted teeth.

A flush of satisfaction coils in my chest. "Jealous?"

"Jealous?" He laughs and the sound is dark. "I am going to hunt down each and every one of the men who ever touched you, and kill them. And as for your ex..." He squeezes his fingers into fists. "If I had my way, I'd slice him from ear-to-ear and grind him into the dirt. Then, I'd throw you down in his blood and fuck you."

Heat blooms low in my belly; my pussy clenches and my toes curl. "How very bloodthirsty of you."

"You have no idea." He bares his teeth. "Are you done talking?"

I nod.

"If you have anything else to say, now would be the time."

"I…" I swallow, "I agree."

His gaze intensifies. "What, exactly, are you agreeing to?"

"For you to be my Dom."

18

Elsa

"Are you sure?"

Why is he asking me that? Why is he giving me a way out? Why can't he simply take what I'm offering? Why can't he just dominate me, overpower me, ride over my wishes, and give me what I need? Why can't he satisfy the ache that crawls in my belly? This emptiness that has been inside me for so long, that has grown over the months and the years, until I can barely feel myself anymore.

"Princess?" He notches his knuckles under my chin and lifts up my head. "What do you say?"

I squeeze my eyes shut and draw in a breath. Then, "Yes," I nod, "yes."

The breath rushes out of him. His muscles seem to relax. Eh? Had he actually thought I would decline his offer? How could I? How could I walk away from him? The fact he gave me a way out only confirms to me I've made the right choice… Did he do it knowing he had a better chance of getting me to agree if he put the power back in my hands? Had he told me I could leave, knowing I wouldn't? Had he left the decision to me, knowing I would stay, and this time, it would be of my own volition, thus effectively, handing the power back to him, and putting myself at his disposal completely? My head spins. Damn it, I am tying myself in knots.

"You made the right decision, Princess." He reaches for a bottle of grappa and pours a thimble-sized portion into a glass. He places it on the counter. I reach for it and he clicks his tongue. "Did I give you permission to touch it yet?"

I shake my head.

"Say it."

"You didn't give me permission to touch it yet."

He glares at me, and my breathing grows ragged. The pulse at the base of my throat flutters.

"No." I swallow. "No, Master."

"Good girl."

I flush, and his gaze intensifies. His nostrils flare, and something like satisfaction settles over his features. He seems so confident, so pleased with himself. Damnit, did I make the right choice? Should I have left when he gave me the chance? I glance from my drink to his empty glass. "Where's yours?"

His lips curl.

"Why are you smiling like that?"

"You'll find out," he murmurs. "Open your mouth."

"What?"

"Open. Your. Mouth. I won't repeat myself again."

I part my lips.

He clamps his fingers around the nape of my neck, then he reaches for the glass of grappa, takes a sip, then leans in, and puts his lips to mine. He dribbles the grappa into my mouth. Heat flushes my skin and my belly flip-flops. My thighs clench and I swallow, so aware I am drinking from him. Oh, my god, this is so filthy. And so hot. So very hot. Why do I find it hot? Why do I not find it more disgusting? That familiar guilt creeps into the back of my mind. I shouldn't find this so sensual, shouldn't need this degradation so much. What's wrong with me that I can't enjoy vanilla sex like most of the population of this planet?

"Don't." He peers into my face. "Don't do it."

"What?"

"Don't berate yourself."

"How do you know—"

"You're so damn transparent, woman." He reaches over and scoops up a drop from the corner of my mouth, then he brings it to his lips and sucks on his finger.

My toes curl and heat sluices through my veins. How can such a simple gesture turn out to be so... so much more?

"Open your mouth, baby."

I oblige.

He takes another sip of the grappa then spits it at my mouth. Some of it hits my tongue and some of it slips down my chin; he follows the trail and licks it up.

He takes a third sip, and this time, he closes the distance between us and fits his mouth to mine. The warm liquid slips across my tongue and he chases it with his own. The alcohol drips into my veins, the scent of him envelops me, the taste of him fills my palate. He tilts his head, deepens the kiss, and a moan bubbles up my throat. My skin feels too tight for my body. My scalp tingles. My entire body seems to be on fire. *Too much, too soon.* He's not just dominating me; he's consuming me. He's going to chew me up and spit me out, and I'll never be able to deny him anything. My heart begins to race and my pulse pounds at my temples. I try to pull away, but he tightens his fingers around the nape of my neck and holds me in place. "Breathe," he murmurs against my lips. "I've got you; I promise."

Does he, though?

What if he decides I'm the cause of Nonna's death? What if he finds out how I am going to betray him? Will he still treat me with such consideration then? My pulse rate speeds up, and my knees tremble. I grip his upper arm and dig my fingernails into his biceps. His muscles are so solid, it's like trying to hold onto a brick wall.

"I don't want you to be gentle," I whisper. "I want you to treat me like I'm your slave. Someone you'll use for your needs and discard after. Someone you don't care about, except to make sure your desires are being taken care of. Can you do that for me?"

A crease wrinkles the space between his eyebrows.

"Please." I lean in, close enough for my breasts to push into the unforgiving expanse of his chest. "Please, Master, use me. Abuse me. Treat me roughly. Tear into my pussy, maul my skin, take my ass, use all my holes for your pleasure, Master."

Color smears his cheeks. His nostrils flare, even as his gaze sharpens on me. His grasp on my neck tightens to the point of pain. Goosebumps pop on my skin.

"You don't know what you're saying."

"I do."

"You have no idea what would happen if I take you at your word."

"I want you to."

"Once I start, there's no backing down. Once you're mine, I'll never release you."

"Are you only going to keep saying that, or will you do something about it, too?"

"Choose a safe word," he growls.

"Eh?" I blink rapidly.

"A safe word," he repeats, "choose a safe word. One you will use when you want me to stop what I'm doing to you. But remember, once you do, it's because you definitely don't want me to continue what I am doing."

"I don't need a safe word," I scoff, "I can take everything you do to me."

"I am not like any of the Doms you may have seen perform at your night-clubs. What I ask of you will not be easy. What I demand you to do for me will be beyond your comfort level. So, I'm telling you again, choose a safe word, Princess."

I hold his gaze, and the intent in his is so potent. So real. The lines radiating out from his eyes seem to have deepened in the last few minutes. The expression on his face is so serious, he seems to be in pain.

"Elsa?" He growls, "Choose. The. Fucking. Safe word."

"Oracle," I burst out.

"Oracle?"

"Oracle," I repeat. "It's oracle."

"Good." He looks me up and down. "Now let's discuss boundaries."

"Boundaries?" I blink.

"Apparently, you haven't been observing carefully on your forays to the BDSM clubs, or you wouldn't be asking me that." He widens his stance. "Boundaries, Princess. Is anything a hard 'no' for you? Anything off-limits for you?"

"Off-limits?" I know I'm repeating his words, but somehow, I seem to have lost the ability to think.

"Not that I encourage it, but I wouldn't be a good Dom if I didn't ask you. Is there anything you don't want me to do to you?" He leans in closer, so the heat from his body seems to increase in intensity, so I can see the fine lines around his eyes, so that masculine scent of his seeps into my skin, and it all goes straight to my head.

"You mean like—"

"Like, can I take your ass, your pussy, your mouth... all at the same time, after having tied you up and flogged you and aroused you until you are so slippery, I can use your cum to ease my way inside your backchannel?"

I swallow. All the moisture seems to have dried from my mouth. The space between my legs, on the other hand, is another matter altogether. Why do I find what he's saying so hot? Why do I want him to do exactly that to me?

"Princess?" he growls. "Still waiting for your answer."

"Yes," I whisper, breathless.

His gaze widens. "Are you sure?"

Jesus, can't he just accept what I am saying and let it be? Does he have to ask me to think through all of my answers?

"Well?" He tilts his head. "You sure about this?"

"Yes," I burst out. "Yes, Master."

"Good girl."

I can't stop the flush that sears my cheeks. All he has to do is praise me, and I'm ready to do anything for him.

"There's one more thing..." He narrows his gaze on me. "What I ask of you won't be limited to the physical."

I frown. "You mean—"

"Your emotions, your feelings. I'll ask you to share your thoughts, your desires, your past." He surveys my features. "Does that scare you?"

My heart stutters and my stomach knots. What does he mean by that? Does he suspect there's something in my past he needs to know about? Does he think I'm hiding something from him? Surely not. I haven't given him any reason to think so, have I? No, this is him taking his duties as a Dom seriously, that's all. Can he see how much I'm shaking?

I tip up my chin, meet his gaze. "No, it doesn't scare me, Master."

"Don't lie to me," he snaps.

I flinch.

"I... I'm not."

"You realize what I am asking, don't you? When I break you down, it will be not just your physical surrender I desire, but your emotional transparency, as well. I'll expect you to share every part of yourself with me. There will be nowhere and nothing you can hide from me. Do you understand?"

A ripple of apprehension squeezes my ribcage. My stomach churns. Now is the time to back away, to say this entire arrangement is a mistake. Now is the time to leave.

"It's not too late to leave if you're scared." It's as if he's read my mind. "If you want to walk away from this agreement, now is your chance." His lips curl.

Goddamn him, he's testing me. He's so sure I won't be able to hold up to whatever he has in store for me. He's trying to scare me off. Or maybe, he knows me too well. Perhaps he suspects if he taunts me, I'll rise to the challenge. Either way, I have come too far. I need to see this through. I need to show him I can go toe-to-toe with him.

"Princess?" His voice softens, "Do you understand?"

I nod.

"I need to hear you say it," he prompts.

"Yes, Master," I breathe, "yes, I understand. You can do as you please with me. You want me to give myself to you physically, emotionally, and mentally. You want me to belong to you completely."

"And you agree?"

"I do."

A flush steals over his features. A nerve throbs at his temple. "And you have your safe word which is..."

"Oracle," I murmur.

"And you'll use it when you want me to stop. And only when you definitely want me to stop. When I have pushed you so far beyond your boundaries you know you can't bend anymore."

I nod.

He draws in a sharp breath. His shoulders seem to expand. Then, without taking his gaze off of me, he reaches down, grips the lapels of my blouse, and yanks them apart.

19

Seb

The buttons of her blouse pop off, hit the floor, and roll away. The lapels of her blouse gape, exposing the tops of her creamy breasts. I grip the edges and pull them further apart, baring her breasts encased in a black lacy bra. There is a bow nestled in the valley between her breasts. I bend, clamp my teeth around the bow, and rip it off.

She screams, "What... what did you do?"

I spit out the bow, then straighten. "Damned if I know." I shake my head. "You fucking mess with my head, you know that?"

"I... I..." She swallows. "Seb, I—"

"Shut up."

"What?" She gapes at me. "What do you mean?"

"I don't want to hear anything from you except for moans, groans, or the sound of you screaming my name as you come, although it will be a while before that last bit happens. So, all I need from you right now is your obedience. Can you give me that?"

She nods.

I peer into her features. "Say it."

"Yes, Sir."

"Good." I study her eyes, as if I'll find the answers hidden there.

Why did she push me to lose control? Why did she taunt me and test my patience? Why did she throw those filthy words back at me, knowing they would arouse me? Knowing they'd send me over the edge.

I drag my thumb across her mouth, and her gaze widens. She stares at me, beseeching me with her gaze. She licks my digit, wraps her lips around my thumb and sucks, and goddamn her, but I feel it all the way to the tip of my cock. I swipe my wet thumb down her chin, down her throat, to the valley between her breasts, push the blouse off one shoulder, then the other.

She shivers and goosebumps rise on her skin.

I reach for the waistband of her skirt, unhook and unzip it, then push it down her legs. She steps out of it, kicks it aside, then stands clad in only her bra and panties.

"You're so fucking beautiful, you know that?"

She places her palm on her stomach. I frown. "Don't hide from me, Princess."

She shakes her head, her gaze wide. I pull her hand to her side and survey the silver stretch marks on her lower belly, the scar from what must have been the caesarean operation of her pregnancy. I sink down to my knees and press my lips to the puckered skin. She flinches, tries to pull away, but I grip her hips and hold her in place. I press tiny kisses across the marks, then sink my nose into the flesh between her legs.

A whine spills from her lips as I inhale deeply, filling my lungs with her essence. I am instantly hard. Goddamnit, where is this tenderness coming from? Why is it, since I laid eyes on her, I've wanted to take care of her and protect her, even as I've wanted to throw her down on her back and thrust deeply inside of her. I grab her buttcheeks and squeeze.

She trembles. I press my lips to the fabric covering her pussy, then close my mouth over her swollen clit. She moans, digs her fingers into my hair and tugs. Pain prickles down my spine and my cock lengthens further. I rub my chin down her pussy lips and she cries out. She thrusts her pelvis forward, chasing the friction as I increase the intensity of my ministrations. I slide a finger under her panties, then inside her soaking wet channel, and she freezes. I close my lips over her pussy and bite down, and that's when her entire body shudders. Her spine bends and the scent of her intensifies. I glance up just as she throws her head back, revealing the curve of her creamy throat. I rise to my feet and she sways. I scoop her up in my arms, walk over to the settee, and drop into it.

She cuddles into me, then turns her head into my chest. "Permission to speak, Sir?"

I nod.

"Why didn't you let me come?" she asks.

"Told you, I'm not going to let you climax easily."

She wriggles around in my lap, and the thick ridge of my arousal digs into her thigh. She freezes, then tips her chin up. "I don't understand. Clearly, you're turned on, so why don't you—"

"Fuck you, and give you what you need?"

She nods.

"I'm not sure."

She holds my gaze, her blue eyes growing stormy. "You don't want me." She tries to pull away, but I hold her in place.

I maneuver her so she straddles me, then fit her firmly over my thickness. "Does it feel like I don't want you?"

She firms her lips. "You said you'd be my Dom. You promised me you'd use my body for your pleasure."

"And I will." I grip her hips, then clamp my palm around her nape so she has no choice but to stay still. Then, I reach over and grab a box from the side table.

I hold it out to her.

"What is it?"

"Open it," I urge her.

She takes the box from me, her gaze wary, then glances at me from under her eyelashes.

"Go on." I allow my lips to kick up. "I promise, it's not anything you won't like."

She opens the box and stares at the pink circular-shaped object inside.

"What is it?"

"Something you're going to enjoy wearing."

"I'm supposed to wear it?"

"Take it out," I order.

She scowls up at me, but reaches for the vibrator and pulls it out. She surveys the comma-shaped gadget. One side broadens out into a balloon-shaped bulb. The other side ends in a slimmer tail.

"Take off your panties."

"What?"

"Go on." I take the vibrator from her and urge her to her feet.

She scowls at me, then tips up her chin. She slides her fingers into the waistband of her panties and shoves them down. She kicks them aside and stands there, dressed only in her bra. "Take that off, too."

"You don't need me to take it off to use the vibrator."

"I want to see how your entire body reacts to it. How your nipples harden in response to the stimulation."

She huffs, then reaches behind to unhook her bra and shrug it off.

I rake my gaze over her creamy shoulders, her swollen breasts. Her nipples so rigid, they seem hard enough to cut through my skin. Her waist is so tiny, I could span it with both palms. Her pussy lips glisten, and the nub of her clit peeks out from its hood. A fat drop of cum slides down her upper thigh, and heat sluices through my veins.

"Come 'ere," I order.

She hesitates.

I raise my gaze to her face. "Don't defy me," I say in a hard voice.

She shivers, takes a step forward, then another, until she comes to a halt in front of me. The scent of cherries, mixed with the sugary, sweet whiff of her arousal envelops me. My groin hardens and my thighs flex. I grip the vibrator in my hand and lean forward to tap the outside of one thigh.

"Open," I growl.

She slides her legs apart, and the scent of her arousal seems to deepen.

Goddamn it. I reach between her legs, and place the head of the vibrator at her entrance. She shudders and another drop of moisture slides down her upper thigh. I scoop it up and bring it to my lips.

"Oh, god," she moans as I suck on my finger and take in her essence.

"You taste like cherries, do you know that?"

"It… it's my favorite fruit," she admits.

My chest tightens, my balls harden, and the discomfort in my groin grows until I'm sure I'm going to burst out of my pants. I thrust the vibrator forward and it slides smoothly into her moist channel.

"Oh," she gasps.

I raise my gaze to her face. "Did it hurt?"

She shakes her head.

I make sure the tail end of it is positioned above her clit. Then, unable to stop myself, I bend and press a kiss to her belly.

"What was that for?"

I glance up at her. "Can't I be affectionate?"

"Why do you want to be affectionate?"

"Something about you, Princess, makes me want to treat you like a queen in public, and a whore in my bed, and like my asset every other time in between."

Her gaze widens. "Is that supposed to be romantic?"

"I wasn't trying to be romantic," I admit.

"But it's the most surprising thing anyone has ever told me."

I slip my hand into my pocket and press down on the remote control.

She stiffens. Her gaze widens. Her shoulders tremble. "Was that—"

"It was." I depress the button on the remote control again, and keep it pressed. Her entire body jolts. She squeezes her thighs together, and her nipples harden into tight buttons of need. The blood rushes to my groin. Desire tightens my balls. My fingers tingle to cup her swelling breasts. To pinch her nipples, and tweak them and intensify her pleasure while I plunder her mouth and suck on her sweet tongue. Instead, I take my finger off the remote and reach for her panties. I hold them out and she steps into them. I drag them back up her legs and over her hips.

"So that's it?" She blinks.

"You won't go anywhere without my permission."

"Eh?" Her forehead scrunches. "So, I have to check with you before I venture out?"

"Is that a problem?" I glare at her.

She juts out her lower lip.

"Something you want to tell me, Princess?"

"What about work?"

"Adrian or Massimo will drive you there and back. Anything else?"

She opens her mouth and shuts it. Then shakes her head.

"Good, you may now wear your clothes."

I lean back and watch as she pulls on her bra, then searches around for her clothes. She fastens her skirt, then dangles her blouse from one finger. "You destroyed my blouse," she whines.

I shrug off my coat and offer it to her. She slips it on. It engulfs her completely and reaches her knees. I do up her buttons, and she frowns down at herself. "I look ridiculous."

"You look adorable."

And completely off-limits to anyone else, since she's dressed in my clothes.

"Now what?" She pouts.

"I'll drive you to work."

She gapes. "So, I wear this… this thing the whole time I'm at work?" She points down between her legs.

I nod.

"And what if you… if you…"

"Activate it while you're at work?"

She nods.

"You'll just have to find out, won't you?"

20

Elsa

Forty-five minutes later, I'm at work at the flower shop.

Seb walked me through the silent nightclub toward his car parked at the curb. Before leaving, he called down and asked the staff to clear the nightclub so he could walk me out the front door without anyone noticing my state of undress. I protested and told him I could walk out the back door. To which he responded I'm more important than profits, and the club could suck up the loss of business for the time needed for us to reach his car.

Uhm, what? Honestly, I was so blown away I couldn't even protest. It was never like this with Fabio. To be fair, there's really no comparison between the two of them.

On the face of it, Fabio was suave and personable. He went to an Ivy League school in the US, then returned to Italy to join the police force, before being posted to London on a special assignment. He's educated, sophisticated, and comes from old money. He's also, as it turned out, a wife beater. Just my luck.

Seb, in contrast, looks rough, with his untamed hair, and the black ink which peeks out from under the collar of his shirt and makes me want to explore just how far down his body they extend. Maybe he has a full sleeve, although I can't tell. So far, every time I've seen him, he's been dressed in one of those suits which, sadly, cover his arms completely.

And so far, Seb has treated me like I'm his. Not that he's a gentleman; far from it. And that's the appeal. He's a man who'll treat me like a queen in real life and a slut in bed. A shiver runs down my back.

He drove me home and insisted on watching as I changed my clothes.

I wanted to protest, but decided against it. If he thought I was going to be embarrassed... Well, I certainly wouldn't let him know if I were. And I was. It had taken everything in me not to flinch as his hot gaze had taken in my curves, alighted on my tits, then slid down my waist to the space between my legs, over my thighs and my legs. By the time he had raised his gaze back to my face, I had been panting. And he was smirking. Bastard knew exactly what he was doing to me.

My finger slips on the rose stem I am trying to trim. The thorn pierces my skin and a drop of blood oozes out. "Damn it." I bring my finger to my mouth and suck on it. Since I met Seb, I've been way too distracted. For the first time I can remember, I'm thinking not of my daughter twenty-four-seven, but of him. I pause. He's managed to wiggle his way under my skin in such a short period of time. If I continue with this charade... Well, not a charade, according to him. If there is no divorce in the *Cosa Nostra*, once I marry him, it's for life. A shiver runs down my spine.

I went into the marriage with Fabio with silly romantic notions in my head. I'd hoped he'd be my Dom... Instead, he turned out to be my abuser. It's only after I started frequenting the BDSM clubs that I saw how a true Dom cares for his sub. Fabio? He simply saw me as an object to slake his lust.

I'd hoped for him to be my husband, my partner, and understand my needs. Instead, he was a monster who knew exactly how to prey on me and my tendency to see the best in people. And my insecurities. He took advantage of my trusting nature and my desire to please him and be all he wanted me to be. But the rules were always changing, so I was never quite sure what he wanted.

He started off so sweet, doting on me, buying me flowers and taking me to romantic places, and telling me how important I was to him. He told me he loved me before it even crossed my mind. He convinced me he would take care of my every need, but when it came down to it, he wanted me to take care of his needs. Except I never really knew what they were. He made me feel so stupid, like I couldn't do anything right, and then I got pregnant. That's when I knew I was trapped.

During the pregnancy, he either treated me like the most precious thing in his life, or forgot about me as he gallivanted around doing god-knows-what with god-knows-who. And he had the nerve to accuse me of cheating on him!

By the time Avery arrived, he'd pretty much lost interest in me and barely showed interest in her. Until he'd discovered he could use her to manipulate me. And he's been doing that ever since.

Of course, with Seb, I know where I stand. Both of us have a practical reason for getting married, only... This damn attraction toward him is potent. Heat flushes my skin. The scent of him, the taste of his skin, the feel of his fingers on my lips, between my thighs, cupping my breasts, thrusting his fingers inside of me... It's like he's marked me as his. With very little effort.

My fingers tremble and the rose stem slips from my grasp. I'm falling for him. Jesus, I'm falling in love with him. *No, no, no, that's not possible.* I barely know him. *You don't need to know a person to be enamored by him.* Damn, why can't I view this as a business transaction without getting my heart involved? Especially when it's the future of my daughter at stake.

And once I'm married to him, I won't be able to hold out against his charm. His presence. His dominance. Maybe that's what drew me to him in the first place. His absolute assurance in knowing what he wants and going after it. He reminds me of the girl I used to be. The one who hadn't hesitated to walk into a BDSM club and watch the others perform.

Somewhere along the way, I lost myself. Lost my conviction and my confidence in myself, as a mother and as a woman. And now, I've begun associating my sexuality with Seb, and I'm not sure I like it. This connection I feel toward him is not healthy. I may be marrying him; doesn't mean I'm going to allow myself to fall for him. If I did, there's no way I'd be able to retain my individuality. And I need to do that—for myself, for the sake of my daughter. What if... he turns out to be like Fabio? What if, like Fabio, I begin to trust him, and then, like my ex, what if Seb turns on me? And once he finds out what my true plans are, he definitely will.

I agreed to share all my thoughts and feelings with him, but it's too dangerous. I can't allow myself to be carried away by him. I need to find a way to hold onto the parts of me that are still left. I worry I will not be able to keep my feelings out of this relationship. That the more I get to know him, the more I'll fall for him, and I cannot bear for that to happen. I need to...

Reassure myself I'm attracted to men other than Seb. That he's not the only man in the world who'll be able to command me. That there are others who I could turn to, to become my Dom, if the need arises. I draw in a breath.

Of course, if Seb finds out what I'm going to do, he won't be happy. But I'll be discreet. I'll make sure I'm not noticed. Besides, he did say this was going to be an open marriage. He's the one who was clear he'd be sleeping with other women. If he thinks that rule applies only to him, he's crazy. And anyway, I'm not going to sleep with anyone else. I'm simply going to reassure myself I haven't been so overpowered with Mr. Grumphole's charisma, I can't be attracted to anyone else.

There are tons of other men out there... *And not one of them can help you get custody of Avery.* No, no. I'm not jeopardizing this chance to build a future with Avery. I'm simply ensuring, at the end of this charade—and it will come to an end when Seb finds out the real reason I agreed to marry him—there's something of me left. A part that has not been completely subsumed by the alphahole.

Yeah, that's all this is about. I'm not committing a crime by wanting to spend one evening away from him, am I?

The bell over the door clangs and I glance up as a woman walks in looking for flowers to purchase for a dinner party. She's followed by a man who wants to buy flowers for a date. I gently guide him away from the carnations and toward the spray of mixed flowers. The traffic picks up, and since I'm the only person in the shop today, I'm run off my feet. By the time it's five p.m., my feet are aching and I'm ready to call it a night.

That's when something vibrates in between my legs. What the—? I gasp, then squeeze my thighs together. The vibrations stop, then there's a second, and another. The woman I'm serving looks at me oddly. "Are you okay?"

"Y-yes."

That thing between my thighs vibrates again—slowly, once, twice, then faster. It speeds up, and a pulse of heat slides up my spine. I grip the edge of the counter, and the customer's gaze widens.

"Are you sure you're okay?"

I grit my teeth, force my lips to kick up. "Yes, I'm sure. Just stomach cramps."

"Oh, I get that. Do you have anything you can take for it? I might have something in my purse..." She begins to rummage in her bag.

"Thanks, but don't worry about it. They'll pass."

"If you're sure..."

The vibrations fade away, and I slump a little. "I am. Thank you. That will be twenty-nine, ninety-nine, please."

She taps the credit card on the machine, and that's when the blasted thing begins vibrating again, this time in a clock-wise motion. Jesus, can this thing also open a bottle of wine, or what? It pauses, then begins to vibrate, this time in a counter-clockwise motion. *What the—!*

Tendrils of pleasure pulse out from my core. My thighs tremble. I must moan a little, for she startles.

I give her a strained smile. "D-do you want your receipt?" I ask.

She shakes her head, then wishes me luck and walks out.

I clutch at the counter and squeeze my legs together. Just need to ride this out.

Except, the damned thing keeps vibrating. My entire body seems to shudder. Oh, hell. At least there's no one in the shop. I bite down on my lower lip and clench my inner muscles as the thing picks up speed—pulsating, throbbing, sending pinpricks of heat squeezing out to my extremities. My nipples harden and my toes curl. I throw my head back, curve my back, and groan. Close, I am so close. I can't believe it. Surely, I can't be close to an orgasm already? I have never come this quickly.

The boyfriend I had before Fabio barely got me to climax once. And Fabio? Well, he was too focused on taking his own pleasure. And this is from an inanimate object. Not that vibrators should be called that, considering how intimately I have gotten to know them of late, but this... Knowing he is at the other end of the remote control, pressing down on the button, knowing exactly what he's doing to me, makes me feel like I'm leashed to him by a virtual chain. That I'm under his control. That he can simply press a button and have me writhing and throbbing and aching for release.

Oh, my god! A whine bleeds from my lips. *Please let me come, please let me come. I'm so close, so close.* I brace myself for the oncoming onslaught of pleasure, even as I cross my legs, trying to hold back the impending climax, when— It stops. What the bloody hell? My climax slinks away. I snap my eyes open, and glance around the now empty shop. Thank god there's no one around to hear my groan of sexual deprivation. No doubt, the jerkalope knows how close I was to the edge. He knew I was on the verge of an orgasm and pulled back.

Argh! I curl my fingers into fists. I turn around with the intention of heading for the restroom, but my steps falter. He told me not to remove the damn thing. I have to keep it in. I have to let him turn it on whenever he feels like it. I have to allow him to bring me to orgasm, without even touching me. Or worse, bring me to the edge and not let me orgasm.

It's bad enough, whenever I see him, I seem to lose my ability to think. A-n-d I did ask him to dominate me, after all. So, in a way, his actions are justified. I can't blame him for trying to turn me on at will. No, it's the effect he has on me when I'm in his presence I resent. He only has to command me in that 'Dom' voice of his, and my body is unable to refuse him. It's a turn-on, but it's also a little scary. I refuse to become a doormat. Refuse to simply do as I'm told, no questions asked. I may want to submit to him... But I'll be damned if I'm going to give in without challenging him. If he wants me to be his submissive, he's bloody well going to have to come after me and tame me!

The blasted thing between my legs finally falls silent. I straighten, then walk to the door and flip the sign to closed. I hurry inside and sweep up the fallen leaves and stems on the floor. Thank god starting next week, we have a cleaner who'll come by every evening to help me. The shop is doing well enough we can afford it.

I take a final look around the place—the gleaming counters, the flowers displayed in the window, and in strategic locations around the shop. One last breath of the rose and honey-suckle scented air, then I grab my bag and step out the door. I have just locked it when something vibrates... in my purse. It's my phone. Not the other thing between my legs. Thank god!

I pull it out of my handbag, glance at the screen, and spot my ex-husband's name. My stomach churns and I grip the phone so tightly, the skin across my knuckles stretches white. The phone continues to vibrate. I grit my teeth and finally answer it. "What do you want?" I snap.

There's silence for a second, then, "Is that how you greet your husband?" Fabio's oily voice sounds in my ear.

"We're divorced," I say tersely.

"How can I forget?" He chuckles. "It's your infidelities which landed you in this mess."

"I never slept with another man, in all the time we were married."

"And what do you call frequenting S&M clubs? Too bad I couldn't beat that proclivity out of you."

My breath comes in pants, my chest hurts, and I lean my shoulder against the door to take in a breath, then another. *He can't harm you. He can't harm you. You got away from him, remember? Now, you just have to do your part, and everything will be fine. You'll get custody of Avery. That's what you want, right? It will all be worth it in the end.*

I square my shoulders, lift my chin. "Why are you calling me?" I demand.

"Are we on track? We'd better be. I'm losing patience."

"A month," I reply, "you said I had a month."

"Forty-eight hours."

"What?" I stiffen. "What do you mean?"

"You have two days to get me the information I need to put the Sovranos behind bars."

"Two days? That's impossible. You told me I had a month!"

"I lied."

"You son of a bitch. There's always something else I have to do, or else. What is it going to take to get you to let go of me and give me Avery?"

"Do you have the information I asked for?" His tone grows more casual. "If you don't get me what I want, I'll do everything in my power to ensure you never see her again."

My guts twist, bile rises in my throat, and I almost throw up. I push the back of my head against the door, close my eyes, and count backward from ten... nine... eight. The world slowly stops spinning. My breathing normalizes.

"Elsa?" His voice cuts through the noise in my head, "You there?"

"Don't make me do this. I can't go through with this... farce."

"Then forget about ever seeing Avery again, you—"

"No." I grip the phone so tightly that pain screeches up my arm.

I push aside the emotions that threaten to overwhelm me, then draw in another breath. "Forty-eight hours," I say in a hard voice, "and you'll get what you need."

"Good," his voice brightens, "I knew I could count on you. Knew I made the right choice when I married you. I—"

"Two days. I get you the information, and then you walk away from us. You never look back."

"First get me what I need, then we'll see."

I grit my teeth. This is so pointless. He always uses Avery to get me to do his bidding, and I always agree to his demands in the hope that he might allow me to see my daughter more often. But he's already filed for full custody. He won't stop until he's stripped me of all of my rights to be with my own daughter. He'll just keep using her against me. He'll always use Avery to make my life a living hell. Worse than what it is now. *Not if I can help it.*

I'm giving Fabio one last chance to come through. I'm going to deliver on what he asked of me. Who am I kidding? Demanded of me. I'm going to get closer to Seb, then use my proximity to spy on the Sovranos. I'll get my ex the information he needs. And if he still doesn't walk away from me and Avery? Then I'm going to fight him with every bone in my body, with my last living breath. I'm going to find a way to protect my daughter from him.

"You take good care of her, you hear me? I'm only leaving her with you because I don't have a choice, you—"

The phone cuts out. My heart twists in my throat and the blood pounds so hard at my temples that specks of black flutter at the edges of my vision. *Focus, focus, you can't faint. Not now. Not when Avery is counting on you. Not when you need to get through this evening.* Apparently, I'm one step ahead of my bastard ex. I already found the perfect way to accelerate events. All I have to do is see this through, and everything will be okay.

There's a touch on my shoulder and I scream. I snap my eyes open, find Adrian holding up his hands, palms facing me.

"Whoa, you okay?" He peers into my features. "You look pale. Did something happen?" He glances up and down the road.

"I'm fine," I clear my throat, "just taking a breather."

"Hmm..." He glances at the phone then back at me. "Seb sent me to pick you up."

Which is perfect. I couldn't have planned this better. I pocket the phone, and paste a smile on my face. "That's great."

"Are you sure you're okay?" His voice softens, "Anything I can help you with?"

Of the seven, Adrian definitely comes across as the most understanding. He's as good-looking as the other Sovrano brothers, as macho in appearance, but something in his eyes hints at more patience. There's a hurt there which seems to stem from something that may have happened to him... Something in his past may have tempered him, so while he's as dangerous as his brothers, there's an empathy in his attitude which invites you to confide in him.

Not that I trust him to keep my secrets. Quite the opposite. I'm confident whatever I tell him will be reported back to Seb. The Sovranos have each other's backs. No matter how much they fight amongst themselves, it's clear that, when it comes to taking care of each other's interests, they'll be there for the other.

It's what gives me the confidence to lower my gaze and say in a low voice, "As a matter of fact, there is something you can help me with."

21

Seb

"She did what?" I tighten my fingers around the phone with such force, pain shoots up my arm. "You mean, she's there, on her own?"

I listen as Adrian tells me my wife-to-be—my fiancée—is at a nightclub. And it's not just any night club, but an S&M Club. One owned by the *Camorra,* our fiercest rivals.

"She wanted to go," he states in a mild voice.

"You couldn't stop her? You could have—"

"Bound her and kept her confined to the house?" he asks.

Cazzo! I drag my fingers through my hair. He has a point there. No one gets to bind her, except me. No one gets to touch her, except me. No one gets to look at her, except me. It's why, when I'd been unable to make it to the flower shop to pick her up, I'd sent Adrian. He's the only one of my brothers I trust with her. Well, he's also one of the only ones available, because Michael, Christian and Axel are married and too busy with their own family dramas. As for Luca and Massimo... Nope. No way am I going to let them get near her. Not that I don't trust them with her...

Okay, I don't trust them not to notice just how gorgeous she is, and fuck if I don't want either of them spending any amount of time with her when I'm not around. Which leaves Adrian. And no, it would be a mistake to think Adrian is less menacing than the others. Bastard is the most unassuming of us seven, but he's also the one most likely to surprise you when you least expect it. In a way, it makes him more dangerous, because people tend to underestimate him, so they never see him coming. Not until he's pulled the rug out from under their feet. All of it done in his easy-going style. Which makes him quite lethal. Exactly the kind of man I'd entrust with protecting what's most dear to me.

"So, you're with her?"

"I am," he replies.

"In the club?"

"*Si*."

"Does she know you're there?"

"Do you think I'm a novice?" A hard note enters his voice.

"Still, I can't understand why you didn't stop her."

"I drove her home from work, left her there, then retreated to keep watch over the house. Sure enough, half an hour later, a car arrives to pick her up."

"*Porca miseria*, I told her not to go anywhere without telling me." I roll my shoulders. "I told her it was dangerous to be out on her own, that she shouldn't be using any transportation, except for the one approved by me."

"And you expected her to obey you?" He chuckles.

"She didn't say she wouldn't." I shuffle my feet.

"You took her silence for assent?"

"Wouldn't you?" I scowl.

He chuckles. "I wouldn't let myself be in a situation where I'd allow a woman to shatter my peace of mind."

"That's why you prefer to watch Cass from afar?"

There's silence on the other end. I sense his anger zinging through the phone and whoa, isn't that interesting? The calm and collected Adrian, getting emotional enough to lose that air of affability he tightens around himself like a coat of armor.

"Keep stalking her without making a move, and one day, someone will come along and sweep her off her feet, from right under your nose Then, we'll talk about peace of mind or any such naive notions you have," I drawl.

"If I were you, I'd be very careful what I say next. Don't forget, I'm the only one here watching out for what's yours," he growls.

I dig my fingers in my hair and tug. "*Dio Santo*, I didn't mean to test you. I'm just stressed, is all."

"I take it meeting with the *Camorra* is not exactly pleasant?"

"It's what Nonna wanted." I squeeze my eyes shut. Still can't believe she's gone. I'd grown up convinced she was immortal, that she'd outlive all of us. Funny how you take people for granted. Then they're gone, and you realize just how much you relied on them. Losing my mother had been a blow, but I'd had Nonna to look up to. Losing my father had been a relief; it had felt like I could finally breathe. And we'd had Nonna, who'd told us it wasn't wrong we didn't feel any remorse about his death. But now that Nonna's gone, who's going to console us? Why does it feel like I've lost a big part of myself? A part of my past. A slice of what anchored me to this life. I never realized how emotionally dependent I was on Nonna, until she passed.

"I miss her, too. The old bat was a force of nature, and a pain in the ass, but she meant well. She looked out for us, used the old ways to guide us, while adapting quickly to the changing times. Guess we never gave her enough credit for how much guidance she gave us," he murmurs.

I squeeze the bridge of my nose. "She wanted us to make amends with the *Camorra*."

"Is that what she told Michael?" he asks.

Before Nonna passed away, she met with Michael and told him she wanted to see all her grandsons married within a month of her passing. She also insisted he bury our long-standing feud with the *Camorra*.

"With the *Bratva* and the Kane Company no longer at loggerheads with us, it leaves only the *Camorra* who pose a threat to us. She made him promise he'd patch up our differences, especially in view of the fact half of us are married, not to mention the babies on the way."

"If she'd had her way, she'd have had the rest of us married within the month," Adrian replies, his tone glum.

"Is that what she made you promise?" I ask.

"What do you think?" He snorts.

"So, you're going to ask Cass too marr—"

"No way," he growls. "Nonna may have asked. Doesn't mean I'm gonna do what she wants."

"You made her a promise on her death bed," I remind him.

"I did it to keep her happy. I have no intention of allowing myself to be manipulated into a marriage I don't want, and especially not by someone from beyond the grave."

"Can't say I blame you," I confess. "But I also feel like I need to follow through with my promise to her. It's the only time she asked something of me, and I can't not give it to her."

"*Cazzo*," he swears softly, "don't guilt trip me, *fratello*. I'm having a hard enough time keeping a handle on my emotions."

"Speak for yourself. I am well and truly in over my head, and if you repeat this to any of the others, I'll deny it."

"Not that I have any interest in your messed up love-life... And speaking of your girlfriend—"

"—fiancée."

"—was just approached by a man."

"*Che cazzo*!" I growl. "What the hell is he doing?"

"Asking her something, by the looks of it."

"And what about her? Is she scared? Is she upset? Why don't you go and intercept him?"

"And make myself known? Not to mention, I'd lose her trust, and then she'll end up hiding her movements from me in the future. Where would that leave us?"

"Fuck," I swear, "what is she doing now?"

"Hmm, she's talking back to him, gaze cast down, chin lowered. Damn, she's a perfect submissive, isn't she?"

"Stop talking about her."

"Just telling you what I see, man," he drawls.

"And now? What is she up to now?"

"He's turned and left the room, and *cazzo*, she's following him out."

"What the—? You keep an eye on her, you get me? I'm on my way."

Forty-five minutes later, I screech to a halt in front of *The Mongoose*. Yep, that's the name of the nightclub run by the *Camorra*. Because the nightclub owned by us is called Venom, so... Snake. Mongoose. Get it? Very original of the *Camorra*. I snort to myself as I point at the valet then at my car. I grab a few notes from my wallet and thrust them at the man, who gasps at me.

"Keep the engine running. I'll be out in ten minutes. And if I'm delayed, you still keep the engine running, you *capisce*?" I growl as I brush past him and walk into the nightclub.

The music hits me at the same time the scent of bodies—of lust and sex—pours over me. I glance around the high-ceilinged room, taking in the bar that stretches from end-to-end on one side. At strategic intervals around the dance floor, there are elevated platforms on which barely dressed men and women—singles, couples, same sex and opposite sex, as well as threesomes—cavort from swings and hang off of each other in various poses that could teach the Kama Sutra a thing or two. Huh.

I've never set foot inside of this place, which is understandable, as it belongs to our arch rivals, after all. But I have to admit, the ambience is over-the-top just enough—with its heaving bodies on the dance floor, the throbbing music that fills my blood, the strobe lights that turn the entire space into a hedonistic experience—that it has me pausing on the threshold.

I scan my gaze across the room. Where the hell is Adrian? I would have come sooner, except it had taken me ten minutes to find a gap in the negotiations which had been taking place between Michael and Salvatore, the leader of the *Camorra*. As it is, Michael hadn't been happy I'd stepped out to call Adrian earlier. Then when I interrupted him to tell him I had to leave, his features hardened, his gaze growing even stonier. That is, until I whispered it was related to Elsa, at which point, he jerked his chin in the direction of the exit. I left them to their discussion of how to bury the bad blood between the two clans, and turned and raced out of there, just catching Massimo and Luca's sniggers as I brushed past them. *Stronzi!*

I pushed my beloved Fornasari to its maximum speed, weaving through traffic, and leaving irate drivers in my wake. This car was created for moments like this. Besides, Italians love nothing more than breaking road rules, while swearing at fellow drivers who flaunt dare-devil driving skills.

But where the devil is Adrian? And more to the point, where is my princess? I rake my gaze across the room, then spot Adrian waving at me from the far corner near the stairs. I shoulder my way through the crowd. The heat presses down on me, the press of bodies pushes me in on all sides, and by the time I reach him, a sheen of sweat covers my brow.

"Where is she?" I snarl.

He jerks his chin up the stairs. "Last door on the left."

He's barely completed the sentence before I've turned and taken the steps, two at a time. I burst onto the landing of the floor, then race down the corridor until I reach the last door on the left. I thrust my shoulder into the door, which swings open. Two spotlights cast their glow on the couple at the back of the semi-dark room.

She is tied to a St. Andrews cross which is attached to the wall. She's spread-eagled, her arms and legs pulled apart, with her wrists and ankles tied to the cross. She's wearing a thin blouse, through which her nipples are clearly visible. It dips at her cleavage. Her skirt is bunched around her thighs, high enough the white of her panties is visible. A man walks around her, coming to a stop at her side. He reaches out to finger a strand of her hair, and anger squeezes my gut. The blood thumps at my temples, my vision tunnels, and a red haze drops over everything. I hear a growl, then realize it's coming from me. Both of them must hear it, too, for they glance toward the door. Even in the dim light, I can see the shock on her face, quickly followed by guilt.

I bare my teeth. She opens and shuts her mouth. I close the distance to the *stronzo* who glances between us. He's shorter than me, somewhat muscular, but with a middle that's flabby.

"Now hold on here." He thrusts out his chest. "This is a private session; this is—"

I bury my fist in his face.

22

Elsa

Seb punches the guy— Is his name Desmond? Dillon? Dixon, maybe? —and I hear a crunch. Ouch. I wince. That must hurt.

Desmond/ Dillon/ Dixon staggers back and slams into the wall. "Ow. ow. Ow." He wails, "What was that for?" He clutches at his face as blood drips from his nose, down his chin, and splatters onto his shirt.

Seb merely closes the distance to him, grabs him by his collar, and hauls him to his feet. "Get out and stay out. If I see you near my fiancée I'll kill you, motherfucker, you get me?"

"Hold on," the man protests, "this was consensual; she asked me to dominate her; she—"

Seb moves so quickly, his movements seem to blur. The next moment, he's pushed a gun into the center of the man's forehead, who freezes.

"You will not come near her again, you feel me? You will not breathe the same air as her. You will not look at her. You will not come within a hundred feet of her. *Capisce*?"

His gaze widens.

"Get the fuck out before I empty this gun in your face." Seb steps back and the man rushes past him and heads to the door, which slams behind him. The music from the nightclub, which had crept into the room, cuts out again.

Silence follows. A beat. Another. Seb stands where he is, still facing the wall. He stalks over to the door and locks it.

My nerves stretch as I wait for him to make a move. I wait for him to say something, anything... When I can't bear it anymore, I clear my throat.

"Seb?" I say softly.

He flinches, but doesn't reply.

"Seb, I'm sorry."

He swings around to face me, the gun pointed at me now. I glance from the barrel to his face. His features are set in stone. The light from above reflects off of his eyes. They seem to glow a golden-orange, lion-like. He takes a step forward, and another, until he's standing in front of me.

He still hasn't said a word. He rakes his gaze down my features, my breasts, pausing at my belly, then between my thighs.

"Did you take it out?" he asks in a soft voice. There's no hint of emotion, nothing in his tone gives away how he's feeling. His shoulder muscles are bunched under his jacket, and his biceps seem to have gotten even bigger, if that's possible.

When I don't answer, he repeats himself. "Did. You. Take. It. Out?" he growls.

"N-no." I swallow, but that doesn't help the dryness in my throat. "You told me not to."

"I also told you not to go anywhere without my permission."

"Oh." My muscles tremble like a jolt of electricity has zapped through my nerve endings.

"Did I, or did I not, warn you not to go anywhere unless you checked in with me first?"

"Yes, but that was a stupid request. Surely, you didn't expect me to obey it?" I shake my hair back from my face.

"Considering you're the one tied up, wearing a skimpy blouse and a skirt, and I'm the one holding a gun, I wouldn't recommend you try to sass me right now," he says in the same tone one might use to ask about the weather.

A shiver courses up my neck. My pulse drumbeats at my temples. Jesus Christ, I've done it now. I've made him not just angry, but furious. If I thought I saw his temper earlier, I'm beginning to suspect I haven't seen anything yet.

"Come to think of it, except for the part when I barged in and you seemed taken aback—a surprise you've recovered from rather quickly, I might add—you've held onto your composure rather well. It's almost as if..." He cocks his head, and I feel like I can see the gears clicking inside before he speaks again. "You were expecting me, weren't you?"

"What?" I bite the inside of my cheek. "Of course not."

"You knew Adrian would be watching the house. You called for a car and came here, knowing full-well he'd report back to me. In fact," his gaze narrows, "this entire scene is for my benefit. You wanted to bring me here. You wanted me to lose my composure. You wanted to push me until I lost control." He leans in until his chest almost brushes my thrust-out breasts. Until his scent deepens and intensifies and swirls around me and goes to my head. Goddam it, why does he always smell so good... so hot... so sexy I want to lick him up from head to toe before I bury my nose in his neck and draw in a lungful of his heady scent?

"I don't know what you are talking about." I lick my lips and his gaze drops to my mouth.

"Don't lie to me," he says, still using that tone which is so casual, it's clear he's plotting something in that sadistic mind of his.

He places the gun against my cheek. "So damn beautiful, you took my breath away the first I saw you at Venom, you know?"

"D-did I?" My breath hitches.

He drags the barrel of the gun down my neck, down the valley between my breasts until it encounters the first button in the front. He pushes down until the button pops. It hits the ground and rolls away. He continues down, pops the second button, then the next and the next, until my blouse gapes in the front. He pushes aside both flaps, until my breasts are bared to his gaze.

"No bra," he says in a conversational tone. "Were you making sure to give an eyeful to the men in the club?"

I shake my head.

"Lying again, Elsa?"

What happened to Princess? Why isn't he calling me Princess? He's really pissed off at me, isn't he? Fear churns my stomach. "I wore a coat and only took it off when I entered this room." I glance at the small closet in the corner of the room. "You can look inside the cupboard."

"I have a better idea." He circles my nipple with the barrel of the gun. My belly flip-flops and my breasts seem to swell. Why am I getting turned on? He's using a gun to play with my nipple, he— He drags the gun to the opposite breast, rubs the barrel of the gun across my nipple, which is as hard as a diamond.

"Turns you on, does it?" He circles my nipple once again with the gun, and my entire body shudders.

"Definitely turns you on." He tilts his head, his gaze curious. "Is it the danger, or the sense of the forbidden that arouses you more, you think? Or is it the fact I'm a Mafioso who's used this gun to kill men, and now I'm holding it to your breast? The same breast with which you fed your daughter, I assume?"

He lowers his gun, only to replace it with his mouth. He closes his lips around my erect nipple and sucks, hard. I feel it all the way to my core.

"Oh, god," I groan, "oh, my god."

He continues to suck on my nipple, pulling at it, tugging on it. He bites down with his teeth and my entire body jerks.

"Please," I whine, "please, Seb, please."

He releases my nipple with a pop and straightens.

"Please what?" he asks, his tone so polite, it's as if he's going to follow up with m'lady. "What do you want me to do?"

"I want you to make me come."

"Negative." One side of his lips twists. "Next?"

I stare at him. "Why won't you let me come? Earlier, you stopped just as I was about to climax."

"Excellent." He bares his teeth. "You're beginning to understand how our relationship is going to play out."

"I don't understand anything," I huff. "If you think you're going to scare me with your gun, think again."

"I'm not going to use my gun to scare you."

"No?" I frown.

"I'm going to use it to fuck you."

My jaw drops. "What do you mean?"

"Exactly that." He hooks the barrel of the gun under my skirt and flips it up. "That's the last time you show your panties to any man other than me."

"That's a thong, and you can't tell me what to do."

"And yet, it's you who came to me and asked me to dominate you."

"Doesn't mean I'm going to submit easily."

"I wouldn't have expected you to." He reaches with his free hand, pinches the delicate strap of my underwear, and tugs. Of course, it snaps. He yanks it off and sniffs it.

My core clenches. "You're an animal."

"You make me an animal. You make me want to throw you down and rut into you. You make me want to forget about the veneer of civilization I'm supposed to present to the world. You make me want to beat my chest and announce to anyone who'll hear me that you're mine. Mine, mine, mine." He snaps his teeth and I jolt. Those golden eyes of his lighten until they seem almost pale yellow. Mesmerizing, animalistic. He seems more beast than man. A thrill grips me.

Is this what I was hoping for when I pranced out of the house and ordered a car to bring me here? He's right, of course. I had no doubt Adrian would be watching the house, and he'd report my whereabouts to Seb. What I hadn't anticipated is how angry it would make him to see me with another man.

For what it's worth, the guy I chose was a wanker. Someone who couldn't hold a candle to him. Someone I wouldn't have wanted to touch me. If he'd tried anything with me... Well, I knew things wouldn't get that far because I had no doubt Seb would come charging in here and pull that entire macho bullshit and throw the guy out.

Stupid plan? Maybe. I hadn't been thinking too clearly after Fabio's call. All I knew was I had to push Seb over the edge, and judging by his flared nostrils, the pulse that tics at his jaw, not to mention the way he's staring at the bared flesh between my legs, I may have succeeded too well.

He tucks the top of my skirt into my waistband, then draws the tip of the gun between my pussy lips. A shudder grips me. My stomach ties itself in knots even as a fat drop of cum slides out from my channel. He scoops up the moisture with his gun and holds it to my mouth.

"Lick it off," he commands.

I part my lips, flick my tongue across the barrel, and his entire body seems to harden. The muscles of his shoulders bulge and the veins stand out at his throat. He seems to grow even bigger. For the first time fear, real fear, visceral and white-hot, grips me.

"Seb, you're scaring me."

23

Elsa

"Good," he growls. He slides his hand into his pocket and pulls out a tiny device. He holds it up so I can see clearly when he presses the button. The thing between my thighs instantly vibrates. A tremor runs up my spine.

"What are you doing?" A groan wells up.

He continues to hold his finger down on the remote and the vibrations intensify. Tendrils of sensation spiral out from where the vibrator throbs inside of me. The warmth intensifies low in my belly, a jolt of heat slingshots up my skin, around my breasts and back toward my clit. I throw my head back and whine, "Please, please, Seb. Please let me come this time."

The oscillations grow in strength, becoming faster, more frequent. Every cell in my body seems to come alive with awareness; every pore on my skin seems to pop. My scalp tingles. My thighs tremble. A shuddering sweeps up from my feet, up my thighs, coils in my belly, and that's when the vibrations cease.

"Noooo!" I flutter my eyes open in time to see him drop the remote control in his pocket. Not again. The jerk-hole, once more, stopped just as I was going to come. Anger flushes my chest. I open my mouth to protest, and that's when he drops to his knees and pushes his face in between my legs. His tongue swirls over my opening. What the hell—? I gasp, try to wriggle away, but he grips my hip and holds me in place. He fits his mouth to my slit and grasps hold of the vibrator, then turns his head and spits. Something clatters to the ground! Holy hell, he pulled it out. He. Pulled. Out. The vibrator. From my cunt. With his mouth. Why is that so hot? Why is that so filthy and forbidden and so very erotic? I'm conscious I'm gaping, even as pleasure pulses out from where he touched his lips to my melting flesh.

He glances up at me from under those dark eyelashes and his eyes gleam.

"You're a monster," I gasp.

"I aim to please." Without taking his gaze off of my face, he rises to his feet, then presses the barrel of his gun to my sopping wet entrance.

I freeze. Goosebumps pop on my skin. My entire body goes rigid, and heat bursts to life in my lower belly. A pulse flares in my cunt as he eases the barrel of the gun inside of me.

Oh, my god. A moan bleeds from my lips as my channel stretches to accommodate the object. It should be scary. I should be petrified, and I would be lying if I said I'm not. But if there's one thing I know, it's that Seb won't hurt me. He's making his point in an extreme fashion, or so the still-thinking part of my brain insists. He's trying to show me who is the Dominant in this relationship—it's him. Something I could have told him for free. All I want is for him to work hard to make me submit. Turns out, making him angry means I pay the price, too.

He holds my gaze as he begins to fuck me with his gun. Each time he sinks it into me, I feel his fingers, grasped around the handle, rubbing against my clit. In-out-in. My breasts seem to swell and my thigh muscles tremble, but I refuse to look away. I refuse to let him see how much he's surprised me; how he's almost succeeded in making me submit. This show of dominance... It's feral and menacing... and wild. And sexy. I shouldn't be turned on by his actions, but I am. What he's doing is so wrong, and yet... There's something indefinably forbidden, something debauched and undeniably titillating. A heaviness settles low in my belly and goosebumps crackle across my skin as he leans into me. Heat spools off of his body and slams into my chest. The force of his dominance pins me down and I gasp.

"Who do your moans belong to, Princess?" he growls.

"You."

He lowers his chin to his chest and his golden eyes seem to slice through more of my defenses.

"You, what?" he growls.

"You... Master," I whisper.

A flush stains his cheeks. A sheen of sweat coats his hairline. He's as turned on as me. As anticipatory of what is to come. As greedy to enjoy my inevitable plummet into submission, as I am to worship his authority over me.

He wraps his arm under my thigh and squeezes, and a jolt of sensation digs its claws into my belly.

"Who does your every breath belong to?" he snaps.

"You... Master."

He bends and locks his lips around a swollen nipple. He sucks on it, then releases it with a pop, before peering up at me. "Who do your breasts belong to?"

"You," I whimper.

"And your cunt? Who does your pussy belong to?"

"You."

"Damn right." A look of fierce satisfaction crosses his features. "You belong to me, Princess. You are mine, and if any man dares look at you again, I'll kill him, do you understand?"

I nod, and color flushes his face. He slides the gun inside of me again, and the friction is too much. A trembling grips me, my back bows, sensations scream up my legs and my thighs, and coalesce in my belly. The climax threatens to overpower me and that's when he pulls his gun back. My orgasm pauses, flutters up my spine, then evaporates.

"No, no, no," I snarl, "you can't do this."

"I can."

"Why won't you let me come?"

"It's called edging, baby."

"I know what it's called."

"Do you, now?" He brings the barrel of the gun to my mouth. "Lick it, Princess."

I curl my tongue around the tip of the gun. The sweet taste of my cum, layered with the metallic taste of the gun, sinks into my taste buds. For some reason, that turns me on even more. He drags the gun down my throat, leaving a trail of my cum and saliva in its wake. This blending of bodily fluids feels filthy, dirty, and hot. Clearly, being with him is bringing out my inner slut. He wipes the gun on my blouse, then slides it into the back of his pants.

He steps back, looks me up and down. "*Cazzo*, you look so fucking hot. If we didn't have to be at City Hall, I'd fuck you right now."

"Why don't you, asshole?"

"Cause we have a date, you and I, darling."

"Date? I didn't agree to any date..." I blink. "Hold on a second, what do you mean by City Hall?"

"Exactly that, sweetheart."

"Don't trust it when you pepper your sentences with endearments," I grumble.

"Maybe you'll trust me, now that I almost made you come?"

"Maybe not," I retort.

"Maybe you will, once you get full custody of your daughter?"

I hold his gaze for a second, then another. "Maybe," I finally whisper.

"I'll hold you to it." He reaches around and lowers the St. Andrews Cross until my feet touch the floor. Then he sinks down to his knees, unties one ankle, making sure I have my balance before he unties my other ankle. I begin to shuffle my feet together, but he stops me.

"Easy, let your blood circulation restore itself." He rubs at my ankles, and the warmth of his hands on my skin sends pinpricks of pleasure racing up my legs. When he's sure that I've reacclimated, he rises to his feet. Then he reaches up and unties my hands. He brings my wrists together in front of me and rubs them between his large, warm fingers. The calluses on his thumbs scrape over my skin and goosebumps pop out. My belly trembles, then flip-flops, and as if he's aware of the effect, he releases me. Then shrugs off his jacket and drapes it over my shoulders.

"I have a jacket," I protest.

"You'll wear mine," he commands in a tone that's so fierce that my insides clench. I thrust my arms into the sleeves, and he proceeds to fasten the buttons.

That masculine, spicy scent of his envelops me. The residual heat of his body trapped in the jacket lining loops about my shoulders, tying me to him further.

Finally, he folds up the sleeves before he steps back and surveys me. "You'll do."

"For what?" I scowl.

"You'll see."

He clasps my wrist and turns just as there is a banging on the door. "Open up! You, in there," a man hollers.

"Why the hell is the door locked?" asks another male voice.

The banging intensifies. We reach the door, and Seb flings it open. A man with his hand raised to knock on the door pauses mid-motion.

"Move," Seb growls.

The man pales. He stumbles back and crashes into his friend, who loses his footing. The two slam into the wall as Seb brushes past them.

"Hey, where are you taking me?" I huff as he hauls me in his wake.

"I've told you already."

"City Hall?" I stumble and try to keep up with his much larger strides. "Why are we going to City Hall?"

"One guess."

My heart begins to thud in my chest and my eyes widen. *It can't be, can it?* "You wouldn't." I gulp.

"Try me," he replies.

He yanks me down the stairs, into a corridor that bypasses the main dance floor, then up a short flight of steps, where he shoulders open the door. The night air hits me as we step out. I shiver. He wraps his arm around me and pulls me into him. His bulk cuts off the breeze and the heat of his body surrounds me. I'm tempted to think he's trying to keep me warm, but I'm pretty sure he's only making sure I don't escape him.

Glancing back at the main door to the nightclub, I notice a queue stretching around the building.

"Won't City Hall be shut at this time of the night?"

"I asked them to keep it open."

"Of course you did." I toss my hair over my shoulder. "What if I don't want to come with you?"

"Too bad." He raises a shoulder.

"I believe I will record my objections on the matter." I set my jaw.

"Noted, and overruled."

"You are not a judge, or a lawyer, for that matter." I scowl.

He glances up and down the street. And goddamn, in profile, he resembles Keanu even more. "Are you waiting for the bus from *Speed*?" I venture.

"What?" He shoots me a sideways glance.

"The bus from *Speed*? When Sandra Bullock drives the bus with Keanu Reeves next to her and the bus has no brakes and—"

The screech of brakes being applied reaches us as a car careens to a stop in front of us. Not just any car; his SUV. The door to the driver's seat opens, and a man in a valet uniform jumps out. Seb slaps a note into his outstretched palm then pushes me into the seat.

"Hey," I protest.

He slides into the car after me, and I scooch over to the passenger's seat. "Could have, at least, allowed me to come around to my side of the car," I grumble.

He slams the door shut and eases the car onto the road.

"So, we're really doing this? We're going to City Hall at—" I peer at the clock on the dashboard. "Eleven p.m. at night."

He glowers at the road ahead, and I take it as his assent.

"Are you going to tell me why? Or should I continue making wild guesses, which I promise you is going to drive you mad. If you thought I was insufferable earlier, you haven't seen me when I'm stressed. Also, as if this were not already obvious, I'm not going to stop talking until you tell me why you're dragging me to City Hall so late at night. I—"

"We're getting married."

24

Seb

I expect her to freak out, but instead, she purses her lips and glowers at me. Probably because she'd already guessed why we're headed there. No other reason to go to City Hall, after all. She opens and shuts her mouth a few times. Then, "You're insane," she says in a low voice.

Only where you're concerned.

"We were supposed to get married in a week, and you didn't want to get married at church, so—" I raise a shoulder. "This way, we can cut to the chase."

She continues to stare at me for a few seconds more, then she glances down at herself. "I'm not dressed for any kind of a wedding."

It wouldn't matter if you were wearing a sack, you'd still look beautiful.

"You're wearing my clothes." A flush of satisfaction fills my chest. Goddam. Since when did I become so possessive about her? It's bad enough I completely lost control when I saw that man toy with her hair. The fact she was tied up—that she'd allowed him to tie her up, that she would allow anyone other than me to tie her up... *Cazzo!* A growl rumbles up my chest. I lost my mind, I admit. I hadn't intended to fuck her with my gun. *Gesù Cristo*, what the hell is wrong with me? How could I have done that? I pulled out the gun to scare off that motherfucker, and I ended up using it to pleasure her. At least, I hope it pleasured her. From her reaction, it certainly seemed that way. I wanted to punish her for how she provoked me, and finding her bound and at my mercy made me lose my head completely.

"Are you okay?" I finally ask.

When she doesn't answer, I glance sideways at her. "Princess, I asked you a question."

She draws in a breath. "Why, are you worried you emotionally scarred me? You don't have to worry; my ex managed to do that just fine."

Anger thuds at my temples. I squeeze the steering wheel, and brake for a red light. The road is empty of traffic. A lone piece of paper blows by in front of us.

"You follow traffic rules, even when there is no real need to," she comments in an offhand voice.

"I am Mafia; I'm always watched by law enforcement. One slip up on my part, and there's no telling where it'd land me. Not that we don't have the cops on the payroll, but I find it best to save my influence for when I need to use it. That way, it's more effective."

The light changes, and I ease the car forward.

"You didn't answer my earlier question."

"I'm fine." She shrugs.

"I'd be lying if I said I'm sorry for what I did. I was fully conscious, and in complete control of all of my faculties when I fucked you with my gun."

"You wanted to teach me a lesson," she says in a low voice.

"I didn't mean to hurt you."

"You didn't. What if I told you what you did took me by surprise… but it was weirdly erotic?"

"I'd say you were lying."

She turns to me. "It pushed me out of my comfort zone."

"That's putting it lightly."

"It was like Keanu Reeves had suddenly decided to get married."

"Eh?" I glance at her, then back at the road. "You have a way of bringing Keanu Reeves into conversations when I least expect it."

"But it's always appropriate. Keanu has a gif for every mood." She nods.

"If you say so." I can't stop my lips from twitching. "Still doesn't answer my question."

She blows out a breath. "It was unexpected, what you did. And a little scary; I won't lie. My heart was in my mouth, but the danger inherent in these situations seems to turn me on even more."

I shoot her a quick glance, then focus on the road.

"I'm not sorry I did it. I won't make excuses for my actions, Elsa. That's the kind of man I am. I live by the gun, will probably die by the gun and—"

"It seems you fuck by the gun, too," she says in a wry tone.

"If you don't want to marry me, now's the time to back out." I come to a halt in front of the steps to City Hall, turn off the ignition, and turn to her. "I can't promise it won't happen again, but I can promise I'll never hurt you."

"Not physically, at least," she murmurs.

"I'm going to ensure you get full custody of your daughter, so I'll be taking care of you emotionally, as well," I point out.

She chuckles. "Tell me about it."

"You can still leave."

"And watch as that asshole wins the case in court and takes my daughter from me?" She squeezes her fingers together in front of her.

Something hot stabs at my chest. Why is it that seeing her get upset makes me want to protect her from whatever is causing her pain? In this case, me. Do I have to protect her from myself? I've never felt so protective about another person before this. But watching her with her daughter was an eye-opener. Once I saw that, I knew I could never let anything or anyone hurt either of them. And the only way to ensure that is to find a way to tether her to me. It's the only way I can safeguard her from her ex, and from this world we live in.

"I will never let that happen," I say in a low voice.

She stills, then searches my features. "Somehow, I believe you. It's why I'm here. Because you are the only one who's been able to promise me the one thing that's more important to me than life itself."

You are more important to me than life itself.

I push open the door, then walk around to open hers. She steps out and wobbles a little on the stilettos she's wearing, before she rights herself. I shut the car door and hold out my arm.

"Shall we?"

Ten minutes later, we're standing in front of the mayor in his office at City Hall.

Adrian and Massimo flank us. I had informed these *stronzi* about my plan to get married today for two reasons. First of all, we need two witnesses. Secondly, and more importantly, I needed Massimo's help in tracking down the mayor and calling in this favor, and I needed Adrian's help to ensure that City Hall opened for us. Sometimes, family can be useful, apparently.

The mayor himself is a short man with jowls and a stomach that strains his shirt, which he seems to have hurriedly donned, given that his buttons are all done up wrong. He rubs his fingers over his head, displacing the long strands of hair that he's combed over to hide the balding spot on the top.

"Uh, are we expecting anyone else?" He glances between us.

Before I can reply, I hear the sound of running footsteps before Theresa bursts in, followed by Axel.

"Oh, my god! We're on time, aren't we?" She runs up to Elsa and hugs her.

Axel rubs his chin. "I had a devil of a time asking her to slow down; woman rushes around like she's not pregnant."

She ignores him and peers into Elsa's face. "You are okay, though? He's not forcing you to do this against your will, right? If you don't want to go through with it, I can ask Axel to intervene."

Her voice is loud enough that I can hear everything. Clearly, she intended me to. I open my mouth to protest, when Elsa shakes her head. Her lips curve into a small smile which is, nevertheless, genuine. "It's fine, really. I want to go through with this. And I'm actually thankful that it's happening so suddenly; gives me less time to stress about it."

"Hmph." Theresa firms her lips. "Whatever the case, just so you know, you have the next few days off from the flower shop."

Elsa stares up at her. "Are you sure?"

"Of course I'm sure, " she scoffs. "You're getting married. You'll need a little time to get your head around everything. And hopefully, have a bit of a honeymoon. You sure you don't want to get hold of a dress, at least?" She steps back and takes in what Elsa is wearing. "You sure you want to get married in that?"

"Absolutely." Elsa pats her shoulder, then steps back. "Thanks for inviting Theresa. It means a lot to have her here," she whispers to me.

I want to deny it, but sadly, she's right. Clearly, I've become soft in my old age, or pussy-whipped before I've even gotten married. Despite the fact that it was last minute, I knew Elsa would appreciate having her friend with her as she gets married.

Elsa shuffles her feet, tugs on her—my jacket, which looks much better on her than it does on me. It also comes to mid-thigh, and the skirt she's wearing below it complements the jacket, so it seems like they're part of the same ensemble. With her flushed cheeks and blonde hair that falls softly about her face, she looks every inch an angel.

I blink. *Dio santo*, I'll be serenading her next. Why is it that every minute I spend in her presence seems to tie me more firmly to her? And nothing will be as permanent as the step I'm about to take. Marriage. I'll be married to her, for better or worse, in sickness and in health, through ups and downs, for the rest of my life. *Che cazzo*, that seems permanent. Maybe too permanent.

I guess I make a noise because Massimo nudges me. "You okay, *fratello*?"

I swallow. "Why wouldn't I be?"

"Seems like you suddenly realized what you're getting into."

I roll my shoulders, trying to ease the tension in my muscles. "Can you ask him to hurry up? *Stronzo* doesn't seem to know his head from his ass. And he's supposed to be the mayor?"

"Sure thing. Anything for you on your wedding day. And by the way, I made sure he's been briefed with your full names, et cetera, et cetera. All the information he needs to marry the two of you. You're welcome." Massimo smirks, then leans forward and claps a hand on the mayor's shoulder.

The man jumps. He has to tilt his head all the way back to meet Massimo's gaze.

"Chop, chop, we don't have all night," Massimo drawls.

Heavy footsteps announce the arrival of Luca. "Someone told me there's a wedding taking place here?"

I groan. That's all I need—my wedding turning into a circus, similar to how it was when first Michael, then Christian, and Axel, got married. How the hell did Luca find out about it, anyway? I shoot Adrian a scowl. He raises his hands as if to say he didn't have a choice. *Bastardo!*

Naturally, within moments, Michael prowls in, with Karma in tow. They're followed by Christian and Aurora.

"Didn't think you could sneak off and get married without my knowing, did you?" Michael smirks.

"Sorry, *fratello*. You get the entire family turning up to your wedding, just like those of us before you." Christian chuckles.

"Anyone else missing? Did you invite the strangers on the road, as well?" I scowl at Adrian.

"Now that you mention it..." Adrian's brow wrinkles.

I glare at him and he chuckles. "I had to inform *la famiglia,* else they never would've forgiven me."

Both Karma and Aurora walk toward Elsa. Karma's face is dominated by a huge smile. She hugs Elsa, then takes a step back. Aurora touches Elsa's shoulder. "If you need anything..." she murmurs.

"I'm good," Elsa reassures her. Her features are pale though.

My fingers tingle to wrap my arm around her and reassure her. Instead, I face the mayor, who's watching the proceedings with a dazed look on his face.

Massimo jerks his chin toward the man. "Get on with it, then."

The mayor mops his brow. He pockets his handkerchief and draws himself up to his full height. As is normal in Italy for a civil ceremony, he reads the three main civil laws and asks us both if we agree to uphold them. Once we agree, he turns to her.

"Do you, Elsa Tara Ducati, take Sebastiano Charles Domenico Sovrano as your husband?"

She stills and the color slides off of her face. She sways and I shoot out my arm to grip her shoulder. "You okay?"

She blinks rapidly. "Your... your second name is Charles?"

"Yes?" I scan her features. "Is everything okay?"

Elsa swallows. "It's also Keanu's middle name."

"Is it, now?"

She nods.

The mayor clears his throat.

She pulls away from me and I release her. She swallows, then tips up her chin at the mayor. "I do," she says softly.

"Do you Sebastiano—"

"I do," I cut him off.

He looks askance. "But I haven't asked the—"

Massimo makes a warning noise at the back of his throat. The mayor pales even more. He mops his forehead, then begins to rattle off words to the effect that he's marrying us as per the laws in this country.

When he's done glancing between us, he says, "Uh, I assume you don't have rings to exchange, in which case—"

"I do, actually." I don't take my gaze off of Elsa. "Hold out your hand."

"What?" She gapes.

I release her, only to reach over and take her left hand to slide the ring onto her ring finger. She glances down at the yellow sapphire embedded in the platinum band, which matches the engagement ring I placed there earlier.

When she looks up at me, her eyes are shining.

The band around my chest tightens. *Don't cry, please don't cry.* If you do, I won't be able to bear it.

"I, uh, now pronounce you man and wife." The mayor's voice seems to come from far away. I close the distance to her, tip her chin up, then bend and touch my lips to hers.

25

Elsa

His lips touch mine. I expect him to kiss me the way he has in the past—with passion, and dominance and the self-assurance I've come to associate with Seb. And it is all that... Yet, it's also different. I share his air as he holds his mouth to mine. His lips are firm, yet soft. He doesn't deepen the kiss. He doesn't touch me anywhere else, either. It's just his mouth, which covers mine. He stays there for a beat, then another. Some of his calmness bleeds into me, and the tension drains from my muscles. I sway toward him, and he breaks the kiss.

He turns to the mayor. "Where do we sign?"

"Eh?" The mayor stares, wide-eyed.

"The marriage certificate," Seb says through gritted teeth.

"Oh, of course." He walks around his desk, then slides a sheet of paper over to us.

Seb reaches over and pulls out a pen from the inside pocket of the jacket he'd draped on me. Then he leans over and signs his name. He hands the pen to me—a fountain pen—who uses fountain pens? Seb, that's who. There's so much I don't know about this man... My husband. Oh, my god, I'm married to him.

If I sign this paper, there will be no way out. The Sovranos don't believe in divorce, which means I'll be married to him for the rest of my life. My heart stutters. What kind of a relationship am I getting into? A transactional one, where each time I do something he doesn't like, he'll warn me I have to obey him or he won't help me get custody of my daughter? He'll help me get Avery back. I know that, but at what cost? Will I lose my sense of self? Will he become my Dominant and overpower me with his personality? Will he break me so thoroughly that I'll no longer be able to think for myself. Oh, I'm strong. I know that. But can I submit to him and also retain my sense of who I am? Will I retain enough independence that I'll be able to function well enough to take care of myself and my daughter? What if he turns out be like Fabio?

No, surely not. He's not like Fabio, at all… He's much stronger—physically, mentally, emotionally. He's got a strength about him that invites me to lean on him; to trust him and unburden my fears to him, and have him soothe me and take care of me, and oh, I'm so tempted to do that. And if I did gravitate toward that… If I did allow myself to become dependent on him… I'd never be able to get over him. He may not divorce me, but no doubt, he's going to be with other women, as he clearly told me. And once more, I'll be in a marriage, in name only. No, no, no. I can't let his charisma seduce me. I can't allow myself to feel anything for him. I need to simply use him… to get access to my daughter and to fulfill my base needs, without allowing my heart and soul to be involved in this relationship. I cannot risk getting hurt again. I owe it to myself and to my daughter. I need to find a way to get through this relationship with my sense of self intact, if it's the last thing I do.

"Princess?" His voice cuts through the thoughts in my head. I glance down to find I am holding his pen poised over the paper. I try to close the gap between the nib and the paper, but my limbs refuse to obey me. My hand trembles. A drop of ink slides out of the nib and blots on the paper. Goddamn it, why can't I do something this simple?

"Breathe," his voice commands. Instantly, oxygen rushes into my lungs. My throat burns. "That's it. Another breath now, slowly," he coaxes.

I follow his order, and my mind clears a little. He places his hand over mine and guides me until the pen touches paper. I scrawl out my signature with his palm still resting over me. When I am done, he slides his hand down, takes the pen from my fingers, then caps it and slides it into his shirt pocket. I straighten and turn to him.

"You did well." He leans in and touches his lips to mine.

A shiver runs down my spine and my nipples tighten. I sway toward him, and this time, he wraps his arm around me and pulls me into his chest. I breathe in his scent, savor the heat that spools off of his body and envelops me. He doesn't deepen the kiss, seeming content to share the air. Then he softens his kiss, until he finally leans back.

He peers into my face. "Okay?"

When I nod, a smile curves his lips. "Good girl." He brushes his lips over mine once more, then grips my hand in his before he turns to face those gathered. "My wife, everyone. Isn't she the most beautiful woman you've ever seen?"

Half an hour later, we are in an Italian restaurant not far from City Hall. I rode here with Seb, and neither of us spoke on the short ride over. Karma informed me the restaurant is owned by the Sovranos. Of course it is. They use it for business meetings and family functions.

Paolo, the chef, walked out to greet us with open arms. He kissed Michael on both cheeks, then took Karma's hands in his, before he turned to us. He congratulated Seb and kissed the knuckles of my fingers, then led us to a table in the center of the restaurant. The food had started arriving almost immediately—baskets of warm bread and olive oil, with bottles of prosecco that had been placed in ice-buckets at strategic intervals around the table.

At the head of the table, Michael grabs the closest prosecco bottle, as do Luca and Massimo. The three pop the bottles, then top up our glasses. After Luca and Massimo take their seats, Michael holds up his prosecco glass and says, "To Sebastian and Elsa, may your marriage be as happy and contented as mine is."

Christian, too, raises his glass, "Never let it be said that the Sovrano brothers take the conventional route to the altar. Going by our track record, it's clear that the more unorthodox the start to the relationship, the happier the final union."

He turns to Axel, who has his arm around Theresa. Axel glances around the table to find the eyes of the crowd are trained on him. "I assume it's my turn to say something, then?" He reaches for his glass and raises it in Seb's direction. "Sebastian, in the little time I've known you, I've come to realize that behind your rather ugly mug, you hide a heart that's mushier than overcooked pasta."

There's laughter around the table.

"You are loyal to a fault, would do anything for your family, and will go out of your way to protect those you care about. I hope you find the kind of contentment that very few of us are lucky enough to say we've found in this lifetime. As for you, Elsa..." He turns to me. "You can rely on Sebastian to be in your corner in your time of need. If there's anyone you need by your side, fighting your battles, it's him. I hope the two of you are very happy." He raises his glass.

"It's my turn now." Theresa leans forward in her seat. "I just want to say that I love Elsa like a sister, and if you hurt her in any way, I'll sic Axel on you."

Axel tilts his head. "You heard the lady. And as you guys already know, the wife is always right. So, I won't have much choice but to come after you and twist your balls if you act out of line."

Next to me, Seb winces. "Spare the family jewels, will ya?" He glances between Axel and Theresa. "I'll do everything possible to make her happy. You have my word. I won't do anything to hurt her."

Everyone claps and he leans in closer to me. "Not unless you ask me to, that is," he says in a voice low enough that only I can hear it.

"Did you just say what I think you did?" I flick him a sideways glance.

"What do you think?" he murmurs.

"I think you are all bark and no bite," I grumble under my breath.

"So, my demonstration back at the nightclub wasn't enough?"

A shudder runs down my spine. I wriggle around in my seat and my core throbs. The space where the vibrator once resided, yawns emptily. I squeeze my thighs together and his lips twist. He knows exactly what I'm feeling right now. That I can't stop thinking of how he sucked the vibrator from my pussy and spit it out; how he replaced it with his gun, how he brought me to the edge, only to pull back.

He whispers, "Tell me, Princess, are you looking forward to being my whore on our wedding night?"

26

Seb

Her breath hitches. Her pupils dilate as she tips up her chin and holds my gaze. Her cheeks flush, and I have no doubt that my words are turning her on. I hadn't meant to say that aloud, but goddamn, seeing her wearing my clothes, with my ring on her finger, with the scent of sex still clinging to her hair, all I want to do is take my wife home and fuck her… But not before I teach her how to become my perfect submissive.

"Two days," I drawl, "that's all I need."

"Two days?" Her forehead furrows. "What happens in two days?"

"You'll have had so many orgasms, you won't be able to think straight. By which time, I'll have broken you, of course."

"What?" Her gaze widens. "How do you mean?"

I allow my lips to twist. "Wouldn't you like to find out?"

Her lips part. Color flushes her cheeks. "You mean… you'll—"

"Make you submit, just like you asked me to."

"I'm not going to make it easy on you."

"I'd be disappointed if you did," I murmur.

Her breathing grows more rapid. Her chest rises and falls. A pulse beats at the base of her throat, and my fingers twitch. I want to press my thumb over that pulse and feel her body respond to my ministrations. I want to press my mouth to the curve of where her neck meets her shoulders and bite down on her skin as I bend her over and spank her, right before I thrust my fingers inside her and feel her flutter around my digits.

"What do you think, Seb?" I hear one of my brothers ask.

"Five minutes," I tell her in a hard voice, "you have five minutes to say your goodbyes."

"Why does that sound like a threat?" She glowers.

"Because after that, the only sounds you'll be making are groans and yelps and moans as I teach you how to behave properly with your Dom."

Her eyes gleam, then she flicks her hair over her shoulder. "Promises, promises."

I know she's doing it to sass me, to test my control, to push my restraint, to see how far I can go without snapping. But she's misjudged me if she thinks I'll let her get to me that easily. *I* am in control of this relationship.

I'm the one who dictates when and how she'll give in to me. I'm the one who intends to take my pleasure from her, after making sure that she's been properly trained. I'm the one who suggested she marry me. I promised Nonna I'd take a wife, and I have. There are no feelings involved here. I'm simply going to enjoy the fringe benefits of being tied down. A submissive of my own—a wife who'll be ready to open her legs to me at my command. And sure, I'll ensure she gets pleasure out of it, too. Pleasure, and full custody of her child. I'll make good on my promise to her. I'm nothing, if not a man of my word.

"Four minutes and thirty seconds," I growl.

"Seb, did you hear what I asked? You—"

"Fine." I turn to Michael. "I'll do it."

"Did you hear the question?" he asks, a knowing look in his eyes.

"You want me to take the lead in Trinity enterprises? I'll do it. I'd like Massimo, Luca, and Adrian to continue to attend, to back me up in the meetings."

Michael places the tips of his fingers together. "Considering the Russians tend to come in a pack, it's not a bad idea."

Next to me, Elsa shifts in her seat. Her cherry scent seems to surround me. The softness of her body beckons to me. I drum my fingers on the table, resist the urge to look at my watch.

"What's JJ's deal?" I force myself to ask. "He comes to these meetings alone; doesn't seem like a man who runs an organized crime gang."

"That's because, technically, he doesn't."

"Eh?" I force myself to give my full attention to what Michael is saying. "He's the head of the Kane Company, isn't he?" I ask.

"You are aware he also runs the biggest media company in Europe..."

"He does?" I sit up straighter. Motherfucker, JJ runs a media company. How was I not aware of it?

"It's called—"

"Kane Media Enterprises," I finish his statement. "How the hell did I not know that?"

"It's not that much of a secret, but it's also not something he talks about too much."

"So, he controls the media in this part of the world. No wonder he's interested in Trinity."

"What does that mean?" Massimo frowns.

"Technology and media overlap so much, they're practically the same side of a coin now," I explain.

"This must be of particular interest to you." Axel leans forward in his seat.

"Is it now?" Michael glances between us. "Care to enlighten us?"

My shoulders tense and I force my muscles to relax.

Axel seems taken aback. I know he's alluding to a conversation the two of us had a while ago; somehow, I hadn't thought he'd remember that particular piece of information. But then, he's an ex-cop, something I hadn't known then. Even if I had, I doubt it would've stopped me from sharing with him. The fact that he hasn't grown up with us, but is yet linked to me by blood, makes it particularly easy for me to trust him. And it's clear he doesn't forget details, either.

"It was a passing remark." I tilt my head. "I mentioned to Axel that my ultimate goal is power, and what better way to grow your influence than by owning a media company?"

"Is that what you want, to control media?" Michael narrows his gaze on me.

"It was a thought," I say slowly.

"Sounded more like an ambition when we spoke, ol' chap," Axel drawls.

I scowl. "I'm beginning to think you raised that particular point on purpose." I stab my finger at him.

"Anything to help you fulfill your dreams and all that." He smirks.

I glower at him. His grin widens.

"As this *stronzo* here has taken such pains to point out, media is something that attracts me. Especially the confluence of media and technology, which I believe is a game changer. Something that will permeate our everyday lives in a big way, given how much social media already plays a big role in influencing opinion."

Michael strokes his chin. "You really are excited about doing something with this, eh?"

"Considering JJ Kane is in the media space, and given Trinity Enterprises is to do with cryptocurrency, there's a sweet spot here I can take advantage of, yes," I reply.

Silence descends upon the table. I glance about the space to find all of them looking at me.

"What?" I scowl.

"The only other time I've seen you this excited is when you spoke about marrying Elsa," Massimo drawls.

I sense Elsa stiffen next to me. She's so close, and yet, not close enough. Giving in to the temptation, I reach for her hand and weave my fingers through hers.

"I do believe you have the perfect opportunity here to do something about your dream," Michael says slowly.

"Are you giving me your blessing?" I train my gaze on Michael.

Elsa tries to pull away, but I tighten my grip on her. The softness of her skin against mine, the brush of my jacket against the skin of her arm, the shuffle of her feet, the brush of her hair over her shoulder... All of it crowds in on me. My every sense is focused on her, even as I once more try to pay attention to the conversation at hand.

"Do you want my blessing?" Michael steeples his fingertips together on the table. Our gazes clash. The silence stretches for a beat, another. Neither of us backs down.

Michael may be my half-brother, but I've never considered him anything less than a brother. We were raised as brothers, and that's the way we all feel about one another. I never wanted the designation of Capo when he took over the position of Don. While I don't hate the Mafia lifestyle, I'm not as enamored by it as Luca is. And unlike Massimo, I've always been sure that, at some point, I'll strike out on my own. Oh, I've been part of the *Cosa Nostra* long enough to know that I'll never be able to leave it behind, but I'm sure I can carve out a life separate from it, while still remaining connected to my brothers in some form. I just never thought my opportunity would come this quickly.

"I want this," I finally say. "The situation holds many possibilities."

"It does." Michael flattens his palms on the table. "You are also my Capo, my second in command."

"And I'm grateful you chose me for that position, but you and I both know there's one person at this table who is better suited to that opportunity."

I turn toward Luca, when I catch a glimpse, a glimmer of something through the window. My heart drops into my stomach; my pulse rate explodes. I open my mouth to yell a warning, and the windows explode.

27

Elsa

One moment, I'm sitting next to Seb; the next, he's thrown himself on top of me. I'm thrown from the chair, and somehow, he manages to get under me and cushion my fall. Then, in a move worthy of Keanu Reeves in *The Matrix*, he flips me over so I hit the ground on my back with his body sprawled over mine.

The breath is knocked out of me, the heat of his body slams into me, and all around me, I hear the sounds of glass breaking, of pops that sound like firecrackers... No, not firecrackers. It's someone shooting at us. As the popping sounds escalate, I realize it's more than one person. Perhaps it's a group of people shooting at us? The sound intensifies until they are coming so close together, it feels like a particularly loud hailstorm, with the hailstones coming at us with such speed that the sound merges together into one continuous screech.

My heart slams into my chest and my pulse pounds at my temples. Above me, Seb grunts and his body shudders. Oh, my god. "Seb," I try to scream, but the sound is stuck in my throat.

The weight of his body seems to grow heavier. Then, just as suddenly as it started, the sounds fade away. Silence descends, broken only by the sound of something falling to the floor and shattering. I flinch; someone screams... One of the women? Is she hurt? More silence follows, then the sound of a car's engine breaks the silence. It seems to galvanize everyone, for I hear the sound of people jumping to their feet, followed by footsteps running out of the room.

"Everyone okay?" a man—Michael?—asks.

Seb jumps to his feet and holds out his hand. I grab it and touch something wet. I retract my hand and see blood on my fingers.

"Seb, you're hurt?" I rake my gaze up his arm, to where blood blots his sleeve. I spring up and my knees seem to give way. He grabs my shoulder with his uninjured arm and hauls me to him. For a second, I rest against his broad chest. Thud-thud-thud. I absorb the beat of his heart against his ribcage. Draw the scent of Seb into my lungs. Some of the tension fades. I'll always be safe with him.

He's promised to break me, and while I hate him for saying it with such confidence, I can't help but look forward to him trying. I can't wait for him to subdue me. Can't wait to stand up to him. But first, he's hurt. OMG, he's hurt. I pull back in his grasp. His grip loosens, and I take in the blood that stains his shirt. I yank at his sleeve and pull it up to reveal the blood oozing from a gash on his bicep. He winces.

"I'm fine," he protests.

"You're bleeding, Seb." I must be yelling, because almost immediately, Aurora appears next to me.

"Sit down," she orders.

He seems like he's about to protest, but Christian appears on the other side of Aurora.

"You heard the doc; sit your ass down, *stronzo*." He pulls a chair upright—the chair I was sitting on before Seb pushed me to the floor. He probably saved my life. Oh, my god, he saved my life. If he hadn't pushed me out of the way... My breath catches in my throat and I whimper.

Seb whips around to face me. "You okay, Princess?"

I don't reply as Christian pushes down on Seb's shoulder. He doesn't have a choice but to sink down into the chair.

I can't take my gaze off of the blood that saturates his shirt sleeve, OMG, he pushed me to the side, and the bullet hit him. It could have killed him. It could have maimed him, or scarred him. My mouth dries, I can feel my heartbeat in my throat. My pulse thuds at my temples, but this time, it's not because I fear for my own safety, but for his. If anything happened to him... I wouldn't be able to bear it. My head spins and I feel faint. In response, Seb pulls me into his lap.

"Wait, what are you doing?"

"Making sure you don't faint and hurt yourself."

He sounds so angry. I glance up into his face and those golden eyes of his bore into me. I flinch, try to pull away, but he winds his good arm around my waist and refuses to let go.

"Give me your jacket," Aurora holds out her hand and Christian pulls off his jacket and hands it to her. She presses it to Seb's wound, then grabs Christian's hand and places it over the jacket. "Hold this in place, please."

Christian complies.

Seb winces. "*Cazzo*, that hurts."

"Don't be a baby," Christian huffs.

Aurora elevates Seb's arm then asks, "Is there a first-aid box in the restaurant?"

"Here." Michael materializes next to us. He's holding Karma's arm as if he can't bear to let go. In his other hand, he has a first-aid box. He places it on the table.

Axel stalks over to join us; his arm is around Theresa. The fabric of his pants over one thigh is ripped and blood stains the fabric surrounding it. He glances at Seb, then at Christian, before turning to Michael.

"This cannot happen again, Don," Axel growls.

Something passes between the four of them. Seb, angry, is an awesome sight. But the four of them together, with the rage pouring off of them, is over-the-top —and that's an understatement. I'm not from this world, but even I know that shooting at the Sovranos when they are together and on their home ground, is nothing less than a call to a full-blown war.

"Somehow, I shouldn't be surprised that this medical kit has all of the supplies I need for stitching this wound," Aurora grumbles under her breath. "By the way, you're next, once I've seen to Seb." She jerks her chin in Axel's direction.

I glance around and take in the broken glasses, plates smashed on the floor, the ripped curtains... The lights seem to have escaped though, which might be the only reason more of us weren't hurt by flying glass. A trembling grips me. His arm around me tightens and he pulls me even closer.

Footsteps crunch on glass as Paolo walks over to us. He places a tray on the table on which are squat glasses filled with a clear liquid; I surmise it's grappa.

"Everyone okay in the kitchen?" Michael asks.

His jaw firms. "One of the chefs was wounded; some of us have scrapes from broken crockery. It's a damn miracle no one is dead."

"This is the second time this has happened." Michael balls his fingers into fists. "I'm going after the *Camorra*. This has their fingerprints all over it."

"I'm not sure that's wise," Seb retorts.

Michael fixes his gaze on my husband. There's such coldness in his eyes that I shiver and cuddle closer to Seb.

"You have something to say, Capo?" His voice is so placid that I wince.

Seb doesn't back down. "Nonna wanted us to build bridges with the *Camorra*."

"If Nonna were here, she'd understand that the only way to win this war is by crushing our opponents."

"Or forming an alliance with them."

"What do you mean?" Christian scowls.

"We were lucky this time. I saw the light reflect off the gun and acted quickly. Next time..." Seb shakes his head. "If anything happens to her..." His grasp on my hip tightens. Pain shudders up my side, but I don't protest. It's a reminder that I'm alive, and so is he. I cuddle closer, not caring that there are people around us. He tucks my head under his chin, and runs his fingers over my hair.

"We can't let this happen again," Seb says in a hard voice.

"Precisely why we need to finish off the *Camorra*," Christian snarls.

"Even if you kill every single person in that clan, someone, somewhere, is going to survive and be back to take vengeance. If not on us, then on our children." Seb glances pointedly at Karma, who places a hand over her belly.

"Be very careful what you say next. You're very close to crossing the line." Michael pushes Karma behind him, blocking her with his body.

"I almost lost my wife. Do you think I don't want to gun them down? Don't you think I want revenge for Nonna?" Seb growls.

"It sure doesn't seem that way from where I am," Christian snaps.

"Firstly, we don't know if it *is* the *Camorra* behind these attacks. It could be that *figlio di puttana*, Freddie," Seb murmurs.

He's referring to the man who was once their father's silent partner, so Theresa mentioned to me. The guy threatened Axel and Theresa in London; he shot at Axel, but Axel managed to scare him off.

"There's a very good chance it is Freddie," Axel admits.

Both Michael and Christian open their mouths to speak, but Seb holds up his hand. "Hear me out, will you? And trust me. I'm only proposing this because it offers a better long-term, permanent solution."

The silence stretches for a few moments. "Speak," Michael growls.

"What I'm going to suggest is a valid consideration, whether the *Camorra* are behind the attacks or not. I propose..." He glances between them. "I propose that one of us marries a *Camorra* princess."

"That's the funniest thing I've ever heard in a long time, you *minchione*." Christian chortles.

Michael, however, doesn't react. He stares at Seb.

Christian glances in Michael's direction, then does a double-take. "You can't be taking this seriously." He rubs his chin. "Even if the *Camorra* were behind the attacks—"

"Especially if the *Camorra* are behind the attacks. There is no better way to transform the bad blood than by arranging a match with one of their women." Seb holds Michael's gaze.

"So, it's true then. The Mafia still believe in arranged marriages?" Axel pulls Theresa closer to him.

"We uphold royal traditions, more than the royal families of today; and you shouldn't talk, you *farabutto*." Christian stabs a finger at Axel. "You agreed to marry Theresa to further your own goals."

"I was already in love with her when I did. I simply didn't know it then."

The men glare at him. Theresa digs her elbow into his side and he winces. "It's true, Sunshine, you know that."

"Oh, how the mighty have fallen." Christian laughs. "Seems Seb's suggestion isn't that far out."

"It certainly has merits," Michael concedes.

"And you were saying you don't want to be Capo?" Axel chuckles.

"I still don't." Seb blows out a breath.

"You still want to focus on the media-tech based idea, and broach it with JJ and Nikolai?" He's referring to Nikolai Solonik, the head of the Bratva and the third of the trifecta who own interests in Trinity.

Seb doesn't reply. Michael glowers at him for a few seconds more, then jerks his chin. "Fine."

"What?" Christian turns on Michael. "You're letting him step down?"

"Who do you propose take over as Capo?" Michael asks.

Luca bursts into the room. His shirt is torn and his nose is bleeding, but his features wear a victorious look.

"Got those *carogne*."

28

Seb

"I'm fine," I insist as I push the car door open and step out with Elsa in my arms. My arm hurts, but I ignore it. She fell asleep in the car on the way home, and no way was I going to wake her up for the short walk to our home.

After Aurora had stitched my wound and then dressed Axel's scratch—both of us had escaped with relatively minor lacerations—my idea of having Luca take over as Capo had been accepted by Michael. To my surprise, he hadn't protested. Maybe he had anticipated this was coming? Perhaps my discussion with Axel had reached him before Axel brought up the idea at the restaurant? Although, I doubt it.

Since his marriage to Theresa, and since giving up his role as an undercover cop with the London Metropolitan Police, Axel had moved to Palermo, started his own security business, and was focused on building it up. He wouldn't have had time to bring it up with Michael. Also, he's not a snitch. He wouldn't have done it behind my back.

Which means, Michael must have known about my aspirations. He must have sensed it. *Stronzo* has instincts which are sharper than a shark sensing its prey in open water. So, not only did he accept my suggestion, he also told Luca, on the spot, that I was stepping down and he was taking over.

Then, before Luca fully recovered, he turned to Massimo, who'd entered the room after Luca, and announced that he's marrying a *Camorra* princess.

Massimo responded by laughing and saying 'no fucking way' is he agreeing to that.

Michael and I exchanged glances, but we didn't push it. There will be enough time to get him to agree to this soon enough.

Adrian, who entered last, surveyed the silent crowd and asked what he had missed.

Elsa replied in a droll voice, "We are all stardust, baby."

Another one of her Keanu Reeves quotes, apparently. Not sure if any of the others got the context, but it seemed apt and broke the silence, and everyone laughed. She started laughing, only to burst into tears. I rocked her as she turned her head into my shoulder. I held her tightly, and to her credit, she managed to get control of herself very quickly. She apologized to everyone, and they all waved her off. We were all shaken up.

We all took it as a sign to break up the post-wedding party. It already seems like ages ago when we made the trip to City Hall and exchanged vows. Michael and the guys agreed that Adrian would drive me home, while the rest of them return to their respective places.

Adrian walks around the car toward me. He takes the keys from me, walks up the steps of my home, and nods at the guards by the door, who straighten to attention as we pass. He unlocks the door, and I precede him into the house. He slaps the keys down on the table by the doorway and turns to me. "You sure you guys are going to be okay? I can stay over in one of the guest rooms, if you want."

"I can take care of my own." I snort.

"I have no doubt, but since you are also hurt, *fratello*..." He gestures toward my blood stained shirt.

"I didn't take any painkillers; I'll be alert enough."

"Of course you will be." He blows out a breath. "Fine, then. I'll leave you guys. If you need anything, you call, yeah?" He scowls at me. "It's okay to ask for help, Seb. You don't always have to be the wise man amongst us who has his shit together, know what I mean?"

If only he knew. I jerk my chin, and with a final clap to my shoulder—my injured side (which I don't wince at, just so you know)—he turns and leaves. The door snicks shut. I slam the deadbolt in place, then I head for the stairs. The adrenaline drains and the pain in my arm ratchets up a notch. *Cazzo!* I walk up to my bedroom and place the sleeping Elsa on my bed. I take off her jacket and ripped shirt. Forcing myself to look away from her creamy breasts, I pull off her shoes and skirt, then cover her up. My muscles feel too heavy and my arms and legs begin to grow numb. I yawn hugely as I shuck off my shoes. My eyes begin to close and I fall onto the bed, on the covers, next to her.

Sleep embraces me almost at once. The glimmer of the light off the gun, the sound of glass breaking... The adrenaline fills my blood as I throw myself on top of her. I know I'm dreaming, but it feels so real. I twist my body to break her fall, then flip her over and throw my body over hers. My heart slams into my ribcage and the blood thuds at my pulse points. *Che cazzo*! If anything happens to her, I'll never forgive myself.

I told myself we'd leave in five minutes. But I allowed myself to be pulled into a discussion with my brothers. Why did I allow my work to take precedence? The lure of my dream was within reach. I knew it was a turning point. I never truly thought I'd be able to move away from the *Cosa Nostra* business and into something I've always wanted to pursue. And I allowed my thirst for power to take control. I thought it wouldn't matter if I stayed a few more minutes before leaving; before taking my wife home to consummate our marriage.

What kind of a man am I, who isn't able to protect his woman? I've faced bullets, and been in the middle of gun fights before... but never when my heart was at the center of it. Never when I had so much to lose. Never when the one thing more important to me than my own life had been under threat.

Wait. Hold on. Where is this coming from? I married her to fulfill my promise to Nonna... Right. Keep fooling yourself, you *testa di cazzo!* You've always known it's more than that. You just didn't want to admit it. And now, here you are, on the verge of falling in love with her. Love. Ha, you're in love with her.

Something slams into my arm. I grunt. White-hot pain slices through my body. Sweat pours down my temples. I glance down to find her features stained with blood. Her eyes are shut. Her body is still. No, no, no, it can't be.

"Seb!"

Someone touches me, and I grab him and throw him down.

"Seb, stop!"

"Elsa." My eyelids snap open. I stare down into blue eyes. Big blue eyes filled with pain, and something else, an emotion I can't place. A tear hovers at the tip of her eyelash. Her chest rises and falls. I look down to find I have my fingers wrapped around her throat. I release her and she gasps for air. The sunlight slants through the window and illuminates her features. The dark circles under her eyes lend her a fragile appearance.

"*Cazzo*, I'm sorry Princess, so sorry. Did I hurt you?"

She shakes her head.

I touch her throat, trace the mark of my fingers on the skin. She draws in a breath.

"Do that again."

"What?" I jerk my gaze to her face. "What did you say?"

"Do it again, Seb," she says in a low voice. "Does it surprise you to hear me say that?"

I search her features. "I'm not sure," I say honestly.

"I told you, I have a craving to be dominated. The harder you give it to me, the more I want it."

I shake my head. "You don't know what you're doing to me right now."

"Don't I?" She places her hand on my crotch.

A growl rumbles up my throat.

She traces the thick column in my pants, and wraps her fingers around the tented fabric. She squeezes and acute pleasure zings up my spine. The wound in my bicep throbs in tandem with the pulse that beats at my temples.

"Is this what you want, Princess?" My voice comes out harsh, "Is it? Tell me, Elsa, that you want me to dominate you."

"I do," she nods.

"Tell me that you want me to break you."

"I..." She swallows. "I want you to break me."

"Tell me that you want me to make you submit, to break you apart and piece you back together in a form that reflects our combined passions."

"I want you to break me apart and piece me back together in a form that reflects your deepest, dirtiest, filthiest fantasies."

"Fuck!" I push back from her, get off the bed and point to the floor in front of me. "Get on the floor, on your hands and knees."

29

Elsa

I hesitate. I pushed him to do this. I asked for this. I knew that once he took on the role of my Dom, he would take his responsibilities seriously. He wouldn't stop until he'd made me his in every way. And I... I'm not going to make it easy for him.

"The simple act of paying attention can take you a long way."

"What?" He blinks.

"It's a Keanu Reeves quote—"

His lips twitch, before he firms them. "Don't ever mention another man when you are with me, you understand?"

I scowl.

"Do you, Princess?" His voice lowers to a hush. A shiver runs down my spine. Oh, my god, when he uses that tone, I can't deny him... but I am going to try. I back away from him on the bed, toward the other side.

His forehead furrows. "What are you doing?"

"Um..." I reach the end of the bed, then throw my legs over the side and stand. My knees support me, at least, so there's that. He watches me as I take a step back, and another.

"Where do you think you're going?" His voice is soft, but underlying it is something dangerous. A shudder grips me. Ohmigod, ohmigod, am I actually going to do this?

"Did you hear what I told you earlier?"

I shake my head. His gaze widens. "You dare sass me?" A growl rumbles up his chest. The sound is so hot, so sexy, so dominant.

OMG, my pussy clenches. Moisture beads between my thighs. I begin to lean toward him, then stop myself. I want to be bad, so he'll discipline me and give me time-outs and talk to me in a stern voice and spank me. Yet, I also want to hold my own against him, just for a little while, so he realizes that he's not going to be able to just walk all over me. I know I'm going to submit to him eventually, but surely, I can make him work for it?

"Princess, come back here."

I shake my head.

"Do as you're told."

"Sometimes life imitates art. It's uh, another Keanu Reeves quote, just in case you were wondering."

His nostrils flare. "Now you've done it."

"Oh?" I pretend to blow on my nails and rub them on my upper arm. Because I don't have my shirt on. Guess he took it off last night before he put me to bed. Oh wow, he put me to bed. And not that he hasn't seen me without clothes on before, but how did I not wake up when he did that? How did I sleep through the act of him stripping me?

"Go." He jerks his chin toward the door.

I blink. "Excuse me?"

"Run, Princess. I'll give you a head start."

"Eh? What do you mean?"

"You're wasting precious time. You broke the very first order I gave you. When I catch you, I'm going to spank you so hard, you won't be able to sit down without feeling my palm print on your ass."

Heat flames in my lower belly and spreads to my extremities.

He takes a step forward. I gasp. My nipples tighten and my breasts hurt. Adrenaline laces my blood. I have this sensation of being hunted by a predator, and it's both scary and thrilling, and it shouldn't turn me on. But oh, god, it does. He's going to catch me, I have no doubt, but I can, at least, try to evade him for as long as possible, right?

He bares his teeth. I shiver. He stalks around the bed. I turn and take off out the door, down the corridor, then down the stairs. I take the steps two at a time, then reach the landing. I hear his footsteps behind me, and my pulse rate ratchets up. I pivot, careen past the living room, and into the kitchen. I round the island and head toward the pantry at the far end. I twist the handle open and step inside. I shut the door behind me and slide back until I'm flush with the wall. The scent of cinnamon and spices fills my senses. It reminds me of his scent... and strangely, that comforts me. My heartbeat slows down. I wrap my arms around myself, and stare at the crack of light in the space between the doors.

I hear the heavy tread of his footsteps approach. The rhythm of his gait tells me he's in no hurry. The footsteps stop, then start again. They come closer, closer. I stiffen, and hold my breath. The crack of light cuts out as he passes in front of the pantry door. I hear him round the island again and head toward the exit. Then I don't hear him anymore.

Wait, what? Is he leaving without opening the pantry door? Did he miss me? It's not possible, is it? Could I have beaten him at his own game? The tension leaks out of my muscles, and I sag against the wall. In the silence, time stands still. When it feels like I've waited long enough, I slowly push the pantry door open. I peek outside, and as far as I can tell, there's no one in the kitchen. I wait for a few seconds more, then slip out.

"There you are."

I hear his voice a second before his heavy hand descends upon my shoulder. I scream, twist my body, and slip from his grasp. I jump forward, but he's too fast. He grabs me around the waist and hauls me to him.

A giggle breaks free, even as heat flushes my chest. Fear twists my belly, and a sliver of anticipation zings under my skin. "Let me go," I pant.

"No." He swings me around so I face his chest. He took the time to change into a fresh T-shirt and sweatpants before coming to look for me? Guess he wasn't kidding when he said he'd give me a head start.

"I'm going to teach you a lesson," he growls.

"You keep saying that." I tip up my chin. "I'm beginning to wonder if you mean—" I yelp as he lifts me up and throws me over his shoulder. My hair falls down over my face, and my nose bumps into his back. I draw in a lungful of Seb and my head spins. I grab at that trim butt of his—to steady myself, of course—and whoa, now I know what they mean by buns of steel. Seriously, this man has not an inch of fat anywhere on him. I dig my fingers into said buns of steel, and that's when his palm connects with my backside. A zing of fire sears up my spine. I scream, "What the hell, you asshole!"

"Language." His voice rumbles up his chest, and via our connection, up my lower belly. My thighs clench, then I gasp as he slaps me on the left cheek, then on the right, and the left, and the right.

"Let me go, let me go!" I squirm in his hold, then cry out when he brings his palm down on the space where my arse meets my upper thighs. Who'd have thought that was such an erogenous zone in my body? But it clearly is, for when he slaps me there again, my pussy clenches. My toes curl. "Oh, god," I groan, "oh, my god!"

He stops spanking me long enough to close the distance to the island.

He grabs my waist and lowers me to the countertop. I barely have time to wince at the contact of my inflamed flesh with the smooth, cold surface when he shoves his bulk between my thighs.

"Will you ever mention another man's name when you are in my bed?"

I purse my lips.

"Will you, Princess?"

I jut out my chin and raise my gaze to his in time to see his lips twitch.

"This is not a joke, you jerk-face."

"No, it isn't. And I shouldn't be jealous of an actor—a man you've never met, and probably never will—but I can't bear to hear you speak of another man."

"Wait, what? You're jealous of Keanu?"

Color flushes his cheeks, then he plants his big palms on either side of me. "You seem to have a crush on him."

"Only because he says the most profound things."

"Right. He's an actor, a creation of the media, an image honed to life from his movies; you know that, right?"

"You *are* jealous of him." My lips curve into a smile. "Aww, so cute. You know, I only quote him because I find what he says quirky."

"Like I care," Seb grumbles. He pushes his face into mine so our eyelashes entangle. "Why can't I stay angry with you for long, even though you refuse to obey my commands?"

"Because you have a thing for me?"

"I have a *thang* for you, all right." He closes the distance between us so the bulge in his sweatpants stabs into my weeping core... Yes, exactly there. Oh, god. A whine bleeds from my lips. His nostrils flare. "Your fictional crush can't do that to you, can he?"

"Seb," I plead, "please, Seb."

"What do you want, Princess? Tell me."

"You." I bite the inside of my cheek. "I want your cock inside me, your fingers in my mouth, in my arse, wherever you want to take me."

"Is that right?" He smirks.

"Anything you want, Seb. Anything."

He holds my gaze for a second longer, then releases me. He leans back. "No," he says in a cold tone.

"Wha... what do you mean, no?"

He pushes away from me, then grasps my waist and lowers me to the floor. "On your knees, Princess."

I sway closer to him and he puts more distance between us. "Get on your knees." He lowers his voice to a hush, and the hair on the nape of my neck rises.

Only when my knees hit the floor do I realize I've obeyed him. I push aside the pain from the impact and peer up at him.

"On all fours," he orders.

I lower my palms to the floor. The ring on my left hand thunks when my fingers connect with the wood. OMG, I'm married to him. I. Am. Married. To this guy who is bent on breaking me down. *I* asked him to make me submit to him, so why do I feel so confused about it? Is it because I'm not used to showing this wanton part of myself to anyone except strangers? Only, he's not a stranger anymore. He's my husband.

"Now, stay there." He walks over to the refrigerator, pulls out eggs, milk, cheese, then places them on the kitchen counter before reaching for a skillet.

"What are you doing?" I snap.

"Making breakfast."

"And you want me to stay here?"

"Right. As you are, baby." He busies himself at the counter. I hear the sound of the whisk clinking against the bowl. Guess he must be beating up the eggs. Then the light *whoomp* as he lights the flame under the skillet. Within minutes, he has a *bialetti* on the flame for espresso, bread in the toaster, and I hear the sound of the egg mixture hitting the skillet. A few more minutes and he pours himself a cup of espresso, plates the omelet, and the toast, brings everything to the island, and draws up the stool nearest to me. He sips the espresso, then balances the cup and saucer on my back.

He's using me as a table. He expects me to stay still and allow him to use me as needed. An inanimate object, in this case. It's demeaning and a classic lesson in subjugation and I, surely, can't find it arousing. Can I? He reaches for the cup of espresso, takes another sip, then places it back on the saucer on my back. The sound of cutlery hitting the plate reaches me, and the scent of the food almost drives me out of my mind. My stomach rumbles and the backs of my thighs and butt feel like they're on fire. The weight of the cup and saucer on my back is a reminder that he expects me to obey him. Anger twists my guts, even as heat flushes my skin. He reaches down and holds out a piece of omelet on a fork to my mouth.

The scent is delicious, but I turn my head away. "How long are you going to make me stay like this?" I snarl.

"Until you've learned your lesson. Eat now," he orders.

I stare at the food, then open my mouth. He pops the piece of omelet between my lips. I chew on it, swallow, then eat the next mouthful of food he feeds me. He continues to feed me until my hunger is assuaged. He takes the cup of espresso and holds it to my lips. Since I can't tilt my head back, I slurp from the surface. The strong taste of the brew revives me. He lets me have another sip, then brings it to his mouth.

I start to straighten, but he places his big palm on the small of my back. He applies enough pressure that I have no choice but to stay down. He removes the saucer from my back, and I hear it clink on the counter. Then, he slides off of the stool and stands in front of me. Wide feet, tidy nails, the edges of his sweatpants that brush his ankles. My belly quivers, my core contracts, a-n-d it's official... I have a foot fetish, and a butt fetish, and a cock fetish—when it comes to this man.

"How are you feeling?" he drawls.

"Like I want to sink my teeth in your skin and bite you," I snap back.

"So damn spirited." There's a note of wonder in his voice. He crouches down then grips the hair at the back of my head and tugs. I have no choice but to tip up my chin.

"You're fucking beautiful, you know that?"

"Let me up and I'll show you just how beautiful I can be," I spit out.

He laughs, then releases me and straightens, only to walk around to stand behind me.

"What are you doing?" I glance over my shoulder to find he's studying my backside. He bends his knees and crouches behind me, then massages the curve of my arse. Pinpricks of awareness dot my skin. "Seb please," I groan as he runs his fingers over my skin and between my legs. He plays with my pussy lips, and a whine bleeds from my lips.

"So fucking wet." He brings his fingers to his mouth and sucks on them. "So sweet."

"Oh, god." I lower my head and squeeze my eyes shut. Pleasure convulses up my spine. My toes curl. So annoying that I find everything he does to me such a turn on.

He runs his fingers down the seam of my pussy, and my entire body jolts. He slides a finger inside my sopping wet channel, then adds another. A moan wells up my throat, and I bite the inside of my cheek. I will not plead with him. Will not. If I do, he's bound to say something stupid like I haven't learned my lesson yet, or something similar. I flex my fingers into the floorboards and push out my butt, trying to chase that sensation of having his fingers inside me.

He chuckles, then begins to weave his fingers in and out of me. Each time he thrusts his digits inside, a shudder grips me. My clit feels swollen, and I try to squeeze my thighs together.

He clicks his tongue. "Don't move, Princess."

He increases the intensity of his movements, adds a third finger, and a fourth. I am so full, so stretched, yet I know having his cock inside me would be so much more satisfying. He curves his fingers inside me and a trembling grips me. My skin feels too tight for my body. My scalp tingles, and heat zings out from my core. I arch my back, knowing I'm close. So close. I angle my butt, trying to hold his fingers inside of me, trying to plug that emptiness that yawns at my center. The climax threatens, and I squeeze my eyes shut, waiting... waiting... He pulls his fingers out.

"What the—! Why did you—?" I snap my eyelids open.

"Consider it a reward for doing as I told you." He pats my bottom, knowing full-well how sensitive my skin is, then walks around to stand in front of me.

He holds out his hand. "Up, Princess."

I grab his hand and lift to my knees, then glance up at him, take in the T-shirt that molds those cut abs, the flat stomach that tapers down to the waistband of his sweatpants. The tent at his crotch, now at eye-level. My mouth waters as I mentally prepare for what I'm sure he's going to demand next.

Instead, he hauls me to my feet, then scoops me up in his arms, bride style. Which is appropriate, considering we were married yesterday. So, he's as affected as me, but it doesn't seem to bother him that he's denying himself. I touch the bandage on his arm. "Does it hurt?"

"A little, but it's fading already."

"So now what?" I lean my head back against his shoulder.

"Now, I'm going to take care of you."

30

Seb

I carry her up the stairs, back to my room, then inside the bathroom. I place her on her feet and study her closely. A rosy hue tints her chest and her face. I can't take my gaze off of her creamy breasts, the perky nipples that jut out... My fingers tingle, and I can't stop myself from cupping her breast. Her breath catches. I lower my mouth to suck on a nipple. I bite down on it, and she gasps. I lick her nipple, and a moan spills from her lips.

"Seb, oh, Seb," she whines, and all the blood empties to my groin.

I turn my head to suckle on her other nipple. I pull on it, tug it inside my mouth, and swirl my tongue around the swollen peak. She buries her fingers in my hair, yanks at the strands, and a shudder runs down my spine. My cock strains against my briefs, begging to be let out. *Che cazzo*, what the hell is wrong with me? I need to take care of her first. I release her nipple with a pop and straighten.

"Why did you stop?" she whines.

"Because I promised to take care of you, didn't I?" I walk over to the sink, and pull out the drawer beside the sink. Pulling out a tube of salve, I turn to her. "Bend over." I jerk my chin toward the counter.

She shoots me a glance.

"I'm only going to make sure I soothe the hurt I inflicted on you."

"Hmph." She presses her lips together. I'm sure she's going to refuse me, but she turns and props her elbows on the counter. Thank fuck. She's naked as the day she was born, the thrust of her gorgeous butt a creamy highway leading down to the promised land. I trace my finger down the valley between her buttcheeks and she shivers. Goosebumps spring up on her skin. This woman is so damn responsive.

My wife. My submissive. She's mine to do with as I want. A hot sensation stabs at my chest. Possessiveness? Selfishness. If only I could hide her away from the world and keep her all to myself. If only I could protect her from the evils lurking out there. The enemies I have made over the years who'll waste no time in coming after her once they find out what she means to me. I need to keep her safe.

What happened last night—actually, this morning? I can never allow it to touch her again. Even if it means I need to guard her day and night. I bend and kiss the curve of her hips. She shudders. Straightening, I squeeze some of the salve onto my fingers and apply it over the reddened skin of her behind.

She sighs, then lowers her head so her hair flows about her shoulders.

"How does it feel?" I murmur.

"Good," she says in a breathy voice.

"You sound surprised," I reply.

"Didn't think you'd have a gentle touch."

"You don't know much about me, do you?"

She turns to survey me over her shoulder. "Less than you know about me, for sure."

I cap the salve, and set it aside. "Why don't you freshen up and get dressed?"

"Oh?" She straightens. "Are we going out somewhere?"

"It's not safe to leave the house. At least, not until we catch whoever shot at us."

"Aww..." Her lips turn down. "It would be nice to get out of the house. You have so many bodyguards. Surely they'd be able to protect us?"

"All of the guards in the world couldn't stop them from getting to us yesterday," I remind her.

"So, you're going to change your way of life? You're going to show them they managed to throw a scare into you?"

"That's not true, and you know it." I scowl.

"Then show it." She draws herself up to her full five-foot, four-inch height, which means she's at eye level with my heart.

She already has my heart. *Cazzo*, when did I fall for her? The feelings crept up on me and I didn't notice. I take a step back.

"I know what you're doing. You're my sub. You're trying to be bratty, poking at me, trying to undermine me, trying to test me and my masculinity."

"Oh?" She flutters her eyelashes. "You're the big, bad Mafia guy. I am but your obedient little wife."

"Right." I snort. "I understand why you do it, though."

"Do you, now?"

I nod. "It turns you on to challenge my authority. You ache to get a reaction out of me, and it's communicating your desire to play. You get off on testing my limits. You adore it when I rise to the occasion and punish you. You can't wait for me to claim mastery over you. The dynamic makes you aware of your sexuality. It reaffirms that you're attractive, the center of my attention. You love the interest and the cerebral connection that comes with the mind play. The feelings it conjures up keep you aroused all day. The words, the orders, the reprimands, the harsh commands, the audacity with which I tell you to turn your body over to me so I can treat you like an object, a thing that is made to pleasure me, a slave whose only goal in life is to service me... No one else can speak to you like this. You'd never allow anyone else to have such access to your mind, your body, your heart—"

"Stop," she whispers, "stop Seb."

"If I touch you now, I'll find you even wetter than before, won't I?"

"Yes." Her chin trembles.

"Yes, Master," I correct her.

"Yes... Master." She bows her head, and in that moment, I fall for her even more. This gorgeous, strong woman who has been through so much, who'd do anything for the well-being of her daughter, who put her trust in me when she asked me to be her Dom, who agreed to marry me because she was confident that I could help her... She lowers her gaze to the floor in front of me.

Does she have any idea just how much she has ensnared me? And it's not only about her looks or her sexy little body... It's her spirit, her ability to roll with the punches and come out on top. It's her little quirks, especially her proclivity to quote from that infernal actor whose name I shall not mention. All of it makes her even more attractive.

And how can I refuse what she wants?

"Okay." I jerk my chin.

"Eh?" She peers up at me from under her eyelashes. "What do you mean, okay?"

"You want to go out, we'll go out."

"But didn't you say it's too dangerous?"

"It is," I raise a shoulder, "but you're right. Now is the time to show we're not afraid. Whoever shot at us wanted to scare us. If we stay inside, we're allowing them to control us. It's time we take a stand instead."

"Wow, so you're actually agreeing I was right?"

"When you are, I have no problem accepting it."

"Didn't think your ego would allow that." She laughs.

"I'm a Sovrano. Of course I have an ego, but that doesn't mean I won't back down when I'm wrong."

"Macho, dominant, *and* reasonable?" She shakes her head. "You're almost too good to be true."

"I'm all of those, and also, if we stay here talking, I'm going to bend you over again. And this time, I'm going to bury myself inside you. And then, I won't be able to stop myself until I've had you over and over again."

"That sounds like a great idea." Her eyes light up.

"No, you wanted to go out, and we're going out."

Her breathing grows erratic, and a shiver runs down her body. "Why is it, everything you say turns me on?"

I raise my gaze to the ceiling. "*Now,* she admits it." Turning her around, I point her in the direction of her bedroom. "Go on, get dressed. I'll meet you downstairs when you're ready."

Half an hour later, I open the door of my Maserati, and usher her inside. I walk around and slide into the driver's seat. "It's still too cold to drive with the top down, but come summer, I promise you're in for a treat."

"Oh, this is already a treat." She glances around the interior of the car with wide eyes. She runs her hand down the leather of the seat, across the console, and *cazzo*, I swear I can feel her touch on my skin. My cock thickens, and heat flushes my chest. I turn on the ignition, then back the car out of the garage and onto the driveway.

I drive out onto the road, and wave to Antonio, Michael's bodyguard who's been assigned to protect us. Michael, of course, has an entire team in place to protect him and Karma. He slides into his car, and is accompanied by another of our men. Behind him, another car starts up, with two more of our men.

"So, they're going to follow us wherever we go?" She turns to me. "Where are we going, anyway?"

"To a place where they have the best pasta, the best gelato, and the best espresso on the Amalfi coast."

"You Italians measure everything in terms of food, don't you?"

"What else is there to life, besides the three F's—food, fucking, and family?"

"Of course," she says dryly.

"You don't agree?"

"It's hard to disagree with it," she admits as I guide the car down the road, and through the streets of Palermo. Another ten minutes and I swing onto the road taking us back toward the coast. I step on the accelerator, then turn to find her watching me. "What?" I smirk. "Admiring the view?"

"I'm not going to say yes, and add to your already inflated opinion of yourself."

"Just admit it; you find me irresistible. You can't resist my charms. It's why you married me, after all."

She snorts. "Don't get ahead of yourself." She fiddles with the dials on the console, and strains of Puccini fill the space.

"Whoa." She straightens. "Opera? I'd never have guessed, but then, even on a day off, you are dressed in a suit, so I suppose it fits the entire Mafioso persona."

I glance down at myself, then raise a shoulder. "This is how I always dress."

"But today's a day off. You could've worn jeans and a T-shirt."

"I do own jeans and a T-shirt." I scowl at her.

"When was the last time you wore them?"

"Huh." I navigate a turn, then stare at the road, considering her observation. "I did dress casually," I point out.

"You're wearing a suit, Seb. That's not casual."

"I didn't wear a tie."

She snorts. "Are you serious?" She peers at my features. "You *are* serious. OMG." She waves a hand toward her knee length skirt and blouse, which she has paired with a sweater. "Now, what I'm wearing is casual."

"Not to mention sexy."

She reddens a little. "Thanks, I guess," she murmurs.

"You could wear a sack and I'd still find it sexy," I admit.

"And I find your suit beyond sexy." She twists her fingers together in front of herself. "Look at us—a mutual admiration society."

"Nothing wrong with being attracted to your spouse," I say in a mild voice. And since when have I become the voice of reason? Somehow, she seems to bring out the worst, and the best, parts of me. When I'm with her, I can't predict anymore how I'm going to behave... And it's both exhilarating, and a little bit annoying. But in a good way.

I suspect, many years down the road, I could be driving with her and she still won't bore me. Is this what they mean by falling in love? Love. Love? Stop that! I shake my head. She's not really your wife. She's someone you married to fulfill your promise to Nonna. But somehow, that doesn't seem to be the truth anymore. The more time I spend with her, the more I'm digging myself into this hole from which there is no escape. I'm completely falling for her, and I haven't even fulfilled my promise to her of making her submit to me first.

"Riding a motorcycle is like being a puppy," she exclaims.

I turn to her. "Excuse me?" I blink. "No, wait. Let me guess—another of your quotes from The-Actor-Who-Shall-Not-Be-Named."

"Good guess. Thought I needed to say something to break the silence." Her lips kick up. "You have to admit, it's rather effective."

"I hate to admit it, but it even fit the occasion." I shake my head. "I can't believe I said that."

"Yay," she cheers, then fist-pumps. "You're getting into the mood. I promise you that The-Actor-Who-Shall-Not-Be-Named has a quote to fit every occasion."

"Hmph." I press my lips together. "I hope that doesn't mean you're going to pepper all of your conversations liberally with his quotes."

"Where would the fun be in that?" She swipes her hair over her shoulder. "It's effective because I choose the occasion of usage. If I dropped quotes too often, they would lose their potency."

"What's losing its potency is the idea of this trip. We should have stayed back at the house where I could have fucked you like a proper Italian husband on the first morning of our married life together."

"Why didn't you?"

"I made you a promise, and I intend to keep it."

"A promise?" Her forehead scrunches. "You mean—"

"I promised that I'd make you submit to me completely, and I intend to do that first."

"So, you'd deprive yourself and me because I asked you to be my Dom?"

"I take my role very seriously, I'll have you know." I turn off the main road and onto an unpaved drive.

"Yes, but you can be both. You can be my Dom and my husband."

"First your Dom, then your husband."

"I can't understand what the difference is."

"You'll see." I bring the car to a halt at the point where the road gives way to a grassy slope. At the very edge is a small structure perched on a ledge, and beyond that, a view of the ocean.

"Wow..." she whispers. "What is this place?"

31

Elsa

"*This* is my favorite place in the entire world," he replies as he leads me toward the gorgeous white-washed structure.

Turns out, it's a Michelin-star restaurant. It has only three tables, and all three were reserved by Seb.

"When did you arrange all this?" I glance away from the breathtaking view and turn my gaze to another breathtaking view—that of his square jaw, his hooked nose, those strong eyebrows, and below that, those golden-brown eyes, which sparkle at me. The sun pours in through the window, picking out flecks of gold in his hair, as well. He seems to absorb the heat and radiate it out, his skin almost sparkling in this light. He seems so much larger-than-life, so perfect. I can't bear to take my gaze off of him.

"While you were in the shower," he says without glancing up from the menu. "And you're doing it again."

"Doing what?"

"Staring at me."

"How do you know? You're not even looking at me."

"Don't need to look at you to know what you're doing, or what you're thinking, for that matter."

"Oh?" I lean back in my chair. "What am I thinking of now?"

"That you want to pour chocolate over my face and lick me up."

"What the—" I gape. "How did you?"

He glances up from his perusal of the menu and smirks at me. Whoa, that's so hot. Why does this bad boy persona of his turn me on so much? I cross my legs, and no, it has nothing to do with the slow throbbing that's flared to life in my core.

His nostrils flare, and he looks so pleased with himself. Damn him, but he knows exactly what he's doing to me.

"The other two tables are empty. You could have invited the bodyguards to eat with us," I point out.

"Then who will protect us?"

"So, you'll make them starve while we eat?"

He looks askance. "Is that a problem?"

"Of course it's a problem."

"If something were to happen to you... Now *that* would be a problem."

I fold my hands in my lap. "I know you want them to do their job and protect us, but it feels weird to be eating when they are starving out there in the cold."

He stares at me. "You're too soft."

"Well, yeah." I scoff. "I'm a mother, after all. Besides," I bite the inside of my cheek, "sometimes we get so caught up in our daily lives, we forget to take the time out to enjoy the beauty in life."

"Don't tell me, that's another quote by The-Actor-Who-Shall-Not-Be-Named?"

"Yep," I laugh. "You're getting into the spirit of things."

"The only way I agreed to bring you out today is if our security stood on guard the entire time."

"If they are inside the restaurant, surely, they could do a better job of protecting us?"

He looks like he is about to protest, then shakes his head. "No winning this battle with you, is there?"

"Nope."

"I suppose you are not going to eat unless I invite them in?"

My lips twitch. "Nope."

"In which case, I'd better take care of my appetizer before I ask them in."

Something in the way he says it, I know he doesn't mean food.

"Wh-what?" I clear my throat. "What do you want for your appetizer?"

"You know what, Princess." He leans back in his seat. "Get your ass up on the table." He pushes away the place-setting and pats the space in front of him.

"Wait, what?" I glance around the space.

"No one's watching us."

"Someone might walk in on us."

"No one will come in, not unless I ask them to," he says with confidence. "Do it, Princess." He lowers his voice to a hush and my nerve-endings crackle. Damn, but when he uses his Dom voice, there's not much I can refuse him, is there? I slip off the chair, round the table and walk toward him. I come to a halt in front of him, and he holds out his palm.

"What?"

"Give me your panties."

"No!" My mouth drops open. "I'm not giving up my panties."

He glares at me, my belly flip-flops, and my knees tremble. I reach under my skirt and push my panties down. Stepping out of them, I hand them over to him. He pockets them, glances at the table, then back at me.

I firm my lips. I want to deny him, want to tell him no, but I can't stop myself from leaning in his direction. He places his hands on my waist, and before I can protest, he's heaved me up and onto the table in front of him. I part my legs, and he pulls me forward so my butt is perched at the edge of the table. He leans forward, flips up the hem of my skirt, then pushes his face into my pussy and inhales deeply.

"Oh, my god." A shiver runs down my spine. My head spins. His action is so primal, so filthy, and yet, so apt.

"H-how do I smell?" I gulp.

"Like you are mine." He bites down on my clit and I cry out.

He places his palm flat on my sternum and applies pressure. I lean back until my spine hits the table.

The heat of his breath sinks into my core and my channel spasms.

"Oh, god, Seb. Oh, my god." I grab at his hair, but he knocks my arm to the side.

"Hold onto the table," he commands.

"Wait, what?"

"Do it," he rumbles against my heated center, and the vibrations pool in my lower belly. My brain cells seem to melt, even as my blood seems to catch fire. I lower my hands to the side, and grip the edge of the table. That's when he slides his big palms under my arse cheeks and squeezes. Fire seems to zing out from where he's touching my already abraded skin.

I can't stop the moan that bubbles up my throat.

He blows lightly on my core and the contrast between that and the colder air of the room almost sends me out of my head.

I tilt my pelvis up, chasing the inevitable intrusion of his tongue... I want it, I need it. Now. *Right now.*

He chuckles lightly, and I want to be mad at him for enjoying my discomfort, but then he grips my arse cheeks, pulls me even closer, bends his head, and licks his way up my seam.

"Jesus," I cry out as he curls his tongue around my swollen nub, then once more, laves me from my back hole to clit.

My back curves, my body jolts, and a whine spills from me. He repeats the action again and again. He circles my clit once more, then stabs his tongue inside my pussy. I squeeze my eyes shut, then groan as he shoves his tongue in and out of me, in and out. I bring my legs up or try to, for he releases my butt cheeks, only to squeeze my inner thighs and hold them apart, as he continues to eat me out. He throws my legs over his shoulders, then slides his palms up under my blouse. He cups my tits and squeezes them as he curls his tongue inside my channel. The combination almost sends me over the edge. Tremors screech up from my feet, up my thighs, then curl in my belly. And once again, he pulls back.

My climax hovers on a knife's edge, then retreats.

I snap open my eyelids.

He releases me and sits back, as I lay there panting. I manage to train my gaze on him, to find he's watching me closely. He wipes the back of his palm across his glistening mouth, then leans over and pulls my skirt down.

"You stopped again," I say through gritted teeth. "I was so close. So close."

"Good." He curls his fingers around my wrists and tugs, so I sit up.

"It's not good," I snarl. "It's bloody frustrating, is what it is."

"You'll learn to deal with it."

"The only thing I want to learn is how to get inside that head of yours. If this is your so-called training, then it's bullshit. You hear me? This is all an excuse not to fuck me. I'm beginning to wonder if you even like girls, you—"

I squeak as he rises to his feet. He plants his hands on either side of me on the table, then thrusts his face into mine. "One more word out of you, and I'll turn you over, and take your ass right now."

I tip up my chin so my mouth is poised right below his. "I dare you to."

What am I doing? Why am I challenging him, knowing it might goad him into doing something I may not like? Or like too much, maybe. He brings out the brat in me. He makes me want to chip away at his control, until he snaps and shows me that dominating side of him. Oh, Seb is always restrained, but it's that sadistic part of him, the one that's so close to the surface that I can all but taste every time I lick him, it's that part I want to reveal. So, I scoff in his face. "Thought so." I place my hand over the bulge in his crotch and squeeze.

His nostrils flare, and the skin around his eyes tightens. The tips of his ears turn white. No, I swear they do. I know, because I'm watching him very closely. I note every change in his expression with great interest, and no small amount of trepidation, to be honest. What would happen if I did push him over the precipice? What would happen if he finally let go of that control which has him bringing me to an almost-climax every time, only to pull back, despite the fact that he is also turned on, and painfully so?

He places his hand over mine, and kneads hard. I gasp as the column in his pants seems to lengthen further. He massages himself with his hand on mine, sliding our joined-up grips up and down the bulge. I don't take my gaze off of his, and marvel as the golden sparks in his eyes seem to catch fire. It's so hot, so erotic. Heat flushes my skin and a bead of sweat trickles down my spine. He seems to grow impossibly bigger, the hard length of him stabbing into my palm.

The emptiness in my core grows and writhes, wanting more, so much more. I wriggle around, trying to squeeze my inner muscles together.

He claps his other palm on the nape of my neck, and squeezes down, holding me in place, even as he continues to get himself off with our joined palms. He compresses his hold with such force that my hand begins to ache. The pressure builds in my lower belly. The hardness at his crotch continues to swell and push up against my fingers. It's incredibly erotic, knowing I have the most sensitive part of him in the palm of my hand. He leans in even closer, until our noses bump, until we share breath, until his lips brush mine. He stares into my eyes as his movements get more frantic. Until his thickness feels so stiff that I'm sure it's going to tear through the fabric of his pants. That's when he pulls my hand away from his crotch. He removes his palm from my neck. He grabs my waist, lowers me to the floor between him and the table, then he flips me over, and pushes me down so my cheek is plastered to the hard surface.

32

Seb

I flip up her skirt, and the creamy globes of her ass are bared to my gaze. So damn tempting. Before I can stop myself, I bend and bite the curve of her ass cheek.

She gasps, then writhes around. Her butt twitches. I straighten, and massage the bite marks on her ass.

"You're so fucking tempting," I growl. I hadn't meant to lose my control, but when she insulted my masculinity, she knew exactly what she was doing. When she touched my raging arousal through my pants, I was a goner.

"You manipulated me." I lean over and place my mouth next to her ear. "You pushed and prodded at my control, knowing if you pressed the right buttons, you'd get a reaction from me."

"I don't know what you're talking about," she taunts.

"Is that right?" I close my teeth around her ear lobe and tug. She moans. I suck on it, then release it, only to drag my tongue around the shell of her ear. Her entire body jerks.

"What are you doing?" she gasps, her voice breathless.

"Making you pay for what you did."

I reach over, grab the bottle of olive oil on the table, then straighten.

"Why do you need that?" She gulps.

"Why do you think?"

She tries to rise up, but I press down on her back. "Stay there," I order.

"But I don't wanna," she pouts.

"Not giving you a choice, Princess." I remove the cork of the bottle with my teeth, and spit it aside. Then I dribble the oil over the valley between her ass cheeks.

"Seb, please," she gasps. "Seb…"

"Do you want me to stop?" I glare at her face.

She glances at me from the corner of her eye.

"Do you?"

She shakes her head.

"Then keep your mouth closed, or I'll do it for you."

She huffs, but doesn't reply. She juts out her lower lip, and *Dio Santo*, I want to fit my mouth on hers and bite down on it.

Holding her gaze, I slide my fingers down the valley between her ass cheeks. She shivers. I play with her puckered hole, and she squeezes her eyes shut.

"Oh, my god," she moans.

I slide one finger inside her back hole, then another. I hook my fingers and she wheezes. Her breath comes in little pants, her forehead scrunches up. She slaps her palm on the table, then slides it over to grab at the edge.

"That… that's different," she pants.

"No shit."

I reach down with my other hand, unhook my belt, then lower my zipper. The rasping sound fills the space and her eyelids flutter.

"Is it going to hurt?" she huffs.

"I'm sure it will," I promise.

She snaps her eyelids open.

I chuckle. "Just kidding."

She scowls at me. "Very funny."

"It may hurt initially," I explain, "but if you relax, it should fade away, and I promise, the orgasm that follows will be intense."

"So you keep saying. Yet you've never let me come."

"Ideally, I wouldn't let you come now, either."

"Why you—" She rears up, but I press down on her back once more.

"Don't move," I warn as I pull out my fingers, then fit myself to the entrance of her back channel. "Ready, Princess?"

"What do you think, you smirking jerkalope, you—"

I angle my hips and thrust into her.

She gasps, then bites down on her lower lip.

I give her time to adjust to my size. I bring my hand around to play with her clit and she parts her legs wider. She thrusts out her hips, and I slip in another centimeter.

"That's it," I croon. "Let me in, Princess."

"You're... you're too big," she groans.

"You can take it."

"Easy for you to say. You're not the one with a monster cock up your arsehole."

I laugh. "Doesn't The-Actor-Who-Shall-Not-Be-Named have a phrase to fit the occasion?"

"He bloody well does." She scowls up at me from under her eyelashes.

"What is it? Are you going to tell me?"

"Are you trying to distract me?"

"Am I succeeding?" I murmur.

"Almost..."

I ease in a little more and push through her ring of muscles. Both of us groan. "Fuck, you're so damn tight, Princess. You're fucking killing me here."

"If you don't open your heart to people, you end up being excluded from the rest of the world," she mumbles under her breath.

"*Gesù Cristo*, it turns me on when you say those quotes, you know that?" My cock throbs, and my balls tighten. The blood rushes to my groin and I have to draw in a breath, then another. I grip her hips as I impale her.

"Oh, god, Seb," she whimpers as I grind my pelvis against the softness of her butt. I pull back, then thrust forward. My balls slap against her flesh. She contracts around me and a groan rumbles up my chest.

"*Cazzo*." I squeeze her hips as I begin to move—pull back, then lunge forward. The entire table shakes. Her body moves forward with the impact.

"Seb," she cries out. Her entire body jolts. "Oh, god, I'm going to—"

"Don't you dare," I growl. "Don't you dare come, Princess."

"Please," she whines. "Please, please, please."

Her thigh muscles spasm as I pull back, then brace my booted feet on the ground, before I plunge forward again. A bead of sweat slides down my temple as I slam into her. I hit a spot deep inside her, and she opens her mouth in a wordless cry. A trembling grips her. Her spine curves. She pulls back her shoulders, and that's when I lean forward and place my cheek against hers.

"Come for me, baby. Come right now."

Her entire body tenses, then she shudders as her inner walls constrict around my shaft, and she shatters. I continue to move in and out of her as the aftershocks grip her. My balls draw up, and I groan as I empty myself inside her. I lower my body to hers, place my cheek against hers, as my orgasm seems to go on and on.

When it finally fades away, I open my eyes and straighten, only to find her still, her breathing almost steady.

"Princess..." I drag my mouth against her lips. "You awake?"

"Hmm?" She flutters her eyes open. Her pupils are dilated, so there's only a ring of blue left around the black.

I pull out of her, and she winces.

"Did I hurt you?"

She shakes her head, her features still wearing a dazed expression. I reach for a napkin from the table and clean myself before tucking myself back in. Then I fold the napkin and run it between her legs.

"What are you doing?" She tries to straighten, but I hold her down. "Hush, let me clean you up, baby."

I complete the job, toss the napkin aside, then flip down her skirt. I reach over, take her hand, and pull her up to standing, then turn her to face me. She sways and I righten her. "You okay?"

"I think so." Her eyes are clearer.

I pull out her panties, then squat down and hold them out. She steps into them and I pull them up her legs, pushing her skirt out of the way. I settle them over her hips, then smooth her skirt down over her legs.

"I'm clean," she murmurs. "I can show you the paperwork."

"Me, too." I tuck a strand of her blonde hair behind her ear. "I also know you're on the pill. Not that it matters this time, but for the future."

"How do you—?" She frowns, then her forehead clears. "You had me checked out?"

"It would have been careless of me if I hadn't before I proposed to you."

She pales, then squares her shoulders. "And?" She firms her lips. "What did you find?"

"Nothing you haven't already told me." If I hadn't been watching her closely, I might not have noticed her shoulders relax. Is she hiding something from me?

She tips up her chin and glowers at me. "Naturally, there's nothing else you could have found; because I told you everything."

Was that too emphatic a statement? Something prickles the edges of my subconscious mind, but I push it away. This is Elsa. There's no way she could be lying to me. Most likely, she's unnerved that I had her checked out, which is understandable.

"I know you have," I interject. "And the only reason I brought up the pill is because, while I've always used condoms in the past, I'd rather not with you."

"Oh." She blinks rapidly. "Okay, then."

"That's it? No arguing with me on this?"

She shakes her head.

"If all it takes to quiet you is to feed you my dick, I would've done it a long time ago."

She flushes, then brushes past me.

I catch her wrist. "Hey," I murmur, "that's a joke."

She hesitates, then nods. "I know."

I pull her to me, then wrap my arm around her. "Are you really okay? I didn't hurt you, did I?"

"It was uncomfortable in the beginning, but you were right. Once I got past that, it was like nothing I've ever experienced before. It probably didn't hurt that you didn't let me come the last few times." She shuffles her feet.

"If it's any consolation, that was the most intense orgasm I've ever had, as well." I cup her cheek. "It's going to get complicated between us, you know that, right?"

She blows out a breath. "I know," she whispers. She holds my gaze for a few seconds more, then drops it. "Uh, I need to go to the bathroom and clean up a little, before eating."

"So do I." I grab the soiled napkins, lead her toward the ladies' room, then walk into the gents' to wash up. I walk out a few seconds later, turn toward the table, then hesitate. I lean a shoulder against the wall and pull out my phone as I wait for her.

There's a message from Michael. "This trip had better be worth it."

I wince. The title of Don has never fit anyone better. Even if he hadn't been born the oldest, he was made for this life. As was Luca. Then there's Massimo, who's never wanted anything else. Xander was the artist... If he had lived, I've no doubt, he'd have broken quite a few of the Mafia rules. Both with his profession and his sexuality. Axel came close to separating himself from the Mafia, considering he's Xander and Christian's triplet, who was not only united with us later, but also turned out to be an undercover cop—now retired. Christian... Well, he seems content with the life, and now he's married, so he's not going to take any risks. Also, he's loyal to Michael. Which leaves Adrian who, while easygoing, should not be underestimated. Although, so far, he hasn't ever said he wants something other than the Mafia life. And me? This opportunity with JJ Kane and Trinity enterprises is the closest I've come to realizing my ambition of making a life beyond the Mafia tradition.

Which still leaves me now married, with a wife and a kid to care for. *Cazzo*, how did things change so quickly?

The door to the ladies' room opens and Elsa steps out. I straighten, and she seems surprised to see me. "You didn't have to wait for me. I could have found my own way back to the table, you know."

"Not when you're with me."

She flushes, her expression somewhere between being delighted and surprised. I escort her back to the table just as the men file in.

Antonio nods in my direction, then they take their seats at diagonal ends of the restaurant, near the windows. That way, they can keep track of what's happening outside, as well.

As if it's a signal, the owner bustles in with baskets of bread. He glances between us. "Ready to order?"

33

Elsa

"That was delicious." I pat my mouth with my napkin. "The pasta was incredible, and the gelato was to-die-for."

"And you ate your pasta in the right way, too." Seb smirks.

"You seem surprised." I raise an eyebrow.

"You'd be amazed at the number of people who get it wrong," he scoffs.

"My mother taught me never to use a knife to cut pasta. She made it clear it must be eaten with a fork. The strands need to be rolled around the tines before being scooped up."

"Your mom was right." His lips kick up. "Are your parents in London?"

"My mother is; my father died when I was very young."

"I'm sorry," he murmurs.

"It was a long time ago." I place the napkin on the table. "My mother loved cooking all kinds of food, but especially Italian food. Probably because it was the easiest to make, considering she had to work and bring me up all on her own."

"What does she do now?"

"She still teaches, a lot of it volunteer based work with kids. I don't think she will stop working until the day she dies."

"You miss her?"

"Yeah." I lower my gaze. "She's a great mom. We didn't have much money, but she made sure we had enough to eat. Supported me when I wanted to learn music. She encouraged me to pursue my interest in playing the piano."

"Were you good?" He raises the wine goblet filled with water to his lips.

"Better than average. If I'd kept at it, perhaps I could've become a performer, but then... I met Fabio when I was eighteen, got married at nineteen, and was pregnant at twenty-one. My mother warned me about him, you know." I twist my fingers in my lap. "I didn't listen to her. I thought she was jealous that I'd met a man who would take care of me. When I got pregnant, she was there for me. I never told her how abusive Fabio could be toward me, but she guessed. She told me to leave him. No, she begged me to leave him, actually. But I didn't. I thought I could make it work."

I raise my hand to the small scar on my wrist, then realize what I'm doing. I drop it, but not before he notices it.

"He did that to you?" Seb's voice is soft, but there is an underlying steel to it that makes me flinch. "Answer me, Princess. Did he do that?"

"It was nothing; just a small scratch. It healed quickly."

"What did he do?" His gaze narrows on me.

I wave my hand. "Seriously, it doesn't matter."

"It does to me." He lowers his voice to a hush, "What did that *carogna* do?"

I hesitate.

"You will tell me." He leaves no room for disagreement, and my belly quivers. A melting sensation assaults my chest, and I feel like I am sinking. When he uses that Dom tone, I cannot refuse him.

"He—" I gulp. "He pushed me away, and I hit the side of the table."

Seb winces. The color drains from his features. His jaw tics and storm clouds gather in his eyes. "He scarred you. He laid his hand on you." His shoulders bunch.

"You have scars, too." I touch the puckered skin at his temple.

"It's not the same thing. My scar is a fallout of my chosen way of life, something I expect in my profession. You, on the other hand, were innocent. He should have protected you. Instead, he hurt you. I'm going to kill the *bastardo*."

Is he angry on my behalf? When was the last time anyone was angry on my behalf? The band around my chest tightens, and the pressure behind my eyes increases. But Avery... I have to think of Avery.

"He's still the father of my child. I'm not saying that to justify anything, but he's her blood. I can't let anything happen to him, knowing how much it could affect her," I say in a low voice.

The skin at the edges of his eyes tightens, and his grip on his goblet of water tightens.

"Seb," I clear my throat, "promise me you'll spare his life."

"*Cazzo.*" His forearms flex. The stem of the wine-goblet breaks, and the remaining water splashes on the table.

"Oh." I lean back in my chair as the goblet part of the glass rolls over and crashes to the floor.

I reach for a towel and try to mop up the water on the table, but Seb places his hand on mine, stopping me. "I can't promise not to teach him a lesson, but..." he blows out a breath, "I'll spare his life."

I jerk my chin in his direction.

"I'm sorry he hurt you, Princess," he says in a gentler voice. "You know I'd never hurt you like that, right?"

I glance away, and his grasp on my hand tightens. "Look at me, Elsa."

I turn my gaze in his direction.

"Tell me you believe me when I say that I'll never lay a hand on you."

I peer between those gorgeous golden eyes of his. "I don't believe—"

His forehead crinkles in a frown.

"That I'll ever have that complaint with you, Seb."

His shoulder muscles unwind a little, but he seems far from satisfied.

"The scenes I set for us, when I'm your Dom and I ask you to do things that a sub should do... I make you perform those actions because I know you need it. I understand that you want to give up your choice to me, of your own volition. I'm aware that, by doing that, you let go of your tensions and stresses, and relax completely into the safe space that I'm creating for you. You understand that I won't judge you. That I'll always be there for you after a scene, to take care of you. That if anytime, anything makes it uncomfortable for you, you simply have to use your safe word and I'll stop. You get me?"

I nod. Something hot stabs at my chest, and my throat feels scratchy. A pressure builds behind my eyes, and I blink away the tears that are on the verge of spilling. Damn it, why does he have to be so understanding, so self-assured, and yet, so caring? How can one man have all of the traits I've been looking for, for so long? The one man I am going to destroy before too long. Why do I have to feel so much for him? Why is it that he couldn't be horrible, someone I would have loved to hate? Why did he turn out to be the kind of person I'm falling in love with instead?

"Elsa?" he prompts. "You understand what I'm saying, right?"

I nod. "I do. I know you'll never hurt me or my daughter. I know you'll do everything to make sure I get custody of her. You're going to be a wonderful husband, Seb."

Just not mine. When you find out what I've been doing to you, when you find out how I've been double-crossing you, you're going to hate me. And then... You'll never want to see me again. But I had no choice. I hope you'll understand, I'm doing what I'm doing because it's the only way to keep my daughter safe.

He peers into my features and the furrow between his eyebrows deepens. "Why do I get the feeling there's something here you're not telling me?"

"There is, actually." I lower my eyelashes, before I raise them back to his face.

"There is?" He leans forward. "Tell me, Princess. You can tell me anything; you know that, right?"

I open my mouth, and god, I'm so tempted to tell him everything. *Everything.* "I'm worried about Fabio." I bite the inside of my cheek. "How do you know he's not the one who arranged to shoot at us at the restaurant? Either way, he's not going to be happy that we're married. There's no telling what he might do next."

Seb firms his lips. "He'll have to get past me to hurt you, and I promise you, that's not going to happen."

"What if he hurts you? If something were to happen to you—"

"Nothing's going to happen to me." He cups my cheek. "Don't you trust me to keep us both safe?"

I search his features, take in the intent that shines in his eyes. I want to believe him; I do. If anyone can ward off the threat posed by Fabio, it's Seb. Besides, there's no way Fabio would actually try to hurt him, would he? Not when he's sent me to Seb to get more information on his family. A shiver snakes up my spine.

"Seb, I..."

He tilts his head, a quizzical look on his features.

"What is it?"

"I... I'm thirsty," I glance away then back at him. "You promised me the best espresso on the Amalfi coast."

As if on cue, Francesco, the owner and chef bustles in with cups of espresso.

Seb draws in a breath and studies me. "This conversation is not over, Princess," he says in a soft voice, but when I pull my hand out from under his, he releases it. Thank god.

Francesco places a tray in front of me, which has the espresso and a small shot glass filled with a clear liquid, as well as a glass of water. He's placed a similar tray in front of Seb, minus the shot glass.

When he's taken his leave, I eye the contents of my tray. "I take it that's grappa?" I point at the shot glass.

"You're meant to pour it into the espresso and then drink it," Seb explains.

"Alcohol and caffeine. Trust you Italians to think of something this explosive." I laugh.

"It's not that unusual. The *carajillo* in Spain is a similar type of coffee-liquor drink, as well as the *kaffekask* and *kaffepunch* in Scandinavia. This combination is called a *caffé corretto*."

"You're not having any?"

"I'm driving." Seb reaches over and pours the contents of the shot glass into my espresso. "Go on; try it."

I pick up my espresso cup and take a sip. The bitterness of the espresso is tempered by the grappa, which lends it a sharp, clean taste. All in all, it doesn't taste too alcoholic, but more like an intense, if concentrated, coffee.

"Well?" he arches an eyebrow. Bet he expects me to say I don't like it.

I firm my lips. The liquid is not too hot. The temperature is just right to down it in a shot. I hesitate then raise my cup. *"Salute!"* I drain the rest of the grappa-espresso combination, then sputter and cough as tears run down my cheeks.

Seb chuckles. "You're supposed to savor it over a few sips, not toss it back."

He hands me the glass of water, and I drink from it. A trail of heat runs down my gullet and expands in my stomach, filling me with a nice warmth.

"Mmm." I smack my lips. "I can definitely see the merits of that. Do you think he'd bring me more, if I ask him?"

"More than that will get you drunk, and I need you in full control of your faculties for what I have planned later."

"And what's that?"

"If I tell you, it won't be a surprise."

34

Elsa

"Oh, it's gorgeous." I gaze up at the mosaic that takes up an entire wall of the ancient Villa Romana in Piazza Armerina, a small town a few hours' drive from the restaurant.

When he said he wanted to surprise me, this was not what I expected. We finished lunch, and two of the men exited the restaurant first and scanned the surroundings to make sure that it was safe before we walked to his car. We drove along the gorgeous coastline. Once more, he switched on the music in the car—more Puccini, then *Aida* by Verdi. The haunting music faded away, to be replaced by the strains of a very familiar tune.

"No, wait." I straightened. "Is that... It can't be, is it?"

Music from Joy Division's *Love Will Tear Us Apart* filled the space.

"Whoa!" I listened to it for a few minutes, then turned to him. "You know what you're playing, right?"

He shot me a glance, as if to say, 'are you really asking me that question?'

"It's Joy Division," I supplied.

He nodded.

"It's *Love Will Tear Us Apart* by Joy Division."

"I'm aware." He frowned.

"You like this song?"

"I *am* playing it," he reminded me. "I assume the song is of some significance to you?"

"It's Kea— I mean, it's the favorite song of The-Actor-Who-Shall-Not-Be-Named."

"Of course it is." He threw me a sideways glance, as if he wasn't quite sure what to make of my reaction.

"It's just..." I shook my head. "I can't believe you're playing it, that's all."

"It's part of a collection I put together," he admitted.

"It's an eclectic collection," I remarked.

"I'm an eclectic man."

"More like a hardheaded, over-the-top, dominant, full-of-himself alphahole."

"I'll take that as a compliment." He snorted.

"*Love Will Tear Us Apart.*" I shook my head again. "I still can't believe it."

"Why do I get the feeling I've passed some kind of test?" he muttered.

"It's nothing like that." I flushed. "I just didn't expect you to play it, is all."

"You don't think The-Actor-Who-Shall-Not-Be-Named and I could have something in common?"

"That's not what I mean," I lied. "It's a surprise. That's all."

"Hmph," he slowed down, then took the turn leading us to Piazza Armerina, which is how we got here.

Now, I turn to face him. "This place is unexpected." I gesture to the vibrant colors on the walls. "I feel like I've been transported into a different dimension."

"I know the feeling. There's so much history around here, it's like we've entered a different world, for sure. For those of us who grew up here, sometimes we take it for granted. It's like you drive through Rome and come across the Colosseum, then turn a corner and find another ruin built in 312 AD. And this place," he gestures to the ancient walls, "was built sometime in fourth century AD. Can you imagine all the history this place has seen? All the events it has witnessed? The people who have walked through this hall before us?"

He turns to find me staring at him.

"What?" He tilts his head.

"You love history, don't you?"

"Eh?" He rubs the back of his neck. "I grew up with it. It's a part of me. It's in me, I suppose." He glances about the space. "I've never thought about it, but you're right. The sense of timelessness in places like this grounds me, I guess. Makes me feel like anything is possible." He laughs a little self-consciously.

I walk over to him and lace my fingers with his. "That was almost poetic."

"More like intellectual masturbation, but then, you like men who are introspective, I take it. Those who are in touch with their emotions and all that shit."

I try to pull away from him, but he doesn't let go.

"That's why you like The-Actor-Who-Shall-Not-Be-Named, isn't it?"

"You're like him, you know," I say, more to throw him off balance than anything else.

He looks askance. "Me? Nah."

"No, really. That's what I thought the first time I saw you—that you're hot, and sexy, and bear more than a passing resemblance to him."

"You think I'm hot and sexy?" His lips curl in a smirk.

Of course, he pretends he didn't hear the last part of what I said.

"Forget I said that; it's only going to swell your already Texas-sized head."

He laughs. "You say the most random things."

"So I've been told." I glance around the space. "Are you going to take me to see the frescoes?"

After admiring the ancient paintings in the next room, we leave the spectacular, dome-shaped building, and drive down the hill on which it's located. We pass through the old town, and back onto the road that curves through the mountain-side, with the blue waters of the sea crashing on the shores not far below. The ride takes my breath away. He follows the winding route up another hill and toward a structure that was built overlooking the waves below.

He escorts me from the car, pausing only to pull a picnic basket out of the boot before guiding me to the gorgeous, white-washed bungalow with pink and white bougainvillea trees flowering around it.

The two cars with the security detail drive up and park at opposite ends of the circular driveway.

When I ask Seb about the basket, he explains that Francesco put it together. He guides me to the door of the bungalow, which is opened by a man who introduces himself as the caretaker. He welcomes us inside, then leaves the house. Seb leads me through the luxurious, yet comfortably-furnished rooms, then up the stairs and to a sheltered patio on the upper floor. I take one look at the view and gasp. The old town is stretched out below us. Beyond that, the translucent waters of the harbor are encircled by the curving hill with homes built into it. The sky is dotted with clouds that already blush with the setting sun.

I turn to find he's laid out a thick blanket. On it, is a bottle of prosecco chilling in a bucket, with two prosecco flutes next to it. There's a plate of cheese, another with pickled artichokes, sun-dried tomatoes and olives, and a third with flatbreads.

"This is quite the spread," I murmur as I walk over to him.

He glances up from placing a bowl of figs, grapes and walnuts, and another with what seems like some kind of jam, next to the flatbreads.

"It's a snack." He pats the rug next to him. "Sit with me, Princess."

I step out of my shoes, then sink down beside him and place my handbag next to me. He puts his arm around me and draws me close. I rest my head on his shoulder, and let the silence wash over me. It's hard to believe we are less than half an hour away from the town center we left behind, and only a few hours out of Palermo.

He pulls me closer and I sink into that wall-like chest. I draw in a breath, and the brine of the sea, laced with the darker, edgier scent of him, teases my nostrils.

"You like being in the Mafia?" I bite my tongue almost as soon as the words are out. What kind of a question is that, anyway?

To his credit, he doesn't seem offended. "It's the only life I know," he admits. "Michael and I were close growing up. He had a lot of responsibilities thrust on him from a very young age. I'm the closest in age to him, so I understood how it felt to try to protect our brothers from the wrath of our father."

I glance up at him. "Your father... Was he—"

"He was a bastard." Seb stares into the distance. "My mother was his mistress. When she passed, he took us in. Any gratefulness I felt toward him dissipated when I realized he was an abusive motherfucker. His wife—Michael and Luca's mother—was too weak to stand up to him. Michael, being the oldest of us, took the brunt of his beatings, until he grew physically strong enough to defend himself. He tried to protect us from our father's wrath, but he wasn't always around. When he turned eighteen, he went to LA to study. In the period of time before we went to join him, our father had free reign. He took out his anger at having Michael escape him by beating up me and Luca, who were the next in age."

"You and Adrian are half-brothers to the rest of the Sovranos?"

"We're half-brothers to Michael and Luca; Christian, Axel, and Xander are half-brothers to all of us. They had a different mother from Michael and Luca's mother, and from my and Adrian's mother."

I widen my gaze. "Your father sure did get around, eh?"

"*Bastardo* couldn't keep it in his pants," Seb agrees.

"So, you and Michael seem to share a special relationship."

"Well, I'm the older sibling, and so is he. We didn't realize that Christian, Axel and Xander shared a different mother until very recently. Luca always had a chip on his shoulder for not being born as the older son. He's always wanted to be Don, for as long as I can remember."

"And now you're handing over your title as Capo to him."

"Michael should have made him Capo when he took over as Don from our father. I never really wanted the title."

"You don't strike me as someone who's selfless." My forehead furrows.

"Oh, trust me, there's nothing particularly selfless about this. My aim has always been to look beyond the Mafia, to bring us into the next century, so to speak."

"Hence, the venture into media and tech?" I interject.

"You were listening in on our conversation?" He doesn't seem upset about it.

"Hard not to listen, considering you guys were talking right in front of me."

"And what do you think of it?"

"Of what?" I blink.

"Of my heading up Trinity Enterprises with the Kane Company and the Bratva, and starting a media venture of my own."

"You're asking me?" I sit up. "You want my opinion?"

"You're my wife. Of course, I want your opinion."

I glance down to where my hand rests on his chest. The ring he gave me catches the sun's rays.

Did Fabio ask my opinion on anything? No, he'd been a typical Italian male, or so I'd thought. Right from the start, he told me he expected me to be a stay-at-home wife to take care of our child and make sure there was a hot dinner waiting for him when he came home. It had been a one-way conversation, that one. No wonder it came as a shock when he discovered my other proclivities.

And now, here's Seb. Also an Italian male. And a Mafia guy, at that. I guess I expected him to be similar. Even though our marriage is only an arrangement, on some level, I thought he'd have the same expectations. At every turn, though, he surprises me. He's shown himself to be far from the chauvinist I pegged him for. Oh sure, he's dominant and has a big ego, but he's also fair and sensitive to my needs. And now, he's asking for my opinion on a possible career shift?

I shake my head. "Are you sure you're for real?"

He laughs. "What's that supposed to mean?"

"Nothing. Forget it." I glance away.

"No, tell me." He notches his knuckles under my chin and tilts my head in his direction. "I want to know." In a firm voice, he adds, "No secrets, Princess. What was that about?"

"You're so dominant, and yet, you're surprisingly... considerate," I finally say.

"Because I asked your opinion on something?"

"Not something. This is a big deal for you, Seb. I get it. You've probably spent a lot of time trying to work out how to make this parallel move, so to speak. And you have the opportunity now, but you ask me for my opinion on it." I shake my head. "It's mind boggling."

"You're my life-partner. It shouldn't surprise you that I ask you to weigh in on changes I'm thinking of making that could affect not only the two of us, but also our daughter."

I know I'm gaping at him, but I can't stop myself. "Are you always this thoughtful? This is a chance for you to pursue your dream career, but you're still thinking of how it would impact me and my daughter?"

"Our daughter," he corrects me. "Why are you so surprised? You should know by now, I'll always do what's best for the two of you, I—"

I throw my arms around him. Honestly, I surprise even myself with the intensity with which I cling to him. "You are incredible, you know that?" I bury my nose in the space between his neck and his shoulder. I draw in a huge lungful of his scent, and hold my breath. I'll never get tired of how good it feels to be plastered to him, to push my breasts into his rock-hard chest, and cling to him.

He rubs my back and it's both soothing and arousing. That's the thing. That's what's different with this guy. Right from the beginning, I've inherently trusted him. I feel safe with him. For the first time since Avery was born, it doesn't feel like the ground below my feet is unsteady. I feel reassured, like I can finally look forward to the future with some level of confidence. Like I can breathe. Like I'm not slowly getting strangled under the weight of my worries. And yet... I'm going to betray him. I shouldn't feel this secure with him when, ultimately, it's not his actions but my own which are going to secure a future for my daughter and myself, right? *Tell him, tell him now. Tell him everything and ask him to help you. And what guarantee do you have that he won't turn on you then? What if he gets upset that you've kept the truth from him this far? What if he decides to walk away from you? Then you'll have lost your one chance to ensure Avery is safe.*

I glance up into his face to find him staring down at me. I reach up and press my lips to his. He doesn't move, doesn't blink, doesn't return the kiss. He simply stays still as I dart my tongue inside his mouth. I swipe my tongue over his teeth, and a groan rumbles up his chest.

His chest planes flex, and *bam-bam-bam*, I feel his heart rate ratchet up. That only emboldens me more. I wind my arms around his neck, tilt my head and deepen the kiss. I suck on his tongue, and begin to grind myself on the thick column between his legs.

Another growl vibrates up his throat. Then he cups my butt and squeezes. A shudder runs up my spine. A pulse flares to life between my legs and I squeeze my thighs around his waist. I try to kiss him even more thoroughly. That's when he flips me over so my back is on the rug, and his weight presses down on me. Without breaking the kiss, he stares into my eyes, then unhooks my arms from around his neck, twists my arms up and above my head, and shackles my wrists together with one hand. He slides the other hand between us and I hear the sound of his belt being unbuckled, his zipper being lowered. He shoves my panties aside, and the next moment, he's inside of me.

One second, I'm empty. The next, he's filling me, stretching me, as his thickness scrapes against my inner walls. He's so big, so deep inside that I swear, I can feel every single ridge of his cock. He stays there for a second, even as his shaft throbs inside of me. He tears his lips from mine, and without taking his gaze off of me, he pulls out. He stays there, poised at my opening, with his dick nudging my slit. Then he lunges forward with enough force that my entire body jolts. He stays there, with his balls pressed against my inner thighs, before he begins to move. Out and in and out again. Every time he fucks me, I move up the rug a little. There's a muffled thud as something hits the ground next to us, the prosecco bottle, probably, but neither of us glance away. He doesn't take his gaze off of mine for a second. Those golden-brown eyes of his are ablaze with so much emotion. So much everything. My throat closes, and a tear squeezes out from the corner of my eye. He bends, licks it up, and for some reason, that's so erotic and so intimate, I can't stop more tears from streaming.

He pulls out, then lunges forward with such force that he hits that special spot deep inside of me. I lock my ankles around his waist and he brings his hand down to cup my face. He peers into my eyes as he slides his thumb inside my mouth. At the same time, he drills into me again, and he goes so deep, I swear, I can feel him in my throat. Another sob wells up, even as the climax swells from our point of contact. It shudders up my spine as he slams into me again and again. The orgasm rips through me and I gasp. A cry wells up. He closes his mouth over mine, and swallows it, even as he continues to fuck me through the climax. My entire body shudders, my core clenches down around his dick. He brings his hand down to squeeze my nipple as he thrusts forward and inside me. I tilt my hips up trying to take him in even deeper. That's when his muscles go solid. His shoulders shudder, as he growls and comes inside me.

35

Seb

My orgasm seems to go on and on. The cherry scent of her, mixed with the sweetness of her arousal, surrounds me. Her thick blonde hair flows about her, a heavenly cloud. The honeyed heat of her pussy is so sweet, so tight, as she flutters around my cock, as she clamps down on my shaft and milks me until I'm sure I'm going to black out. Dark spots flash at the corners of my vision as I slump against her. The softness of her breasts cushion my chest, and her thighs wrap around me. At some point, I released her arms, and she winds them around my neck. She runs her fingers down my back and I can sense her touch through the shirt and jacket that I am wearing.

"Take off your clothes," she whispers, her voice muffled against my throat.

"All in good time." I push up, holding my weight off of her with my arms planted on either side of her.

I glance into her flushed face, the trail of tears down her cheeks, the swollen lips, her hair tangled about her face, and I can't stop myself from bending and brushing my lips over hers again and again.

"You're so gorgeous, it hurts me." I hear the words and can't believe I said them. Who is this lovestruck, pussy-whipped *stronzo* who can't keep his gaze, his lips, his hands off of this woman?

"Elsa," I clear my throat, "I..." I shake my head. Am I actually going to do this? Make myself so completely vulnerable to another. I had loved my mother, at least, for the time I had known her. Other than Nonna, she's the only other person I've felt protective about. Michael and Luca's mother? She had taken care of us, but she'd had her hands full, trying to manage our father, and trying to come to grips with the fact that her husband had not only been unfaithful, but also expected her to take care of his children with his other women. Adrian and I had each other, of course. And the rest of the Sovranos are my family.

But none of them belong to me as completely as this woman. She needs me, and she touches that primal part of me I can't control around her. As her Dom, as her husband, and hopefully, as the father to her child, she demands of me the kinds of roles I hadn't thought I had in me to fulfill. Oh, I've set scenes with other subs at the club, but none of them were mine. I've never experienced the kind of intimacy I felt with her when I made love to her now. And that's what it was. It wasn't just fucking. It went beyond the carnal act of sex. There was so much emotion in the act when it was with her... It makes my head spin.

I push a strand of hair behind her ear, then kiss her on her lips again. *"Ti amo, Principessa."* When I try to pull away, she doesn't let me. She clings to me with her arms and her legs as she rains kisses on my mouth, my cheeks, my nose. She arches up, presses kisses over my eyelids.

"I love you, Seb. Please don't forget that. Whatever happens, promise me, you'll always remember me."

I frown. "What do you mean? What could happen, Elsa? You—"

She flexes her inner muscles around my cock, and instantly, it comes to life inside her.

"Cazzo," I growl as I struggle to complete my train of thought. That's when she reaches up and kisses me. She thrusts her tongue in between my lips, presses herself even closer against me, if that were possible, and angles her hips as she slides up and down my dick.

"Elsa," I say through gritted teeth, "you're fucking killing me."

She makes a sound deep in her throat, and digs her heels into my back. Using it for leverage, she hauls herself up my dick which is, by now, fully erect inside of her.

"Gesù Cristo, woman, you're insatiable, you know that?" I pry her arms from around my neck and shove them up and over her head.

A glint of satisfaction in her eyes makes me pause, but then she arches up and buries her teeth in the side of my neck and *cazzo*, I feel that all the way to the tip of my cock. I shackle her wrists together as I pull out, then piston my hips and thrust into her with such force that she yells. Her entire body jolts, her pupils dilate, and she releases her hold on my neck, only to latch onto my mouth again. I glare into her baby blues, and see desperation... and something else. Fear?

I try to pull back, but she follows me, deepening the kiss as she tilts her hips so I slide even deeper inside her melting cunt. Liquid heat flares in my veins. Something inside of me seems to detonate. My scalp tingles, my balls tighten, and every pore in my body seems to awaken as I thrust forward and into her again and again. I fuck her in earnest, until whatever I had seen in her eyes fades away, replaced by lust. Then, even that disappears, and all that's left is my face reflected in her eyes, as she begins to flutter around me, as her flesh seems to melt even more, as her core accepts all of me. Her spine bends, a shudder grips her, and she shatters as I empty myself inside her.

When I rouse myself next, I push off of her, then pull out my handkerchief and clean between her legs. She protests half-heartedly, then watches as I clean myself up and pocket the handkerchief. I fix her panties, then her skirt, before I put myself in order. Then I pull her up against me, and reaching for the prosecco, pour out two glasses. We toast each other silently, and sip from the bubbling frothy liquid. I feed her an olive; she feeds me some of the antipasto. We manage to make our way through most of the food while drinking the prosecco, as we watch the sun go down.

As the shadows lengthen across the harbor, I wonder if the darkness in her eyes also grows more intense. But each time I want to ask her about it, I don't. Why spoil the evening? There'll be time later. She's mine. Mine to protect. Mine to cherish. Mine to dominate and please. Mine to keep safe, along with her daughter.

When the sun has dipped completely under the horizon, we stay for a few more seconds watching the pink and purple colors that flood the clouds.

"It's beautiful," she murmurs.

"Fucking gorgeous," I agree as I take in the play of light across her face.

She glances up at me and her cheeks grow pink. "I meant the sunset." Her lips twitch.

"So did I." I smirk.

"Liar," she says lightly.

"Never." I bend and kiss her again. That's when my phone begins to vibrate. I see Antonio's name on the screen before I answer it.

"Yeah?" I snap.

"Sorry, Seb. We need to be getting back home. Once it gets dark, it'll be more difficult to keep both of you safe. You know the drill," he adds.

"We'll be there shortly." I disconnect and pocket the phone.

"We need to get going?" she guesses.

"In a few minutes."

"It's safer if we get back before it gets too dark, right?" She begins to rise, but I hold her back.

"What's the hurry? I promise, nothing will happen to you as long as you're with me."

"It's not me I'm worried about; it's—" That's when I hear a whirring sound behind me. Before I can turn, something slams into my shoulder.

36

Elsa

"No," I scream as Seb's gaze widens. His entire body shudders. I glance past him to find what looks like a drone hovering just beyond the parapet of the decking we're on. "No, no, no." I try to hold him up, but he's too heavy. He begins to slide down, and I manage to lower him to the rug on his side. I can just about hold his shoulder to stop him from being slumped completely.

There's a surprised expression on his face as he takes in my features. "I think I'm hit," he finally says in a calm voice.

"Seb." Terror wells up. My stomach twists. I touch the back of his shoulder, and my fingers come away wet. At least it's the shoulder of his unhurt arm. I manage to sit up and lean over to find blood oozing from a wound in his shoulder. It's blotting the rug and spreading out. As I watch, more of the scarlet spills out. My head spins. My chest hurts. My pulse is beating so hard, I can hear the blood pumping in my ears.

"Seb, oh, my god, Seb," I blubber as his eyelids flutter shut. His body twitches, then he slumps onto the rug. I hear voices yelling and footsteps running, and turn to find Antonio and the man who'd gotten into the car with him bursting onto the deck.

He glances at us, then at the drone that hovers beyond us. He pulls out his gun, and in response, lights flicker on the device. The drone makes that whirring noise again.

"No, no, no." I throw myself over Seb as it fires. A man yells something—someone hits the floor. The sound of bullets fills the space. When it pauses, I hear the whirring sound again, a second before bullets pepper across the deck. I scream as I hold onto Seb, trying to cover him as best I can. There's the sound of more footsteps, more yelling, and more shots being fired. Then, silence. *Bam-bam-bam.* My heart slams against my rib cage. I hold onto Seb as tears slide down my cheeks. I stay that way for a few more seconds.

When I glance up, the drone still hovers in the same place. I scan the patio, then cry out when I find all four of the men who comprised our security detail, including Antonio, sprawled out on the floor. Blood pools under one of the men. The rest of them are so silent, surely, they must be dead. Are they dead? Seb. Oh, my god, Seb. I touch his face, which already feels cool to the touch. And he's pale, so pale. I hear the whirring sound, and once more, throw myself over him.

"No," I yell at the drone. "No, I won't let you kill him! You hear me? Not unless you kill me first, motherfucker!"

The drone hovers there silently, then swings away and out of sight.

"Seb! Jesus! Help me, God. Please, please, please don't let him... Don't let him die." I sit back, tear off my jacket, bundle it, and press it against the wound. *Help. I need help.*

I glance around, spot my handbag, and leap toward it. I pull out my phone, but it's dead. "Fuuuck!" I yell. Why, oh, why did I forget to charge it? I throw it aside, then turn back to Seb. I pat around in his jacket pockets. Don't find anything. *No, no, no.* My stomach caves in on itself and bile bubbles up. I swallow it down, then reach for his pants pocket. *There.* My fingers brush the phone.

I pull it out, but it's locked. Of course it's locked. "Fuck, fuck, fuck," I yell as I rise to my feet. My knees almost give way before I steady myself. I stumble over to Antonio, who's collapsed on his front, check his jacket pockets, and find his phone. Locked. *No, no, no, this can't be happening. Please, please, God, don't let anything happen to my Seb. Please let him survive this, and I'll confess everything to him. Everything. I promise.* I check the pockets of the next guy; no phone. And the next; his phone is locked, too. I approach the fourth guy, who's body is twisted in such a way that I can't help but think he must be dead. The blood pooling under him has spread out even more. I don't have a choice. I step into his blood, then reach for his jacket pocket. *Bingo.* I pull out his phone. *Please, please, please let this be unlocked. Please.* I snap open the old-fashioned device... Is it a burner phone? It's unlocked. *Thank you, God!* I reach for the keypad, and dial the only number I know from memory.

. . .

Two hours later, I pace the floor of the waiting room in the hospital in Palermo. I called the number of the flower shop, hoping and praying someone would pick up. The first time, the call went to voice mail. Damn it, I wished I'd memorized Theresa's mobile number, or knew the number of one of the Sovrano brothers, but I didn't. I tried the number of the shop again, and this time, Theresa picked up. I almost burst into tears as I explained what'd happened. To Theresa's credit, she snapped to attention right away. She reassured me that I'd done the right thing by calling her instead of directly calling the ambulance or the police—which, to be honest, hadn't even occurred to me. I may have only just married into a Mafia family, but being married to Fabio had instilled a healthy distrust for the cops, and common sense had told me that calling an ambulance service directly might not be wise, given the nature of the incident which had taken place. Apparently, even though I'd been dazed, some part of me had been thinking clearly.

She took the details of my location and made me stay on the line while she called Axel and told him what had transpired.

She came back on the call with me and told me someone would be with me very soon.

Within seconds, Aurora called her on her cell phone, and she put Aurora on speaker.

Aurora assured me she was already en route with Christian and some of the other Sovrano brothers in an air-ambulance. How they got hold of an air-ambulance so quickly, I have no idea. Maybe they have one on standby, given the nature of the business the brothers are in? Either way, Aurora walked me through some basic first-aid steps on how to keep the pressure on the wound to stem the flow of blood, while checking for his pulse—which had been sluggish. She then cut the call, with the promise they'd be there very soon.

Theresa stayed on the line with me, and fifteen minutes later, I heard the whoomp-whoomp-whoomp of an approaching chopper.

Within five minutes of that, Aurora and Christian burst onto the patio, along with two paramedics.

Aurora and the paramedics took over. I watched numbly as they placed the oxygen mask over Seb, cut through his jacket, and kept the pressure steady as they loaded him onto a stretcher.

Then I heard the sound of another chopper and realized one of them had the foresight to call for reinforcements.

Massimo and Luca arrived with four more paramedics. Together, they worked in what seemed to be a well-rehearsed operation of patching up and loading the other guys onto the second chopper.

Within fifteen minutes, we were all loaded up, and both choppers were on their way to the hospital.

Less than an hour after I called Theresa, Seb and the other men were in surgery. By some miracle, all four of the guys, while injured, were breathing. As for Seb, the doctor had yet to tell us the extent of his injury.

Theresa stayed with me. Thankfully, she'd hired a temporary employee to take my place while I was away.

Now, I watch as she talks to Axel in one corner of the room.

Massimo and Luca huddle together with Adrian and Christian in another corner.

Aurora went into the operating theatre to assist the doctors.

As for me? I can't get rid of the sight of Seb's face—the surprise in his eyes, followed by the realization that he'd been hit—before he lost consciousness.

I sink down into a seat from where I have a direct view of the door, and fold my fingers together. I don't think I've prayed this much in a long time... Not since I went into labor with Avery, and then I'd been in too much pain to remember to pray after a while. No, this time I am in possession of all of my faculties. I can't take my gaze off of the doorway.

Someone presses a cup of something hot into my hands. The scent of coffee reaches me, and my stomach churns. I shake my head, and Theresa sits down next to me. "Have a sip," she urges me.

I take a sip, and my stomach protests. "No more." I place the cup on the table next to me.

"Drink some water, at least." She uncaps a bottle and hands it to me. I sip from it and my stomach, thankfully, doesn't react to that. I take a few more sips, then hand it back to her.

"I got you some clothes." She hands me a cloth bag.

"Clothes?"

"You need to change, Elsa." She jerks her chin toward me. I glance down to find my blouse and skirt are stained with blood. His blood? My belly knots. Tears squeeze out from the corners of my eyes, and I wipe the back of my hand across my face.

"Come on, Elsa." She rises and draws me up to my feet. "I'll help you." She leads me through the waiting room to a door at the far end I hadn't noticed. "Go on." She pushes the door open, places the cloth bag next to the sink, and guides me inside. "I'll be waiting outside. Call if you need anything." The door shuts behind her.

I glance at my face in the mirror, notice the droplets of blood across my cheek, and burst out crying.

"Elsa, are you okay?" Theresa knocks on the door. "Do you need me to come in."

"No," I say through my sobs, "I'll be fine." I turn on the tap, scoop some water in my hands, and splash it on my face several times. I manage to choke down my sobs, turn off the tap, shrug out of my clothes, and slip into the dress she brought me. I stuff my clothes into the bag, and run my fingers through my hair trying to restore some semblance of order to the strands. With a last look at myself in the mirror, I head out.

"How are you feeling?" Theresa peers into my features.

"Not great." I glance around, wondering what to do with the bag, when she holds out her hand.

"I'll take care of that for you."

I hand her the bag, and allow her to lead me back to a seat in the waiting room.

"He'll be fine," she reassures me as we sit down.

"What if the bullet does permanent damage to him?" I swallow, "I'll never forgive myself if it did. And those men who were hurt. What if they die?" My entire body trembles. My hands and feet are so numb, I can barely feel them. "This is all my fault, Theresa. It's my fault."

"No, it's not. You couldn't have known that someone was going to shoot at you guys."

"I knew he was in danger, and yet, I asked him to take me on the trip. I was the one who said I wanted to leave the house. He told me it was dangerous, but I still insisted." A sob blocks my throat, and I swallow it down. "I knew this was going to happen. I knew it, and I didn't stop it. This is all my fault."

"What do you mean?"

I glance up to find Axel has come over to stand next to us.

"How could you know that this would happen?" he asks.

"I..." I bite the inside of my cheek. How can I explain something I am, only now, trying to get my head around?

"Axel," Theresa scowls at him, "stop trying to scare her."

Axel glances between us. When his gaze alights on Theresa, it thaws a little. "I'm only trying to understand how she knew that something was going to happen to Seb."

"It's just a figure of speech, Axel. She's feeling guilty that she coaxed Seb to take her out today. She had no idea something like this would happen."

"That's not what I'm understanding from what she's saying." Axel narrows his gaze on me.

"It's only because she's worried and confused." Theresa turns to me. "Isn't that right Elsa? You had no idea that something like this could happen, right?"

I glance at her and then away. Oh, god, what am I going to tell them? This is not how everything was supposed to turn out. If I'd known that Seb would end up getting hurt like this... Would I have agreed to what Fabio asked? Was there any other way to protect my daughter? My head spins. I lean back against the wall, close my eyes, and lock my fingers together.

"Elsa, honey, are you okay?" Theresa asks.

Footsteps head in my direction. I snap my eyes open, searching for the figure of the doctor, but it's Karma who sweeps in. "Elsa!" She walks over to me, places a bag on the side table, then reaches for my hands. "You poor, poor thing," She rubs my cold palms between her warmer ones. "I'm so sorry this happened, Elsa. Are you okay?"

I nod. Tears bite the backs of my eyes, and another sob wells up my throat.

"How's Seb?"

I shake my head, unable to form the words.

"The doctors, and Aurora, too... They're all in there with him. They haven't told us the status yet," Theresa replies.

"And Antonio, and the rest of the team?" Karma asks.

"They're alive, but that's all we know right now," Axel interjects.

The tension in the room ratchets up, and I turn to find Michael's broad shoulders filling the doorway. He stalks inside, his tread measured, then glances over to where Massimo and Luca are huddled together. Something passes between the men, then Massimo and Luca walk over to the doorway and leave the room.

Michael prowls over to stand behind Karma.

I glance up at his features, and my heart stutters. *He knows. Oh, my god. He knows.*

Seb

The scent of antiseptic hurts my nostrils. I draw in a breath and my lungs rattle. I try to raise my eyelids, but they seem like they're weighed down. My mouth is so dry, my tongue feels like it's stuck to the roof. I try to raise my arm, but find I'm unable to move it. *Cazzo!* I flutter my eyelids open, and the brightness seems to pierce my brain.

"Porca miseria," I growl, "what the fuck happened?" My heart slams into my ribcage. Shot. I have no doubt I was shot. And her? What happened to her? "Elsa?" I cough. "Where are you?"

"Seb." A woman's voice reaches me.

"Elsa." I strain in the direction of the voice.

Cool fingers touch my hand. "It's Aurora."

"Where's Elsa?" I swallow down the ball of emotion that's lodged in my throat. "Is she okay? Is she hurt?"

"She's not hurt; she's fine," Aurora reassures me.

The tension drains out of my muscles. "Where is she?" My throat hurts and my shoulder feels numb. I try to knit my thoughts together, but my brain cells feel like they're coated in white fog. Everything in my body hurts, but as if from behind a curtain, a clear indication that there are enough drugs running through my body to keep the worst of the pain at bay.

"Elsa. I want to see her."

"Uh, I'm not sure that's advisable," Aurora murmurs.

My pulse rate shoots up. "What do you mean? Is she okay? You said she was okay. So why isn't she here with me?"

"Doc," the voice of one of my brothers interrupts, "why don't you take a break?"

"I'll be right outside." Aurora pats my hand, then I hear her step away.

"How are you doing, *fratello*?" Massimo's face fills my line of sight.

"The fuck you doing here?" I try to sit up, but my body refuses to comply. "The fuck is wrong with me?" I pant.

"You got shot, bro. The bullet went right through. But you lost a lot of blood. It's a good thing we got to you when we did. A few minutes more and—" He shakes his head. "You gave us a scare, Sebastian."

O-k-a-y, Massimo never calls me by my full name. Never. So, this must be really serious. I sink back against the pillows. "Where's Elsa? If she's not hurt, why isn't she here with me?"

"It's... complicated." Massimo pulls up a chair and sinks into it.

"She's my wife; she needs to be by my side. What's complicated about that?"

"How much do you know about Elsa?"

"What do you mean?" I scowl.

"You met her at a bar. Do you know how she came to be there?"

"She was there with Theresa." I raise my shoulder, or try to, but my body protests. "What the fuck is this all about? I married her, she's my wife, and I need her here. End of discussion."

"Is it?"

Something in Massimo's voice alerts me. A heaviness grips my chest and the hair on my forearms rises.

"The fuck is happening? You going to tell me, or are you playing games with me?"

"No games," Luca says from the doorway. He walks inside, followed by

Adrian, who shuts the door behind him and walks over to stand on the side of the bed opposite Massimo. Luca positions himself at the foot of my bed.

I glance from Luca to Adrian, then finally rest my gaze on Massimo. "The fuck is going on?" I ask in a hard voice. "Why the hell are the three of you in my room? And where is Elsa?"

"Firstly, let us reassure you, again, that Elsa is safe," Adrian replies.

"So why isn't she here?"

"That's what we're here to talk to you about," Adrian says in a calm voice.

"*Gesù Cristo.*" I try to sit up again, then gasp when my entire body seems to seize up. "*Cazzo*, if any of you have harmed her—"

"She's safe, Seb," Massimo rumbles, "I promise you."

"You'll see her soon, *fratello*, but first there's something you need to know." Adrian leans forward on the balls of his feet.

I train my gaze on Luca, who hasn't spoken a word since he entered the room. "I assume you're behind this?"

"I'm the Capo, but the decision was not mine alone. Michael agreed to it."

"Where is she, you *testa di cazzo*?"

Luca's features harden, but he doesn't rise to the bait. Imagine that. Apparently, even he has to grow up some day. Too bad he's chosen me to fuck with on his first piece of business as Capo.

"She knew who shot you."

"What?" I blink. "That's not possible. Besides, it was a drone that shot at me."

"She mentioned that." Luca folds his arms across his chest. "She also told us who was operating the drone."

I shake my head. "There's some misunderstanding here. Perhaps you put pressure on her. Did you?" I glance from Luca to Massimo, then Adrian. "Was she coerced into this confession?"

Adrian shakes his head. "She volunteered the information to Michael."

If there's anyone I believe, it's Adrian. Not only is he the most level headed of all of us, he's also the one with the least to lose. He's never been interested in the *Cosa Nostra*. He's always been clear that he's there to support Michael, but doesn't want a stake in the business. He's built himself a life separate from ours. At one time, I'd thought he was being disloyal to us. And yet, I'd envied him for it. I've never been able to tear myself away from the *Cosa Nostra* long enough to follow his example. And now, when I'm about to carve out my own path, with the love of my life at my side... Turns out, she's been an illusion all along.

No. What am I actually thinking? I trusted her. My instincts couldn't be that wrong, could they? "I don't believe any of this."

"Better believe it. She confirmed that her ex is the person behind the shooting. Turns out, she was colluding with him all along. She only agreed to marry you so she could spy on you and on the rest of the family. She was using you to get close to the *famiglia*. She was going to pass information to him that would have put us behind bars," Luca states blandly.

"Hold on." Sweat beads my hairline. My head spins. I take a breath, then another to try to clear my mind. "So she was working with Fabio to put us away?"

"So it would seem," Massimo murmurs.

"And she thinks he's the one who set the drone on me?"

All three of them nod.

"So why didn't he kill me? Why am I still alive?"

"That is the question." Luca rubs his jaw. "For whatever reason, the drone did not fire to kill you."

"And Antonio, and my bodyguards?"

"They're all alive. Antonio escaped with a wounded knee. Of the other three, one's in a coma, and the other two have already regained consciousness." Massimo widens his stance.

"So, no deaths?"

"No deaths," Luca says slowly. "It may have been an oversight. Clearly, the drone intended to kill."

"But no one died," I snap.

Massimo and Luca exchange looks.

"He has a point. Fabio is the police commissioner; he's not a fool. If he was behind the attacks, what stopped him from completing what he started? Doesn't that simply put him in a dangerous position?" Massimo finally offers.

"I agree with Massimo." Adrian turns to Luca. "The attack may have started with the intention of killing, but for some reason, that didn't happen."

"Also, she wasn't hurt," Luca interjects. "All of you were injured and she— Not a scratch on her, despite the fact that she was right there with you when the shooting started."

Silence descends on the room. The pain in my shoulder turns up a notch. My stomach cramps, and I'm sure I'm going to be sick. I swallow down the bile, and glare at Luca. "I want to speak to my wife."

Luca hesitates.

"She married me; she is under my protection," I remind him.

Luca firms his lips. "She will not be harmed; you have my word," he finally offers.

"Not that I don't believe you, but..." I set my jaw. "I. Want. To. See. Her."

37

Elsa

I run my palm down the fabric of my dress. Why am I sweating? I didn't do anything wrong. Whatever I did was to protect my child. It's what any mother would have done.

And you almost got him killed. I raise my hand to knock on the door of the hospital room, then pause. I flatten my palm against the door instead. My husband's in there. Is he still my husband, after everything that happened, or is this like the shortest marriage in history? No, that accomplishment belongs to Britney Spears and Jason Alexander, who were married for fifty-five hours. And didn't a couple in Kuwait stay married for just three minutes? And why are these random facts popping into my head? No doubt, it's Summer's influence. Not only was she a movie buff but she also loved to quote random trivia facts, something which rubbed off on me. It's also where my Keanu Reeves obsession comes from.

We lost touch when I married Fabio, and while I feel lucky to have met Theresa, the fact is, she married into the *Cosa Nostra*, as well. If only I could speak to someone like Summer, who has nothing to do with this life. Maybe that would provide some perspective on my situation. She must be very busy though, for the last I heard, she's happily married to Sinclair Sterling, once the most notorious playboy in London; now, by all accounts, her loyal husband. I saw a photo of them in the tabloids, where one of the paparazzi had clicked them attending a Christmas party at one of their friend's places. They both seemed very happy, hand-in-hand, big smiles on their faces.

No, it wouldn't do to disturb her.

"Elsa," Massimo says gently from behind me, "you ready to see him?"

No.

No.

"Yes," I nod.

He reaches over and knocks on the door. "Go on," he says in an encouraging tone, "I know he's looking forward to seeing you."

I take a deep breath. Here goes. I push the door open and enter. My gaze is instantly drawn to the man on the bed. His shoulder is swathed in bandages, and his left arm is in a sling that goes around his neck. The bandages are stark white against the tan of his skin. His big body dwarfs the bed. Surrounded by the white sheets, he seems so out of place there. *You put him there. It's your fault he was hit. Your fault he's hurting now.*

He watches me with a brooding gaze as I move toward him. My knees tremble, but I force myself to put one foot in front of the other. I come to a halt in front of him. This close, I can see the dark circles under his eyes; the hollows under his cheekbones are more pronounced than I remember. There are new creases radiating out from the edges of his eyes that I don't recall. Somehow, that only adds to his sexiness. Even wrapped in bandages, he's the most virile man I've ever met. I'll never love anyone else like I do him. And I lost him. The band around my chest tightens, a ball of emotion twists my stomach with such force that I am sure I am going to be sick.

"Seb," I clear my throat, "Seb, I'm so sorry."

His features harden, then he firms his lips. He peers into my features as if searching for something. He holds my watery gaze, and I want to look away. I try to lower my eyelids and not allow him to search through my emotions, but I can't. I owe him this. I stare into those golden-brown orbs of his, now dulled with pain. A pain that I caused. My stomach hurts. My knees tremble. I grab the back of a chair and steady myself.

"Seb... Avery... I..."

"I forgive you."

"What?" I gape.

"You're a mother first, Elsa. You'd do anything to protect your child. It's the first thing I noticed about you. How you'd hold her close and never take your gaze off of her when you were with her. And more than anything, I wanted that. I wanted your attention just as focused on me, to the exclusion of anything else. The fact that you could put her before anything else, even yourself... It's that complete selflessness that drew me to you. How can I now blame you for following that instinct? How can I hate you for putting your child first, when it was that very quality that drew me to you?"

"Seb?" My heart seems to expand in my chest. At the same time, the hair on the back of my neck rises. What have I done? Did I actually think I could hurt this man and live with myself afterward? Couldn't I have found a way to safeguard my child and also spare him from being hurt? How was I so weak I allowed Fabio to manipulate me into doing something I didn't want to do? Couldn't I have trusted my husband with the truth? And now, it's too late.

"Oh, Seb." My voice cracks, and I lower my chin to my chest. A tear drop squeezes out of the corner of my eyes, and goddamn it, I've had enough. This crying, sniveling mess I have become, who bends too easily to other people's will, is not me. I may have allowed Fabio to use my weakness—Avery—against me, but that ends here.

Seb had done that, too, though. He'd used the fact that I'd do anything for Avery's happiness to cajole me into marrying him. The only difference is, I'd known what I was getting into. Known that this would help me set him up so Fabio could get access to him. I feel so dirty.

"I had no idea that he was going to shoot at you. If I did—"

"You'd have still done it."

This time, I glance away. He's right. I didn't have a choice, though, did I?

"I would have helped you." Seb curls the fingers of his unbandaged hand into a fist. "All you had to do was tell me what he was forcing you to do, and I'd have found a way to protect you and Avery."

"He has Avery with him during the week. Every time I drop her off, I'm convinced it's the last time I'll see her. There's nothing stopping him from never allowing her to see me again."

"I would have found a solution. I would have done anything it took to ensure that you never had to see him again."

"He had. Avery. With him." I grip the back of the chair so hard that the edges of the wood dig into my palms. "How could I risk going against him, when he had my daughter in his grasp?" Anger licks through my veins. "It's so easy for you to ask me to trust you, isn't it? So easy for you to wave a hand and get your people to take care of the situation."

"I never would have asked anyone else for help. I would have taken care of this personally."

"I couldn't risk it, don't you understand? He had Avery in his home, under his roof. What if he did something to her?"

"And yet, you don't want me to kill him?"

"God knows, I do... But he's still her father." I squeeze my eyes shut. "When she grows up and asks me about her father, what would I tell her?"

"That I'm her father."

I snap my eyelids open. I see his face, take in the clarity in those gorgeous eyes of his. Oh, my god, I've been such a fool. This man... He would have done anything... Anything for me and my daughter. He would've died before allowing anything to happen to her. He never would've allowed Fabio to hurt her. He would've used everything in his power to ensure that Fabio would never see her again. He would've ensured I had full custody of her, just like he had promised. He actually loves me. He loves me. And while I'd told him I loved him... I hadn't fully internalized it. I didn't love him enough to trust him. The pressure behind my eyes builds, and I blink away the moisture. I will not cry, not again. Shit. I'm doing it again. I tip up my chin and meet his gaze as tears stream down my cheeks. "I am truly so, so sorry, Seb."

38

A week later

Elsa

I clutch the window sill of my apartment and peer out. Any moment now, she'll be here. Any moment, I'll get to see my heart, my angel, here again.

A car draws up. Massimo gets out of the driver's side, while Axel emerges from the passenger side. Both glance up and down the road, and when they're satisfied, Axel raps his knuckles against the window of the back door, which is pushed open. Theresa slides out. She reaches in, hiding whoever is in the backseat with her, then straightens with Avery in her arms.

I rush out of my apartment, down the hallway, and toward the front door. I fling it open, step out, and the two guards instantly block my way.

I stop and hold out my arms as Theresa walks up the pathway. She reaches us, and Avery spots me.

Her face scrunches up. "Mama," she begins to cry. "Mama."

"Don't cry, sweetie pie." Tears well up, and I swallow them down. *No crying again, remember? You did this. Now, be strong. Do what needs to be done, and don't let* your emotions muddy the waters. Focus on the end goal—your daughter's happiness. That's what's important. It doesn't matter if you have to give up everything, even if you end up hating yourself in the process. As long as Avery is safe, everything will have been worth it.

As soon as Theresa reaches me, Avery leaps out of her arms and into mine. I clasp her to my chest and rock her. "My baby, my sweet little baby."

She cries harder, and my heart feels like it's going to break. I turn and walk back inside and down the hallway, Theresa following closely behind me. I head for Avery's nursery, aware of the men walking into the house behind us, as well. The door snicks shut as I enter the nursery. I head for the rocking-chair I used when I was nursing her and sit down, holding her in my arms. I rock back and forth, holding her close.

A few minutes later, the door opens and Theresa walks in with a bowl of the food I prepared for Avery.

"Thank you, T." She stands next to me, holding the bowl as I feed Avery. After a few mouthfuls, my baby shakes her head, and instead, burrows into me.

"You sure you don't want to eat, pumpkin?" I feed her another mouthful, then she turns her face away again.

"It's fine." I jerk my head toward the table. "Why don't you leave it there for now? This is her nap time anyway."

Avery yawns again, and I hold her close and pat her back as I rock in the chair. Within a few minutes, she's fast asleep. I bury my nose in her hair and draw in her baby smell, which is already fading. Soon, she'll become her own person, and I'll have missed so much of her childhood. If only I had trusted Sebastian. If only I had told him everything.

Avery's breathing deepens. I rock back and forth a few more times, then rising to my feet, I place her in the crib and cover her up. Drawing the curtains, I pick up the baby monitor and follow Theresa out. We walk to the living room to find Massimo and Axel deep in conversation.

Massimo points to the bag with Avery's essentials that he has placed by the sofa.

"Thank you." I glance between them. "How is... Seb doing?"

"He's much better." Massimo leans forward a little. "They're discharging him tomorrow."

"Oh..." I swallow. After that conversation with Seb, I had walked out of the hospital room, and Adrian had driven me home to my old apartment. He'd explained that the Sovranos had decided I should move back here and stay here for now. I wasn't allowed out; not even to pick up Avery. Theresa and Axel would be the ones who'd pick her up and drop her back with Fabio.

After I had confessed everything to Michael that day in the hospital, he hadn't seemed too surprised. Maybe he'd suspected it all along. Maybe he's just seen so much in his life, this latest twist didn't come as a shock to him.

After the doctor reassured us Seb was going to be fine, I was allowed to peek in on him in the recovery room. He was sleeping. I wanted to stay with him, but after everything I'd just told Michael, it didn't seem like I had the right to ask to do so.

Instead, I agreed to being driven to my place, where I crashed. When I woke up, Theresa arrived with food; along with Axel and Massimo. Which is when they conveyed to me that, for now, I'll be staying here. All of my needs will be taken care of. I'm not allowed to leave the house.

I was allowed to call Fabio and tell him that I was unwell and Axel and Theresa would arrive to pick up Avery. Fabio had met Theresa at the flower shop, so she wasn't a stranger to him. I had expected Fabio to be uncooperative, but he hadn't asked too many questions. After that, my phone had been taken, and I didn't have access to internet in the house.

Other than that, I'm allowed to do whatever I want. Which basically means, I'm under a kind of house arrest. Clearly, the Sovranos don't trust me. Not that I blame them. After what happened to Seb, I'm surprised they didn't do something worse... although I'm still under Seb's protection, so they're not going to kill me. They told me that nothing will be decided about me or my future until Seb is back on his feet. That includes not moving against Fabio, for now. Seb was adamant about that.

That was two days ago, and now, Seb is being discharged.

"When... when do I get to see him?"

Axel and Massimo glance at each other.

"When he asks for you," Massimo replies.

Of all the Sovranos, he's the one who speaks the least, he's also the most tatted.

Seb too has tattoos. I've seen them peek out from under his collar though I don't know what they are about. But then I've never seen my husband without his shirt on, either. He is still my husband, right? I play with the ring on my finger. I'm still married to him, technically, at least.

"I want to see him." I set my jaw. "I want to be there when he arrives home."

Massimo and Axel exchange glances. At least Luca isn't here. If he were, there's no doubt, he'd shut down that suggestion right away.

"I'm still his wife; he'll want to see me when he's back from the hospital." *I hope.* I bite the inside of my cheek. "Besides, he'll need help, since he's hurt. I can be there for him."

The doorbell rings.

Theresa turns to me. "Will that wake up Avery?"

I shake my head. "Once she's asleep, she's not disturbed by noises." I take a step toward the door, but Massimo beats me to it. Of course, I'm not allowed to open the door to my own apartment. I'm under house arrest, after all. I lock my fingers together as Massimo reaches the door and throws it open. Karma walks in, followed by Aurora. Michael and Christian follow in their wake.

Both of the women make a beeline toward me.

"Elsa..." Karma throws her arms around me. "How are you?"

Aurora pats my shoulder, then hovers next to us, while Theresa flanks me on the other side.

I'm not worried that the Sovrano brothers would hurt me. They're too loyal to Seb for that, but it still feels good to have the women in my corner.

"I'm fine," I sniffle as I hug Karma back.

"Are you?" She leans back and peers into my face. "You don't look fine, babe." She turns to Michael. "Don, this is not right." Her voice takes on a pleading tone, "Elsa's one of us. She also told you the truth of her own accord. Surely, she shouldn't be punished for it?"

I draw in a breath. She's questioning the Don in front of us? Sure, she's his wife, and it's only close family who're around, but still... You'd think the Don would be unhappy about this, right? I expect Michael to tell her off. Instead, he drums his fingers on his chest. "She may have told the truth, but it doesn't excuse what she did. Seb was hurt because of her, as were the other men."

"I didn't know that's what would happen." Tears press down at the backs of my eyes, and I blink them away. "If I'd any idea that Seb would be hurt... If I'd known that's what he intended, I wouldn't have agreed. I would have... stayed away from Seb. I never would've agreed to marry him. Please, believe me."

Michael's gaze intensifies, but there's no change of expression on his face.

Karma draws in a breath, while Aurora grips my shoulder before looking toward Christian. "She needs her family even more right now. She's away from home, trying to do what's best for her child. If we don't help her, who will?"

"We trusted her last time, and see what happened? Seb landed in the hospital. He almost died."

I gasp and bite back a sob.

Christian rubs the back of his neck. "Next time, it could be you who's hurt, and you know I could never let that happen."

"This is not right." Theresa grips Axel's arm. "You know she's not the guilty party here.

"She's also not innocent," Axel retorts.

"She's already explained she hadn't expected Seb to be hurt. Surely, she should, be allowed to be at Seb's home waiting for him, when he returns from the hospital?" Aurora insists. "You know that's what Seb would want too."

The guys glance at each other, then Michael jerks his chin. He turns to us. "I'll talk to Luca."

39

Seb

I push the car door open and step out onto the driveway in front of my house. My knees tremble, but they don't give way, thank fuck. I refused to leave the hospital in a wheelchair. Even though I'm still weak, I insisted on walking out on my own two feet, albeit with Massimo and Luca's help.

A stony-faced Luca told me that he and Michael had spoken, and he'd agreed to back down on holding Elsa under house arrest in her apartment. Apparently, the women had staged an intervention on behalf of Elsa, and asked that she be allowed to move back in with me.

Now she's in there, in my home, waiting for me.

I can't wait to see her which is why I'd insisted on being discharged from the hospital. While the wound is painful, it's not life-threatening, and the doctors agreed to let me go.

Massimo drove me back to my home, while Luca said that he and the others would be coming by to catch up with me soon. Something I wasn't looking forward to. For the first time, I didn't want my brothers with me.

I appreciate that they're looking out for me, and while I'll always defend Elsa to them, the truth is, I need to understand the motivation behind her actions. Did she not believe I'd keep my word to her? Did she not trust me enough when I promised I would help her get full custody of her daughter? Is she... I pause halfway up the path to my home. Is she still in love with that *stronzo*, Fabio? Is that why she colluded with him?

Next to me, Massimo pauses. I refused to let him help me, but he insists on walking me to my door. Like I'm a fucking weakling. "You okay, *fratello*?" he murmurs.

"Why the hell wouldn't I be?"

"You don't have to hide your disappointment from me." He grips my shoulder. "I know you're a stubborn *bastardo*—hell, we all are. But to find out your wife has been colluding with someone else behind your back... It's got to hurt."

"You know nothing," I reply through gritted teeth.

"I know that you would have done anything for her. I know that you're in love with her."

I whip my head around in his direction. My shoulder protests, but I ignore it.

"You married her, didn't you? You may have fooled the others with your talk of doing it to honor your promise to Nonna. You may have even fooled yourself. But I've seen the way you look at her. I've noticed how you can't take your gaze off of her. You want to protect her and her child. It's natural. It's why you want her to move back in with you; so you can get to the bottom of what actually happened."

"That's no secret." I shake off his hand. "As for the rest... Yeah, it hurts, but she's my wife. I believe in her. My instincts couldn't have been completely wrong. There's a reason for what she did, and I'm going to find out what it is. She would not have knowingly harmed me."

"I agree."

I narrow my gaze on him. "You do?"

"We all do. We may have our differences of opinion, but one thing we all agree on is that family comes first. We'd do anything to protect what is ours, so on some level, we understand why she did what she did." He chuckles. "And that includes that *stronzo*, Luca."

"I may have made a mistake, giving up my title of Capo. Not because it's what I want, but now that Luca's Capo, he feels like he gets to make decisions for the rest of us. It's why he's doing his best to control what happens with Elsa. It's why he's so opposed to having Elsa stay with me."

"He's watching out for you." Massimo's lips quirk. "Sure, he has a pigheaded way of showing it, but underneath all that bluster, you know he's loyal to us."

"That may be the only thing he has going for him." I rub the back of my neck. "Still, I can't believe he insisted on Elsa moving back to her place, and then he put her under virtual house arrest."

"He did allow her to be with her daughter," Massimo points out. "And once he realized his mistake moved her back in to your home."

"It's the only reason I haven't taken a gun to the *coglione*'s head." I turn and begin to walk toward my front door.

"He was only watching out for you. You can't blame him for being careful."

"You, too?" I stiffen. "I thought you were in my corner."

"We're all in your corner," he says in a low voice, "but you have to admit, the fact that she wasn't shot, while everyone else on that patio was injured, is suspicious."

"I know how it looks, but I swear she isn't guilty of what happened," I retort.

"I believe you..." He shuffles his feet. "But I would be remiss if I didn't tell you to watch your back."

"She's my wife." I glare at him. "Do you understand that?"

"And wives have killed their husband's for less." He tilts his head. "I'm not saying she's responsible for what happened, but she admitted to colluding with her ex. Regardless of what you wish were the case, it doesn't exactly exonerate her from what happened."

"The fact that she admitted to it should show that she's ready to repent for what happened."

"And if you had died—?"

"I didn't," I point out.

"What if she admitted to being guilty to lull us into complacency?"

I scowl. "You're not going to stop until you hold her responsible for what happened, are you?"

"Not at all." He rolls his shoulders. "I want to believe her. If it turns out she really had no idea that *minchione*, Fabio, would come after you, then no one will be happier than me."

"But—"

"But," he blows out a breath, "it still doesn't negate the fact that she was in cahoots with her ex. I'm just not sure if she's as innocent as she claims to be, *fratello*."

"And I have no doubt that there's an honest explanation for everything." I set my lips.

"You're her husband. Of course you believe her." His lips kick up. "I wouldn't have expected anything less from you. All I am saying is, stay on guard."

The door to the house opens, and I turn toward it.

40

Elsa

I open the door and glance between the two men. Clearly, they'd been in the middle of an argument. No doubt, the argument had something to do with me, going by how both of them shut up and turn to me.

I take in Seb's drawn features. There are hollows under his cheekbones. His usual bright, golden eyes are mired in pain. He's wearing a shirt, which has been buttoned over his arm in a sling, and over that, a jacket with one sleeve hanging loose. He's wearing faded jeans that cling to his muscular thighs, and on his feet are worn boots. I've never seen Seb this casually dressed. Almost every other time I've seen him, he's worn a suit and a tie. Today, he's also unshaven. The scruff on his chin is, at least, a few days old. His hair is uncombed. I've never seen it this messy. The scar on his temple lends him an air of mystery.

Anger, and something else... Tension... Frustration, maybe? All of it vibrates off of him, so the air is thick with unspoken emotions. All in all, he looks like a dangerous criminal. Which is how he'd be viewed by some people, given what he does for a living. Somehow, I've never seen him that way, though. Right from the beginning, he's always been Seb. It doesn't matter that he's part of the *Cosa Nostra*, or that he's one of the Sovranos, that his reputation precedes him in this city... He's just someone I noticed and connected with. He and I may not have exactly hit it off in the beginning but I never could have ignored him. Not then;

not now. Not when he looked like a model about to walk a Milan runway, and not now, when he looks like he's going to star in the next instalment of *John Wick*.

He rakes his gaze across my features, down my chest, my waist, my legs, before he raises his head and meets my gaze again. A frown mars his forehead.

"You look terrible," he says flatly.

"Gee, thanks." I scowl back at him. "You don't look so hot, either," I lie.

Massimo glances between us. "Um, where should I put this?" He holds out a paper bag. "This has his medicines and prescriptions for more."

Both Seb and I reach for it, but I get to it first. "Thanks," I murmur as Seb's frown deepens.

"I can take care of myself," he grumbles.

"And I want to make sure that you do." I set my jaw.

We stare at each other, and his scowl intensifies even more. The skin around his eyes stretches. The silence extends for a beat, then another.

Massimo clears his throat. "Guess I'll be going then." He pats Seb on his unhurt shoulder and mutters, "*In bocca al lupo.*"

I've picked up enough Italian to know that it means good luck.

Neither of us reply as he spins around and walks back the way they came.

Our staring match continues, then, "Elsa." Seb lowers his voice to a hush.

A shiver runs down my back. My thighs clench. Bloody hell, he's using that Dom voice of his.

I step back and Seb walks in. As he brushes past me, that spicy, masculine scent of his fills my nostrils. My heart stutters and my pussy clenches. Goddamn. Even wounded and tired, he's a force to be reckoned with. He stalks forward and into the living room, then comes to a halt. His gaze is entranced by the child in the area I have cordoned off in a corner of the room. Avery sits there, surrounded by her toys.

"I hope you don't mind." I come to a halt next to him. "I needed to keep an eye on her while I work on some billing for the flower shop, so I thought I could move her to the living room and—"

"Stop," he says in a tight voice.

"I'm sorry. I guess I should have asked you. I didn't think you'd mind though, so—"

"Elsa," he warns me.

Out of the corner of my eyes, I see him clench his fist... The fist which belongs to the arm that isn't in a sling.

"I'll... I'll take her back into the nursery." I take a step forward and he grips my wrist.

"Stop, Elsa," he states. "Do you really think I'd be angry that you set up a play area for Avery in the living room?"

"I should have checked with you; I know it's your house and—"

"You're my wife, Elsa." He turns toward me. "I don't know what this *coglione* Fabio did to you, but have I ever given you reason to think that this house is not your own?"

I bite the inside of my cheek.

"Have I?" He glares at me. "Tell me, Elsa."

I shake my head.

"So why are you acting like I'll disapprove of what you did?"

"Because," I take a deep breath before I continue, "it's my fault you were shot, Seb. It's my fault those men, whose job it was to protect us, are still in the hospital. It's my fault I didn't trust you enough to tell you I was still trying to negotiate with Fabio, that he wanted me to spy on you and your brothers and pass him information of what you all were up to. I should have told you Seb." I swallow. "I'm so sorry I didn't."

"Elsa, I—" He shakes his head. "You should've trusted me."

"I… do," I insist.

"But you didn't earlier."

"I thought I did, Seb. I was going to tell you about what he'd asked me to do."

"But you didn't." He peers into my face. "You said you loved me."

"I… I did… I mean, I *do*."

"I'm not so sure. If you did, you'd have come clean to me."

"I should have. It's just…" I glance toward Avery. "I leave her with Fabio during the week. What do you think he'd have done if I'd told you, and somehow, he found out? What do you think he would have done to her and to me? He'd have never allowed me to see her again."

"I would have ensured that never happened."

"You don't know him." I tighten my hold on the paper bag.

"No, you don't know me," he growls. "You don't know what I'm capable of. You asked me not to kill him, and I won't. But after what he did, my brothers and I will make sure he loses everything. This much, I promise you."

"He's dangerous, Seb, you saw what he did already."

"No, what you're not realizing is that I am far more of a threat than he is. He dared to open fire when you were with me. He could have hit you."

"He hurt you." I turn to him. "He injured you."

"He could have killed you," we both say at the same time.

"Seb," I swallow, "if something had happened to you—" I shake my head. "I never would have been able to live with myself."

"I'm not going to die that easily." His voice hardens, "Fabio has fucked with the wrong people." His tone is that of a person who has come to a decision. I look into his eyes and I see the anger, the coldness in them. Cold fire. He's Keanu on a mission to get revenge. No wonder I thought of him as John Wick when I first saw him.

"What are you going to do?"

"Show him that he can't touch what's mine anymore."

"What do you mean?"

"You are not going to drop off Avery with him anymore."

I stiffen. "It's a court order. If I go against it, he'll make sure I lose all rights to her."

"I'd like to see him try." Seb firms his lips. "You and Avery are not going anywhere near him."

"But—"

Seb holds up his hand. "You said that you trust me. Do you mean it this time?"

"I…" I gaze into his eyes. *Do I trust him? Do I really trust him?* "Seb, please don't ask me to do this."

"So, you don't trust me?"

"That's not what I mean."

"You trusted me enough to put your body in my hands when you asked me to be your Dom," he points out.

"It's just, this is about my child, Seb… Please…" *How can I make him understand?*

"Either you do or you don't trust me, Elsa." He draws himself up to his full height. "Which one is it?"

"I…" I shake my head as tears spring to my eyes. "I'm not sure."

41

Seb

She still doesn't trust me. Oh, she trusts me with her body; just not with her child. What does that say about me? Am I wrong in asking her to trust me so quickly? And if she didn't trust me, why did she marry me? Our entire union is based on the fact that she trusted me to find a way for her to get full custody of her daughter. Did she ever mean it? Did she get married to me simply because she wanted to stay close to me, because she wanted to feed information to her ex? Is that all our relationship means to her?

Avery stands up and begins to walk toward us. She holds out a toy and warbles.

Elsa is instantly beside her. She lifts up the toddler and holds her close. "Hey, baby, what've you got there, sweetheart?"

She says something in her baby speak and Elsa laughs. "I know, that's your favorite bunny, huh?"

She kisses the child, and my chest heats. She rubs noses with the toddler, who giggles, then squeals when Elsa blows a raspberry on her tummy. The bunny slips out of the toddler's hands and falls to the floor. I close the distance between us, pick up the bunny, which is frayed at the ears and hand it back to her.

Avery accepts it, and her blue gaze falls on my face. She stares, unblinking, then reaches for me. I glance at Elsa, who asks, "You sure you'll be able to carry her? Your arm is in a sling."

When I don't reply, she waits for a beat longer, then hands the child over to me. I carry her with my free arm as she continues to stare at me with her big blue eyes. So innocent, so clear. My heart stutters in my chest. Our staring match continues, then she smiles. A big smile that lights up her features and makes her seem even more like her mother. The band around my chest tightens. She grins, showing her tiny baby teeth, then offers me her doll.

"You keep it, sweetheart," I chuckle, "it's all yours."

Avery frowns, then thrusts the ragged doll in my face again.

I huff, then peek around the doll and waggle my eyebrows at the little girl, who laughs. She warbles again.

"She wants you to have her doll," Elsa says in a surprised voice. "It's her favorite toy." She shakes her head.

I glance at her, and she holds my gaze.

"I'm sorry about what I said earlier, Seb. It's just, when it comes to Avery, I'm constantly second-guessing myself when it comes to what's best for her."

"You can share your thoughts with me; it's why I'm here. I can help lighten the load... if you'll let me."

Her forehead furrows. She bites down on her lower lip, and my gaze drops there. I want to reach over and release the plump flesh from between her teeth, but my hand is in a sling, goddamnit. I glance around, then walk over to the settee and drop into it, then balance Avery in my lap. The toddler wriggles around and settles herself, then reaches up and pokes her finger into my cheek. She warbles again, and I bounce her a little.

Elsa walks over to sit down next to me. She reaches out and circles Avery's wrist with her fingers. "Hey, Bubu, whatcha doin'? You like Seb, huh?"

Avery turns her big blue eyes back on me. She stares at me with solemn intent, then blows a spit bubble. I laugh, then can't stop myself from kissing her cheek. The fresh scent of her baby's skin, combined with the faint cherry scent I've come to associate with Elsa, fills my lungs. A fierce protectiveness grips me and I lean back.

Avery glances up at me, then pats my cheek, before digging her fingernails in.

"Avery, don't hurt Sebastian."

"She's not." I smile down at the child, who presses her tiny palm into my cheek. I turn my face and kiss her little fingers, and she laughs at me.

A tiredness washes over me, and I lean back into the settee, and with my arm around Avery, balancing her on my chest. She bounces a little, then smacks my forehead.

"Avery," Elsa scolds her.

"She's fine," I laugh a little as the toddler warbles again, then thrusts her bunny in my face.

"I think she wants you to kiss her toy." Elsa smiles at her daughter.

"Is that right, hmm?" I lean forward and kiss the bunny, and Avery laughs again. She bounces on my chest, then blinks a little, before she turns to Elsa.

"You hungry, Bubu, or thirsty maybe? Want some water?" Elsa coos.

Avery blinks at Elsa, who rises and walks into the other room, returning almost immediately with a sippy cup. She sits down next to me and holds it up to Avery, who sips from it. Some of the water drops onto my shirt.

"Oh, sorry." Elsa tries to brush off the water that's dripped onto my skin in the opening between the lapels of my shirt. The touch of her fingers on my chest sends a trail of goosebumps down my spine. The blood drains to my cock, and goddamn it, this is wrong, isn't it? I'm holding her child, and I'm also turned on.

As if she senses the impact of her touch, she flickers her gaze up to my face. Whatever she sees there makes her breath catch. Her throat moves as she swallows. The tension in the air ratchets up. She flicks out her tongue to touch her lower lip, and a groan rumbles up my chest. This is wrong, so wrong.

"I think you need to take her." I lean over to bring Avery close to her. She places the sippy cup on the side table, then takes Avery from me. Her fingers brush my chest, and my cock perks up. *Cazzo*, how the hell can I go from caring for her daughter to being turned on by her in such a short period of time? How can I ask her to trust me, when even as I'm holding her daughter, all I can think about is also holding her mother in my arms.

I rise to my feet and put distance between us, as she holds the sippy cup up to Avery's lips. Avery takes a few more sips, then turns her head in my direction again.

I watch as Elsa places the cup on the table, and rises to her feet with the toddler in her arms. The sippy cup overbalances and hits the floor; some of the water spills out.

"Oh, god, I'm so sorry," Elsa gasps as she stops halfway to the play area.

"Stop apologizing, for fu— please." I stalk over to the settee, snatch up the sippy cup and place it on the side table, then pull out a few tissues from the tissue box placed there, and mop up the water. I walk into the kitchen and deposit the used tissues in the wastepaper basket. By the time I re-enter the living room, she's placed Avery in the play area, and the little girl is playing with building blocks… Or rather, crashing the blocks into each other.

Elsa rises to her feet and glances at me. "I'm sorry we're messing up your space," she murmurs.

"Didn't I tell you to stop saying sorry?" I say through gritted teeth.

"I thought it would be a good idea to be back here when you returned from the hospital, but now, I'm not so sure."

"Because some water spilled on the floor?" I scowl at her. "You have a child Elsa, these things happen."

"It's just..." She wrings her fingers together and sighs. "I got so used to apologizing for every noise, every mess. Really, anytime Avery's presence became noticeable in any way. I never knew when he was going to blow up. And now..."

I growl and she looks up at me. "I'm just really confused about what to do, Seb."

"What do your instincts say?"

"I... I'm not sure." She shakes her head. "When Axel and Theresa went to pick up Avery from Fabio, I was so sure he wasn't going to hand her over. Each time I return her to him, after the weekend is over, it's like I lose a piece of myself. Every time, I'm scared senseless that this is the time he'll decide he's not going to let me pick her up again. Every single time, I worry that this is the last time I'm going to see her. It's killing me, Seb."

I close the distance between us. "This is how he continues to abuse you, Elsa. And I'm giving you a way out. I told you, I'll make sure that *tes*— man will never get close to your daughter again."

"I know." She shuffles her feet. "But how will you do it? Will you bribe the courts? Is that what you're thinking?"

"Why don't you leave that to me?" I take in her pinched features. "I'm part of the *Cosa Nostra*; my family has owned this town for decades. I admit, the fact that Fabio is the police commissioner means things could get messy, but I'm not going to shy away from it."

"He already tried to kill you, Seb, and that's my fault. It's not something I'll ever forgive myself for. If something happens to you again... I'll... I'm not sure if I can take it."

"I survived, didn't I?" I nod toward my sling. "I'm a little battered, but I'm fine. I'm not going to be that easy to get rid of. Also, when it comes to choosing between my life and the future of your daughter, I know what's more important."

"Seb," she tilts up her chin, "you're both important to me."

"And you are more than important to me. You're my heart, Princess, and nobody comes between my heart and me."

"Do you mean it?"

"Of course I do."

"So, you'll do anything I ask?" A strange look comes into her eyes.

The hair on the nape of my neck rises. What is she up to? Whatever it is, I'm not going to be happy about it. I hesitate.

"You said I could trust you, Seb," she reminds me.

Am I going to regret the words? Am I going to regret asking her to do so?

"Elsa," I warn, but she shakes her head.

"You said I could trust you. Surely, you can return the favor?"

I blow out a breath. "Fine," I say, knowing I'm going to regret it. And it's not that I don't trust her. It's just... I'll do anything to take care of her, and knowing how much she loves Avery, and how she'll do anything to protect her daughter... Somehow, I know she's planning to do something that's going to make it very difficult for me to keep her safe.

"Okay." She blows out a breath.

"Okay," I nod, "what do you want from me?"

"I want to meet Fabio."

42

Elsa

"No! Absolutely not. You want to meet the man who tried to kill me? Who might very well have shot you, too? And what would have happened if he succeeded, Elsa? What would have happened to our daughter? Have you even thought of that?"

I wince. The blood rushes from my face, and I know I've gone pale. Truthfully, I hadn't thought of that possibility. Not that Fabio didn't beat me when we were together, but the thought of him killing me... Somehow, it didn't occur to me. It's why I'd thrown myself on top of Seb when that drone had started firing, sensing that it wouldn't hurt me. I could have been wrong, but instinct had told me that he'd spare me. Oh, I don't doubt he wouldn't care if he'd shot and wounded me. Sure, I'd known that was a possibility, but would he have tried to kill me?

Well, who knows. Fabio is unpredictable. All he cares about is having control over me. It's why he came up with this arrangement, where I only get to see Avery on weekends. He's trying to throw me just enough crumbs to keep me hankering for more, while also being grateful that I actually get to spend some time with her, when really, I'm her mother, and she should be staying with me all the time. She's a toddler, almost two years old, and she needs me. And I'm going to make sure I no longer have to drop her back with Fabio when the weekend is over. But I'm going to do this my way.

I'm her mother, goddamn it, and I can do what's needed to take care of my child, can't I?

And he's your husband. He wants to help you. But if I involve him, he may get hurt again, and that, I can't bear. He told me he loved me and I believe him. And I... I love him. It's why I need to confront Fabio, once and for all. I can't let him or anyone else be a casualty in this fight between Fabio and me.

"I..." I swallow. "I don't think Fabio's going to kill me."

"You don't *think* he's going to kill you?" He peers into my features. "You think he's still in love with you, so he won't hurt you?"

"Oh, he's hurt me plenty already." I touch the scar on my wrist, and his gaze intensifies. "Besides, I don't think he actually knows what love means, anyway. But if he kills me, he'll lose his hold on me, and that's not his pattern."

"He sent you to get information from me, so why would he shoot at me?" He scowls.

"Maybe," I glance away, "because he found out that you married me?"

"And how would that have happened? The only people at the wedding were my brothers, their wives, and the mayor, who knows better than to talk about it to anyone else." He rubs his jaw, then adds, "And then, someone shot at us at the restaurant afterward."

"When that failed, he came after you again."

"And failed again." He looks around the room, as if the answer is somehow hidden there. Then he sighs. "It makes no sense. He could have killed me there, and he didn't."

"It's why I threw myself over you. I was banking on Fabio not wanting to kill me. Besides, I think he wanted to send me a warning." I twist my fingers together. "Already, too many people have been hurt, Seb. Can't you see? I need to confront him; it's the only way to stop this."

"Absolutely not." He crosses his arms in front of his chest. "There's no way I'm letting you go to him."

"I will not have the blood of more people on my hands," I argue. "If any of the bodyguards had died, I would have never been able to forgive myself. It's a miracle they survived. I'm afraid next time we won't be so lucky."

"There will not be a next time, because I'm going to make sure that asshole never comes near you or any of our family again."

"The only way to put an end to this peacefully is if I speak to him," I insist.

"And what will you say to him? Do you think if you ask him nicely, he's going to back off and leave you alone?"

I bite the inside of my cheek. "I can try. All this time, I've been afraid of him, and maybe that's the mistake I made. I gave him power over me. You know, many times when a bully's confronted, he backs down. If I stand up to him, it's possible he'll leave us alone."

"Surely, you know better than that. It's more likely he'll respond violently, thinking if he can't have you, no one can. That's what abusers do, Elsa." He drags his fingers through his hair. "Goddamn it, I'm not letting you meet him, and that's that."

"But, Seb—"

"No, you will not see him, and my decision is final."

"But—"

He slashes his palm through the air. "I don't want to hear another thing about it."

He pivots and walks toward the staircase.

A few hours later, after I've put Avery down for her afternoon nap, I walk into the kitchen and find Cass.

"Hey..." I pause halfway across the floor. "I didn't hear you come in."

"I wanted to come by and make sure you guys don't starve." She turns to me.

"We do have a housekeeper to cook for us, you know," I murmur.

"Oh, pfft." She waves her hand in the air. "I wanted to see you. Besides, my *Pasta alla Norma* is just what you need."

My stomach rumbles as she mentions it, and I walk over to her and hug her. "Thank you," I whisper, "you shouldn't have, but I'm glad you did."

She hugs me, then pulls back to look at my face. "Everything okay?"

Tears prick at the backs of my eyes at her concern, and once again, I blink them away. "I'm not sure," I reply honestly.

"Why don't I make you a plate, and you can tell me as you eat?"

"What about Seb?"

"I already took a tray up to him."

"Oh." I glance away.

"You guys have a fight or something?" she guesses.

"Kind of..." I shuffle my feet. "It was more like, I suggested something, and Seb dismissed my idea and told me he doesn't want to hear about it again."

"Do you want to tell me about it?" She retrieves the plate of food from the warmer and sets it down on the breakfast nook counter. I clamber onto a stool, and place the baby monitor next to me on the counter. She slides the cutlery over to me, and I pick up a fork and dig into the pasta dish.

"This is good." I work my way through half of the contents of my plate before I finally glance up. "Really good." I lick my lips.

"Thanks, I'm glad you're enjoying it." She pours me a glass of water, then slides onto the stool beside me, props her elbow on the counter, and leans her chin on her hand. "So, tell me everything."

I proceed to tell her about my earlier conversation with Seb. By the time I wipe my plate clean and sit back, she's looking at me with concern in her gaze.

"I can understand why he was upset. It seems to me you'd be taking an unnecessary risk by meeting with Fabio."

"I need to confront him. It's the only way he'll stop trying to ruin my life. All of these years, I've been afraid of him. It's why he's always managed to ride rough-shod over me."

"So, what changed now? Why do you feel as if you can confront him now?"

"He shot at Seb; he hurt Seb." I grip the side of the counter. "Fabio hates Seb. He won't stop until he's taken Seb out, and I can't let that happen. I will not see him get hurt again, Cass." I reach for the glass of water and sip from it.

"Firstly, Seb can take care of himself—"

"Like he did when the drone shot at him?"

Cass purses her lips. "That was an aberration. Likely, he was taken by surprise. Doesn't mean it will happen again."

"I can't take that risk." I fold my arms about my waist. "You don't know how scary it was when that bullet hit him and he started bleeding. He passed out, and I was sure I was going to lose him. I can't let that happen, Cass." My guts churn, bile rushes up my throat, and I swallow it down. "He's my chance at happiness. He's the man who should have been Avery's father. It's my fault he got hurt, and I can't risk that happening again. This is the only way, Cass. It's time I shook free of Fabio's hold on my life and Avery's future, once and for all. " I shake my head, unable to continue.

I slide off of the stool, take my plate, and head for the sink. I rinse it off and place it in the dishwasher.

"Either way, Seb is right about one thing. I can't take Avery back to Fabio."

"That, I understand," Cass finishes wiping the counter then turns to me. "I don't agree with your going to confront Fabio but," she draws in a breath, "but I was a mother once. I know what it feels like to want to protect your child against the world. Whatever you are thinking of doing, I know it's because you think that's the best way to protect your daughter."

I scan her features. "You said you were a mother, once...?" I don't want to probe, but Cass raised the topic, so I assume it's okay to ask.

She turns to straighten the cutlery drying on the board near the sink. "I lost him when he was a year old. It took me a long time to get over it." She glances away, then back at me. "I haven't told anyone else," she murmurs.

"And I won't breathe a word of it, either," I close the distance between us and take her hands in mine, "I am so sorry for your loss."

One side of her lips twists. "I hated the universe for taking Ray from me. Then... I realized I should be happy that I had, at least, that much time with him. He was a gorgeous little baby; never cried, never troubled me at night. And when he smiled, it was as if the sun had poured its radiance over me. He was too good for this world, I guess." A tear runs down her cheek. "The stories we tell ourselves, eh?" She wipes her cheek on her shoulder. "So you see, I understand why what you're planning to do may seem crazy, but why it also makes sense to me."

"Thanks, Cass." I squeeze her hands. "So, you'll help me?"

43

Seb

I come awake with a start. It's dark in the room, and I blink, disoriented. I know I'm back in my room, and I remember eating the lunch Cass brought me. Later, she came by to clear my tray, and I fell asleep after that. I must have slept clear through the afternoon, for the light has faded outside. I reach for my lamp and flip it on, then check the time on my phone.

It's seven p.m. Damn. I must have been more tired than I realized. I sit up, and while there's a dull throb in my shoulder, it's not as painful as it was this morning. I ease my arm out of my sling and stretch it out. Pain shivers up my arm and I wince.

"Are you supposed to do that?"

I glance up to find Elsa hovering by the door. In one arm, she has Avery. In the other, she holds a familiar paper bag filled with my medicines. She walks over and places the paper bag on the table near the bed.

Avery fusses and reaches for me.

"No, baby. Seb's still recovering from being hurt."

"I'm fine." I hold out the arm attached to my unhurt shoulder. "The sling is just a precaution, to keep me from moving my arm around. It helps it heal faster."

"Eb," Avery warbles. "Eb."

"Did she say my name?" I stare at the little girl, who smiles back at me, showing the gaps between her teeth.

Elsa looks at me, an expression of surprise on her features. "I guess she likes you."

"Me and Avery... We understand each other, don't we, sweetheart?"

Avery all but jumps out of Elsa's grasp. I rise to my feet and take her in my arm. She stares at me, then bumps her fist into my cheek.

"Or maybe, she thinks I'm a punching bag, of sorts." I chuckle.

She flattens her other palm against my mouth then warbles something.

"What's she saying?"

"I have no idea." Elsa shakes her head. "This girl talks to anyone and anything. If she thought she'd get a response, I swear she'd talk to the furniture."

"You're fu— I mean, very clever, aren't you, doll?" I pretend to bite her finger and she bursts out laughing again. "You're such a smarty-pants, aren't you? So clever; such a performer. Love attention, don't you, Bubu?" I realize I've called her by the same pet name Elsa used earlier.

Avery bumps her head against my chin. "Seb." This time, it's unmistakable she's saying my name. A flurry of emotions coil in my chest.

I lift her shirt and plant a raspberry on her tummy. She screams with pleasure, then laughs again. I glance up to find Elsa watching the two of us with a strange look on her face.

"What?" I growl.

"It's just," she shakes her head, "you're really good with her."

"Why do you sound so surprised?"

She pulls out a bottle of pills, then shakes off two and offers them to me, along with a glass of water.

I glance down at Avery and at my other hand, which, I hate to admit, is already growing tired since I slid it out from the sling.

"Here," she urges me.

I open my mouth, and she drops the pills onto my tongue. Her fingertips brush my lips, and a shiver runs down my spine. My belly hardens and my cock twitches. Her chest rises and falls, and she avoids my gaze as she raises the glass of water to my lips. I sip from it, without taking my gaze off of her.

Avery chooses that moment to slap her hand down on the glass. Water splashes on my shirt and on her.

"Sorry, sorry. Oh, Avery, look what you did?" Elsa frowns at the toddler, who glances between us. Her face crumples, and she takes in a deep breath.

"Hey, hey, it's okay, Bubu; it's fine. No harm done. It's water; it will dry, right?" I walk away as I jiggle her and try to distract her. She glances at me, her features frozen as she eyes me, then her face crumples again.

"Aww, come on, baby, don't cry." I begin to pace as I move her up and down in my grasp. Goddamn arm, if it were functional, I could use it to distract her.

She blinks, a teardrop balanced at the edge of her delicate eyelashes. She opens her mouth, but before she can make a sound, I whistle. She blinks again, and watches me, entranced. I whistle under my breath, then vary the tone, and she slowly shuts her mouth. I whistle once more. This time, she lands her fist in my mouth.

"A-n-d, normal service is resumed." I snicker. "Crisis averted. For now, at least."

An hour later, Elsa has given Avery a bath—which Avery insisted I watch. She refused to let go of my sleeve, so I had to accompany them to the small room connecting to the guest bedroom Elsa had occupied—and read a bedtime story to her, during which time, she insisted on holding onto my finger as she finally fell asleep. After that, we stand next to her crib and gaze down at the sleeping child.

"Wow," I breathe as a wave of tiredness washes over me, "she's really something."

"She never stops," Elsa agrees. "You caught her as she was winding down."

"That's her winding down?" I wince.

"You should see her in the mornings. She springs up, ready to face the day, and doesn't stop until I put her down for her afternoon nap, at which time, she often refuses to sleep." Elsa shakes her head. "At this age, they're still learning how to sleep, you know?" she says softly. Then she bends and kisses Avery on her forehead before she straightens and catches me watching her.

"Do you want to kiss her goodnight?"

"Me?" I catch myself gaping, and promptly shut my mouth.

"Yes, you." Elsa smiles a little. "You earned it."

I lower myself and bring my face close to the sleeping child's. Her features are flushed, her lips slightly parted. Her chest rises and falls quickly. I push aside the strand of hair over her forehead, then bend and kiss her cheek.

"Goodnight, Bubu," I whisper.

I straighten and my gaze connects with Elsa's. Once more, awareness hums between us. We've always had that connection, the chemistry that thrummed between us from the moment we met... but this... This is different. A shared experience, of taking care of Avery this evening, unites us. It changes the flavor of our interaction, deepens it, adds an edge to it. Laces it with tenderness, weaves it with an awareness that's both soft and potent, both erotic and intense, innocent and yet, so deep. It strengthens what already existed between us, helps me understand her more completely—as a woman, a mother, a nurturer, and someone who deserves every pleasure I can give her. And more.

Avery murmurs something, and we both shift our gazes to her face. She turns over on her side, but continues sleeping. When she doesn't move for a few more minutes, the breath I hadn't been aware I was holding slides out. Tension drains from my shoulders. Goddamn, and all this because I was worried we might have woken her up?

Elsa puts a finger to her lips, then jerks her head toward the doorway. She picks up the baby monitor and sidles toward the door. I follow her, when she pauses and turns to me. "Watch out for the—"

I step on a floorboard that creaks.

"—floorboard," she completes her statement.

I freeze, glance over my shoulder... to find Avery is still asleep. Whew! I turn to Elsa, who seems as relieved as me. She beckons to me, switching off the overhead light as I follow her out of the room, this time, without incident.

The nightlight illuminates the space as she closes the door, leaving it a little ajar. I follow her into her bedroom, and the breath I am not aware of holding rushes out.

"Is it always like that?" I whisper.

"Like what?"

"Like a major incident has been averted every time you put her to bed?"

She chuckles. "Once she's asleep, she wouldn't wake up if a freight train passed through her room. It's just those few minutes before she tips over into deep sleep that you have to be careful of."

"Right." I peer down into her face. "You are an amazing mother, Elsa."

She flushes. "So you keep saying."

"Only because every time I watch you with her, I can see how much she means to you, how much you'd give up to be with her."

"When I first gave birth to her, I was depressed. No one tells you how hard it is to take care of a child. Nothing prepares you for how the child takes over your life completely. And my ex, let's just say, he wasn't very understanding." She swallows. "He told me it was my problem, and I had to handle it on my own."

"That *figlio di puttana*." Anger flushes my skin. No wonder she's so nervous every time Avery does something wrong. She's afraid I'll yell at her, or worse. I clench my fists by my sides, and by god, if I had any doubts about what I was going to do to that *pezzo di merda*, *after* what she's just told me, it has convinced me not to hold back.

She glances past me, through the crack in the door, to make sure Avery's asleep. Then, she turns and walks over to the window and glances out.

"Those months were rough. My mother helped me with Avery, but it wasn't enough. I felt so trapped, like it was the end of my life, my identity. The fact that I could no longer move around freely, or pursue my career as a pianist... I couldn't see any help in sight. I knew what I needed to do was see a Dom. Someone in whom I could put my trust and hand over control, at least for a little time. When it felt like everything in my life was going to shit, I felt like I needed that little window of space when I could just forget about my responsibilities. It's why, at the first chance I got, I slipped off to that underground club. It's because I couldn't stop thinking of myself. Because I was so selfish, I didn't realize how my one move could hurt Avery and put us in this situation."

Her grip around the baby monitor tightens.

"Princess," I wrap my fingers around the nape of her neck, "you didn't do anything wrong. You were trying to be both a mother and a woman, and that's understandable."

"No, I made a mistake, I—"

"Listen to me." I squeeze my fingers, and her breath hitches. I apply enough pressure so she has to turn her head to face me. "You made only one mistake."

Her color fades. "I did?"

I nod. "You allowed someone else to touch you before I met you. You married someone else before I could put a ring on your finger. You searched for some other man to become your Dom, when you should have waited for me."

44

Elsa

"Did you... did you just say what I think you did?" I stare at him.

"I never say something unless I mean it." His thumb presses down on the pulse that beats at the hollow of my throat.

"I... " I try to form the words, but it's like my brain cells have all fused together. How can he be so presumptuous? How can he assume that I should've saved myself for him? How can he say I should've waited for him to become my Dom? How can he... expect that I wouldn't have married anyone else and waited for him to come along? And yet, the fact that he thinks this, and with such authority, only reinforces his power over me. His possessiveness, the way he clasped—is still clasping—his fingers around the nape of my neck like he owns me, only adds more intensity to his words.

"Seb," I swallow, "sometimes I don't know what to make of you. You barge into my life, turn it upside down and then you... you..."

"Tell you the truth."

I glance away. That's the issue here. The fact that I can't disagree with him. That every part of me wishes I had waited for him. That I had heeded my mother's words and not rushed to marry Fabio... But he'd swept me off my feet, and when he'd asked me to marry him, I got carried away. Then I got pregnant with

Avery. *And if I hadn't met him, I wouldn't have Avery. And I wouldn't have moved to Palermo and met Seb, either.*

"Admit it, Princess." He applies just enough pressure on the nape of my neck that I raise my gaze to his. "Tell me I'm right." His golden-brown eyes flare with that intensity I'm coming to associate with him. It's like he's gathered all of the emotions he holds inside of himself, twisted them into a knot, and lodged it behind his eyes. And now, I can see it, sense it... smell the frustration that coats his features. "Do you know how many times I've wanted to kill that motherfucker for putting his hands on you? Every time I think about him holding you, touching you... Kissing you." His gaze drops to my mouth and stays there. "I want to fuck you and keep fucking you, until the only thing you can see, hear, taste, touch, smell is me... Only me."

My breath hitches.

"I don't want to stop until you're mine."

"But I am yours," I whisper. "Since the first time I set eyes on you, there has been no one else but you."

"And yet, you didn't trust me to take care of your daughter?"

"I..." I bite the inside of my cheek. "I'm sorry."

"Do you know what I would give for that little girl in there to be mine?"

"She is... She is yours," I say in a low voice.

"I don't think I heard you," he says in a hard voice.

"She is yours, Seb. So am I." I tip up my chin. "I made some bad decisions. I made choices I'm not proud of, but if I hadn't, I wouldn't have Avery, and because of that, I can't regret everything. I'd give anything for her to be yours by blood, but spiritually, it's clear you're connected."

His jaw tics.

"She's never taken to anyone as quickly as she's taken to you, Seb. She's never asked for anyone else—not even her blood father—to stay with her as I bathe her and read to her and put her to bed. She asked for you, Seb. She asked. For you."

He peers into my eyes and a multitude of emotions seem to pass over his features. Then he drags me forward. I fall against him and he grunts.

"Sorry," I exclaim, "I totally forgot that you're wounded."

"The real wounds are the ones you inflicted on my heart when you didn't trust me enough to tell me that you were colluding with him."

"I'm sorry, Seb," I whisper, "so sorry for having hurt you." *And if I have to do it again to make sure you're safe, then I will.*

"What are you thinking?" He glances between my eyes. "What's going on in that mind of yours, Elsa?"

Damn, but he knows me so well, and in such a short period of time. Maybe I shouldn't go ahead with my plan; maybe I should tell him what I'm planning to do. I open my mouth, but what comes out is, "...that Avery's asleep, and if she does wake up, I have this—" I raise my hand and show him the baby monitor receiver. "So—"

"So…?

"So, I think we should move to your room, and make sure you get settled, so you can rest up, considering you're still recovering from your injury."

"Is that all you were thinking about?"

I swallow.

"Tell me, Princess."

"Y-yes," I stutter.

He bends his knees so he's at eye level with me. "Liar." His lips pull up in a smirk. "But I'll let you get away with it… this time."

He releases me, then straightens and walks toward the door of my bedroom. I follow him down the corridor and to the next bedroom at the far end. He pushes the door open, walks in, then heads for his bed. He turns to glance at me over his shoulder and asks, "Coming?"

I follow him as he walks over to sit down on the bed. He toes off his shoes, then stretches out on the mattress.

Some of the tension seems to leave his big body, and he watches me from under his eyelashes as I walk around to the other side of the bed. I place the baby monitor on the nightstand, then stretch out next to him, over the covers.

For a few seconds, we lay there. Then he reaches into the pocket of his jeans and hands me something. "Here."

I glance over to find my phone in his hand.

"You're returning my phone to me?"

"I trust you," he says simply, and my heart nearly shatters. Jesus, is it possible for this man to break me further? He said he'd wear me down by being my Dom, but it's his words, his gestures, the way he looks at me like he wants to scold me one second, and the next second fuck me… It's his heart that's winning me over, and he's not even aware of it. I thought an alpha male was someone who holds power over you, who can make you shiver with a look, a touch, a single tilt of his lips… And Seb has all that and more. And yet, it's his empathy that slays me every time. He seems to understand what I need to hear from him. He knows what I need without my having to spell it out for him. He understands Avery like he's her blood father, better than her blood father, and all I've given him in return is a bullet to his shoulder.

I reach for the phone and place it on the side table, then lower my legs to the ground. I walk around to stand on his side of the bed so he has an unfettered view of me. Then I grip the hem of my sweater and pull it off. His breath catches, and I raise my gaze to find him watching as I reach down, lower the zipper of my jeans, and push them off, along with my sneakers and my socks. Clad only in my panties and bra, I straighten.

He rakes his gaze down my face, my breasts, my hips, my thighs, down to my toes. By the time he's raised his gaze back to mine, my breathing has grown shallow. My skin feels too tight for my body and my scalp tingles. I reach behind me, unhook my bra, and let it drop to the floor. My nipples instantly peak. Every pore in my body seems to have opened, and is ready and open and willing to be filled by him. He's controlling me and he doesn't even have to say a word. I slide my fingers into the waistband of my panties and push them down my legs without breaking the connection of our eyes.

I straighten, and he takes another leisurely visual tour of my body. He circles his finger. A flush blooms on my face and creeps down my body as I turn slowly, then stop to face him, with my hand on my hip.

"What do you want, Princess?"

"I want to see you naked."

45

Seb

She's killing me. The way she undressed with such confidence, while the flush on her features, and the way her hands trembled as she pushed those pale pink panties down her legs, hinted at her nervousness. She didn't pause though; she went through with it, and now, she stands in front of me—naked, gorgeous, beautiful. And did I mention? Not a stitch of clothing on her. Nothing except the ring I gave her.

The blood drains to my groin. My shoulder throbs, reminding me I'm not in peak condition to do everything I want to her. Not to mention, I still have my arm in this goddamn sling.

"You want to see me naked? Why don't you undress me yourself?" I drawl.

Her throat moves as she swallows. She takes one step forward, then another. She reaches the bed and places one knee on the mattress. She swings her other leg over my waist and pauses, kneeling over me. Then she bends and begins to undo the first button on my shirt. Her fingers brush my chest as she unbuttons the next one, and the third. She doesn't stop until she's reached the end, then swallows.

She takes in the skin bared to her gaze, and the blood drains from her face. She traces the lines of the letters that run down the bifurcation of my pecs, and reads the letters that spell out:

. . .

Fortis Fortuna Adiuvat

Her chin wobbles. "What's this?"

"It's Latin for *Fortune Favors the Bold*," I reply.

"I know what it stands for. The question is, why do you have *this* tattoo?" she bursts out.

"I had it done when I was fourteen."

"Fourteen?" She blinks rapidly. "You were barely a teenager."

"It's when Michael left us and moved to the US to study. That's when our father unleashed the full impact of his wrath on us. I was the oldest amongst the brothers left behind. Of course, I wasn't his legitimate son." My lips twist. "I was one of his bastard sons, and he'd taken me in with Adrian. Not that it mattered when it came to his beatings. He beat me and Luca, the second oldest of his legitimate sons, equally. You'd think that'd forge a certain level of kinship among us, but it turns out, it only shamed us so much we'd never speak of it afterward. If anything, we went out of our way to avoid each other after each of the beatings. It was what made me realize that I didn't want to ever become my father. It's when I knew I needed to find a life beyond the *Cosa Nostra*. It was during this time that I got the tattoo. Not long after, Michael returned to visit from the US—probably because our grandmother finally told him what was happening—and he moved all of us to LA. Our father didn't protest. God only knows why. In fact, he agreed to pay for the education of all of us."

"Did getting the tattoo help?"

"It's a reminder to be courageous. To never give up." I tilt my head. "Now your turn."

"What do you mean?" Goosebumps dot her skin. She turns her head away.

I click my tongue. "Look at me, Elsa."

She hesitates.

"Now," I lower my voice to a hush and her shoulders shake, but she turns to meet my gaze.

"Why did the sight of my tattoo elicit that reaction from you?" I ask.

"You don't know?" She half-laughs, then drags her fingers through her hair. Of course, the action results in her breasts being pushed out, and of course, my eyes drop to her chest. In response, she plays with her breasts, drags her fingers across those dusky areolae of hers, then down toward her pussy. My cock jerks in response. A part of me knows what she's doing. She's distracting me. The same thing she did before I was shot by the drone. She's trying to divert my attention;

and succeeding, for I can't stop my gaze from following her movements. She plays with her pussy lips, and *Cazzo*, my dick almost pokes a hole in the crotch of my boxers. She slides a finger inside her sopping wet channel and my breath catches. It fucking catches. Heat suffuses my skin, and my fingertips tingle to reach out and push away her fingers, and replace it with my own. Followed by my tongue. And then my shaft, with which I'm going to impale her and...

Fucking hell, stop this right now. I tear my gaze away from her juicy core and up to her face. "Nice try, but it won't work," I growl.

"What do you mean?" She holds out her glistening fingers, and *Gesù Cristo...* Clearly, He hates me, which is why He's forcing me to watch this vixen tempt me, knowing I must not give in. Must not give in.

"Princess," I warn.

Her hand wavers, then she flips her hair over her shoulder. "You don't want to taste me? Fine." She brings her fingers to her mouth and sucks on them.

"*Cazzo.*" I grit my teeth. "You will tell me, right now, why my tattoo disturbed you."

"It didn't disturb me," she protests.

"Don't lie. You looked like you'd seen a ghost."

"Or a scene from a movie."

"Explain," I order.

"Kea—"

I glare at her.

"The-Actor-Who-Shall-Not-Be-Named in John Wick..." She tips up her chin. "He had the same tattoo across his back."

"And he was part of a Mafia gang in the movie?"

She nods. "A Russian clan."

"That explains it. It's not uncommon for some of us to choose this as a tattoo."

"First, I find out that your second name is the same as the middle name of The-Actor-Who-Shall-Not-Be-Named. Then, you play his favorite song. Now, it turns out you sport a tattoo his character wore in John Wick... It's," she shakes her head, "it's mind-boggling."

"Or maybe, The-Actor-Who-Shall-Not-Be-Named is giving you his blessing? Maybe it's a sign from him that he approves of us."

"Eh?" She scrunches her eyebrows.

"Think about it. You have a thing for him, and now, I'm your movie boyfriend, come to life."

"Hmph..." She twists her lips. "You may have a point."

"I always have a point, baby, and in this case, a very big, blunt point... in my pants."

Her gaze drops to my crotch and she flushes.

"See how much I want you? You haven't even touched me, and I'm so hard for you, Princess."

She reaches down and lowers my zipper, then pushes down my pants, along with my boxer briefs. My cock springs free, and a gasp slips from her lips. A flush blooms over her cheeks, down her neck, to swoop down her breasts—her gorgeous, plump tits, with nipples so peaked that they resemble Johnny Utah's upright surfboard in Point Break.

A-n-d I have officially lost it. I'm comparing her nipples to surfboards? And not just any surfboard, but to the character's surfboard in the movie of The-Actor-Who-Shall-Not-Be-Named that I saw. And have seen... many times. *What? It's Point Break.* It has nothing to do with the fact that *he's* in it. Besides, I was young. I didn't know any better then.

She trails her fingers up my cock and my balls tighten. She raises her gaze to mine, and whatever she sees there causes her to part her lips. She gulps and I hold her gaze.

"Just because I allowed you to undress me, doesn't mean I'm going to let you direct the proceedings."

A shiver runs down her body. Her breathing grows ragged and her pupils dilate. She's perfect. She loves it when I command her. When I dominate her. When I order her to follow my directions.

"Suck me off, Princess."

She firms her lips, even as her eyes gleam. She wants to do what I ask of her, but something in her resists. And it's that stubborn core of hers which attracts me to her. It's that obstinacy in her that pushes her to stand firm in the face of my overpowering personality. It's the fact that, even after everything we've been through, she still hasn't taken that final step of putting her faith in me. Which frustrates me, and intrigues me, and pushes me to find a way to wear her down. To break her. To make her mine over and over again.

"Wrap those pretty pink lips around my cock."

46

Elsa

"What?" I hear the word that slips from my lips, and a part of me wonders why I even bother with the token protest. I know what he wants. Hell, I want it. I want to oblige him with what he wants, and yet, something in me insists that I hold out. That I don't let him see how easy it would be for him to control me. How compelled I am to do as he says. How close I am to giving in and allowing him to direct me and manipulate my body, and my mind, and my heart into doing what he wants me to do.

"You heard me." He lowers his voice to a hush, and a buzz of electricity races under my skin. He's using that Dom voice of his. OMG, soon I'll be helpless to resist him.

I firm my lips, and he glances down at his crotch, then back to my face. "You will do as I say," he growls.

My breath catches. My mouth waters. It would be so easy to bend down, to lock my lips around that thick, gorgeous dick of his, to lick and suck and draw him into my mouth. To take him down my throat and show him just how much I want him. And I do… I want to pleasure him, to make him realize there's no one else but me who can give him what he wants. That, even if he can't forgive me for what I'm going to do next… He'll always remember my spectacular blowjob.

I glance up, hold his gaze, then dip my head toward his crotch. I close my fingers around the root of his shaft, then drag my tongue from base to head. His stomach muscles clench, his chest planes flex, and his dick lengthens even further.

Color suffuses his cheeks, his lips part, and a groan rumbles up his throat. "*Cazzo*," his jaw tics, "don't fucking stop."

I close my mouth around the head, and the tangy, salty taste of his pre-cum explodes on my palate. My sex stutters and my belly ties itself in knots. Moisture seeps out from between my thighs. I bob my head to take him deeper inside my mouth, and his entire body seems to go solid.

His gaze intensifies as I pull back until he's poised between my lips, then I tilt my head and take him down my throat.

"*Cristo Santo, così fottutamente buono,*" he says in a rough voice. A melting sensation grips my chest. I could listen to him speak Italian all day, even if I have no idea what he's saying.

I swallow, and his hips seem to rise of their own accord. His cock slips down further, and I gag. Tears run down my cheeks, but I refuse to look away from him.

His nostrils flare. The next second, he wraps his fingers around my throat. He holds me in place, and I have no choice but to gasp and try to breathe through my nose as he tilts his head.

"Do you know how much it turns me on to feel my cock down your throat as you swallow?"

My pussy clamps down and comes up empty. More moisture coats my slit. That is the hottest, filthiest thing I have ever heard. He applies enough pressure so I pull back until his cock is poised between my lips. Then he draws me forward and his shaft, once more, slips down my throat. This time, I slacken my jaw so my gag reflex doesn't engage. He glares at me as if he wants to squeeze down further, until I'm out of breath, before he kisses my mouth. He hauls me back, then forward again, as he begins to fuck my throat with slow, measured movements. Each time he glides down my throat, sensations swell the column and roll over his palm. Each time he pulls me back, his chest heaves in tandem. A bead of sweat slides down the demarcation of his pecs.

It's uncomfortable, and yet, strangely erotic as he tugs me back, then eases me forward again. His cock thickens, filling my throat. My lungs feel like they are going to burst into flames any moment. More tears slide down my cheeks and drip from my chin. And his shoulders roll forward.

"I am going to come down your throat, and you are going to swallow every drop, Princess, you hear me?"

His movements intensify, and I grip his legs and dig my fingers into the fabric of his pants, which are twisted around his lower thighs, as he continues to use my mouth, my throat, and my tongue for his pleasure. As his breathing grows even more ragged, as his chest planes shift under his tanned skin, as his thigh muscles roll and his hips jerk forward, he shoots his load down my throat.

He holds me there with his fingers still around my throat for a beat, another, then pulls out. Only to draw me up and fix his lips on mine. He kisses my mouth like he fucked my face, with thoroughness, precision, and a cold intent that is so single-minded, it leaves no doubt he wants to extract every last drop of pleasure from this connection. He keeps his eyes open, and I can't close mine, either. I watch the golden-yellow sparks catch fire in the depths of his irises as he claims my mouth with his as thoroughly as he possessed it with his shaft.

The taste of him, laced with something sweeter, more evocative—my cum—coats my palate. A trembling grips my chest and spreads out, bending, twisting, swirling, until it reaches my extremities, until it flows over me, threatening to consume me.

When he finally releases my mouth, I draw in a breath—his breath. The taste of him clings to my tongue and my lips, the scent of him in my nostrils, his touch around my neck a brand that I'll never erase.

"Seb," I open my mouth, but no other words come out. What else is there to say? What else can I say?

That's when he flips me over. "I'm going to fuck you now."

"Eh?" If I'd been speechless before, all of my brain cells seem to melt now, leaving behind a soft, mushy puddle which bears just one name—his.

One side of his lips twists, then he leans back, pushes himself off the bed, and shoves his pants and his boxers down his legs. He kicks them aside, then shrugs off the sling and tosses it to the ground.

"Wait, what are you doing?" I begin to sit up, but he clicks his tongue.

"Lay back, Princess."

As I lay slumped back against the covers, I realize I've obeyed him again. "Your shoulder... You were shot, Seb. Shouldn't you keep the sling on?"

"Nothing comes between us," he replies in a hard voice.

A flush courses through my veins, and my entire body feels like it's aflame. "That," I clear my throat, "that has got to be the most romantic thing anyone has ever said to me."

"I'm just getting started, baby." He lowers his chin to his chest, and I take in his wide shoulders, his thick biceps, that gorgeously sculpted chest with that tattoo scrawled from one end to the other, the wound on his shoulder covered in a white bandage which is startling against his darker skin, the slim waist, that beautiful cock of his that stands to attention, against his stomach—already!—the corded thighs, those muscled calves, and his feet. Oh, my god, his feet. They are big and wide, with such shapely toes.

Hold on, can a guy's toes be shapely? I know Kea—I mean The-Actor-Who-Shall-Not-Be-Named has beautiful toes. I saw them in *Point Break*. But Seb? In all honesty, he puts up stiff competition, and not just in the toes department. Right now, he's winning on so many fronts... And not only because he's real and here and sporting a boner the size of a courgette. No, it's because he might actually be more handsome than my idol, and that's something I've never admitted to myself before. Damn. Apparently, my fixation with a screen actor is being replaced by my obsession with a real-life man... Who also happens to be my husband. Clearly, I'm doomed.

He closes the distance to the bed, then positions himself between my legs. He plants his uninjured hand next to my shoulder; the other one, he keeps tucked into his side. Then he glares into my eyes. "Wrap your fingers around my dick," he commands.

"And if I don't?"

"Do it," he lowers his voice again, and my nerve-endings seem to catch fire. "Elsa," he growls. Before my name is out of his mouth, I've curled my fingers around his dick.

"Good girl. Now, position me at your entrance."

I do so, and the blunt end of his cock nudges my opening. A pulse flares to life in my lower belly, mirroring the bam-bam-bam of my heart in my ribcage. A groan bleeds from my lips, and his mouth seems to firm further. A pulse flares to life at his temple and his jaw tics. He grits his teeth as he stays there, poised at my slit.

"Do you want me, Elsa?" he asks in a harsh voice. "Do you?"

I nod.

"Want me to fuck you?"

I open my mouth, then close it, then shake my head. "No Seb." I search his features. "I want you to make love to me."

47

Seb

"*Cazzo.*" Heat constricts my chest, wraps around my ribs, and squeezes until spots of darkness flicker at the edges of my vision. And I'm not even inside her. "The things you say to me... You're going to make me come right now." Only I won't, because I'm waiting to be inside her sweet cunt, inside her fleshy, hot, melting pussy, wrapped in that hot, tight channel of hers as she milks me. I place my other arm—the one attached to my injured shoulder—on the other side of her. I lean my weight on it, and it throbs, but not too badly—thank fuck—then I lunge forward.

She gasps as I slam into her, fill her, stretch her... As I hit that elusive place deep inside of her. My balls slap against her skin, as my cock thickens inside of her.

"Oh, my god." She bites her lower lip. "Seb, you're too big."

"You can take it." Inch-by-inch, I pull out of her, then thrust forward with enough force that her body slides up. Her head hits the headboard and the bed jolts. At the same time, pain squeezes my shoulder, and I shove it aside. "Grab the headboard."

"What?"

"Not going to repeat myself, babe."

She sets her jaw, then does as she is told, thank fuck.

"Now wrap your legs around my waist."

"Are you going to direct me at every turn?" She huffs.

How cute. If she thinks she's going to direct the proceedings because I'm hurt... Well, she has no idea what's in store for her.

I glare at her, and some of her color fades. I tilt my head, and she blinks rapidly. Her chest rises and falls, then she tips up her chin, and winds first one leg, then the other, around my waist.

"Good girl," I say in a low voice. Her cheeks redden. Her pupils dilate further. She parts her lips, and goddamn, I can't stop myself from pushing into her even deeper, until once more, I am embedded balls-deep in her. Right where I belong. I begin to fuck her in long, slow, smooth strokes, in and out of her, then slant my hips, so when I next thrust into her, I hit her clit.

"Oh, god." Her eyes roll back in her head. Her eyelids flutter, and I repeat the action again. Her entire body jolts. The bed slams into the wall again, and she arches back and raises her hips so I slide even deeper inside of her.

"Seb, oh, my god, Seb," she whimpers as the tension at the base of my spine tightens, knots, folds in on itself, and I know I'm not far behind.

"Eyes on me, Princess."

She raises those heavy eyelids and gazes up and into me, pupils blown, the dark so wide, there's only a thin circle of blue around it. I did this to her. She's so turned on for me. Only me. I plunge into her again as I hold her gaze. "Come with me," I order, "come all over my cock. Right now, Princess."

Her spine curves, she thrusts up her breasts, and I can't stop myself from lowering my mouth and biting down on a nipple. That's when she opens her mouth in a silent scream. I release her breast, only to fit my mouth over hers and absorb the sounds she makes as wetness gushes out to envelop my cock. I continue to fuck her through the aftershocks as her body convulses, as her pussy clamps down on my dick, and finally I come inside of her.

Dark spots flicker at the edges of my vision, and sweat runs down my temples. I tear my mouth from hers, and peer into her features. Her eyelids half-closed, she holds my gaze. My shoulder begins to throb in earnest, matching the throbbing in my balls.

"*Gesù Cristo*," I whisper, "I love you."

She chuckles weakly. "You do know, declarations of love right after sex are notoriously unreliable."

"Or the most honest?"

"Maybe." She doesn't sound convinced. A pulse of agony whips through my mind, and a groan wells up my throat. I swallow it, push away from her to collapse on my back. And a low cry emerges from the baby monitor.

"*Cazzo!*" I snap my eyes open. "Is that—"

"It is," she confirms as she sits up, then swings her legs over. She glances around for something to wear, when I hold up my hand.

"Wait, let me go."

She turns to face me. "You?"

"Why not?"

She glances away, then back at me. "You're still hurt. You need your rest, especially after those exertions." She pushes off of the bed, reaches for my shirt, and pulls it on. "I'm assuming it's okay to borrow your shirt?"

I take in her curvy body swathed in my shirt that comes to just above her knees. "It looks much better on you." I settle back against the pillow as she heads out the door and toward Avery's room.

Either she doesn't trust me yet with her daughter or… Something's still stopping her from seeing me in the role of father. On the other hand, she wore my shirt. Tiredness tugs at my senses. I fight against the sleep that wraps around my mind.

"Hey, Bubu," her voice comes through the baby monitor. There's the rustle of fabric as she picks Avery up in her arms, no doubt. Another sleepy cry from the child, then Elsa says, "P.U. You seriously need a diaper change, Bubu."

I hear her move about the room as she gathers what she needs. Then, the sound of Velcro being pulled apart filters through the speaker, followed by, "Oh, god, Avery. That's a poonami."

I chuckle a little and close my eyes as she clucks her tongue. Avery gurgles, then there are more sounds, before Elsa begins to hum softly. It's a song I don't recognize, but her voice is soothing. She continues to sing in a low voice, as darkness overwhelms me.

My eyelids snap open. I'm not sure what wakes me. I glance around the darkened room. Starlight streams in through the open curtains. "Elsa?" I reach for her, but the bed is empty. I sit up and the cover falls about my waist. "Elsa? Princess?" *Did she cover me up? Where did she go?* I spot the baby monitor. Of course, she went to put Avery back to sleep. Perhaps she's still in her room? I swing my legs over the side of the bed, stand up, and head for the door, then stop.

"*Cazzo!*" I need to put on my clothes before I go in there. I snatch my pants from the floor, then grunt when my shoulder protests. Still, the pain seems to have settled into a dull throb, which is an improvement. I sit down on the bed and pull them on, then zip up my pants, before I head for the door. I step out into the corridor and head toward Avery's room. I walk in and find the baby fast asleep in her crib. The nightlight is on, and the stars on the ceiling glitter in their reflected glory. There's no sign of Elsa, though. I turn and head out the door, making sure to avoid the creaky floorboard this time. Then I duck into Elsa's room. There's no one there. Eh? I cross the floor to the ensuite bathroom, push open the door to find it all empty. What the—? My heartbeat speeds up. The hair on my forearms prickle. Where could she be?

I head back to my room, snatch up my phone, and that's when I see her message, "I'm sorry, Seb."

48

Elsa

"Thank you." I push open the door of the car I called earlier using the phone that Seb gave me. The phone that Seb gave me because he trusts me. And I betrayed his trust. Again. But it's for a good reason this time. This is the only way to put an end to the nightmare that's been dogging my heels for the past couple of years. This is the only way to get my life back, and to get my daughter back, without hurting anyone else in the process.

I step onto the driveway that leads up to Fabio's house. Bastard's an insomniac. Bet he's still awake, plotting more ways to make my life miserable. The car that drove me here pulls away. Its engine fades into the distance, and then there's only me and the still, dark night around me.

I hummed to Avery until she fell asleep again, then sat with her while her breathing deepened. The little mite lay on her back, arms and legs stretched out in that starfish shape she often assumes when she's exhausted. Her little chest rose and fell, her features flushed, tracks of tears drying on her cheeks. I reached over and wiped away the moisture, then kissed her forehead.

As I padded out of her room and toward Seb's room, I felt too wired to sleep. I walked into Seb's room and found him fast asleep, one arm flung out on the mattress, as if he were reaching for me in his sleep. The covers were twisted around his waist, the bandage over his shoulder a stark contrast with the rest of his body. His chest barely moved; he was sleeping that deeply. No doubt, he was worn out from his injury. Not to mention, the way he'd exerted himself when he'd fucked me. Like I'd done with Avery, I watched him for a few more seconds, then bent down and brushed my lips over his. He didn't move.

I straightened, then walked out of his room and back to mine, where I changed. I waited until the security guard at the back door dozed off. Then I slipped past him and down to the beach that runs parallel to the property. Seb has security cameras on the doorway, but by the time he or his guards notice, hopefully I'll be gone. I walked down the beach, keeping to the shadows until three houses down. Then, I located the path that ran from the beach up to the main road, something I'd noticed on one of my infrequent walks when I first moved in here. I walked onto the road, and finally, called for a pick-up. My mind was made up, so I hadn't had time to be nervous, not until the car dropped me off here.

Now, I walk up the driveway toward the silent house, then take the steps one at a time, until I'm at the main door. I stare at it. *There's time; you can turn around and leave. You don't have to do this. If you let Seb, he'll take care of it for you.* But that's the thing. I don't want to be dependent on a man who's my husband again. This time, I'm going to take care of things in my own way. All I have to do is look Fabio in the eye and tell him to back off. I can't be afraid of him. He's a bully; he thrives on fear. If I show him I'm no longer afraid of him, he'll leave me alone.

The phone in my jeans' pocket buzzes. I pull it out.

Alphahole calling.

Of course it is. He must have woken up and missed me. I hesitate, then decline the call. It starts to vibrate again almost instantly with a call from him again. I decline the call again, then switch the ringer and the buzzer off and slide it into my jacket pocket.

I raise my hand to rap on the door, and am not surprised when it's wrenched open.

Fabio stands there, wearing a pair of pants and no shirt. The house is still dark, but the silvery moonlight is bright enough that I can make out his features. His chest is smooth... unmarked. A wave of disgust slithers under my skin. How had I ever thought of him as attractive?

"Elsa." His face breaks into a smile. I'd almost believe he's happy to see me, except for the fact that his smile never reaches those dark eyes of his. He watches me with that unblinking gaze I've come to expect. I used to think it was because he likes to give me his undivided focus. Now, I know it's because he's watching me for any sign of weakness. He's waiting to trip me up, so he can reinforce the sense that something is wrong with me. It took me a while to figure out that, behind that charming façade lies a snake. One who loves to use my insecurities against me. And I'm not going to give him that opportunity again.

"I knew you'd come." His voice drips with satisfaction.

"Did you?" I tip my chin up.

"You missed me, didn't you? Missed what only I can give you. Face it, my darling wife, you want the kind of satisfaction that comes from being beaten to within an inch of your life."

"What? No." I take a step back. "And I am *not* your wife anymore. You lost the right to call me that a long time ago."

"I'm still the father of your child." He chuckles.

"Not for much longer," I say through gritted teeth.

"What do you mean?" He seems taken aback enough that he blinks. A first.

I draw myself up through the length of my spine. "You are not going to bother me again, Fabio."

"I'm not?"

I shake my head. "You're going to leave me and Avery alone. You're not going to come near us. You're done scaring me with your browbeating. You're not going to petition the court for sole custody of our daughter. You don't want her anyway. You know it's best if she stays with me. You don't love her; not like I do. You will walk away from us, and not come near us again, do you her me?"

He gapes a little. "Let me get this right. You want me to turn my back on you and my daughter, and let you get on with your life with your new husband. Is that what you want?"

I nod.

"That's why you came to my house? To tell me to leave you alone?"

"You don't want Avery. You never wanted me or my daughter. I was merely a pawn for you. Someone you intimidate and control because it feeds your ego. It's the only reason you keep me around."

"Now that you mention it—" He rubs his chin. "You're probably right."

"I know I am. You married me, not because you loved me, but because you wanted someone you could push around. It made you feel good to have me dependent on you, and then when I had Avery, you had someone you could threaten me with. You used her to make me feel even more helpless."

"When you lay it all out that way, I can see how badly I've treated you. I did you an injustice by keeping you away from Avery. You're her mother, after all. She needs you more than anyone. You've made your case with such passion, I have no choice but to accept that you're right. You don't need to bring Avery back to me after this weekend. You can have sole custody of her."

Hope buoys me, and a flush rises under my skin. I did it. I stood up to Fabio and told him off. I knew if I faced him, he would back off. I knew it.

"Thank you." I dip my chin at him. "I'm going to leave now."

I pivot on my heels when I hear, "Where are you going?" His voice follows me.

I turn around to face him. "I need to get back home before Avery wakes up."

"Why don't you come in, have something to drink before you leave?"

"No thanks." I take a step back. "I think it's best I leave now."

I sense him move, know what he's going to do, even before he reaches for my wrist. I evade him, then reach into my purse and pull out the handgun Cass sourced for me. I point it at him.

He freezes, and his gaze widens. He glances from the gun to my face, then back to the gun. "Now, let's not be hasty," he cajoles, "you know I was only trying to be hospitable."

"Were you?" I cock the gun and the sound seems to blast through the quiet night. "Put your hands up," I snap.

"Come on, Elsa, honey—"

"Don't you 'honey' me, you bastard."

"Elsa, sweetheart, do you even know how to use that?" He takes a step forward, and adrenaline spikes my blood. My heart collides with my ribcage. I depress the trigger.

Despite the silencer, the sound of the shot slaps me in the face, and ricochets around my ears, but I hold firm.

"Fuck," Fabio curses. Droplets of blood dot his side. It's only a graze, but still! I shot him. I fucking shot him. Something like exhilaration fills my chest. I toss my handbag to the ground, then grip the fingers of both of my hands around the weapon. So, this is why men prefer to shoot first and ask questions later. The power, the absolute certainty that you have the upper hand, it's as if the most addictive drug has been injected into my brain.

"Put your goddamn hands up, you motherfucker," I snap.

Asshole seems shaken, but this time, he complies.

"Good." I wave the gun in the direction of the front room. "Get the fuck inside. Now."

He sidles back.

I keep the gun trained on him. "Further back, you piece of shit."

He stumbles back a step, then another, and another. When he pauses, I wave the gun at him, and he moves all the way into the room until the back of his legs touch a chair.

"Sit the fuck down."

"Now, Elsa, be reasonable, I—"

"Say another word and I swear I'll shoot you again." He firms his lips, and I allow mine to curve. "Good. Now, where were we?" I tilt my head. "You will not come near me or my daughter, or my husband, or anyone in my extended family again, you get me?"

He jerks his chin. "Anything you say; whatever you want. Now, will you lower the gun?"

"Why should I?" I narrow my gaze on him. "I like the feeling of having control over you for a change. How do you like it?" I don't wait for him to answer. "I like having control over my own destiny, something which you denied me for so long. I realize now, I never should have given you my power. I should have claimed it for myself."

"Like you are doing now?" he interjects.

"Stop trying to talk down to me. I thought your life should be spared because you're Avery's father. Now, I know that I was wrong. You add nothing of value to her life. You're more like a cancer that should be cut out of our lives. I should have killed you much sooner. I should have—"

The skin around his eyes tightens, and his shoulders flex. I squeeze down on the trigger, but he's already grabbed my arm and pushed it up. The bullet hits the ceiling and bits of plaster rain down on us.

"Let me go." I try to pull free of his grasp, but he tightens his grip around my arm. Pain whips through my brain, and spots of black race across my line of sight. My fingers go numb, and then he's snatched the gun.

He points it at me. "You thought you could point a gun at me with no repercussions? You thought you could shoot me? You don't think I'm letting you leave without paying a price, do you?" he growls.

My heartbeat booms with such force, it brushes my throat. My stomach churns, bile coats my tongue, and I'm sure I am going to throw up.

"You're not going to shoot me," I say in a hard voice.

He looks me up and down and a crafty look enters his eyes. "You're right. I have other plans for you."

My skin crawls, and the hair on the back of my neck springs up. *I am not going to let him touch him. I will not let him touch me.*

I rush forward, but he grabs my arm and twists me around so I am pulled up against him. The heat of his body pours over me, and every part of my body shrinks. I can feel my heartbeat in my stomach, feel the blood pound at my temples. My chest feels so tight, it's like a snake has tied itself around me and is squeezing the breath out of me.

"I knew you couldn't stay away from me." He presses his cheek to mine and the sickening-sweet smell of rum, which is the alcohol this bastard favors, clogs my senses.

No, no, no. He's been drinking, something he did far too often when we were married. It means he'll be even more unpredictable than usual. I shouldn't have come. I should have stayed back and... What? Allowed him to find a way to take Avery from me? Given him another chance to hurt Seb? No, I have to do this. I have to see this through.

"Let me go!" I snarl.

"You came here of your own volition, remember?"

"I came here to tell you to leave me and my daughter alone."

"And I heard you out, didn't I? Now it's my turn." His grip around my waist tightens, and flickers of black fleck my vision. I raise my leg and bring my booted heel down on his bare foot.

"Fuck!" he yells. His hold on me loosens, and I dig my teeth into his arm.

"*Cazzo di puttana!*" he howls, but I don't let go. The metallic taste of blood fills my mouth, I still don't let go. My stomach heaves; sweat beads my hairline. I. Still. Don't. Let. Go.

"Fuck," he screams.

The gun slips from his grasp. It hits the floor and skids to the side. He grabs my hair and yanks with such force that I see stars. He flings me aside, and my body arcs through the air. I manage to throw my arm up to shield my face at the last moment before I hit the floor. The breath whooshes out of me, and my entire body trembles. My shoulder screams in agony. I can't feel my fingers or my toes. *Avery. Think of Avery. Of Seb.* I am not going to die—not like this. The *thud-thud-thud* of footsteps approaches me, and my heart leaps into my throat. Adrenaline pumps through my veins. I force my eyes open and spot the gun. The gun! I grab it, then push myself up to standing.

"I'm going to teach you a lesson you won't forget, *stupida cagna*," he snarls.

I fire at him, miss, fire again. This time, the bullet grazes his other side. "That's for Seb, you monster."

He yells and lurches toward me.

I scream, fire once more, but the shot is wide. I careen back out of his reach and depress the trigger, but an empty click sounds.

"No, no, no, no." I cry out. *This can't be happening. Not now. Not when I am so close to being free.*

Fabio's mouth seems frozen in a grimace. "I've changed my mind. I'm going to kill you." He stumbles in my direction. I fling the gun at him, then pivot and race toward the doorway, but he rushes forward and grabs my arm. I scream, try to pull away, but he hauls me close to him. Once again, the heat of his body overwhelms me, and my skin crawls. Bile rises up my throat.

"But first... I'm going to teach you a lesson. You will *never* be rid of me, Elsa; not as long as both of us are alive. I'll never be far from you. I'll always be watching. I'll never let go of you and Avery. Never."

Anger rips through my veins. All the hair on my body stands on end. A current of energy grips me, and adrenaline spikes my blood. "Damn you." I snap my head back and connect with his chin. He yells out, releases me again, and I stumble back. He grabs at my jacket, and I pull away, leaving it behind in his grasp. Anger twists my guts, and fear courses through my veins. I am not going to let him get to me. I'm going to make sure he never has a chance to come near me or Avery, ever again. I leap forward, out of the living room, down a short corridor that leads past a sun room, toward the back of the house. I spot the entrance to a room and dart inside, then slam the door behind me and lock it. Almost instantly, a heavy weight slams into the barrier from the other side, and the entire frame shakes.

My breath catches in my chest. A shiver of fear runs down my spine. I spin around, searching for a weapon, just as his weight hits the door again, and the frame shudders. *No, no, no, it's not going to hold.*

"Open the goddam door, Elsa, or you're going to regret locking me out even more," he bellows.

Clearly, his housekeeper isn't here; or she'd have made an appearance by now.

I slide my hand inside the pocket of my pants, but there's no phone. Shit, I put it in my jacket pocket. Fear stabs at my chest. My ribcage feels like it's constricting my lungs. *Oh, my god! What have I done? How could I have been so stupid? How could I have put myself in danger like this?* I walked out of the house without thinking. Without worrying about Avery. I knew Seb would be there with her. I trusted him to take care of her... Or at least, my subconscious did. It didn't even occur to me to think otherwise. I thought I was so clever. Why didn't I stop to think? Why didn't I wake him up and speak to him instead?

I continue searching for some kind of weapon I can use. I spot the poker near the fire and race toward it, and that's when the door flies open.

With a scream, I leap back, then round the coffee table in the center of the room and put it between me and him. Not that it's going to help. It's one more thing blocking my escape. And I don't have a weapon.

I glance at the poker, then back at him.

He laughs. "Oh, no you don't." Blood stains his shirt and he staggers toward me.

I hold up my hands. "Don't touch me," I snarl.

His gaze falls to the ring on my finger, and his features contort. "You married him. You thought his influence with the Mafia would scare me off. It'll take more than some two-bit criminal to stop me from getting to you."

"He's not a two-bit criminal. His family owns this country, and you know it. Touch me, and the entire Sovrano family will be after you."

"Oh, I'm going to do more than touch you. I'm going to mess you up so much, he's not going to be able to recognize your pretty face again. And then he won't want you anymore. He'll throw you away like the trash you are."

He throws himself over the table. I scream and scramble away again. The chair behind me hits the wall and crashes to the floor. I glance around again for something, anything to defend myself with.

I spot a drawer, pull it open, and find a gun. I snatch it up and point it at him as he straightens. He freezes instantly. It's amazing what a gun in the right hands can do. Just like before, his gaze ping-pongs between the gun and my face.

"Oh, so you're going to try that again?" he asks, his tone so condescending, I instinctively curve my finger around the trigger.

By god, how I want to squeeze down and be done with him. "What I do know is that I have the gun, and you are on the wrong end of the barrel." I wave the gun at him. "Step back, or I promise, I'll shoot you."

"I've seen your shooting," he scoffs.

I look pointedly at the blood staining his side, and he balks. "I'll do it." My chin trembles, and I clamp my lips together. I will not let him see how afraid I am right now.

"No you won't. After all, I'm the father of your child."

"Seb has been more of a father to Avery in the few days he's been with her than you ever have."

His jaw hardens. "You dare compare me to that Mafioso vermin?"

"That man has done more for Avery in a few weeks than you have in all the time you've been her father. You never held her after she was born. You never even looked at her. You never cared about her, or me. She was just another tool you could use to control me."

"What's wrong with that?" He raises a shoulder. "I thought you wanted someone to control you." He smirks. "Everything was working out so well. I encouraged you to be with him so you could get me information that would help me put him and his brothers behind bars. I'm the one who orchestrated the series of events that led to you knocking on his nonna's door and asking for help in the first place."

I pale. "That was you? You were behind the cars that crowded me so I had no choice but to take the road that led to his nonna's house?"

He half bows. "Clever, eh? Knew he wouldn't be able to resist a damsel in distress. All the Sovranos think they're these big bad guys, but they can't pass up the opportunity to play a knight in shining armor."

My pulse thuds at my temples. Sweat beads my brow. "You're the one who shot and killed his nonna?"

"Not me, but one of my men. It wasn't intended, but I have to admit, the payoff from it was much sweeter. Nothing like upping the stakes so emotions run high and make people more vulnerable. It accelerated the chain of events and led to him proposing to you. Even I couldn't have planned it so well."

Anger squeezes my chest with such force that I can't breathe.

He puffs out his chest. "And then, it was my magnanimity that allowed you to marry him so he'd trust you enough to let his guard down with you. But you made the mistake of falling for him."

"Did that make you jealous? Is that why you tried to kill him with the drone attack?"

"Drone?" He chuckles. "I think you've been watching too many movies. If I were going to shoot him, I'd do it the old-fashioned way, a bullet to the back of the head, and preferably, without getting my hands dirty."

Something clicks in my brain. "The shooting at the restaurant. That was you, wasn't it?"

His expression flickers for just a second, but it's enough.

"It *was* you. Did you put the *Camorra* up to it?"

"Guilty as charged. Too bad the *faccia di merda* escaped."

My heart jackhammers in my chest. The pressure builds behind my eyes.

"You tried to kill him. Hell, you could have killed me while you were at it. But I guess you wanted to make enough of a statement so I'd come to you. Well, here I am."

"And now, I'm going to kill you. If I can't have you, no one else will. I'm never letting go of you Elsa. Never."

He reaches for the gun.

I shoot, or at least, try to, but the gun doesn't fire.

His features light up and his eyes gleam. He jumps forward. I yell and dash around the table and toward the door, but he grabs hold of my shirt and pulls. I scream, then turn around and bring the gun down on his head.

I hear the sound of something cracking. He sways, then crumples to the floor. My fingers tremble. The gun slips from my grasp, hits the floor, and bounces once.

"Elsa?"

I turn to find Seb at the door.

49

Seb

"You came!" Her features crumple, Then she throws herself across the room and into my arms. I pull her close to me and lift her off the floor as I examine her features. "You're okay? Did he hurt you? If he dared touch a hair on your head, I'm going to kill him, notwithstanding my promise to you. Elsa?"

She hiccups, opens her mouth to say something, then closes it. Tears pour down her cheeks, as she shakes her head.

"Elsa, baby?"

"I'm fine," she rasps. Then, she pushes her face into the crook of my neck and bursts out crying. "I was so scared, Seb. I thought he was going to kill me, or do something worse. You should have seen his eyes, Seb. He was crazy. I should have listened to you. I never should have come here. I'm so sorry I didn't tell you."

"It's okay." I rub circles over her back. "It's fine, I've got you. And I'm never letting you go now."

She nods, hiccups again, then pulls back. "Avery, is she—"

"She's fine. Massimo is with her."

"How did you know where to find me?"

"I tracked your phone."

"My phone." She swallows. "You tracked my phone? Is that why you returned it to me, so you'd know where I was?"

I survey her features as she glances away, then back at me. "I'm glad you did."

"When I woke up, and you were gone... You have no idea how worried I was. If he had done anything to you—" I shake my head. "What were you thinking, coming here on your own?"

"I wasn't," she admits.

"How did you get here?"

"I... I walked up the beach, past the next two houses, then followed the path to the road before I called a car."

"You called a car at this time of night?" Anger suffuses my skin. My stomach feels like I've swallowed a rock. "*Cazzo*, Princess, do you realize the risks you took tonight? It's a good thing Massimo saw you."

"Massimo saw me?"

"The path you took led by his house."

"His house?" She scowls. "You mean, the path I took to get to the road from the beach led by his house?"

"Didn't I tell you? The rest of my brothers have their houses along the same strip of beach that borders mine."

"Ah," she bites the inside of her cheek, "you didn't tell me that. Or did you decide to keep it quiet, just in case I did something as stupid as what I did today?"

"I didn't keep it from you consciously," I bring my hand up to cup her cheek, "but I also decided I wasn't going to bring it up, unless there was a specific reason."

She draws in a breath. "I'm glad you didn't tell me. And I'm glad Massimo saw me."

"He called me, and I waited until he came over to be with Avery before leaving the house."

"So how did you get here? Who drove you?"

"I drove myself. I knew you were in danger, and trust me, nothing could stop me from getting to you. Certainly not a bullet wound." I cup her cheek. "I'm so sorry I didn't make it earlier, and I was selfish enough that I didn't want anyone but me to come get you. I should have told you about the rest of my brothers occupying the other houses; it might have stopped you from acting so rashly. It might have deterred you from coming here." I press my forehead into hers. "I may never forgive myself for not doing so."

"Stop, Seb." She glances into my eyes. "This is my fault, not yours. And you're here now, and that's all that matters."

I lower my lips to hers and kiss her hard... Then I catch movement out of the corner of my eye. I straighten, use my unhurt arm to shove her behind me, then reach for the gun tucked into the small of my back. But the pain that slices through my shoulder slows me down. "*Cazzo!*" I growl as that *pezzo di merda*, Fabio, points his gun at me.

"No," she cries from behind me. She tries to move past me, but I hold her back.

"Don't move," I say in a low voice.

"Yes, don't move, Elsa. Let me shoot him, so I can make you a widow this time around." Fabio laughs.

"Stop it! Don't do this, Fabio." Fear pours off of her. "Please, don't hurt him."

"Put down the gun and let us go, and you'll live," I snap.

"Oh, I'm going to live all right, but you... You're not going to walk away from here. In fact, I'm going to kill both of you today, you hear me, Elsa? You married him; now die with him. I'm going to raise Avery on my own. I'm going to tell her how depraved her mother was. I'm going to tell her how she chose to die with her new husband, rather than stick around for her own daughter, I'm going to—"

The retort of a bullet being fired fills the space before he glances down at the blood that blooms at his chest. He looks up at me and his hand shakes. I look to my side and realize she grabbed my gun, stepped around me, and fired. As he begins to crumple, he fires his gun again. The bullet goes wide, hits the ceiling, and his body jerks again. She holds her finger down on the trigger, and another bullet slams into him, and another. He hits the floor and lays still as she brushes past me. She reaches him, points the gun at him, and fires again.

"Goddamn you," she snarls, then fires again. A clicking sound fills the space as I close the distance to her.

"Princess..." I place my hand on hers, take the gun from her, and she doesn't protest. "Elsa..." I pull her into my arms and she stands there stiffly. "Baby?" I pat her back with the arm attached to my uninjured shoulder as I rub soothing circles over her back. "Are you okay, darling?"

She remains silent.

Massimo bursts into the room, followed by Luca.

"Che cazzo?" Massimo growls as he draws abreast.

"Did you?" He glances at the gun in my hand; I shake my head.

His gaze moves to her, then back at me. The creases around his eyes intensify.

"Good riddance." Luca prowls over to us. "This one was so goddamn corrupt, he was given a wide berth, even by his own men."

"He has friends in high places; there'll be a fallout from this," Massimo warns.

"Avery. Who's with Avery?" she croaks.

"Axel and Theresa are with her," Massimo replies in a gentle voice.

A trembling grips her, and I pull her even closer.

"You mind?" I hold the gun out to Massimo, who grips it with his gloved fingers.

"I assume this needs to be disposed of?"

I nod.

"And what about this piece of trash?" Luca stabs the foot of his pointed boot into the fallen Fabio's chest.

Elsa stiffens in my arms. She tips up her chin and meets my gaze. "Burn him."

An hour later, I wrap a blanket around her as I put her to bed.

Massimo drove both of us back, while Luca stayed behind to take care of the details. Before we reached home, Luca called us to say it was done. After making sure there was no one else in the house, he set the place on fire. I spoke to Michael, and he promised me he would reach out to his sources within the police to ensure his death would not be investigated. Paradoxically, with Fabio out of the way, it was much easier for his contacts to do what was needed.

After we got home, she went straight to Avery's room, where she and Theresa had quietly embraced beside the sleeping little girl. She didn't say anything to Theresa, but her best friend seemed to understand that something major had gone down. In just a few words, I conveyed to Axel what had happened. His features turned grim, and he told me he'd double the number of people guarding our place. Then, he and Theresa left. I led her into the bathroom, stripped her, and bathed her, and she still hadn't spoken a word. Then I dried her, and myself, dropped an old T-shirt of mine over her shoulders, and helped her into bed.

Now, as I slide out of bed, she grabs my arm. "Stay," she says in a hollow voice, "don't leave me alone."

"Just going to check on Avery one last time. I'll be right back."

50

Elsa

A few seconds later, he returns, then undresses, his movements slow because of his injured shoulder. Finally, he slides under the covers, wearing only his boxers.

"How's the shoulder," I ask.

"It's healing fast." He pulls me into his arms and I place my cheek against the thud-thud-thud of his heartbeat. If only I could, I'd bottle this sound, and carry it around with me, and take it out and listen every time I needed a pick me up.

"How are you feeling?" He tucks my head under his chin. He wanted me to see a doctor, but I refused. I wasn't really hurt, and once I had a shower, all I wanted was to crawl into bed with him and have him hold me.

"Shaken." Tears prick the backs of my eyes, and I turn my face into his chest. "You know what's the worst thing?" I swallow. "I went there, hoping to have an excuse to kill him, and put an end to this torture he's put me through."

He runs his fingers through my hair, the gesture soothing.

"You had a gun with you?"

I nod. "Cass procured it for me."

He stills, and I pull back. I glance up into his face. "Please don't blame her. I'm the one who asked her to procure it for me."

"And she did." His lips thin. "She endangered your life."

"She helped me out. She was there for me when I needed a friend."

"And if you'd been killed? What then? Did you think about what would happen to me and Avery if that *stronzo* had hurt you?"

"I wasn't going to let that happen. I knew I was going to get out of there alive."

"You almost didn't," he says in a low voice.

"But I did." I cup his face. "Don't you see? There was too much at stake for me. No way was I going to lose. No way would I have let anything happen to me. I knew you were waiting for me. I knew I was going to see Avery grow up. I knew I was going to walk out of there alive."

He peers into my face, then draws in a breath. "I believe you." He wraps his arms around me. "But I still can't forgive Cass for getting you a gun."

"Would you have given me a gun if I'd asked you?"

He hesitates.

"That's what I thought."

"If she hadn't given you a gun, you wouldn't have gone."

"If she hadn't given me a gun, I would have gone unprepared, and then..." I swallow. "Then I wouldn't have been able to protect myself." I lean in close enough for us to share breath. "And when he pointed his gun at you, I knew he'd kill you, and then I didn't think at all."

A shiver grips my shoulders.

"You know what else?" I glance away. "I don't feel sorry, at all. I'm relieved I don't have to face him again. I don't have to take Avery over and leave her for the rest of the week with that... that... Monster. I don't need to look at him and remember how he used to beat me up, how he made me feel helpless, how he used her to get me to do whatever he wanted, how he would taunt me about my skills as a mother, as a woman. How he made me feel weak, and stupid, and undesirable, and unwanted, and—"

"I love you." He notches his knuckles under my chin so I have no choice but to look up at him. "You are the strongest, most gorgeous, most beautiful woman I've ever met, and I don't mean only in the physical fashion, although—" his lips quirk, "—I mean that, too, of course."

I look between those golden eyes of his—and my heart flutters. I'll never get used to how he looks at me, like I'm his entire world.

"It's your heart, your soul, your spirit that attracts me to you. Your quick mind, the depth of your love for Avery, how you'd do anything for her, how you killed the man who would have taken her away from you and scarred her for life. You did what had to be done to protect your daughter, and I not only respect you for that, but I fell in love with you all over again for what you did."

I draw in a breath, not sure what to say. His words... They wash over me, through me, and wash away the stain of what I did, that I thought I would carry forever. He absolves me of the guilt I thought I was destined to endure. He lightens the load that had already begun to settle on me, the dread that had begun to seep into my soul. The anger at myself for what I did, knowing I'd do it all over again. The helplessness that had begun to bind me in its shackles fades away, leaving in its place... Freedom. A lightness. A sense of rightness, of being here in his bed. With him. And yet, the tears flow down my cheeks... Not tears of sorrow, but an acknowledgement that my life as I know it is just starting. With him. The man of my dreams. My husband. The one. The only.

"Seb," I whisper, "please fuck me. Please dominate me. Now, more than ever, I need you to take my choice away from me."

He searches my features. "Are you sure?" he asks.

"More than sure. I need you to show me that I'm alive, that you're alive, that everything I hold dear to me is here in this house with me. That I'm not alone anymore, Seb. Can you do that for me?"

His gaze narrows, and something flickers deep within those leonine eyes. Then, those beautiful lips of his twist. He lowers his lips and brushes mine once, twice. I open my mouth, and he sweeps his tongue inside and deepens the kiss. He pours himself, his taste, his strength, his heart... his love... I feel all of it in that kiss as he slides his tongue over mine.

Then he pulls away and moves off the bed. He walks over to the door at the end of the room which I assume leads to his closet. The light comes on inside, then switches off as he steps back into the room. Between his fingers, he holds swatches of fabric. A tie? He brought out a tie? No, more than one tie... He has a couple of ties... Three, maybe? Why does he need three ties? He walks over to me and rakes his gaze over my body. My nipples instantly bead, my belly flutters, liquid heat erupts low in my stomach, and I can't stop myself from squeezing my thighs together.

He jerks his chin at me. "Arms over your head. Grip the headboard, Princess."

A shiver of heat blooms in my chest. I do as he orders. I hook my fingers through the slats in the headboard. The mattress dips as he climbs on. With slow movements that hint his shoulder is slowing him down, he knots the first tie around my wrists and secures them to the headboard. He climbs off of the bed again and walks to the end of it. He circles his fingers around one ankle, and goosebumps dot my skin. He pulls my leg to the side, uses the second tie to secure my leg to the bed, then does the same with the other.

The T-shirt I'm wearing—his T-shirt—rides up my waist. Cool air flows over my bare pussy and goosebumps dot my skin.

When he finishes, he stands back and surveys my spread-out position. A flush steals over his cheeks and that golden gaze of his seems to catch fire.

He shoves his boxers down his legs and kicks them aside. His cock juts up, thick and fat and proud. Pre-cum glistens at the slit of the head. He wraps his fingers around his shaft and pumps once, twice. A pulse flares to life between my legs. I try to tug my legs together, but they're held apart.

"Seb, please," I gasp.

"What do you want, Princess?"

"You. I want you inside of me. I need to feel your cock thickening in me, please," I whine.

His breath catches. His chest, with that beautiful tattoo scrawled across it, rises and falls. His shoulders seem to grow even bigger as he, once more, mounts the bed and settles in between them. I try to wind my arm around his neck, but end up tugging at my restraints.

"So impatient, baby?"

He cups my tit in his hand, then bends and bites down on my nipple. My pussy instantly clenches. More moisture squeezes out between my legs.

"Oh, god, please, please, please-please-please."

He laughs. That trademark, mean, hard laugh of his, that settles somewhere deep inside of me. That angers me and turns me on even more. He brings his mouth to my other breast, then wraps his tongue around my nipple.

A melting feeling coats my insides, and my brain cells feel like they have turned to mush. He pulls back. I push my chest up, trying to chase that sensation of having him suckle at my teat. He obliges by sucking hard, and my head spins. My eyes roll back in my head, and I almost come right then.

He releases my breast at once, his breath hot on my skin. He slides his hand down between us and thrusts his fingers inside my channel. He works them in and out of me. My body trembles and pinpricks of lust ladder up my spine. I try to shift away, even as I push my upper body into him. He pulls his fingers out, then slides down and pushes his face into my cunt.

"Seb," I whisper-scream as he thrusts his tongue inside me. He weaves it in and out of me, stabbing at me, dragging it over my inner walls, before he drags his tongue up my slit and closes his mouth around my pussy. He bites down on my clit, and that's when I explode. The orgasm bursts out from my center to my extremities. Spots of black dot my eyesight, and by the time I recover, he's moved up my body again and presses his lips to mine.

"Two more orgasms, baby."

"What?" I rasp, " I can't."

"You can," he stares into my eyes, "and you will."

He slides his fingers inside my already swollen cunt, and adds a third finger for good measure, filling me, stretching me. He curves them inside of me and I moan. Heat scours my veins and my toes curl. He kisses me deeply, thrusting his tongue inside my mouth, dragging it over my teeth. He pulls his fingers from my pussy, then drags them around to the valley between my arse cheeks. He strokes the forbidden little knot of flesh there, and I freeze. My gaze widens and is caught by his golden gaze. Something flares deep inside them as he tears his lips from mine. Once more, he moves down my body. He drags his tongue from back hole to clit, and then does it again. He curves his tongue around my swollen bud, as he slips his finger inside my back channel. The sensations are weird and strange, and then he drags his whiskered jaw across my pussy, and I gasp, writhe, try to evade that source of absolute pleasure as he rubs the rough skin of his jaw across my tender skin.

"S-e-b," I yell, as my entire body bucks and jolts, and I squirm and twist. I try to get away, while I also want more. He leans more of his weight on me, holding me captive as he increases the intensity of his movements. He strokes his jaw across my clit, and sparks explode behind my eyes.

This time, the orgasm slams into me, overpowers me, and sweeps me away. I black out for a few seconds, and when I come to, his face is positioned over mine, watching me, wearing a very satisfied look on his features.

"You okay?" he asks.

I nod, not trusting my voice. My throat feels raw, and I vaguely recall screaming.

"Ready for your third one?" He smirks.

I don't have the strength to either nod or deny him as he kisses me softly, and works his finger in my arse, in and out of me. The pleasure unfurls slowly in my lower belly. And honestly, if it weren't happening, I wouldn't have thought it were possible for my body to continue to respond the way it does. At this stage, I'm not trying to control anything. He's playing me like Neo controls the matrix. Like John Wick knows exactly where his nemesis is hiding and laser targets their position... That's how he hones in on my pleasure points. Clearly, I'm losing my mind completely, or I'm so punch-drunk on the pleasure he's wringing from my poor body, I'm beginning to confuse a lot of things in my mind.

"Last one, babe." Jerkhole kicks up his lips. One hard kiss, and then he dives down between my legs again.

"Oh, Jesus!" I gasp as he sticks his tongue inside my channel again.

He tears his mouth from my pussy and I almost cry out in frustration.

"I don't want anyone else's name passing through your lips but mine, you hear me?"

I gulp.

"Do you hear me, Princess?"

"Yes," I moan.

"Yes, Seb," he snaps.

"Yes, Seb."

Even before I've completed the statement, he's fitted his mouth back to my core. He slurps up the cum from my entrance, then he grips my hips and hitches me up as he begins to eat me out with gusto.

Lust curls in my lower belly, my toes arch, and my scalp tingles. My skin feels too tight for the rest of my body, as he slides his palm behind my butt cheek and squeezes, even as he slides a second finger inside my back hole.

"Seb," I yell, as he curls his tongue inside my channel. Then, suddenly, he's removed his tongue and replaced it with his cock. He rises up on his knees between my legs. He balances himself on his elbow, the one attached to his hurt shoulder. He winces, then just as quickly, the pain is gone from his face, replaced by lust and intent, and that singular focus that I find so appealing about him.

"Okay?" he whispers against my lips.

"I will be, when you're inside me."

A groan rumbles up his chest. His eyes gleam, then he lunges forward and buries himself inside me.

51

Seb

Hot. Warm. So tight. Her channel contracts around my dick, and goddamn, but I'm in heaven. And in hell, from how much I want her. And home. I'm home. I pull out, then stay poised at the entrance to her slippery channel. Her eyelids flutter. She jerks her hips forward, chasing my cock, and I can't stop the smile that curls my lips.

Her forehead knits and she pouts. "You're an asshole, you know that?"

"Always and forever, baby." I lunge forward, and thrust into her with enough force that her entire body jerks. The headboard slams into the wall. Behind me, I hear something crash to the floor. "Oops." I chuckle.

She blinks, then her gaze widens. "Did you make something fall down?"

"Seems that way." I peer into her eyes as I tilt my hips. Her lips part, and a soft breath whooshes out. "I'm going to fuck you now."

Her gaze widens as I thrust deep into her, again and again. I piston my hips and bury myself balls-deep in her again and again. A trembling winds up her body. Her features flush, and her pupils dilate. She arches her back, and I know she's close. I lower my head to hers until our eyelashes tangle, until our breaths mingle, until my lips brush hers. "Come for me, Princess. Come all over my cock," I command.

It's as if she was waiting for my words, for her chest heaves, a low keening cry slips from her lips, then moisture bathes my cock as her cunt flutters around my shaft. Her breasts tremble, her hips jerk, and she shatters under me. I continue to fuck her through her climax, then my balls draw up, and I come inside her.

Her eyelids begin to close, and I click my tongue. "Look at me, Princess."

She raises her eyelashes, holds my gaze, and together, we come down from the high.

"Seb," she whispers.

I lower my head and bump my nose with hers. "Hmm?" I kiss her lips. "Are you okay?"

She chuckles. "I may be a little out of my head with the orgasms, but otherwise... Wow."

I laugh. "That's the idea." I kiss her hard, then reach up and undo her restraints. I pull out of her, then swing my legs over the side of the bed. Straightening, I walk over to the foot of it, and undo the knots around her ankles. She brings up her knees, parts her legs wide, and holds out her arms.

"*Cazzo*," I blow out a breath, "you completely undo me, baby." I slide in between her thighs, then flip over, so she's nestled on my chest. "Sleep now."

She pushes her cheek into my chest, and I feel my heartbeat against her skin. She stays there for a few seconds, then traces the outline of the bandage over my shoulder. "This doesn't bother you too much, does it?"

"Now that you mention it..." A dull pain throbs down my side. "But when I'm with you, I tend to forget about everything else, baby."

She turns her face into my chest and kisses me. "Will I ever be able to forgive myself for what I did?"

I tug my fingers down her tresses. "The first one is always the worst," I reply honestly. "You probably won't ever forget what you did. But like grief, the memory dulls with time. It's always there, under the surface, lurking around and ready to spring forward during your weakest times... But you know why you did it, and you need to hold onto that reason. You know, if you hadn't done it, he would have hurt you and our daughter."

She swallows. "You've been so good to her, from the moment you met her."

"I've always known she's mine, like you are, from the moment I set eyes on you."

"I don't regret what I did."

"Good." I notch my knuckles under her chin. "You shouldn't. I just wish you had let me do it for you. I would do anything to spare you the weight of what you'll carry for the rest of your life."

"It had to be me, to make sure he'd never bother us again. You understand that, right? I had to make sure he could no longer hurt us."

I blow out a breath. "I understand; doesn't mean I agree." I lower my chin and press my lips to hers. "And never again, are you allowed to put yourself at such risk, you understand?"

She nods. "When I met you, I didn't understand how you could do what you do. How you straddle this line between light and dark, between life and death, so casually. How you accept death is so much a part of your life." She draws in a breath. "Now I do."

"I wish you didn't have to." I cup her cheek. "But I can't deny that it makes the bond between us stronger, and for that, I'm grateful."

"You know I'll never use the safe word, right?" She searches my features. "I know that you'll never give me an occasion to use it. You're so attentive, so caring, so everything I've ever wanted in a Dom. I never dreamed that I could have someone as protective as you for my husband."

"I'll always be there for you and Avery," I vow.

"It's fun to be hopelessly in love. It's dangerous, but it's fun," she murmurs.

"Let me guess." I tilt my head. "That's another quote from The-Actor-Who-Shall-Not-Be-Named?"

Her lips kick up. "It's also a not very thinly veiled code for I love you."

A warmth fills my chest. "*Ti amo. Sono pazzo di te. Sei la cosa più bella che mi sia mai capitata.*"

I flip her over. My shoulder twinges, but I ignore it. "From now on, you let me deal with the darkness." I bend over her. "You and Avery deserve the light. You deserve every happiness I can provide for you. I want to fulfill your every wish; I want to make sure you and Avery never have to fear anything, for as long as you live."

A shadow crosses her features.

"What is it?" I frown.

She bites the inside of her cheek. "It may be nothing… but there's something he said that I just remembered."

"Which is?" I scrutinize her features.

"That he wasn't the one behind the attempt on your life."

"He wasn't?"

"That's what he said." She holds my gaze. "At first, I didn't believe it, either. But when I asked him again, he insisted he wasn't the one who tried to take your life. Which means—"

"The real killer is still out there somewhere."

Abruptly, the security app on my phone goes off.

"*Cazzo.*" I roll off of her and onto my feet. My shoulder protests. I ignore it as I march to my phone and grab it up from the nightstand. The app that controls the security on my phone has a notification. I click on it, and the video shows the guards outside with their guns trained on a man on the ground.

52

Seb

Half an hour later, I pace the floor of the garage of the warehouse. Earlier—after making sure my wife and our daughter were safely at home, and tripling the number of guards outside our house—I marched to the car with the man who had been captured trying to break in. No way was I going to take him into the house, especially with Avery there. And while Michael has been known to interrogate men in the basement of his house, things have changed since he got married. So, we now have a safe house on the outskirts of Palermo, precisely to be used as a place where we can hold those disloyal to us and interrogate them, if needed. Which is where I brought the intruder, after alerting my brothers.

I drove to the warehouse, and as I parked, Massimo, then Luca, and Adrian arrived.

Now, I look toward where Luca glares at the intruder. The man sits on a chair, his arms and legs restrained.

"Who sent you?" Luca asks in a hard voice. "You can make this go much easier on yourself if you give up your employer."

"And risk you killing me?" The man bares his teeth. "I think not."

Luca buries his fist in the man's face, and blood blooms from his nose. He slumps back in the chair, and blood splatters on his clothes and on the floor.

"Easy, *fratello*," Massimo cautions him, "if you knock out all of his teeth, he won't be able to speak."

"*Cazzo!*" Luca shakes his head, then steps back. "You're right," he murmurs, much to my shock. The hot-headed Luca, actually reining in his anger? Whoa, it's as hard to believe as Elsa not mentioning The-Actor-Who-Shall-Not-Be-Named in conversation for an entire day.

A-n-d, now I'm the one thinking of him, and without Elsa's prompting. I close the distance to Luca, then grip his shoulder "May I?" I jerk my chin in the man's direction.

"Have at him." Luca shakes out his arm as he walks out of the circle of yellow the spotlight casts over the man.

Outside, it's daylight already. The sun was rising as I drove here. But here in the basement of the safe house, perpetual darkness shrouds the space.

I pause in front of the man, who glances at me from under swollen eyelids.

"Look man, we have nothing against you. We simply want to know if it was Freddie Nielsen who sent you."

The man stiffens, before his features, once more, assume the look of boring aloofness that he's worn since being captured.

"So, it was Freddie, eh?"

He stays still.

"Your body language gave you away. Your muscles tightened there for a second, and I caught it. So, you may as well give up the pretense."

His gaze widens for a fraction of a second, but he still doesn't say anything.

"What does the bastard have over you? If he's threatening a family member, we can help you."

The corners of his eyes tighten. Again, it's only a minute tell, and I might have missed it, if not for the fact that I've been watching him so closely.

"Who is it that he is threatening? Your wife? Children?" His jaw tics and this time he glowers at me.

"I have a daughter, and I'd do anything for her, too." I sense my brothers glancing toward me, but I keep my gaze trained on the man's face. "It's why I understand why you must have felt compelled to do as he asked. It's why we're here talking, and I haven't shot you yet."

The man's throat moves as he swallows.

"Girl or boy?" I ask.

He blows out a breath then closes his eyes. "One of each." The muscles of his shoulders bunch.

"Does Freddie have them?"

"And my wife." He swallows.

"What did he ask you to do?" I lean forward on the balls of my feet.

He opens his eyes. "He wanted me to simply draw your attention. He wanted me to attempt to break in—"

"—knowing that you would be caught?"

"Maybe." His forehead wrinkles. "If I got through, I had to mess up your house enough that it threw a scare into you. If I'd known you have a daughter, I would've... been more careful. As it is, I'm glad your security caught me before I broke in."

I rub the back of my neck. "We need to rescue your family."

His features slacken. "You... you'll help me get to them?"

"Provided you help *me*."

"Anything." He straightens. "Anything you want."

"You sure you want to join forces with a man who was sent to break into your house?" Luca asks.

"Look at him. Does he look like he's going to hurt us further?" I ask.

"I don't know." Luca crosses his arms across his chest. "I'm not sure I'd trust him quite so easily."

"What do you think?" I look the man up and down. "Can I trust you on this?"

"You can." He glances from me to Luca. "I have everything to lose here, if I'm lying. And this is my family we're talking about. I'd do anything to save them."

"Do we even know where the *stronzo*'s taken them? Or are we going to have to track them down first?"

"I have an idea where they could be." He turns to me. "Look, there's no reason for you to believe me, but I think I know where he's taken them."

"Where?" Massimo asks.

"To my laboratory. It's a very secure place, since I work on stuff that can be potentially life-threatening. Which means, you'll need me to get in there."

"If it's that secure, could Freddie get in?" Adrian shoots back.

"He has access to the best hackers in the world. I know because I introduced him to them. Unfortunately. " He winces. "You could also use a hacker, I suppose." He raises a shoulder. "But it'd be a lot easier if you took me along."

"Hold on. If he took them to the laboratory, wouldn't there be other people there, as well?" Luca growls.

"I work alone." He glances away, then back at us. "What I work on is top-secret and privately-financed. Not even the government knows about the kind of research I conduct."

"Privately-financed, eh? By whom?" Massimo snaps.

"I don't know."

"He's lying." Luca takes a step in his direction, but Adrian grabs his shoulder. "Hold on, bro, let's hear him out first."

Adrian stabs a finger at the man. "Start talking before Luca here, loses his patience and decides to shoot you, or worse, rough you up further. It's a miracle he hasn't lost his cool so far."

The man pales. "It's the truth. I get all of my directions by email from a secure server which is impossible to trace. I know because my hacker friends tried. Whoever they are, they pay me very well. Each month, the money is credited to my bank account. And no, we haven't been able to trace that, either."

Luca takes a step in his direction, and he leans as far back in the chair as he can. "It's the truth. I promise you on the lives of my children."

Luca hesitates. "If you're lying, I'll shove your head so far up your ass, you'll never be able to speak again."

Sweat beads the man's hairline. "I'm not lying."

Massimo blows out a breath. "So, you want to come along for the mission because, I assume, we'll need your fingerprint or your retinal scan to gain entry into this place?"

He nods. "I specialize in weapons technology. Freddie asked me to sell him some of my patented technology."

"But you refused?"

He nods again. "Not that it mattered. He took my drone technology, then took my family as hostage, for good measure."

"So, the drone he used to shoot at me was designed by you."

He seems surprised. "Shit, I didn't know. I'm sorry about that, man."

"Maybe it's time you found a different way of making a living, eh?" Luca scowls at him.

Massimo, Adrian, and I exchange looks.

"Ah, Luca, considering we're not exactly the good guys here, it might be a bit much asking him to change his occupation," Adrian murmurs.

"Speak for yourself. As far as I'm concerned, we go out of our way to make sure we help those who come to us. If it weren't for us, this country wouldn't be able to function. Have you seen how corrupt the politicians are? Compared to them, we always deliver on our promises. And we get justice for those who are wronged."

Massimo rolls his shoulders. "He has a point."

"He fucking does," Adrian grumbles.

"Can we get back to the issue at hand?" I squeeze the bridge of my nose. "This Freddie guy is one massive pain in the ass. Why the hell is he targeting me anyway?"

"He's coming after you because he's pissed at the lot of you," the man interjects.

All of us turn in his direction.

"How the hell do you know that?" I glare at him.

"You working with him? Is that why you're pretending to help us, so you can betray us to Freddie?" Luca closes the distance to him and grabs his collar. "If there's something you haven't told us, then I suggest you do so while you can still speak, *stronzo!*"

The man opens his mouth, and ends up choking.

"I suggest you loosen your grip on him so he can speak," Adrian offers.

Luca must do so, for the man draws in a breath, then coughs. "I... I overheard him talking on his phone to someone." His chin trembles. "He mentioned how the Sovranos had betrayed him by taking all of the credit for the kidnapping of the Seven, when he was the mastermind. Then, one of you infiltrated his gang, and that was a blow to his ego. He seemed very upset, and swore he wouldn't rest until he's killed every last one of you."

For a moment, none of us have anything to say, until Luca breaks the silence.

"If you're lying, I'm going to pound your face into the earth, you understand?"

"I'm not lying. In fact, I'm telling you this so you know I'm on your side. This is my family's future at stake, and I know you guys are my only chance to save them," the man says in a firm voice.

Luca glares at him for a few seconds more, then releases his grip on the man's shirt.

"Cazzo." I rub the back of my neck. "Remind me why we haven't managed to track him down yet?"

"Maybe it's because the lot of you have been too busy falling in love, getting married, and getting pregnant?" Luca says in a tone indicating just how good an idea he thinks that is.

"You should try it; you might find you like it," I retort mildly.

"No thanks," he scoffs. "Marriage is for pussies. No offense."

"None taken." I exchange a look with the guy in the chair, who looks vaguely amused by Luca's outburst.

"You," I jerk my chin in the intruder's direction, "what's your name?"

"Ricardo," the man replies.

"Ricardo, I'm going to untie you," I declare.

"You are?" he says at the same time as Luca.

I move toward Ricardo, pull a knife from my pocket, and slice through his restraints. He shakes off the ropes, and I turn to Massimo and Luca. Both of them are watching me with varying degrees of incredulity.

"You sure about this?" Massimo asks slowly.

I raise a shoulder. "I have an instinct about this; one I don't want to ignore."

"You're pussy-whipped." Luca rolls his shoulders.

"Maybe." I half smile. "But I'll wager this gets us to Freddie faster than anything else, and the only thing I want right now, is to shut down the bastard before he does something else to hurt one of us."

Massimo cracks his neck. "Okay, so I guess we're going to the fucking source to smoke this rat out."

"We are."

"You?" Luca stabs his finger at me. "You get back to your wife. Leave this one to Massimo, Adrian and me."

EPILOGUE

Elsa

"She's so cute." Karma blows a raspberry on Avery's stomach. My daughter giggles, then bursts into laughter. Karma glances at her, an adoring expression on her face. "You gorgeous little thing." She rubs noses with Avery, who grabs at Karma's hair and tugs.

"She's a handful. Once she gets hold of your hair, she's not going to let go of it easily," I warn.

"And I'm not going to let go of you, either, am I?" She blows another raspberry, and Avery giggles. She babbles words in her own special language.

"What did she say?" Karma turns to me.

"I believe she's saying, fair's fair." I walk over to rescue Karma's hair from Avery, which results in Avery throwing her other arm around my neck. She holds onto both of us with a fierceness that belies her little frame.

"So, are things good with you and Seb?" Karma searches my features. "I assume they are, but you know, I have to ask. As the Don's wife, by default, it makes me the senior-most female in the family, and all that."

"I'm great," I smile at her. "Seb hasn't let us out of his sight since the night the intruder tried to break in. Not that I'm complaining. I'd rather have him for eye-candy, if you know what I mean."

"Oh, trust me, I do. And what about her? How's she doing with Seb, and all the changes?" She nods toward Avery, who is following our conversation with avid attention. You'd think the girl understood every single word we speak, which I'm fairly sure she doesn't. But once she starts speaking and picking up words, I'll have to watch myself around her.

"Oh, she and Seb have a mutual love affair going on. She has him wrapped around her little finger. From the time she wakes up in the morning, until she goes to bed, she has him doting on her. And he does it willingly. He's arranged his entire life around her. He works from home so he can be sure to eat his meals with her. And he bathes her, then reads to her, and puts her to bed at night, and she… Laps it up."

"Sounds like the three of you are getting along really well."

"We are."

"Sounds like you're happy," she says in a soft voice.

Tears prick my eyes, which is silly. "I am," I agree. "I'm happier than I've ever been in my life."

"You deserve it." She gives me her full attention. "You really do."

"Thanks." Avery releases Karma's hair and wraps both of her arms around my neck. I swing her into my arms, then plant her on my hip. "And what about you? How's the pregnancy going?"

"It's fine… so far." Her face clouds.

"So far?" I take in her features. "What does that mean?"

"Just that…" She glances away, then back at me. "I need to tell this to somebody, I guess."

"What?"

"I don't know why it feels like it's okay to tell you… Maybe because you have a child, so I think you'll understand."

"What is it?" Avery wriggles in my arms and I shush her. "You can tell me anything Karma. I can keep a secret."

"I have this heart condition. It's one of those things which is not life-threatening, unless it is."

"Like… when you're pregnant, you mean?"

"There's a chance it could flare up and turn life-threatening," she admits.

"Does Michael know about it?"

She locks her fingers together, then shakes her head.

"Are you going to tell him?"

She shakes her head again.

"What about Aurora?"

"No, absolutely not. If I told her, she'd have me admitted to the hospital, strap me to the bed, and have me monitored day and night."

"If it's life-threatening—"

"That's the thing. It's not. There's a chance I pull off the entire pregnancy without anything happening."

"What are the chances of it happening?"

"It's a good chance." She chews on her lower lip. "Believe me, I'm not taking a stupid chance... Or maybe I am. I don't know. All I know is I want this child so badly. I want Michael to have an heir, you know."

"But do you think he'd be happy if something were to happen to you, Karma?"

Her shoulders sag a little. "No. When I lost my child from my last pregnancy, it was terrible. It was like something had been taken from me which I didn't even know I wanted, and then I realized I really did want it. A lot. And then I found out I was pregnant again, and it was like the universe had answered. I mean, if I weren't supposed to have this child, why would I get pregnant again, right?"

"Karma." I reach over and wrap my arm around her. "I completely understand how much you want this child. When I became pregnant with Avery, my life changed. Suddenly, it wasn't about me or my problems anymore. It was about her, about what was best for her. About her future. It's all I could think of. It's why... When Seb came into my life, I thought—"

"That you were being disloyal to her?"

I wince. "I didn't think it was possible for me to be a mother and my own person... someone with my own preferences, and my own identity, but Seb showed me otherwise. It's because of him, I'm standing here today, holding my daughter and planning my future. I couldn't have done it without him. It's why," I search her features before continuing, "you need to tell Michael about this."

"If I do, it'll worry him."

"If you don't tell him, and he finds out anyway, he's going to be a lot more than worried. He'll be hurt."

She looks down at her feet. "I know, but I can't bring myself to tell him. A part of me hopes this entire pregnancy will pass without my having to tell him, you know?"

"I hope it does," I murmur. Avery chooses that moment to press her palm into Karma's cheek.

"Aww, baby," she coos, "you're such a sweetheart."

"There are my girls." Seb walks over to us. And of course, as soon as Avery spots him, she holds her arms out to him. Seb reaches us, and Avery all but jumps into his arms. Avery begins to babble to him, and Seb listens patiently. "Yes, we'll go home soon Avery."

"Home." Avery bounces excitedly. "Story, Dog. Eb."

"I'll read you the story about the Big Blue Dog, too." He confirms.

Avery snuggles into him and glances at me with a big smile on her face.

"You're spoiling her." I laugh.

"She deserves to be spoiled, as do you." Seb wraps his other arm around me, and pulls me close. I melt into him.

Karma glances between us, a big smile on her face. Michael walks over to wrap his arm around her.

"Hmm..." She rubs her cheek against his sleeve. "You smell sooo good, baby."

Michael chuckles. "So you keep saying."

I marvel at how adoring Michael is with her. It gives me hope that when Seb tells Michael about Cass' role in Fabio's death, he'll find it in himself to go easy on her. I pleaded with Seb not to tell Michael, but Seb said he owed it to Michael to tell him the truth. He insisted Cass had put me in danger, and Michael needed to be informed of it. I'll have to find a way to help Cass. I already have some ideas on that, and can't wait to put them into action.

Michael's phone rings and he pulls it out. "*Pronto.*" He uses the Italian word for 'Hello,' then listens. He glances toward Seb, whose muscles stiffen.

"Is that right?" Something passes between the two of them. He jerks his chin, then cuts the call.

The silent dialogue between the two men continues. Even Avery must sense the tension in the air, for she falls silent and watches Michael with big eyes.

"Wha-what is it?" I clear my throat.

Neither man responds.

"Michael?" Karma reaches up to pat his cheek. "What's happening?"

"It's probably nothing you should worry about," he replies.

"Now don't give me that." She purses her lips. "You promised you'd always share what's happening with your business, remember?"

Michael blows out a breath, then turns his gaze on her. "If you recall, Luca, Massimo, and Adrian went off with the intruder to help save his family."

Seb's grip around me tightens.

"Things didn't go according to plan." Michael sets his jaw. "Luca's missing."

To find out what happens next, get Mafia Obsession, Luca and Jeanne's story HERE

Read an excerpt

Jeanne

"Let me the F out of here." *Can't even let yourself use the f-word when you've been kidnapped, eh?* Goddam politeness that's been drilled into me since childhood. Ma was unequivocal that no occasion, no matter how frustrating, warrants the use of four-letter words. But then, I doubt she was ever held against her will.

On the bright side, I haven't seen any more of my captor; not since he held something sweet-smelling to my face. Ether, I'm guessing. I was walking home from the bus stop in Palermo, and even though it was past ten pm, there was still a smattering of people on the road, enough for me to feel safe. That was until someone darted out from behind a telephone booth—yep they still have them in Italy— I'm fairly certain he was wearing a mask. I seem to recall a black mask, a thick neck, large shoulders, and the man was overweight, and definitely not very tall. I tried to yell, but whatever was in that handkerchief got into my blood stream with just one inhalation. I blacked out and woken up here, with a headache.

At least someone left a bottle of water, which I've been sipping for the last two days. I think it's been two days because the light that comes in from the window set high in the ceiling has shown me the passage of two nights. *Goddamn, I am not spending another day cooped up in here.*

Food has been delivered via a small panel in the lower half of the door that gets pushed open, but only once a day, yesterday and today. And there's a small bathroom attached to the room with decent enough facilities. Thank god! There's no shower in there, but at least there's running water. I bring my arm to my nose and sniff. Ugh, I stink. No way can I go another day without taking a shower.

And the performance... I should be on stage for my first performance as the lead actress in a musical, and I'm not going to be able to make it now.

I bang my fists against the door again. "Let me the hell out, you...you... Twerp." *Is that the best insult I can come up with? Who even uses twerp anymore? I do, that's who.* I hammer on the door again. My wrists ache, and the edges of my palms protest. One of my nails is chipped. Argh, I stare at it. Hate when that happens.

"Nails are the windows to your soul." That was the mantra my mom lived by. We never had much money, but it didn't stop my ma from making sure that she and both of her daughters always had well-manicured nails. Even if we had to take turns pampering one another. At least they didn't tie my arms or legs. I have to be thankful for that. And of course, there's a bed in the room, with a mattress that doesn't smell too funky. On the other hand, there isn't much room in this space for walking. And there's nothing else to do.

"Let me the hell out of here... Please!" I wince. *Really, you had to add please at the end?*

I bring my fist down on the door, when it's wrenched open, and a man is shoved in my direction. A big man. A big, tall man. So tall, I have to crane my head all the way back to try to make out his features. His bulk collides with me.

The scent of dark chocolate and coffee, laced with that masculine scent I just call 'man,' fills my senses, and I stumble back.

"Hey—" My voice is cut off when the man begins to slump into me. The full weight of his body pushes me down. My knees begin to give way. Whoever pushed him in here, gives him another shove. Of course, I take the brunt of his weight, and both of us go tumbling down. I manage to swerve out of his way, then wince when he hits the floor with a crash and stays there. The door to the room is slammed shut.

"Come back!" I jump up, leap toward the door and hammer my fists on it. "Let me out of here. You can't do this. You can't keep me locked up here without any explanation. There are people looking for me, you nincompoops. What do you gain by keeping me in here? Let me out, and I promise I won't go to the police when I get out of here." My voice cracks a little, and I pause. There's no one out there listening to me. Whoever shoved the man in here is gone—

Oh, wait. They shoved someone else in here... in my already tiny room. I turn to find the monster of a guy who hit the floor face down still hasn't moved. Not good; this is not good. I step over his feet and walk over to stand near his face. I prod his massive shoulder with the tip of my boot. He doesn't move. Doesn't even stir.

"Hey, mister," my voice echoes in the space. "Hey!" I prod him with a little more force. Same response. Is he breathing? Yes, I can hear it now. I sink down on one knee and touch his shoulder. When there's no movement, I touch his hair. It's soft, springy. I run my fingers through the thick strands, and a weird heat trickles up my spine. *Umm, no, it's just hair.* So what if it seems to belong to the head attached to a particularly impressive torso. The man's jacket clings to his shoulders, stretches across a broad back that tapers down to a narrow waist. His T-shirt has been pulled up, due to the fall, and a narrow strip of skin is visible above the waistband of his dark pants. I reach for the strip of skin, then pull back. *Eh, stop it. What are you doing, touching this guy without his permission, anyway?*

I turn my attention back to his head. Thick dark hair that's long enough to brush the collar of his jacket. Unruly enough to have fallen over his forehead. Thick eyelashes, strong nose, square jaw, from what I can make out of his face. High cheekbones, and the hollows under them lend definition to his features. My breath catches in my chest. Whoever he is, he's gorgeous. He has the kind of good looks that wouldn't be out of place on the big screen. He could have been the star of the next Godfather, if someone ever decided to reboot the movie franchise; though admittedly, it would take someone with huge balls to touch cinematic history. I reach for the strand of hair that's fallen over his forehead and push it back. That's when his eyelids snap open.

Bright blue eyes. Like the sky at the peak of summer. Like water freshly melted from snow. Like freshly-laundered white which is so intense, you'd be forgiven for mistaking it for blue. He reaches out a hand. I scream, scramble back, but he locks his fingers around my ankle and pulls me closer.

"Let me go," I screech, "let me the hell go."

His grasp tightens. I reach over, try to pry his fingers off, but he doesn't let go. He continues to stare at my face like he's unable to tear his gaze away.

My heart slams into my rib cage. My blood thumps so loudly in my ears, I think I'm going to faint. "Please," I gulp, "please let me go." A tear squeezes out from the corner of my eye. It slides down my cheek and plops on his face.

His forehead furrows and he releases his grip on my leg. I scoot back as he raises his arm in my direction.

"Angel," he whispers, "don't cry." Then his eyelids flutter down again, and his arm falls by his side.

I ease away from him until my back connects with the wall. I take in his face, eyes now closed again, the way his dark eyelashes sweep down until the tips seem to sweep his cheekbones. That patrician nose I noticed earlier, the thick upper lip, the pouty lower one, the square jaw of his that hints at the power coiled under his skin. Even unconscious, the man exudes a raw power that thrums around him, that draws my attention, a presence that seems to suck all of the oxygen in the room, leaving me lightheaded.

I hope he didn't hurt himself when he fell. Was he drugged, like me? Is that why he's out cold? It would have taken more than one man to overpower him, more like a crowd of them to take him down, given his size. Did he resist them as they hauled him here? Did he fight before they finally managed to overwhelm him?

I watch him for a few more seconds, but he doesn't stir. Guess I'll have to leave him on the floor. No way am I going to be able to move him. And after the last time I touched him, when he'd snapped his eyes open so suddenly, I'm not going to risk that again. I guess I could cover him up with a sheet, at least. I rise to my feet, then shuffle alongside the wall, clinging to it as I make my way around him. When I reach the bed, I pull the cover from it, then walk over and drape it over him. I step back until the backs of my knees hit the bed, then sit down on it. I watch him for a few more seconds, until a yawn surprises me. Tiredness drags at the edge of my conscious mind. I lay down facing him, back to the wall, and bring my knees up to my chest. I fold my arms and watch the back of his head until I fall asleep.

The next time I open my eyes, it's to meet that piercing blue gaze of his. No... Not completely blue. There are specks of grey, almost black, around his pupils. I part my lips to scream, and he clamps his palm across my mouth. I raise my hand, and he grabs my wrist and wrenches it over my head. My heart pounds in my ribcage, and my pulse-rate goes through the roof. Fear twists my guts, and my breath locks in my chest. What the hell is he doing? Why is he trying to restrain me? If he thinks I'm going to give up without a fight, he doesn't know who he's dealing with. I bring my knee up, intent on kicking him, when he drops onto the bed, on top of me.

Luca

The hell are you doing? She's scared out of her mind, and instead of calming her down, I climb onto the bed, between her legs, and lean my weight on top of her. Not because I want to scare her, but because I can't afford to be kneed by her or hit by her flailing arms. It's the only reason I have my hand over her mouth, and am trying to hold her down without hurting her.

"Stay quiet," I growl.

Her gaze widens. She begins to writhe under me, trying to get away, but it only brings her in closer contact with the hardness between my thighs. She instantly freezes, her eyes growing even bigger. Color smears her cheeks. She begins to wriggle with even more ferocity. She bites down on my fingers, which I've clamped over her mouth, and goddamn, but I feel the pinch all the way to the tip of my cock. The blood rushes to my groin, and the column in my pants grows even thicker. Which, in turn, seems to inject a fresh dose of terror through her veins because now, she begins to fight me in earnest. She lashes out with her free hand and catches me in the face. I grunt. The bump at the back of my head, where one of the men must have hit me, throbs. Pain slices through my mind, and for a second, I see stars. Then she manages to work one of her legs free and kicks me in the shoulder. It doesn't really hurt me, but goddam, I have had enough.

"Stop fighting me, you little hellcat; they have cameras on us here."

She continues to thrash around, then grows still, as if my words have suddenly sunk in.

I nod, then jerk my chin toward the ceiling. She follows my gaze, takes in the corners of the ceiling, and stills. Then she brings her gaze back to my face.

"Yeah, see what I mean?" I say in a low voice. "They're watching us, and I wager, they have microphones on us, as well."

Her throat moves as she swallows. The tension that pours off of her body seems to intensify. Her shoulders hunch, and every muscle in her body seems to coil with nervousness. Her chest rises and falls, and a bead of sweat runs down her throat. I follow its path down to the valley between her breasts until it disappears.

Heat sluices through my veins. Goddamn, her tits are perfectly round. The nipples are so hard that their outline is visible through both the bra and the shirt she's wearing. The band around my chest tightens. I only realize I've leaned in closer to her when a jolt runs through her body. I raise my gaze to her face to find those green pupils of hers are almost fully dilated. The black of her irises has expanded until only a circle of green is visible around them.

"I'll remove my hand from your mouth, if you promise you won't scream," I caution.

She stills for a second, then nods.

Goddam, I don't trust her. Bet she's going to scream as soon as I take my hand off of her mouth. And how long am I going to stay in this position, trying to keep her quiet, while the proximity to her body, the sweet scent of her, the softness of her skin, the warmth of her core—all of it ensures that my pants are getting tighter by the moment?

Cazzo! I remove my hand from her face, and instantly, she screams. So I do the only thing I can in these circumstances; I close my mouth over hers. Her entire body freezes. I absorb the sound, draw it into me as I thrust my tongue in between her lips, and kiss her soundly.

She stays still for a beat, then another. Then, she bites down on my lower lip, and *cazzo*, my cock jerks in my pants. I tilt my head, deepen the kiss, and she pushes her breasts up into my chest. She juts out her chin, opens her mouth, and I slide my tongue in deeper. The taste of her is sweet and complex, with a bite, the scent of her like crushed rose petals, the feel of her curves so soft, so lush, so goddamn sumptuous. My head spins. She wriggles under me, and the hard column in my pants nestles into her core. My balls tighten. A hot sensation fills my chest, and my ribcage hurts. I squeeze her chin to hold her face where I want it as I swipe my tongue across her teeth, as I drink from her, and suck on her tongue, and my entire body goes on alert.

The hair on the back of my neck rises, and the muscles of my shoulders coil. I tear my mouth from hers and stare into her flushed face. Into those green eyes with pupils so blown, I can see myself reflected in the blackness.

She stares back, the surprise I feel reflected in her features. Then, she raises her hand—and to be honest, I see what's coming, but I do nothing to avoid it—and her palm connects with my cheek. My head jolts back, and yet, I can't take my gaze off of her. Something electric crackles in the air between us, coils itself around my chest, and squeezes until I can't breathe. Can't think. Can't do anything but gape at her.

"Get off of me," she snarls.

"Only if you promise to listen," I shoot back.

"First, you get off me."

"First, *you* promise to listen."

"I'll do no such thing."

"In which case..." I place more of my weight on her, and her gaze widens.

"You wouldn't." She scowls.

"Try me." I allow my lips to curve in a smirk. Using my weight to hold her captive while I try to make her listen to me? It's a dick move, but fuck that. We're in trouble, and the only way out is if I get her to follow my directions.

Her face pales a little, then her lips firm. "Fine," she says in a low voice.

"I didn't hear you," I drawl.

"Asshole," she murmurs under her breath.

"Heard it, and it's alphahole to you."

She opens and shuts her mouth. "You have an inflated opinion about yourself, don't you?"

"Not the only thing that's inflated, Angel."

"Don't call me that."

"I'll call you anything I want." I allow my grin to widen.

Her scowl deepens. "You... you... dickwaffle!"

I blink, then can't stop the chuckle that rolls up my throat. I laugh so hard, my whole body shakes, and as a result, she shakes under me. "That's a creative insult, I'll give you that."

"I'm just getting started," she shoots back.

"You and I are going to have fun, I can feel it," I tease her.

"Oh, sod off." She slaps my shoulder, and the vibrations shudder through my brain. The back of my head begins to throb in earnest. I touch the space and my fingers come away wet.

"Is that blood?" She stares at it, then at my face. "Does it hurt?"

"Are you concerned?" I narrow my gaze on her.

"Of course not. But since we are, clearly, having a conversation, can you please get off of me now?"

"We are, aren't we?" I roll off of her, and once on my feet, extend my arm to her. "Luca Sovrano."

She sits up, then pushes off the bed and stands facing me.

"What the hell did you think you were doing earlier?"

"Trying to distract you so you wouldn't scream and make those guys come in here again."

She pales a little, and her gaze flicks to the door. "Did they take you, as well? I mean, obviously they did take you... But how did they overpower you? You seem—"

"Strong? Virile? Sexy?"

She darts me an annoyed look. "Does everything always have to be about you?"

"Not always... but mostly." I wiggle my fingers. "At least shake my hand, will you?"

"If you think I want to be your friend after what you did earlier, you are sadly mistaken."

"Considering we've already exchanged saliva, a handshake doesn't seem that far-fetched."

She throws up her hands. "You're gross."

"And you're cute when you are angry."

"Eh?" She opens and shuts her mouth. "Who are you again?"

"Luca Sovrano, part of the Sovrano Seven?"

"What are you, some kind of underground Mafia gang?"

"How'd you guess?"

"You're joking, right?" She begins to laugh, but she must notice the look on my face, for her lips firm. "You're *not* joking."

"Not at all," I confirm.

"Oh for F's sake." She takes a step back, as if she's just realized the predicament she's in. *Too late, baby. I've already set my sights on you, and I'm not letting go that easily.*

"So, you're part of a Mafia outfit?"

"I *am* the Mafia." I widen my stance. "And you're trapped with me in this cell."

To find out what happens next get Mafia Obsession, HERE

Want to be the first to find out when L. Steele's next book releases? Subscribe to her newsletter HERE

Read Michael & Karma's story in Mafia King HERE

Read an excerpt from mafia king

Karma

"Morn came and went—and came, and brought no day..."

Tears prick the backs of my eyes. Goddamn Byron. His words creep up on me when I am at my weakest. Not that I am a poetry addict, by any measure, but words are my jam. The one consolation I have is that, when everything else in the world is wrong, I can turn to them, and they'll be there, friendly, steady, waiting with open arms.

And this particular poem had laced my blood, crawled into my gut when I'd first read it. Darkness had folded within me like an insidious snake, that raises its head when I least expect it. Like now, when I look out on the still sleeping city of London, from the grassy slope of Waterlow Park.

Somewhere out there, the Mafia is hunting me, apparently. It's why my sister Summer and her new husband Sinclair Sterling had insisted that I have my own security detail. I had agreed...only to appease them...then given my bodyguard the slip this morning. I had decided to come running here because it's not a place I'd normally go... Not so early in the morning, anyway. They won't think to look for me here. At least, not for a while longer.

I purse my lips, close my eyes. Silence. The rustle of the wind between the leaves. The faint tinkle of the water from the nearby spring.

I could be the last person on this planet, alone, unsung, bound for the grave.

Ugh! Stop. Right there. I drag the back of my hand across my nose. Try it again, focus, get the words out, one after the other, like the steps of my sorry life.

"*Morn came and went—and came, and... and...*" My voice breaks. "Bloody asinine hell." I dig my fingers into the grass and grab a handful and fling it out. Again. From the top.

"*Morn came and went—and came, and—*"

"*...brought no day.*"

A gravelly voice completes my sentence.

I whip my head around. His silhouette fills my line of sight. He's sitting on the same knoll as me, yet I have to crane my neck back to see his profile. The sun is at his back, so I can't make out his features. Can't see his eyes... Can only take in his dark hair, combed back by a ruthless hand that brooked no measure.

My throat dries.

Thick dark hair, shot through with grey at the temples. He wears his age like a badge. I don't know why, but I know his years have not been easy. That he's seen more, indulged in more, reveled in the consequences of his actions, however extreme they might have been. He's not a normal, everyday person, this man. Not a nine-to-fiver, not someone who lives an average life. Definitely not a man who returns home to his wife and home at the end of the day. He is...different, unique, evil... Monstrous. Yes, he is a beast, one who sports the face of a man but who harbors the kind of darkness inside that speaks to me. I gulp.

His face boasts a hooked nose, a thin upper lip, a fleshy lower lip. One that hints at hidden desires, Heat. Lust. The sensuous scrape of that whiskered jaw over my innermost places. Across my inner thigh, reaching toward that core of me that throbs, clenches, melts to feel the stab of his tongue, the thrust of his hardness as he impales me, takes me, makes me his. Goosebumps pop on my skin.

I drag my gaze away from his mouth down to the scar that slashes across his throat. A cold sensation coils in my chest. What or who had hurt him in such a cruel fashion?

"Of this their desolation; and all hearts
Were chill'd into a selfish prayer for light..."

He continues in that rasping guttural tone. Is it the wound that caused that scar that makes his voice so...gravelly... So dèep...so...so, hot?

Sweat beads my palms and the hairs on my nape rise. "Who are you?"

He stares ahead as his lips move,

"Forests were set on fire—but hour by hour
They fell and faded—and the crackling trunks
Extinguish'd with a crash—and all was black."

I swallow, moisture gathers in my core. How can I be wet by the mere cadence of this stranger's voice?

I spring up to my feet.

"Sit down," he commands.

His voice is unhurried, lazy even, his spine erect. The cut of his black jacket stretches across the width of his massive shoulders. His hair... I was mistaken—there are threads of dark gold woven between the darkness that pours down to brush the nape of his neck. A strand of hair falls over his brow. As I watch, he raises his hand and brushes it away. Somehow, the gesture lends an air of vulnerability to him. Something so at odds with the rest of his persona that, surely, I am mistaken?

My scalp itches. I take in a breath and my lungs burn. This man... He's sucked up all the oxygen in this open space as if he owns it, the master of all he surveys. The master of me. My death. My life. A shiver ladders along my spine. *Get away, get away now, while you still can.*

I angle my body, ready to spring away from him.

"I won't ask again."

Ask. Command. Force me to do as he wants. He'll have me on my back, bent over, on my side, on my knees, over him, under him. He'll surround me, overwhelm me, pin me down with the force of his personality. His charisma, his larger-than-life essence will crush everything else out of me and I... I'll love it.

"No."

"Yes."

A fact. A statement of intent, spoken aloud. So true. So real. Too real. Too much. Too fast. All of my nightmares...my dreams come to life. Everything I've wanted is here in front of me. I'll die a thousand deaths before he'll be done with me... And then? Will I be reborn? For him. For me. For myself.

I live, first and foremost, to be the woman I was...am meant to be.

"You want to run?"

No.

No.

I nod my head.

He turns his, and all the breath leaves my lungs. Blue eyes—cerulean, dark like the morning skies, deep like the nighttime...hidden corners, secrets that I don't dare uncover. He'll destroy me, have my heart, and break it so casually.

My throat burns and a boiling sensation squeezes my chest.

"Go then, my beauty, fly. You have until I count to five. If I catch you, you are mine."

"If you don't?"

"Then I'll come after you, stalk your every living moment, possess your nightmares, and steal you away in the dead of night, and then…"

I draw in a shuddering breath as liquid heat drips from between my legs. "Then?" I whisper.

"Then, I'll ensure you'll never belong to anyone else, you'll never see the light of day again, for your every breath, your every waking second, your thoughts, your actions…and all your words, every single last one, will belong to me." He peels back his lips, and his teeth glint in the first rays of the morning light. "Only me." He straightens to his feet and rises, and rises.

This man… He is massive. A monster who always gets his way. My guts churn. My toes curl. Something primeval inside of me insists I hold my own. I cannot give in to him. Cannot let him win whatever this is. I need to stake my ground, in some form. *Say something. Anything. Show him you're not afraid of this.*

"Why?" I tilt my head back, all the way back. "Why are you doing this?"

He tilts his head, his ears almost canine in the way they are silhouetted against his profile.

"Is it because you can? Is it a…a," I blink, "a debt of some kind?"

He stills.

"My father, this is about how he betrayed the Mafia, right? You're one of them?"

"Lucky guess." His lips twist, "It is about your father, and how he promised you to me. He reneged on his promise, and now, I am here to collect."

"No." I swallow… *No, no, no.*

"Yes." His jaw hardens.

All expression is wiped clean of his face, and I know then, that he speaks the truth. It's always about the past. My sorry shambles of a past… Why does it always catch up with me? *You can run, but you can never hide.*

"Tick-tock, Beauty." He angles his body and his shoulders shut out the sight of the sun, the dawn skies, the horizon, the city in the distance, the rustle of the grass, the trees, the rustle of the leaves. All of it fades and leaves just me and him. Us. *Run.*

"Five." He jerks his chin, straightens the cuffs of his sleeves.

My knees wobble.

"Four."

My pulse rate spikes. I should go. Leave. But my feet are planted in this earth. This piece of land where we first met. What am I, but a speck in the larger scheme of things? To be hurt. To be forgotten. To be taken without an ounce of retribution. To be punished...by him.

"Three." He thrusts out his chest, widens his stance, every muscle in his body relaxed. "Two."

I swallow. The pulse beats at my temples. My blood thrums.

"One."

To find out what happens next read Mafia King HERE

Read Summer & Sinclair Sterling's story HERE in The Billionaire's Fake Wife

Read an excerpt from Summer & Sinclair's story

Summer

"Slap, slap, kiss, kiss."

"Huh?" I stare up at the bartender.

"Aka, there's a thin line between love and hate." He shakes out the crimson liquid into my glass.

"Nah." I snort. "Why would she allow him to control her, and after he insulted her?"

"It's the chemistry between them." He lowers his head, "You have to admit that when the man is arrogant and the woman resists, it's a challenge to both of them, to see who blinks first, huh?"

"Why?" I wave my hand in the air, "Because they hate each other?"

"Because," he chuckles, "the girl in school whose braids I pulled and teased mercilessly, is the one who I—"

"Proposed to?" I huff.

His face lights up. "You get it now?"

Yeah. No. A headache begins to pound at my temples. This crash course in pop psychology is not why I came to my favorite bar in Islington, to meet my best friend, who is—I glance at the face of my phone—thirty minutes late.

I inhale the drink, and his eyebrows rise.

"What?" I glower up at the bartender. "I can barely taste the alcohol. Besides, it's free drinks at happy hour for women, right?"

"Which ends in precisely" he holds up five fingers, "minutes."

"Oh! Yay!" I mock fist pump. "Time enough for one more, at least."

A hiccough swells my throat and I swallow it back, nod.

One has to do what one has to do... when everything else in the world is going to shit.

A hot sensation stabs behind my eyes; my chest tightens. Is this what people call growing up?

The bartender tips his mixing flask, strains out a fresh batch of the ruby red liquid onto the glass in front of me.

"Salut." I nod my thanks, then toss it back. It hits my stomach and tendrils of fire crawl up my spine, I cough.

My head spins. Warmth sears my chest, spreads to my extremities. I can't feel my fingers or toes. Good. Almost there. "Top me up."

"You sure?"

"Yes." I square my shoulders and reach for the drink.

"No. She's had enough."

"What the—?" I pivot on the bar stool.

Indigo eyes bore into me.

Fathomless. Black at the bottom, the intensity in their depths grips me. He swoops out his arm, grabs the glass and holds it up. Thick fingers dwarf the glass. Tapered at the edges. The nails short and buff. *All the better to grab you with.* I gulp.

"Like what you see?"

I flush, peer up into his face.

Hard cheekbones, hollows under them, and a tiny scar that slashes at his left eyebrow. *How did he get that?* Not that I care. My gaze slides to his mouth. Thin upper lip, a lower lip that is full and cushioned. Pouty with a hint of bad boy. *Oh!* My toes curl. My thighs clench.

The corner of his mouth kicks up. *Asshole.*

Bet he thinks life is one big smug-fest. I glower, reach for my glass, and he holds it up and out of my reach.

I scowl, "Gimme that."

He shakes his head.

"That's my drink."

"Not anymore." He shoves my glass at the bartender. "Water for her. Get me a whiskey, neat."

I splutter, then reach for my drink again. The barstool tips, in his direction. This is when I fall against him, and my breasts slam into his hard chest, sculpted planes with layers upon layers of muscle that ripple and writhe as he turns aside, flattens himself against the bar. The floor rises up to meet me.

What the actual hell?

I twist my torso at the last second and my butt connects with the surface. *Ow!*

The breath rushes out of me. My hair swirls around my face. I scrabble for purchase, and my knee connects with his leg.

"Watch it." He steps around, stands in front of me.

"You stepped aside?" I splutter. "You let me fall?"

"Hmph."

I tilt my chin back, all the way back, look up the expanse of muscled thigh that stretches the silken material of his suit. *What is he wearing? Could any suit fit a man with such precision?* Hand crafted on Saville Row, no doubt. I glance at the bulge that tents the fabric between his legs. *Oh!* I blink.

Look away, look away. I hold out my arm. He'll help me up at least, won't he?

He glances at my palm, then turns away. *No, he didn't do that, no way.*

A glass of amber liquid appears in front of him. He lifts the tumbler to his sculpted mouth.

His throat moves, strong tendons flexing. He tilts his head back, and the column of his neck moves as he swallows. Dark hair covers his chin—it's a discordant chord in that clean-cut profile, I shiver. He would scrape that rough skin down my core. He'd mark my inner thigh, lick my core, thrust his tongue inside my melting channel and drink from my pussy. *Oh! God.* Goosebumps rise on my skin.

No one has the right to look this beautiful, this achingly gorgeous. Too magnificent for his own good. Anger coils in my chest.

"Arrogant wanker."

"I'll take that under advisement."

"You're a jerk, you know that?"

He presses his lips together. The grooves on either side of his mouth deepen. Jesus, clearly the man has never laughed a single day in his life. Bet that stick up his arse is uncomfortable. I chuckle.

He runs his gaze down my features, my chest, down to my toes, then yawns.

The hell! I will not let him provoke me. Will not. "Like what you see?" I jut out my chin.

"Sorry, you're not my type." He slides a hand into the pocket of those perfectly cut pants, stretching it across that heavy bulge.

Heat curls low in my belly.

Not fair, that he could afford a wardrobe that clearly shouts his status and what amounts to the economy of a small third-world country. A hot feeling stabs in my chest.

He reeks of privilege, of taking his status in life for granted.

While I've had to fight every inch of the way. Hell, I am still battling to hold onto the last of my equilibrium.

"Last chance—" I wiggle my fingers, from where I am sprawled out on the floor at his feet, "—to redeem yourself..."

"You have me there." He places the glass on the counter, then bends and holds out his hand. The hint of discolored steel at his wrist catches my attention. Huh?

He wears a cheap-ass watch?

That's got to bring down the net worth of his presence by more than 1000% percent. Weird.

I reach up and he straightens.

I lurch back.

"Oops, I changed my mind." His lips curl.

A hot burning sensation claws at my stomach. I am not a violent person, honestly. But Smirky Pants here, he needs to be taught a lesson.

I swipe out my legs, kicking his out from under him.

Sinclair

My knees give way, and I hurtle toward the ground.

What the—? I twist around, thrust out my arms. My palms hit the floor. The impact jostles up my elbows. I firm my biceps and come to a halt planked above her.

A huffing sound fills my ear.

I turn to find my whippet, Max, panting with his mouth open. I scowl and he flattens his ears.

All of my businesses are dog-friendly. Before you draw conclusions about me being the caring sort or some such shit—it attracts footfall.

Max scrutinizes the girl, then glances at me. *Huh?* He hates women, but not her, apparently.

I straighten and my nose grazes hers.

My arms are on either side of her head. Her chest heaves. The fabric of her dress stretches across her gorgeous breasts. My fingers tingle; my palms ache to cup those tits, squeeze those hard nipples outlined against the—hold on, what is she wearing? A tunic shirt in a sparkly pink... and are those shoulder pads she has on?

I glance up, and a squeak escapes her lips.

Pink hair surrounds her face. *Pink? Who dyes their hair that color past the age of eighteen?*

I stare at her face. *How old is she?* Un-furrowed forehead, dark eyelashes that flutter against pale cheeks. Tiny nose, and that mouth—luscious, tempting. A whiff of her scent, cherries and caramel, assails my senses. My mouth waters. *What the hell?*

She opens her eyes and our eyelashes brush. Her gaze widens. Green, like the leaves of the evergreens, flickers of gold sparkling in their depths. "What?" She glowers. "You're demonstrating the plank position?"

"Actually," I lower my weight onto her, the ridge of my hardness thrusting into the softness between her legs, "I was thinking of something else, altogether."

She gulps and her pupils dilate. *Ah, so she feels it, too?*

I drop my head toward her, closer, closer.

Color floods the creamy expanse of her neck. Her eyelids flutter down. She tilts her chin up.

I push up and off of her.

"That... Sweetheart, is an emphatic 'no thank you' to whatever you are offering."

Her eyelids spring open and pink stains her cheeks. Adorable. Such a range of emotions across those gorgeous features in a few seconds? What else is hidden under that exquisite exterior of hers?

She scrambles up, eyes blazing.

Ah! The little bird is trying to spread her wings? My dick twitches. My groin hardens, *Why does her anger turn me on so, huh?*

She steps forward, thrusts a finger in my chest.

My heart begins to thud.

She peers up from under those hooded eyelashes. "Wake up and taste the wasabi, asshole."

"What does that even mean?"

She makes a sound deep in her throat. My dick twitches. My pulse speeds up.

She pivots, grabs a half-full beer mug sitting on the bar counter.

I growl, "Oh, no, you don't."

She turns, swings it at me. The smell of hops envelops the space.

I stare down at the beer-splattered shirt, the lapels of my camel colored jacket deepening to a dull brown. Anger squeezes my guts.

I fist my fingers at my side, broaden my stance.

She snickers.

I tip my chin up. "You're going to regret that."

The smile fades from her face. "Umm." She places the now empty mug on the bar.

I take a step forward and she skitters back. "It's only clothes." She gulps, "They'll wash."

I glare at her and she swallows, wiggles her fingers in the air, "I should have known that you wouldn't have a sense of humor."

I thrust out my jaw, "That's a ten-thousand-pound suit you destroyed."

She blanches, then straightens her shoulders, "Must have been some hot date you were trying to impress, huh?"

"Actually," I flick some of the offending liquid from my lapels, "it's you I was after."

"Me?" She frowns.

"We need to speak."

She glances toward the bartender who's on the other side of the bar. "I don't know you." She chews on her lower lip, biting off some of the hot pink. How would she look, with that pouty mouth fastened on my cock?

The blood rushes to my groin so quickly that my head spins. My pulse rate ratchets up. Focus, focus on the task you came here for.

"This will take only a few seconds." I take a step forward.

She moves aside.

I frown, "You want to hear this, I promise."

"Go to hell." She pivots and darts forward.

I let her go, a step, another, because... I can? Besides it's fun to create the illusion of freedom first; makes the hunt so much more entertaining, huh?

I swoop forward, loop an arm around her waist, and yank her toward me.

She yelps. "Release me."

Good thing the bar is not yet full. It's too early for the usual officegoers to stop by. And the staff...? Well they are well aware of who cuts their paychecks.

I spin her around and against the bar, then release her. "You will listen to me."

She swallows; she glances left to right.

Not letting you go yet, little Bird. I move into her space, crowd her.

She tips her chin up. "Whatever you're selling, I'm not interested."

I allow my lips to curl, "You don't fool me."

A flush steals up her throat, sears her cheeks. So tiny, so innocent. Such a good little liar. I narrow my gaze, "Every action has its consequences."

"Are you daft?" She blinks.

"This pretense of yours?" I thrust my face into hers, "It's not working."

She blinks, then color suffuses her cheeks, "You're certifiably mad—"

"Getting tired of your insults."

"It's true, everything I said." She scrapes back the hair from her face.

Her fingernails are painted... You guessed it, pink.

"And here's something else. You are a selfish, egotistical jackass."

I smirk. "You're beginning to repeat your insults and I haven't even kissed you yet."

"Don't you dare." She gulps.

I tilt my head, "Is that a challenge?"

"It's a..." she scans the crowded space, then turns to me. Her lips firm, "...a warning. You're delusional, you jackass." She inhales a deep breath, "Your ego is bigger than the size of a black hole." She snickers, "Bet it's to compensate for your lack of balls."

A-n-d, that's it. I've had enough of her mouth that threatens to never stop spewing words. How many insults can one tiny woman hurl my way? Answer: too many to count.

"You—"

I lower my chin, touch my lips to hers.

Heat, sweetness, the honey of her essence explodes on my palate. My dick twitches. I tilt my head, deepen the kiss, reaching for that something more... more... of whatever scent she's wearing on her skin, infused with that breath of hers that crowds my senses, rushes down my spine. My groin hardens; my cock lengthens. I thrust my tongue between those infuriating lips.

She makes a sound deep in her throat and my heart begins to pound.

So innocent, yet so crafty. Beautiful and feisty. The kind of complication I don't need in my life.

I prefer the straight and narrow. Gray and black, that's how I choose to define my world. She, with her flashes of color—pink hair and lips that threaten to drive me to the edge of distraction—is exactly what I hate.

Give me a female who has her priorities set in life. To pleasure me, get me off, then walk away before her emotions engage. Yeah. That's what I prefer.

Not this... this bundle of craziness who flings her arms around my shoulders, thrusts her breasts up and into my chest, tips up her chin, opens her mouth, and invites me to take and take.

Does she have no self-preservation? Does she think I am going to fall for her wide-eyed appeal? She has another think coming.

I tear my mouth away and she protests.

She twines her leg with mine, pushes up her hips, so that melting softness between her thighs cradles my aching hardness.

I glare into her face and she holds my gaze.

Trains her green eyes on me. Her cheeks flush a bright red. Her lips fall open and a moan bleeds into the air. The blood rushes to my dick, which instantly thickens. *Fuck*.

Time to put distance between myself and the situation.

It's how I prefer to manage things. Stay in control, always. Cut out anything that threatens to impinge on my equilibrium. Shut it down or buy them off. Reduce it to a transaction. That I understand.

The power of money, to be able to buy and sell—numbers, logic. That's what's worked for me so far.

"How much?"

Her forehead furrows.

"Whatever it is, I can afford it."

Her jaw slackens. "You think... you—"

"A million?"

"What?"

"Pounds, dollars... You name the currency, and it will be in your account."

Her jaw slackens, "You're offering me money?"

"For your time, and for you to fall in line with my plan."

She reddens, "You think I am for sale?"

"Everyone is."

"Not me."

Here we go again. "Is that a challenge?"

Color fades from her face, "Get away from me."

"Are you shy, is that what this is?" I frown. "You can write your price down on a piece of paper if you prefer," I glance up, notice the bartender watching us. I jerk my chin toward the napkins. He grabs one, then offers it to her.

She glowers at him, "Did you buy him too?"

"What do you think?"

She glances around, "I think everyone here is ignoring us."

"It's what I'd expect."

"Why is that?"

I wave the tissue in front of her face, "Why do you think?"

"You own the place?"

"As I am going to own you."

She sets her jaw, "Let me leave and you won't regret this."

A chuckle bubbles up. I swallow it away. This is no laughing matter. I never smile during a transaction. Especially not when I am negotiating a new acquisition. And that's all she is. The final piece in the puzzle I am building.

"No one threatens me."

"You're right."

"Huh?"

"I'd rather act on my instinct."

Her lips twist, her gaze narrows. All of my senses scream a warning.

No, she wouldn't, no way—pain slices through my middle and sparks explode behind my eyes.

TO FIND OUT WHAT HAPPENS NEXT READ SUMMER & SINCLAIR STERLING'S STORY **HERE**

WANT TO BE THE FIRST TO FIND OUT ABOUT L. STEELE'S NEW RELEASES? JOIN HER NEWSLETTER **HERE**

READ ABOUT THE SEVEN IN THE BIG BAD BILLIONAIRES SERIES
US
UK
OTHER COUNTRIES
CLAIM YOUR **FREE** CONTEMPORARY ROMANCE BOXSET **HERE**
CLAIM YOUR **FREE** PARANORMAL ROMANCE BOXSET **HERE**
FOLLOW L. STEELE ON **AMAZON**
FOLLOW L. STEELE ON BOOKBUB
FOLLOW L. STEELE ON GOODREADS
FOLLOW L. STEELE ON FACEBOOK
FOLLOW L. STEELE ON INSTAGRAM
JOIN L. STEELE'S SECRET FACEBOOK READER GROUP
FOR MORE BOOKS BY L. STEELE CLICK **HERE**

AFTERWORD

From L. Steele (Laxmi)

Hope you enjoyed Seb and Elsa's story. You can also read Michael & Karma's story in Mafia King, Christian & Aurora's story in A Very Mafia Christmas and Axel & Thersa's story in Mafia Crown.

The Arranged Marriage Mafia series starts after *The Billionaire's Fake Wife* in the Big Bad Billionaire Series and the two series then run parallel. They dovetail with Liam and Isla's story which his next in the Big Bad Billionaire Series.

When I wrote *The Billionaire's Fake Wife* I didn't realize I was actually writing two series. The Seven Billionaires in the Big Bad Billionaires Series, and the Seven Sovrano brothers in the Arranged Marriage Mafia series. And yes I promise a scene at some point when all fourteen alphaholes are in one room... is that even possible? Will their big egos even fit under one roof? :) Wait and see.

Thank you to my editor Elizabeth Connor, my alpha reader Li Iacobacci, my publicist Sarah Ferguson of Social Butterfly PR who has been so supportive, and my reader group who always cheer me on.

Have an opinion on the Sovranos? Share them in my reader group, join Laxmi's team HERE.

FREE BOOK

Claim your free contemporary romance book from L. Steele. Scan the QR code

How to scan a QR code?
    1. Open the camera app on your phone or tablet.
    2. Point the camera at the QR code.

3. Tap the banner that appears on your phone or tablet.
4. Follow the instructions on the screen to finish signing in.

©2021 Laxmi Hariharan. All rights reserved under the International and Pan-American Copyright Conventions. No part of this book may be reproduced or transmitted in any form or by any means, electronic or mechanical, including photocopying, recording, or by any information storage and retrieval system, without permission in writing from the publisher.

This is a work of fiction. Names, places, characters and incidents are either the product of the author's imagination or are used fictitiously, and any resemblance to any actual persons, living or dead, organizations, events or locales is entirely coincidental.

Warning: the unauthorized reproduction or distribution of this copyrighted work is illegal. Criminal copyright infringement, including infringement without monetary gain, is investigated by the FBI and is punishable by up to 5 years in prison and a fine of $250,000.

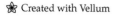 Created with Vellum

www.ingramcontent.com/pod-product-compliance
Lightning Source LLC
LaVergne TN
LVHW012155100225
803455LV00008B/211